Where We Belong

K.L. Grayson ♡

K.L. GRAYSON

Where We Belong
Copyright ©2014 K.L. Grayson

All rights reserved. Without limiting the rights under copyright reserved above, no part of this publication may be reproduced, stored in or introduced into retrieval system, or transmitted, in any form, or by any means (electronic, mechanical, photocopying, recording, or otherwise) without the prior written permission of both the copyright owner and the above publisher of this book.

This is a work of fiction. Names, characters, places, brands, media, and incidents are either the products of the author's imagination or are used fictitiously. The author acknowledges the trademarked status and trademark owners of various products referenced in this work of fiction, which have been used without permission. The publication/use of these trademarks is not authorized, associated with, or sponsored by the trademark owners.

Cover Photographer: Tess J Photography
Cover Designer: Wicked By Design
Editor: S.G. Thomas
Bio Pic Photographer: Elisabeth Wiseman Photography
Formatting by Champagne Formats

ISBN: 978-0-9907955-1-3

Dedication

Writing this book is a dream come true for me, but I absolutely could not have done it without the help of some amazingly wonderful women. Each and every one of you stepped up and offered me your help, advice, expertise, and guidance without batting an eye and I am truly grateful. Alexis Durbin, Nevaeh Lee, Mia Kayla, B.A. Wolfe, Michelle Lynn, Livia Jamerlan, A.L. Zaun, Elisabeth Grace, K. Langston, and Mia Sheridan…thank you—from the bottom of my heart—thank you.

Prologue

Harley

"HOLY SHIT, THAT BURNS!" I crinkle my nose up at the fire the tequila leaves behind.

"Pussy." Quinn laughs, handing me a lemon and popping one in her mouth.

Flipping her off, I swivel in my seat, watching all the sweaty bodies fight for attention on the dance floor. Adam Levine's seductive voice croons through the speakers, and I sway to the beat.

My eyes wander over to the pool table, landing on Ty. Reaching up, he runs his fingers through his shaggy, brown hair and laughs at something someone says. His dimples take root, and his smile lights up his face. I tilt my head to the side, a deep sigh rushing from my lips. *Ty.*

We're friends.

Best friends.

That's it.

Tyson and I grew up together. Literally. Our mothers have been best friends since the day my family moved in next door. At the ripe age of twelve months, Tyson and I became friends. We not only learned how to walk together, we learned how to do *every-*

thing together. He was my preschool buddy, my co-conspirator in detention, and he survived my attempts at learning how to drive.

Tonight, we are celebrating because this morning, we graduated from college together. Me, with a degree in nursing, and Ty with his bachelor's in biology—Pre-Med.

Quinn nudges my shoulder. "You love him. You need to tell him or you're going to regret it." She thinks she's helping, but she's not. Some things should just stay the way they are...I think.

"Quinn," I say, raising my glass to the server with a quick nod, letting her know I want another. "It's complicated."

She shakes her head with a sarcastic laugh. "Only because you're making it. Why you two are in the friend zone is beyond me."

The server sets down another round of shots. "Shut up and drink. To friends!" I raise my glass, tap it against hers, and down the shot. I stare at my empty shot glass. My head spins, signaling the beginning of a nice buzz. I wasn't planning on getting drunk tonight, but after the bomb Tyson dropped on me a couple of hours ago, I need this.

Tyson is standing in the doorway to my bedroom, his hands tucked deep in his pockets. He looks off to the side. "Harley, we need to talk." His voice is pained, and he hasn't made a move to come in. I can tell I'm not going to like this. My heart drops into the pit of my stomach because I can feel it in my bones...something is off.

"Okaaaay, shoot." I train my eyes on the suitcase in front of me as I begin to pull out clothes. He reaches for me, but I turn away and stuff some T-shirts in my drawer.

"A lot changes when you go away to college for four years," he says, running his hand down the back of his neck.

"Yes, it can." Opening the closet door, I stare into the dark empty space. "Moving back home is going to take some getting used to. I'm definitely finding a place of my own right after I find a job."

"Brit and I decided not to stay at Wash U for medical school," he blurts. "She wants to be closer to her family." Ty wipes his hands on his jeans and fidgets as he sits on my bed. I take a deep breath and close my eyes.

Ty shifts toward me, reaching for my hand. This time, I don't pull away. "Please look at me, Harley. I want you to understand what I'm saying."

I blow out the breath I didn't know I was holding and stare at my suitcase for a few more seconds before I look up. "Doesn't Brit's family live in New York?"

"They do," he nods, "as soon as she told me she wanted to be near them, we applied to the medical school at Columbia, and we've both been accepted. We, ummm, we leave next week."

"What?" I gasp, jumping up, my eyes nearly popping out of my head. "You can't be serious." My voice rises with each word. "Just like that?" I shake my head, refusing to accept this. "You're just going to up and leave?" I shove a drawer closed harder than I intend, causing the mirror to shake violently. "One week? That's it?" Tears gather in my eyes and I look away, blinking rapidly to keep them at bay.

I will not cry.
I will not cry.

"I'm sorry, Harley," Tyson's voice cracks. "I didn't know how to tell you." He sighs heavily, dropping his head. "I didn't want to tell you." His hands shake in his lap, and some of my anger dissipates. The magnetic pull we've always had draws me closer to him. My fingers itch to dive into his hair and pull him against me. To comfort him. To comfort me. Something—anything—to slow down whatever storm he's battling...but . . . I don't.

"Wow," I whisper, sitting on the bed next to him. "I'm not really sure what to say." I look up, and our eyes meet in the mirror. "Is this what you want? I mean, she isn't pressuring you to do this. Right?"

He shakes his head slowly. "No, she isn't." I reach over and grab his hand, entwining my fingers with his, and he squeezes his eyes shut with the contact. "She's my future, Harley," he says, looking up. "This is my future. Please tell me you understand." He clutches my hand, a silent plea for me to accept the path he's chosen.

Don't go.

Stay.

Don't do this.

"Of course," I whisper, my heart breaking at the lie. Unable to hold back the tears, I let them fall silently down my cheeks while my mind yells at me to say or do something to make him stay.

"Earth to Harley," Quinn says, jolting me out of my trip across the minefield I walked through today.

I glance over at the pool table again. Tyson's arm hangs loosely around Brit's neck. Her arms are wrapped tightly around his body. Me. That should be me.

I watch as he wraps her perfectly straight, blond hair around his hand and tugs her beautifully sculpted face to his. He leans down, placing a gentle kiss on her pouty lips, and when she smiles, I swear, I'm blinded by her sparkling blue eyes. I, on the other hand, was gifted with an unruly brown rat's nest on top of my head and a pair of mossy green eyes with a tiny button nose. Side by side, we are the princess and the frog.

Okay, I may be exaggerating a bit. I'm cute, or so I've been told. But Brit is every man's dream. She can have any guy she wants, but she wants Tyson—*my* Tyson.

I sigh as he pulls her in closer. The worst part is that he wants her, too.

I hate her.

They began dating our sophomore year in college, and my relationship with Brit has been rocky at best. She's frequently upset with the amount of time that Ty and I spend together. Despite our reassurances that we're just friends, she doesn't buy it. On more than one occasion, she has tried to convince Ty that I've been harboring secret feelings for him. She even went so far as to accuse me of using our friendship as an excuse to spend extra time with him.

And although Tyson never believed her, she was right. I do have feelings for Ty. I've loved that boy since I was nine years old. The minute he punched Jimmy Tallen in the nose for calling me ugly, my heart belonged to him.

Telling him about my feelings just didn't seem like an option. He never seemed to be into me, and I wasn't willing to risk losing our friendship. So I sat back, watching quietly as he dated girl after girl. I nursed his broken hearts and encouraged him to get back on the dating wagon, as any good friend would do. Then Brit literally stumbled into our lives and everything changed. I didn't like it at all.

Tyson used to know everything about me. He knew all of my secrets, lies, and insecurities. But that isn't the case anymore. He doesn't know my biggest secret—he doesn't know that I'm in love with him.

Something began to happen though when he told me he was moving. It took me all afternoon to recover from the bomb he dropped and I'm not sure what it was, but it's like a puzzle piece was put into place. Everything became crystal clear. *He can't leave without knowing the truth.*

"One more shot," I say, raising my glass to Quinn.

Her lips curl into a devious smile. "Someone is getting brave."

"I need all the liquid courage I can get." We tap and chug.

"It's about damn time." She has been trying to get me to confess my undying love for Ty for the past four years.

My head spins when I move to stand, but it's not because I'm drunk. Confrontations have never been my strong suit. Not that I'm going to confront Ty in a bad way, but until now, I've always been able to predict how Tyson will react to things. This…well, I honestly have no idea how he is going to respond to this.

On unsteady legs, I make my way across the bar. Ty is playing pool with Levi and Cooper, his college roommates. This is the perfect time to approach him since Brit is standing at an adjacent table talking to some of her friends. I would prefer her not to be present for this conversation.

Levi greets my intrusion with a hug. "Hello, gorgeous." His hand roams down to the small of my back, and I smack it away playfully.

Poking his chest, I give him a firm look. "No ass grabbing tonight," I scold.

I lean against the back wall and watch as Cooper sweeps the table. That's my cue. Wasting no time, I kick off the wall and approach Ty. "Hey, got a sec?"

He cocks his head to the side, giving me a lopsided grin that makes my insides melt and my knees wobble. "Anything for you, you know that."

Taking a deep cleansing breath, I calm my nerves. "Can we step outside? Maybe somewhere a little more quiet?"

Tyson purses his lips, but he doesn't protest. Instead he places his hand at the small of my back and steers me toward the side door.

"I think there are some tables outside in the back," he says quietly.

I nod once and continue for the exit. Tyson opens the door and a rush of hot air greets us before he guides me to the right and toward the back of the building, where we locate a group of picnic tables. We walk quietly side-by-side while I give myself a pep talk.

Breathe.
You can do it.
Breathe.
What's the worst that could happen?
Don't forget to breathe.

We stop by one of the tables and I grab Ty's arm, preventing him from sitting. "I think you're going to want to stand for this."

I know him all too well, and I'm sure that within the next two minutes he'll be pacing like a bull.

"Okay. You're starting to make me nervous, Harley. Is everything okay?" He runs his hand through his hair, giving it that I-just-had-wild-monkey-sex look, and then he shoves both hands into his pockets.

I take a deep breath and blow it out slowly. *It's now or never.* "I love you."

Smiling sweetly, he replies, "I love you, too."

I shake my head, pinning him with my stare, trying to convey how much my feelings have morphed from friendship into something more. "No. I *love you*, love you, Ty."

At first he just looks at me, and I'm not completely sure he understands what I'm saying.

But then I see it.

Acceptance, relief, and fear flash quickly through his eyes, before settling on the one thing that makes this all worth it: love. Pure love.

My body sags with relief. *This was the right move.*

My small bubble of hope is quickly popped as Tyson's expression changes. His face turns cold. His eyebrows narrow. He shakes his head slowly. He looks over at me and then stares at the ground, clenching his fists. When his eyes land back on mine, the love that I saw a second ago is gone. But it was there. I saw the adoration in his eyes. He can fight it all he wants, but it *was* there.

"Don't leave. Please don't leave," I beg, my voice panicky. Desperation takes over. I cling to his arms, trying to get him to look at me, but he shrugs me away. "Stay. Please stay. Stay here with me. I love you." My words rush out, tumbling over each other. I can't stop them. "I know you're my best friend, but I love you. I'm *in* love with you. I want to be with you, Ty. Give me a chance...give us a chance." I reach slowly for his hand, needing to make some sort of contact, but he pushes me away. With his fingers tightly laced together, he placed his hands on his head and paces in circles.

"I know I'm asking a lot," I say, my voice thick with emotion. "I should have told you a long time ago, but I didn't, and I can't change that now."

Tyson keeps walking in circles, clenching and unclenching his fists.

I take a hesitant step toward him. "I know that this is incredibly selfish of me. I know I'm asking you to give up everything, but—"

"I can't believe this is happening," he interrupts. I don't respond because he doesn't give me the chance. "How long, Harley? How long have you felt like this?"

"Years."

"Years?" he asks incredulously, his eyebrows arched.

I nod my head, swallowing hard, suppressing the tears threatening to fall.

His head drops down. His voice is quiet but full of curiosity. "Why now, Harley? Why not a year ago, a month ago, or hell, a week ago? Why now?"

"Because you're too important to me, Ty. I was scared." My voice cracks when I say his name and a fat tear streaks down my cheek. "I didn't want to risk our friendship. I didn't want to lose everything we have if you didn't feel the same way." I squeeze my eyes shut and hang my head in regret. I should have told him sooner, but I've come this far, and I'm sure as hell not giving up now. Wiping away the wetness under my eyes, I step in Ty's path, preventing further pacing. "Would it have mattered? If I would have told you a year ago, a month ago, or a week ago...would it have mattered?"

His eyes are downcast, his lips tilted in a frown. My chest tightens and my hand twitches, wanting to touch him, but I don't.

"Yes," he whispers, looking up at me. "It would have mattered."

"Then it matters now!" I snap. "If it would have mattered

then, then it matters now. We can do this, Ty. You just have to take the chance. Please take the chance. Please," I beg.

His emotions shift once again, anger and resentment visibly overtaking the sadness. Reaching for his head, Ty grips his hair tightly and a deep growl rips from his throat. "Damn it, Harley." His voice is low and hard. My eyes widen in shock at the menacing glare he shoots at me. "What the fuck do you want me to say to that? You're doing this because I told you I'm leaving. Do you realize what you're asking? You're asking me to uproot my entire life. Do you know the work it took to transfer medical schools? And what about Brit?" His mouth parts and a look of horror overcomes his features. "Brit," he mutters to himself. "Fuuuuuck. Brit was right."

He begins to mumble and I'm not sure if he is talking to himself or to me. "Brit told me you had feelings for me. I didn't listen. I defended you. I mean...I had hoped you did, but I didn't know. I told her she was wrong and that she was just jealous." He looks at me, eyes wide with shock. "But she *was* right. My God! All those times I left her to spend time with you..." His words drop off but quickly resume. "I told her there was no way you felt that way about me because you're my best friend." He stops pacing and turns to face me, but his eyes are trained on the ground.

Silence consumes us. Tension fills the air.

"Ty, say something please," I whisper. "Please tell me what you're thinking. You're my best friend, and I know you feel like I'm just throwing this at—"

"But you are," he interrupts loudly. "You are just throwing this at me, Harley!"

I grip my hands tightly in front of me, wringing my fingers together in pure desperation. My heart slams in my chest. I know he feels the same way. He loves me. I saw it in his eyes. I just have to convince him that this is right. I wait patiently for him to continue, but when his hard gaze lands on me, my hope vanishes into thin air and my heart plummets to the ground. His lips are set in a firm line, and his eyebrows are dipped low in disappointment.

"I'm with Brit," he states firmly. "And I'm not going to hurt her...I can't." He shakes his head. "She hasn't done anything to deserve this," he says, waving his hand between the two of us. The pacing continues, back and forth in front of me until he finally removes his hands from his hair and places them on his hips. He turns to face me. There is a finality in his eyes that causes my resolve to crumble. I throw a hand to my mouth, but I can't stop the sob that slips out.

"Harley..." His voice trails off while his eyes search mine—for what, I'm not sure. "Harley, I can't do this. I'm sorry, but I can't." He pauses again, taking a second to sit down on the table. Placing his elbows on his knees, he bends forward and lowers his head. His voice is so soft that I almost don't hear his next devastating words. "We need to step back and take a break...from our friendship, Harley. We need to take a step back from our friendship."

I cry, and my body trembles. "No." My hands shake, my mind working furiously to find a way to fix this. "No," I repeat desperately. "We don't need to take a step back. We need to move forward." I crouch down in front of Ty and grip his fisted hands in mine. "Please give me a chance. I know you're scared, but I promise, you won't regret it. You won't regret me." My eyes flicker across his face, pleading with him to take this leap.

He exhales loudly and raises his head. "I can't believe you're doing this to me—to Brit. Now. When I'm suppose to be moving to New York in a week. A fucking week, Harley!" Standing abruptly, his eyes lock onto something over my left shoulder, but I can't tear my eyes away from him to find out what it is. "I can't do this. I won't do it." A cold shiver of realization trembles through me. "I'm leaving next week for New York—with Brit. It's best for my relationship with her if you and I don't talk...at least not until I can sort through all of this in my head."

His words hit me like a knife to the chest. He can't mean that. He's just in shock. "We can't be friends?" I hiccup, gripping my chest where I'm sure there's a gaping whole from his words.

"Please don't do this. Please, Ty! I'm sorry." I grab his arm, forcing him to face me. "I'm so sorry. Please forget I said anything. I *can't* lose you...I *won't* lose you." My tears fall freely. I've stopped wiping them away; there's just no point.

I startle when I hear someone behind me clear their voice. I turn slowly and find myself face-to-face with Brit. I'm not sure how long she's been standing there, but based on the look on her face, I'd say she pretty much knows what's going on.

Ty moves to walk around me, and I quickly grab his wrist. "Please, Ty," I whisper. Gently removing my hand, he reaches for Brit, entwining his fingers with hers. Without a backward glance, they walk away.

Slumping down onto the picnic table, I close my eyes, praying that this was all a bad dream and I just have to wake up. Realistically, I know it's not, but there is always that small window of time right after something horrible happens when you feel like if you hope and pray hard enough, you can actually rewind time and undo what's been done.

I grip my hair tightly at the scalp and watch as my tears cascade off my face and hit the table below. I'm not sure how long I sit, but eventually I get up and pace the alley behind the bar, trying to wrap my head around everything that just happened. This is why I never told him before...for exactly this reason.

What on earth have I done?
He can't seriously end our friendship.
He can't really walk away.
There is way too much history for him to do that. Right?

A gravelly, slurred voice interrupts my thoughts. "Harley? That you?" The hair on the back of my neck stands up, and I squint through my tears, trying to see whom the drunken voice belongs to. Relief washes over me at the familiar face. I try to respond, but a deep sob comes out instead. He moves to my side quickly. "You're crying," he says, putting a comforting hand to my back. "Please don't cry."

I normally wouldn't get this close to someone who isn't Tyson or Quinn, but right now I need the familiarity and comfort he offers. In a desperate move, I wrap my arms around his middle, bury my face in his chest, and cry like I've never cried before.

The stench of smoke deeply rooted in his shirt fills my nostrils and the stale odor of liquor makes me sick as he whispers calming words in my ear. I should be worried. I've heard that he's gotten into some heavier drugs recently, but I know I'm safe.

We stand there for several minutes, neither of us saying a word. His body sways slightly to the left. I grip him tightly to steady his balance and raise my eyes to his. "Are you okay?"

His red-rimmed, glossy eyes lock onto mine, but he doesn't respond. I watch as his expression changes. A shiver runs up my spine as goose bumps immediately cover my body. "Are you okay?" I repeat, trying to keep the fear out of my voice. Loosening my grip, I attempt to step back, but his arms tighten around me.

"You always smell so good," he slurs, his eyes roaming my face. His hand slides up my back and to my neck. He wraps his fingers around my hair and tugs, forcing my head to snap back. Leaning into me, he runs his nose along the side of my neck, and my stomach churns. "I would have given you anything. But I wasn't good enough for you, was I?" I don't respond and he yanks my hair again, arching my back. "Was I?" he seethes.

I've never been in a situation where I feel legitimately uncomfortable in the presence of another human being, but right here...in this second...I am terrified. Adrenalin courses through my body. My heart slams violently in my chest and my muscles tense as terror washes through me. I squeeze my eyes tightly shut. A sharp pain rips through my scalp. My face smacks the ground, and a metallic taste fills my mouth.

Please, God. Please let me survive this.

Tyson

MY HAND GRIPS BRIT'S so tightly that I let go in fear of actually hurting her. She follows me across the dance floor, past Levi and Cooper at the pool tables, and to the bar. Flagging down the bartender, I order a bottle of Bud Light. I turn to Brit, raising my eyebrows and cocking my head toward the bar.

"I'm good," she replies quietly.

The bartender grabs a beer from behind the bar, pops the top, and slides it to me. I raise the bottle and begin to drink, my eyes landing on the door we just walked through.

Brit stands there, absently rubbing my arm. She is giving me time and space, but her stare begs me to say something. To be completely honest, I am absolutely dumbfounded at what just happened. When Harley asked to talk to me, I was expecting her to tell me she's going to miss me but supports me regardless. I was *not* expecting her to tell me she loves me and beg me to stay here to give "us" a chance. She completely caught me off-guard. At first, all I felt was relief. She finally said the words I've wanted to hear for so long.

I shouldn't have gotten mad that she didn't tell me sooner. That just makes me a hypocrite because I never told her how I felt either. I didn't mean to yell at her, and her tears were almost my undoing. I've never yelled at Harley—ever.

The other part of me feels horrible for Brit. I was ready to tell Harley I loved her too. I itched to pull her into me, bury my face in her thick brown hair, and tell her how happy she'd made me. But that split-second thought quickly vanished when Brit's face popped in my head.

I'm not sure when I started looking at Harley differently, but by the time I realized that I harbored some feelings for her, I was in college and the last thing I wanted to do was tie myself down. It makes me a prick, but it's the truth. I didn't want to be shackled to the girl next door—the girl who had naked pictures of my butt and took baths with me when I was growing up. I'm a guy. I wanted to drink beer with my friends and fuck hot girls, even if the girl next door was hot.

I wasn't expecting to meet Brit. In fact, she literally stumbled into my life when she tripped on the sidewalk and landed conveniently in my lap. But I sure as hell wasn't complaining. She was new and exciting, and she looked at me like I was a shiny toy that she couldn't wait to play with. And I wanted to be played with.

It was nice being around someone who didn't already know everything about me. I enjoyed telling her stories and having her ask me things, rather than just knowing me inside and out like Harley.

Fuck. I made the right choice...right? I mean...I've worked so hard to get where I am. It took a lot of work to switch medical schools. I just can't veer off course right now. And then there's Brit. I love Brit. Am I ready to just walk away from her? No. I will not second-guess myself. I made the right choice.

Brit rests her hand on my forearm, pulling me from my thoughts, and I turn to meet her eyes. "You okay?" she whispers.

"I feel like I should be asking you that."

She links her fingers between mine. "Do you..." She hesitates, her eyes frantically searching mine. "Do you want to stay? Here? With Harley?" Her eyes drop to the floor.

Gripping her chin between my thumb and forefinger, I lift her gaze back to mine. "No. Absolutely not. I love you, Brit," I say, brushing my lips gently against hers.

She nods, accepting my answer. "We still need to talk about what happened. If you choose me, then you need to choose me, one hundred percent." Lifting her hand, she runs her fingers behind my ear into my hair, rubbing my cheek with her thumb. Rising onto her toes, her lips meet mine, and then with absolute resolve, she says, "I'm sorry about what happened earlier, but I'm done sharing. I will not share you with her anymore. We'll never make it if I have to."

Taking a long swig of my beer, I set the bottle down and wrap her in my arms, pulling her close. I need to comfort her. I need her to comfort me.

"I know," I whisper into her ear.

Making our way over to Levi and Cooper, we quietly join in the conversation. Brit starts chatting with one of her friends while I stand there and pretend that my life didn't just completely change.

I can't help it. I continue to stare at the back door of the bar, waiting for Harley to come back in. I need to see her and make sure that she's okay. I practically tossed her out of my life, and I feel like a complete asshole for that. Right now, though, I would give anything to rewind time by a few minutes and change my wording a little bit. If I could, I'd be less harsh and maybe tell her something to ease the blow, if that were even possible.

The thought of not talking to Harley every day scares the shit out of me. It's an indescribable feeling, but if I had to try, I'd say that the thought of her not being a part of my life leaves me feeling...lost.

I'm not sure how much time passes, but Brit and I hang out with Levi and Cooper while I nurse another beer and lose another game of pool. A part of me is concerned that I still haven't seen Harley come back in, but I also don't see Quinn anywhere, so it's possible that Quinn met her outside and they left. I want so badly to go search for her and talk this out, but Brit deserves better than that.

"Come on, Brit," I say, grabbing her hand. "Let's go home." Halfway through the bar, she tugs on my arm and I turn to her, raising my eyebrows in silent question.

"Do you want to go find her? You know, to, umm, to make sure she's okay?"

I tighten my grip around her hand and pull her in for a tight hug. "You are amazing, do you know that?" I mumble into her hair.

She looks up at me and smiles sadly. I kiss her nose and whisper, "Let's go home. I can talk to Harley later. Tonight, I need to be with you."

Proceeding through the bar, we exit out into the warm summer heat. I open the passenger door to my truck, allowing Brit to slide in. Shutting her door, I jog around the front, anxious to get home so that I can show Brit *exactly* how much she means to me.

My truck roars to life and I reach over with my right hand to grab onto Brit's, entwining our fingers and bringing them to rest on my thigh. She smiles sweetly. I know Brit feels bad about what happened with Harley tonight because she knows how much Harley means to me. But I also know Brit will have plenty to say about it when we get home—she's never really cared for Harley.

Pulling up to the road, I signal to take a left turn, and for no particular reason, I glance into my rearview mirror. My gaze catches on Harley's red Mustang, and I furrow my brow in confusion.

If she's still there, where is she?

Chapter 1

5 Years Later

Harley

"MAX, PLEASE COME IN here so we can put your shoes on. We really need to get going, buddy."

Getting out of the house in the morning would be so much easier if I were actually organized. But...I'm not. I could probably speed up the Harley and Max morning extrication process if I would pre-select our clothes the night before and pre-make our lunches. Unfortunately for me, by the time I get home from work, make dinner, play with Max, bathe Max, and coerce Max into going to bed, I'm simply too exhausted to plan for the next day. Therefore, every morning I'm running around the house like a chicken with my head cut off while I try to get us out the door in a timely fashion.

"Wee oooo, weeee oooo, weeeee oooo." Max comes flying into the kitchen, sliding across the floor in his socks. "Officer Max toooooo the rescuuuuue!"

"Oh, thank God you're here, Officer Max," I croon. "I have

a huge emergency." I exaggerate my movements and point to his tennis shoes, which are sitting by the refrigerator. "See those shoes? They need feet! Do you have feet?"

"Yes ma'am, I do," he says, nodding his head curtly.

"You, Officer Max, will save my whole entire day if you will put those shoes on your feet!"

"No, mom!" he whines, rolling his eyes. *Do they seriously start that this early?* "I'm here to rescue, not save the day." Sliding his feet into his shoes, he leans back onto his hands, presenting me with his feet. "Double knot this time, mom. They always untie."

"You got it, Officer Max." I make quick work of tying his shoes, then ruffle his hair and grab his lunch box.

I've never been a morning person. I'd consider myself more of a night owl, but there is just something about the cool morning air that always makes me happy. It symbolizes the start of another day...a *new* day. There was once a time when I would dread the start of a new day. But I pulled through. I survived, and now I live for new days.

I wish I could say my journey to this happy place was an easy one, but I'd be lying. It was a bitch. My soul was tried and tested, along with the patience of the people I love most in my life. But with their persistence and support, I was able to find peace and smile once again.

Once we're in the car and buckled in, my eyes find Max in the rearview mirror. "Finger out of the nose, please."

"Geez, how do you do that?" he whines.

"Do what?"

"Catch me."

"I have eyes in the back of my head," I deadpan, my smile bursting to break free.

"What?" he gasps. "You do?"

"Yup, mommies see everything. Remember that, okay?"

He nods solemnly. "Okay, but can you see through doors?"

"Sometimes. I just have to concentrate reaaaally hard."

"Someday, can I see through doors and grow eyes in the back

of my head?"

Chuckling softly, I respond, "Someday, buddy. Probably when you become a daddy."

He scrunches his brows. "Huh?"

Oh Lord, I couldn't keep my damn mouth shut. Haven't I learned my lesson yet? Every answer results in another question, and another question and another question...

"Alright buddy, we're here," I announce, grateful that the trip to Max's daycare is a short one. Hopping out of the car, I reach into the back and unhook Max from his booster seat. Grabbing his lunch box, I hurriedly walk him to the door. "Okay, Max. Mommy loves you. I'll see you when I get off work." I bend to hug him, but he's already bouncing off to where his friends are sitting down, playing with fire trucks.

His teacher, Maria, walks up and smiles as she reaches for his lunch box. "Have a good day, Harley. We'll see you tonight."

CRANKING UP THE RADIO, I settle in my seat for the commute to work. I live in Illinois but drive across the river into Missouri for my job. There are hospitals that are definitely closer, but none that pay quite as well with the same benefits as the city hospitals. I work at a larger university hospital where I've been employed as a staff nurse for the past five years.

Two years ago, I was given the opportunity to take on a 'float' position. There are several perks to being a float nurse. First and foremost, it allows me to work eight-hour shifts rather than the usual twelve hours. I still have to work every third weekend, but all in all, the hours are great and it allows me to be home with Max in the evenings.

Plus, I'm never bored at work. I'm constantly being pulled from one floor or one department to the next, which keeps things interesting. I am able to meet so many people that I wouldn't have met otherwise. It's also allowed me to greatly expand my medical knowledge base.

My dream is to one day become a nursing educator and teach the next generation of nurses. I want to guide them into becoming the silent heroes that they are destined to be. But my dream is just that...a dream. Going back to school isn't an option right now.

It took a long time to get where I needed to be financially, but I feel like I'm finally getting there. Last year, I signed the paperwork and bought the first real home Max and I have ever had. Leaving my parents' house was hard, but it was something I had to do—not only for myself, but for Max as well.

I was in such a bad place mentally and emotionally after he was born that it literally took two years to dig, scratch, and claw my way back—but I did it. Then,

I worked my ass off for the next three years to save enough money for a down payment on a home, all while providing for my son. Aside from the day Max came into this world, the day I bought our house was the proudest I've ever been.

The faint buzzing of my phone snaps me out of the fog. Sliding my finger across the phone, I allow my Bluetooth to accept the call.

"Hello, Levi," I answer while picking up my cup to take a drink of my tea.

"Good morning, beautiful. Max in the car?"

"Nope, you're all clear. What's up?" That's one thing I love about Levi; he always asks if Max is in the car before he starts talking. Levi has been present since the day Max was born. He understands how quickly Max's little ears pick up on something. I'll never forget how that lesson was learned.

Max was two, and Levi and I were in the car, taking him to the zoo. A car cut us off. Levi slammed on his breaks and murmured *'asshole'* under his breath. Needless to say, we spent the entire day trying to stop Max from calling everyone at the zoo an asshole. It was one of those times when—as a mom—I felt horrible that my son was cussing, but it was also one of those hilarious moments that we'd never forget.

"Can I get Max later? That Disney movie he wanted to see came out this week. I'd like to take him, if that's okay with you?" Pots were clanging in the background; Levi was most likely opening the restaurant for the day.

"Absolutely. Max would love that," I answer, smiling softly to myself. I couldn't ask for a better male figure in Max's life. Well, other than my dad.

"Great! I can't wait. We always have so much fun. Plus, he's a great wingman." His deep chuckle rings rich through the line, bringing a warm feeling to my heart.

"Thanks, Levi," I say, exhaling loudly. Some things are just too difficult to put into words. "For everything." The last part is whispered, but he hears it—he always hears it.

"No need to thank me, baby girl. No need at all," he says, his voice softening, followed by a beat of silence. "See you tonight."

I swallow past the lump in my throat, determined to keep myself together. "Yup. See you tonight.".

Aside from Quinn, Levi has been the most amazing friend I could ever ask for. If I were a smart girl—which obviously I'm not—I would grab onto everything that Levi has offered me, and I would hold on damn tight. But I can't let myself do that. I've already lost one friend; I'm not willing to lose another.

My relationship with Levi is so complicated, yet so easy. To put it simply, we each act as a crutch for the other. I'm there for him when he needs someone, both emotionally and physically, and vice versa. But we aren't *together,* and both of our hearts are closed off to the rest of the world.

It took a long time before I let a man touch me after the attack. The insecurities that I harbored prevented any of my relationships from growing—until Levi. As my relationship with Levi developed, so did my comfort level around him. To be honest, if it weren't for him, I'm afraid I may have never let another man touch me again.

Levi was there for me the day my life irreversibly changed,

and he has stayed by my side through it all. He held me after the doctors cleaned me up, comforted me after every panic attack, dried my tears when there was no hope for them to stop, and eventually yelled at me to get my ass back into gear. Then, because he is such an amazing friend, he went through Lamaze class with me and held my hand during Max's birth. To top off every incredible thing he has already done, he continues to be a part of our lives and has essentially taken on a fatherly role with Max. To put it mildly, I owe Levi my life and sanity.

I wish I could kick myself in the ass, not only for allowing Levi to do everything he has done and for leaning on him so much, but because I haven't been completely honest with him. There are things from that horrific night five years ago that I haven't told anyone—not Levi, not Quinn, and most certainly not the police. Shame and embarrassment have plagued my sleep for the past five years, and I can't share those details with anyone else.

Ever.

My day at work flies by like usual. Today, I worked in the emergency room. Of all the departments, ER is my least favorite, so thank the Lord this day is over, because I have wonderful things planned for tonight. After Levi picks Max up, I have a date with my Kindle and bathtub, and if I'm feeling really frisky, I may even throw in a bottle of wine.

Yay for me!

Four hours later, two loads of laundry, and a sinkful of dishes later, I find myself submerged in a sudsy paradise while electronically lusting after my current book boyfriend, Jax. My Kindle in one hand and a glass of sweet Moscato in the other, life can't get much better than this. Well, maybe it could...especially if I had a hard warm body in the form of a man sitting in here with me to act out some of these smokin' hot sex scenes.

Damn sex scenes.

Reaching over the edge of the tub, I set my Kindle and wine glass down. I lean my head back on my bath pillow and slink down further into the tub, allowing the bubbles to conform to my curves. Closing my eyes, I glide my hand down the planes of my stomach toward my core, which is now throbbing incessantly. My fingers easily slide through my entrance, and my lips part in a low moan at the intrusion. Using the heel of my hand, I gently apply pressure to my clit, allowing the deep warmth in the pit of my stomach to take form.

Sliding my free hand to my breast, I begin kneading and pinching my hardened nipple, starting gently and then slowly applying more pressure until the most amazing sensations shoot straight to my toes.

My heart rate increases and a fine sheen of sweat forms across my forehead as my orgasm builds. My back arches and I push my hips down, using the added force to my advantage.

Ahhhh...so close.

Moving my hand and fingers fervently, I bring myself closer and closer to the place I'm so desperately trying to re—

"Were home," Max sings loudly from the entryway.

No no no no no...

Max flings the bathroom door open and I still my hand under the water, my breath coming out in labored pants. I want nothing more than to rub the ache that I have built up, the ache that's on the verge of exploding. It takes every ounce of willpower I have to remain still and unaffected.

This is not happening.

This is not happening.

Repeating this mantra over and over again will surely make this situation go away, right?

I purposely slow my breathing and try to appear relaxed. I open my eyes in time to see Levi come barreling into the bathroom behind Max.

"Max, what are you—" Levi's words die off as he bumps into Max, propelling him forward. Levi cocks his head to the side and his lips slowly curve into a devastating grin.

Oh, dear Lord.

Grabbing onto Max's shoulders, Levi steers him into the hall.

"Buddy, why don't you go to your room and get your pajamas on and then crawl into bed? I'll be there in a couple minutes to read you a book, and we'll let your mom finish her bath." Levi's gaze never wavers from mine as Max bounces out of the room without a backward glance.

Levi shuts the door, the click of the lock echoing loudly in my ears.

Stalking over to the tub, he sits on the edge and simply stares at me contemplatively. When he finally speaks, his voice is equal parts amusement and desire.

"Harley?"

"Yes?" I squeak.

"What are you doing?"

"Taking a bath," I half question, half state.

"What else are you doing, Harley?"

Dropping to his knees, Levi leans in closely, brushing his lips against the outer rim of my ear. His voice is a hoarse whisper and oozes sex. "Don't even answer that. I know *exactly* what Max walked in on because it's written all over your face."

His cerulean eyes and deep voice are hypnotizing and have me completely paralyzed. Using the back of his hand, he slides his fingers over my cheek. "You're flushed," he says softly as his hands trail down my neck, "and your pulse is racing." As his fingertips reach the swell of my breast, he murmurs, "And you're breathless."

Fuck me running. This guy is sex on a stick and I'm horny as hell.

Levi leans down, the stubble on his square jaw tickling me as he nuzzles the soft spot below my ear. Dropping my head, I can't help but watch as his hand descends past my breast and under the soapy water.

Keep going, you're almost there.

His hand is no longer visible, but I can sure as hell feel every inch of skin it's grazing under the water. His touch is leaving behind a tingly goodness that is quickly building the tension back up in my body. I tilt my head up, offering him my mouth, and he quickly accepts the invitation. Molding his soft lips to mine, I allow him in and our tongues begin to slide against one another effortlessly.

His fingers slide into me and I groan, fisting a hand in his thick black hair. Slowly, he begins to push them deep and then pull them out and back up over my clit, circling it with perfect rhythm. My pleasure begins to rip through me, eliciting a loud gasp from my wanton body.

Oh Shit! Max!

Sitting up abruptly, I dislodge Levi's hand from between my legs. "We can't do this. I have to go get Max. I don't want him wond—"

"Shhh...Max is fine," he whispers, gently pushing his hand back between my thighs, which willingly allow him entrance.

Damn traitorous thighs, I knew you couldn't be trusted.

He growls deep in his throat as his mouth attacks my breast. Using his tongue and teeth, he flicks and nips my hardened nipple, alternating from one breast to the next. A deep warmth takes over my body and my hips begin to move in sync with his fingers as the tension starts to build low in my abdomen.

Increasing the pace of his movements, Levi starts a persistent attack against my clit.

"Oh God," I moan, a deep flush crawling up my neck. "Please don't stop." Throwing my head back, I give Levi complete control of my body. Waves of pleasure begin to crash through me, sending pulsating bliss straight to my core. My fingers dig into his back as I hold on for dear life.

Levi continues to rub, his movements slowing and the pressure lightening while I come down from my post-orgasmic high.

Lifting his head, he places a gentle kiss to my nose. "That was the sexiest fucking thing I've ever seen." Removing his arm from the water, he uses my towel to dry it off and walks to the door. Flicking the lock, he turns the knob and then stops, turns slightly, and gives me a wink before sauntering out.

I stare at myself in the mirror. My lips are red and swollen and my neck is excoriated from the stubble on Levi's face. I should be elated, considering a gorgeous man just gave me an amazing orgasm...but I'm not. I feel nothing. I don't get goose bumps when Levi walks into the room and no butterflies flutter around my belly when he touches me. Am I okay with that? I run the tips of my fingers across my swollen lips and consider the fact that maybe Levi and I shouldn't be doing this.

I finger comb my hair and throw it into a messy ponytail. Slipping on my favorite yoga pants and T-shirt, I make my way out into the hall before sneaking a peek in Max's room. He's already asleep. Tiptoeing quietly to his bed, I brush his hair back from his face and place a kiss on his forehead. "Love you, buddy," I whisper softly.

Walking into the living room, I find Levi sprawled out on the couch with a beer in his hand. "Max was already asleep by the time I left the bathroom, so you'll have to brush his teeth twice in the morning," he says, giving me a cheeky smile.

I make my way to the couch and curl up next to Levi, resting my head on his arm. Shifting the beer to his right hand, he encircles my shoulders and hugs me tightly. "Why is it that this should feel weird with you, but it doesn't?" I ask.

"What do you mean?" he says with a frown.

Straightening my back, I shrug off his arm and sit up, turning to face him. Levi mimics my position and rests his hand on my thigh. Taking a deep breath, I respond, "You just got me off in the bathtub—" He grins and I slap his chest playfully. "And then we come out here and sit like nothing ever happened. You aren't even upset that you didn't get off."

"Oh no, I'm actually really pissed about that," he says with a wide smile while reaching down to unbutton his pants. "In fact, get down on your knees."

I roll my eyes, not acknowledging his feeble attempt at amusement. "See, I'm trying to have a real conversation with you and all you—"

"I'm sorry, I'm sorry," he cuts me off. "I won't joke anymore. You want to talk, we'll talk."

"Thank you. Now where was I? Oh yeah...you don't think it's weird that we have been intimate in every way possible for a man and woman, and yet afterward, we so easily fall right back into our friendship like nothing ever happened?"

"Oh no, we're definitely fucked up. But it's us, so who cares?" He takes a long swig of his beer, emptying the bottle and then setting it down on the table. Grabbing my hands, he continues, "This works for us because I'm not your prince."

"I don't need rescuing," I scoff.

Levi's gaze softens and he raises his hand to gently brush the side of my cheek. "I know you don't *need* a prince, Harley, but that's what you deserve. You *deserve* a prince."

"Well, I'm not your princess," I say with a light smile.

He nods once. "Exactly. I love you, Harley, but I'm not *in love* with you, just like you're not *in love* with me. We have filled a void for each other, but that's all it is. That's all it'll ever be."

Laying my head against the back of the couch, I raise my eyebrows, urging him to continue, and he chuckles softly. "Because someday you'll find your prince. But that's not going to change anything; it's not going to change how I feel about you. You will always be my best friend and I will always be here for you...even if I'm not the one making you come on a regular basis." His smile is infectious and I can tell he's trying to get a rise out of me, but this is my chance and I'm taking it.

"And you'll find your princess."

"Huh?"

"You said some day I'll find my prince, and I'm saying that someday you'll find your princess."

"Sorry, sweetheart," he says, closing his eyes as he leans his head back and runs a hand down his face, "that ship sailed a long time ago."

I cock my head. "I don't understand."

He scoffs but continues, "I've already found my princess,

Harley." My eyes widen, doing a piss-poor job at hiding my shock. Levi has never talked about his past girlfriends, and he's never alluded to having already found *the one*.

"Levi..."

"Listen," he scolds, holding up his hand. "I'm only going to talk about this once and then it's over...got it?"

I nod once.

"I gave my heart away a long time ago. That's why it's so easy to be with you—or anyone else I meet—without getting attached, because I don't have a heart to give away. I don't even know where my heart is right now; all I know is that she walked away with it and for the life of me, I can't seem to get it back."

Reaching out, I lock my hand around his forearm. "Do you want to tell me about her?"

"Nope," he shakes his head. "But that's why we work. Some day the 'benefits' portion of our friendship will end, and that's okay. But until that day comes..." he trails off, wiggling his eyebrows in a suggestive manner.

"Down boy," I chuckle, knowing good and well that he has just ended that conversation. Closing my eyes, I lean my head back on the couch, silently enjoying the camaraderie that Levi and I share. Finally able to relax, I allow myself to feel at peace, not knowing that what's about to come out of Levi's mouth is going to rock my world to its core.

"So...ummm..." Levi clears his throat and swallows hard. "I ran into Tyson before picking up Max. I, uh, I thought that you should know. He moved back home, Harley."

I inhale quickly, sitting up and locking my eyes onto Levi's. My heart starts racing and a rush of adrenaline shoots through my body. I want to know everything. How did he look? Who was he with? Where was he? But mostly, I want to know if he asked about me. My questions remain trapped as my worried eyes search Levi's face, trying to come to grips with what he just told me.

Tyson is home.

Chapter 2

Tyson

"HEY, BRO! I KNOW it's been awhile since I've been by to see you...okay, it's been five years and I feel horrible about that." With a deep breath, I resolve to say all of the things that I've had holed up in my damn head for the past five years.

"God, Dallas. I was so angry with you. Angry about the things you did. Angry about the things you didn't do. Angry that you didn't try harder...for me."

I begin pacing back and forth. Reaching up with my hands, I grip my hair and tug roughly. My next words come out harsh and loud. "I fucking looked up to you, Dallas. You're my big brother and I idolized you. Not only that, I defended you! When everyone else had something bad to say, I was the one sticking up for you. I was the one telling everyone how wrong they were."

Taking a deep breath, I close my eyes. I've got to let this go. Sitting here and yelling at someone who can't yell back isn't going to do a damn thing for anybody.

"So I ran into Levi a few nights ago," I breathe, trying to let go of my anger. "You remember Levi, don't you? Anyway, I was walking into the grocery store and, lo and behold, there he was."

It took me all of about two seconds to feel like a complete idiot. Levi was one of my best friends for years. After Brit and I left for New York, Levi and I kept in contact fairly regularly, but the further I got into medical school, the harder it became to make time for anyone. Before I knew it, almost an entire year had passed and I hadn't once talked to Levi or Cooper.

When I finally pulled my head out of my ass and called him, things were strained. He wanted to talk about Harley, and well...I didn't. But it wasn't because I didn't want to hear about her. Nope, it was the complete opposite. I wanted to know everything about her; I was just too chicken-shit to ask.

"You remember Harley, right? Of course you do," I say, chuckling lightly to myself. "You had such a crush on her. I remember when she would come over, and you would always find a way to involve yourself in our conversations or our plans. You were so persistent, always trying to get her to go out with you. But she never would. She always told you that her dad wouldn't let her date an older boy." I shake my head, smiling. "That was a freakin' lie."

Sitting down, I take off my jacket and lay it on the soft green grass. I lie back, folding my arms under my head and close my eyes. Taking a deep breath, I allow myself to be sucked in by the memories.

"I never told you, but Harley and I got into a huge fight our junior year of high school. I told her that she was being stupid and she should give you a chance. That maybe you guys would hit it off. But she wouldn't do it. She always said that if something went south with the two of you, that it would put me in a bad spot and she wasn't willing to risk losing our friendship."

Harley.

God, I miss her.

I was a terrible friend. I'll never forget the look on her face the night I walked away from her. Her tears and the sound of her voice as she begged me to stay are forever burned into my brain.

But walking away from her that night isn't my biggest regret.

My biggest regret is never making it right. Those first two days after our big fight, my phone was inundated with texts and voicemails from Levi, Quinn, and even Harley's mom. When Harley started calling, that's when I turned off my phone and left it off.

At the time, I hadn't been ready to talk to her, or anyone else for that matter. I was simply trying to absorb what Harley's confession meant for me...for us...for Brit. My plan had been to make the move to New York, allow things to calm down, and then reach out to Harley. But that never happened.

The day after I walked away from her, Brit and I began packing for New York. Then, before I knew it, it was time to leave. The move and subsequent unpacking kept me busy, and before I knew it, two weeks had passed. When I finally took the time to listen to the voicemails on my phone, I discovered that they were mostly from Levi and Quinn. Harley had only left one. It's still saved in my phone.

"Tyson (sniff, sniff), please talk to me (sniff)." Her voice had been low and gravelly, most likely raw from crying. "Something happened and I—I need you. Please, Ty. I know I messed up. I know I put you in a bad spot and I would give anything—anything—to fix this, but that's not why I'm calling." She pauses, sobbing into the phone. "Please. I need you to call me, Ty. Please."

I never called her back.

Two weeks had already passed, and I had no clue what to say to Harley. Then, shortly after listening to her voicemail, I got the call about Dallas. That call fucking destroyed me.

Closing my eyes, I reach out with my right hand, allowing my fingers to graze over the lettering on the cool marble.

DALLAS THOMAS GRAWE
FEBRUARY 3, 1981 – JUNE 05, 2008
IN LOVING MEMORY OF OUR SON AND
BROTHER

My vision blurs and I blink rapidly, effectively stopping the tears. Turning away, I tilt my head to the sky.

"God, Dallas, you were my idol. You showed me how to throw that perfect spiral...and remember when I dinged dad's new car with my bike?" I laugh humorlessly. "You covered for me, just like you always had my back. I miss you so much, big brother."

I lower my head, pressing my fingers against my temples. It's so hard to remember the good times but not the bad. It's hard to forget how quickly things went to hell. The fraternity. Drinking. Drugs. Women. It all got the best of him.

I was so naive, telling myself that he was only doing what every other college kid was doing...experimenting, messing around, having fun. But Dallas was taking it too far. He quit coming home and stopped calling. Mom and Dad were a complete wreck and tried several times to reach out and get Dallas the help he so desperately needed.

One night after a raging party, Dallas called Dad. He was drunk and high, begging my Dad to come get him up.

My parents picked him up, and he spent the next nine months in and out of rehab. But none of that mattered. He relapsed. When Dallas died, the level of alcohol and drugs in his system was astonishing. The perfect amount of drugs...followed by alcohol...followed by more drugs...it was too much for his body to handle. I've often wondered whether or not it was accidental or if he knew the combination would be too much.

Coming home for the funeral was tough. Harley showed up with Levi and Quinn, and I didn't say a word to any of them. I was trying so desperately to wrap my head around everything that had happened with Dallas that I didn't want to talk to anyone about anything.

My teeth grind at the thought of the unknown and I stand hastily, shaking myself out of the path my head was going. Picking up my coat, I dust off the leaves that fall has left behind and I lay my hand atop Dallas' tombstone. "I've got to go. Levi and some of his friends are going out for drinks tonight and he invited me along. I promise I won't wait another five years. You'll be seeing a lot more of me." Slowly turning to walk away, my final words are but a whisper, "rest in peace, brother."

I PULL UP TO Blue, the upscale bar that Levi owns. It's attached to Flame, a restaurant that he owns with his dad. Pushing through the heavy steel door, I take in my surroundings. *Fuck, this place is awesome.* I make my way to the third level, where Levi said they would be sitting.

A young woman is standing at the top of the stairs, a clipboard in hand. She is gorgeous in her tight, tuxedo-style shirt, black pencil skirt, and red stilettos, but I wouldn't expect anything less coming from Levi. She reminds me of a librarian, and I instantly picture her with black-rimmed glasses and a wooden stick. *Shit. Now I'm hard.*

She smiles. "Your name please."

"Tyson Grawe," I reply, giving her an easy smile.

She glances briefly at her clipboard. "Right this way, Mr. Grawe." Her voice is low and seductive, and when she turns around, I have to adjust myself. "Your party is right over here. Can I start you off with something to drink?"

"Yes, Bud Light bottle." She grins and moves closer.

"Anything for you, Mr. Grawe. Please have a seat and I'll be right back with your drink."

Reaching out, I grab her hand before she walks away.

"I didn't catch your name."

Her eyes shine brightly. "Blaire," she states, giving a quick wink as she turns toward the bar.

Levi, Cooper, and Levi's brother, Mason, are situated around a high-top table."Tyson!" Levi booms, standing to shake my hand. "Goddamn, I missed your ugly face." He snakes his arm around my back and pounds a few times.

I sit down as Blaire returns with my beer.

"I see you met Blaire," Cooper says, leaning back in his chair to watch her ass as she walks away.

"Coop," Levi scolds, slapping Cooper in the chest. "Leave that poor girl alone."

"Trust me," Cooper says, leveling Levi with a glare while pointing in the direction of Blaire. "She is not a *poor* girl. Blaire's mouth—"

"Enough." Levi rolls his eyes and takes a pull from his bottle. "You know I can't sit here and talk about my staff like that. And I certainly don't need to know which of my girls you're luring into your bed," he says, shaking his head. He turns to me as Cooper reaches over to high-five Mason.

Damn, I've missed these guys.

"Where are you staying, bro?" Levi asks, tipping his beer at me.

"I'm renting a sweet-ass condo a few blocks from the hospital," I answer, picking at the label of my beer bottle.

"So you're not too far from here, then? You'll have to swing by sometime for lunch." I nod in agreement but don't get a chance to respond.

"So what the fuck happened with Brit?" Mason asks, leaning his elbows on the table. "Last we heard, the two of you were tying the knot." Before I can say anything, Levi and Cooper pipe in at the same time.

"I never liked her."

"She was a bitch."

I shake my head at the easy banter, amazed that we're all sitting around like no time has passed.

I raise my bottle, signaling for another beer. "Nah, we broke up."

"See," Levi says, "I knew I didn't like her." He lifts his bottle and we all salute. "To dodged bullets!" he says with a grin.

I chug what's left of my beer and a knot forms in my stomach. I wonder if Harley thinks of me as a 'dodged bullet.'

"Whatever happened to your parents?" Levi asks.

I sigh heavily. "They moved. Not far, but they were struggling after Dallas died. They needed to get out of town."

Levi nods in understanding and the table goes quiet. I hate this. Everyone does this when they talk to me about Dallas. Time for a subject change.

"This place is amazing," I say, reclining back in the leather chair. I look down and over the edge at the bar, admiring how stunning he made this place is. Stunning isn't even the right word... sexy is more like it. This place is fucking sexy.

"Thanks, man! That means a lot. She's my baby." I can hear the pride in his voice...and he damn well should feel that way.

"What are those?" I ask, pointing to three steel contraptions hanging from the ceiling.

"Those are God's gift to men," Cooper answers.

"Levi's girls dance in there," Mason says with a playful smile. "It was an ingenious idea. Everyone fucking loves it."

Interesting. "So your bartenders go in there, or patrons?" I ask, wondering briefly if Harley has ever stepped foot in one.

"Mostly the staff, but only if they want to. They get paid extra and then men usually tip really well afterward, so most of them aren't complaining." Levi turns back to the table and when Blaire returns with my beer, he orders a round of shots.

"Quinn gets in there," Cooper states, displaying a wide grin. "That girl is fucking hot." Mason shoots Cooper an irritated glare. "We've been telling Levi that he should hire her to come dance in one of those cages every weekend. The crowd that girl can draw is unbelievable!"

I watch curiously as Mason's jaw noticeably clenches. He opens his mouth to say something, then stops short. Pushing away from the table forcefully, he stalks off toward the bar. Okay, there is definitely a story there. I'll have to remember to ask Levi about that later.

"Knock it off," Levi says, his tone sharp.

"Oh, come on," Cooper defends. "Like you don't find it fucking hilarious."

"Has Harley been in there?" I interrupt, letting my gaze wander. I'm hoping like hell that question came off as indifferent, but when I glance back at Coop's face, I know I didn't succeed. His smirk is slow and easy, his eyes knowing. But what surprises me is the searing look I get from Levi, pinning me to the chair. I can't help but wonder if I just pissed on someone else's territory.

The sound of hysterical laughter breaks the tension and we turn in our seats, just in time to see a tall, willowy, beautiful woman come stumbling into the room.

Quinn. I smile softly to myself—she's always been a bit of a klutz.

Two seconds later, she is followed by...

Harley.

The sight of her causes my heart to start slamming wildly against my ribcage and my throat grows thick.

Christ, she looks incredible. Who am I kidding? She's always looked amazing, but her body has matured over the past five years in the most mind-blowing—and dick-throbbing—way. Her dark brown hair flows in long, thick waves past her shoulders. A yellow halter dress hugs her curves in all the right places and black stilettos show off her toned, mile-long legs. She looks absolutely perfect.

I keep telling myself to stop staring, but for the life of me I can't. For the past five years I've thought of her, and now here she is. Sliding my chair back, I begin to stand, the need to be closer to her pulling at me like a fucking magnet. I don't know what the hell I'm doing, but I know I've got to do something—say something.

Looking up from her phone, Harley spies Levi and her face lights up like a kid on Christmas morning. *What the fuck is that about?* As her eyes move across the rest of the table, she continues to laugh at something unknown. When her gaze lands on mine, the energy in the room shifts instantly. The air becomes heavy, and for a split second I find it hard to breathe.

Harley's face falls. The beautiful smile that had formed on

her face just seconds before is gone. Her eyes dart frantically to Levi and then back to me. Without a word, she spins on her heel and heads back out the same way she came in.

I need to go after her. There are so many things I need to tell her, starting with 'I'm sorry.' Before I can move, Levi grips my forearm. "I got this." He nods for me to sit and takes off toward the only place I want to be.

Fuck this, I haven't waited five years to just sit here. I push up from my seat and a round of cheers echo from my table. If I'm not mistaken, I hear Quinn mumble 'it's about damn time' as I stride past her.

Chapter 3

Harley

PISSED...I'M PISSED. NO, I'm beyond pissed. I'm furious. How could Levi do this to me? I trusted him, and he just invited Ty here without even—

Suddenly my arm is locked in a tight grip, another wrapping firmly around my stomach. Yanking at the hold, I attempt to propel myself forward but my body is quickly hauled up against a hard chest. Closing my eyes, I inhale deeply, a feeble attempt at calming myself. I don't need to turn around to know who my captor is; I would recognize his scent anywhere. He smells of old spice deodorant and peppermint and...Tyson.

He's panting, obviously having run out here after me, and his breath is hot against my ear, causing me to shiver. *Fuck.* I hate that he can still do this to me.

"Wha—" My voice comes out strained so I take a few deep breaths, trying to school my thoughts. My hands tremble at the feel of his arms wrapped around me, and my heart is slamming so hard in my chest that I'm slightly terrified it may tumble right out. "What are you doing here?"

To my surprise, he doesn't respond but continues to hold on

to me without a word. God, he smells so good. He *feels* so good. How did I ever think I could get over—?

Nope, not going there.

Twisting from his grasp, I turn, shoving at his chest. He doesn't budge. When did he get so...so...big? My God, this boy is ripped! Pissed that he didn't budge, I shove him again. This time his hands encircle my wrists and he uses his momentum to pull me toward him.

My glare is hard, but I can feel myself melting as I take in the man standing before me. Tyson has always been buff, but now he is downright sculpted. His black Henley stretches across his wide chest, and I swear I can see the definition of his pecs through the material. *That can't be right. Tyson doesn't have pecs.* His sleeves are bunched around his elbows and when his grip tightens on my wrists, I watch as the muscles in his forearms flex. A surge of unwelcome warmth shoots through my body and I yank at his hold, but it's useless...he's too strong. I puff out a hard breath, blowing a strand of hair out of my eye.

I know for a fact that he's hiding two perfectly placed dimples behind the firm look that he's giving me. I also know that I most likely won't be seeing them anytime soon.

His hair is still the same, only longer. His once carefully manicured locks now fall in light brown waves across his forehead and curl at the tops of his ears. It takes all the strength I have not to reach up and run my fingers through his hair to see if it's as soft as it looks. Not that I could right now even if I tried, since it's obvious he has no intention of letting go of my wrists.

Plus...what the hell is wrong with me?

I don't want to stroke his hair...I want to pull it! And not in the hot, sexy kind of way either.

"I'm sorry." Tyson swallows hard. "I hurt you, Harley, and I'm so sorry." His voice is sincere and his eyes are soft—which only pisses me off even more.

I flinch at his words. "You're sorry?" I ask incredulously, a sarcastic laugh quickly making its way out of my mouth. I repeat myself, only this time it's not a question. "You're sorry. Tell me, Tyson, what exactly are you sorry for?" Wrenching myself free from his grip, I continue with my rant without giving him a chance to reply.

"Are you sorry for showing up tonight? Are you sorry that I'm upset about seeing you? Are you sorry that I'm even here?" *Are you sorry that I haven't stopped loving you after all this time? Are you sorry that you broke my fucking heart?*

I can feel my body flush in frustration. My jaw clenches and tears burn my eyes, threatening to fall.

He grimaces at my words. A haunted look flashes across his face and he drops his head, staring down at his feet. He tucks his hands in his pockets, and I watch his shoulders rise and fall with a long, slow sigh.

I close my eyes tightly. *This has to end.* All of this anger and hurt that I've been harboring has got to go. As much as I don't want to do this, I know that I need to. I've waited five years to make peace. If there's any chance of me getting past this and moving on, then now's the time. I allow my tears to fall silently down my cheeks. There's no sense in wiping them away—he needs to know how much he hurt me.

"Or are you sorry for how things ended?" I murmur. "Is that it? After five long years, you've finally decided that you need to apologize for throwing away our friendship like it was *nothing*?"

His head snaps up, a painful expression marring his beautiful face. "You—"

"I know!" I snap, cutting him off. "I know I fucked up, okay?" My voice trembles and I wipe angrily at my tears. "I tried to apologize but you wouldn't listen to me," I yell, my voice cracking on the last word.

"I know but—" He tries to explain, but again I don't give him the chance. He didn't *once* give me the opportunity to tell him how I felt in the past five years, so there's no stopping me now.

"No! You *don't* know, Tyson. You don't know what I went through." Using my fist, I pound against my chest. "You don't know how bad your leaving hurt me. Because it did—it destroyed me. I needed you and you weren't there. I trusted you, Tyson. I trusted you with my friendship and my heart, and you ripped them both to shreds without a second thought." My chest is heaving and Tyson's face contorts as though he's in pain.

We both stand there, staring at each other. Tyson's shoulders droop and his arms hang loose at his sides. My chin quivers and tears continue to stream down my cheeks. Through my watery vision, I can see the pain and sadness in his eyes. I know that I hurt him when I confessed my feelings; I know he felt betrayed. But he's the one that walked away from me and never looked back, so what nerve does he have to stand there and look upset?

When he speaks, his voice is soft and hesitant but firm. "I don't know what you went through. And I know that I wasn't there for you, nor did I give you the chance to explain or apologize, but you don't know what I went through either." When I start to respond, he holds up his hands, urging me to let him continue. I snap my mouth closed, actually wanting to hear what he has to say.

"I'm sorry for everything, Harley. Everything." My heart squeezes at the words that I've waited so long to hear. "I'm sorry for all of it. Please, Harley. Please..." he begs, holding his hands out to me. "I need you to forgive me. I need you to give me another chance." His words sound firmer at the end and he straightens his back, standing tall. "I'm going to redeem myself for how I've acted the past five years. I want to know you again, Harley. I want our friendship back."

Wrong answer, buddy.

"Are you serious? What? You think that you can move home, tell me you're sorry, and POOF, everything is back to the way it was?" *God. Oh God.* I want that so badly—more than I ever want to admit. Just seeing him and being this close to him reminds me of everything that we've been through together, both good and bad. Only he wasn't there for the *really* bad, and whose fault was that?

"Give me *one* reason," I state firmly. "Give me one reason

why I should forgive you for walking away from me and our friendship so easily. One reason why I should forgive you for abandoning me at the darkest time of my life."

His response is immediate. "Because you promised to always forgive me."

I throw my hands in the air. "I was nine," I shout in frustration.

He shakes his head. "It was still a promise," he says. Clearing his throat, he runs his hands through his tousled hair. Little does he know that he's only making it look that much better, but Lord knows I'm not going to tell him that.

Jesus, Harley. What is wrong with you? You're pissed, remember? Pissed!

Neither one of us speaks for several minutes. When Tyson finally breaks the silence, his voice is thick with emotion. "I can't make this better if you won't let me. You have to give me the chance, Harley. Please. I know this won't be easy, and I know that it will be a long road, but I *need* you to give me the chance that I never gave you." His eyebrows dip low and his lips part. He looks...pained.

I hold his gaze firmly, but I can feel my resolve slipping. I hate to even think it, but when he says I need to give him the chance he never gave me, is he talking about more than friendship? I shake my head quickly, clearing my thoughts. I can't even let myself go there. *Never again.*

His eyes shimmer in the moonlight, tears begging to be let free. Who am I kidding? Of course I'm going to give Ty the chance. It might very well ruin me though. I survived Ty once, but I'm not so sure I will survive him again.

"Okay," I whisper, feeling defeated.

"Okay?" he quickly asks in response, his mouth morphing slowly from a small grin into a full-blown smile. My mouth, obviously now acting on its own, smiles back.

Damn mouth.

"Okay."

I LEFT THE BAR after talking to Tyson. There was no way I could go back in there and drink and carry on like nothing had happened.

Coming home to an empty house sucks. Max is with my mom and It's too quiet. Tossing my keys on the dresser, I strip out of my dress, slide into my cami and boy shorts, and curl up in bed. Pulling the covers up to my chin, I close my eyes. Reflecting on what happened tonight isn't easy when all I can think about is how sexy Tyson smelled and how good it felt to have his arms wrapped around me. I just wish it were under different circumstances, like—oh, I don't know—passion rather than desperation.

I can't believe this.

Tyson is really home.

When I walked into the bar and caught sight of him, my stomach dropped. Literally. I had always known that we would see each other again, but it was unexpected. What was even more unexpected was how quickly all the feelings that had been so neatly tucked away came flooding back, hitting me at full force.

I was both surprised and relieved that Tyson was the one who followed me out—I fully expected it to be Levi. I'll have to remember to ask Levi about that.

My determination had been holding up fairly well—or so I had thought—until he broke out the big guns. Of course, he had to use a childhood promise to make me agree to his request. Damn bastard knows how sentimental I am.

"You can't play with us." I could tell it was Jimmy talking. Anyone could hear that squeaky voice coming a mile away.

I had been playing in my backyard when I heard some kids playing on the sidewalk out front. Peeking around the garage, I saw that it was Ty with four other boys from our neighborhood.

Jimmy was a bully; I never understood why Ty wanted to be friends with him.

"Well, why not?" I heard Ty ask.

"Because, you hang out with that fat girl. What's her name?"

"Harley. And she's not fat," Ty replied. I felt myself smile. I always knew Ty would stick up for me.

"Well, we don't like her. She's fat and she stinks," Jimmy said, waving his hand in front of his face as though he smelled something awful.

"She does stink, doesn't she?" Ty said, laughing.

Wait, what?

I tiptoed closer, trying to hear more.

"Are you gonna stop playin' with her?" Jimmy asks, tucking his basketball under his arm.

"If you're gonna start lettin' me play ball with you guys, I will."

I didn't even stay to hear the rest of the conversation. I ran into my house, through the back door, and straight up to my room. I cried to my mom about what I heard and she soothed me the way any great mom would, assuring me that everything would work itself out. I had her turn Ty away both times when he stopped by that weekend, and then on Monday I ignored him all day at school.

Monday night I was playing in the yard and Ty came stomping over. "What's your problem? You ignored me all day," he said.

"You said I stink," I yelled, fighting back tears.

"Huh?"

"I heard you tell Jimmy that I stink, and then you said you'd stop playing with me if he let you play basketball with him." I began to cry. Using my fists, I furiously wiped my tears away. "So go away, Ty, we're not friends anymore."

His eyes widened. "But I punched him for you."

"You what?"

"We were playing basketball and he kept talking bad about you. I got mad, and then he called you ugly and I punched him. I came to your house to tell ya, but your mom said you couldn't

play."

    I stood there staring at Ty. I wasn't sure what to say. I was mad that he said I was stinky, but I was glad that he punched Jimmy for talking bad about me.

    "So you forgive me? I don't wanna play with Jimmy and his friends. I wanna play with you," he said, sitting down on the swing next to me.

    "But you said I stink."

    "I'm sorry, Harley. You don't stink. Now do you forgive me?"

    "Yeah," I replied. "I forgive you."

    "Good. My dad says I'm gonna mess up a lot since I'm a gonna be a man, so you gotta promise you'll always forgive me."

    "Okay, I promise. As long as you always apologize, I'll always forgive you."

    Damn my nine-year-old self.

Chapter 4

Harley

BEEP BEEP BEEP

September in the Midwest usually provides fairly mild weather, and Max and I have been taking full advantage. Sunday flew by as we spent the entire day hopping from park to park, ending our adventurous afternoon at the local sno-cone stand.

Beep Beep Beep

My parents think that I spoil Max, but isn't that what I'm supposed to do? In all honesty, I've harbored feelings of guilt for the past five years toward the way I reacted about the news of my pregnancy. To say that I was devastated when I found out I was pregnant would be a severe understatement. I know…I know. Everyone told me that it was expected for me to act that way after such a traumatic experience. *Blah, blah, blah.* But what bothers me most is that for the first six months of Max's life, I was completely disconnected from him.

Beep Beep Beep

Sure, I would feed and change him and see to his basic needs, but that was pretty much the extent of it. It sickens me when I recall how many times I laid Max down or put him in the swing, just so I wouldn't have to look into his eyes—the eyes that are the mirror image of his father's. I allowed my past and my insecurities to keep me from forming that mother-child bond right from the start. It took me a long time to forgive myself for that, and I hope that one day Max will forgive me too.

Beep Beep Beep

It nauseates me to think about all of the precious moments that I didn't allow myself to have with Max, and that is exactly why I treasure every single minute with him now. I understand that I can't get those six months back, but I sure as hell can try my damnedest to make up for it.

Hence the spoiling.

Beep Beep Beep

Swiping the talk button, my phone connects to Bluetooth. "Jesus! Can you not take a hint?" I yell.

"No! You're being fucking childish."

"Are you serious? I'm being childish?" My left hand on the steering wheel, I begin to flail my right hand as though he can actually see me. "Levi...how could you do that to me?"

"Damn! Your feistiness is a huge fucking turn-on right now." I can hear the smile in his voice and that pisses me off even more. He's trying to make light of the situation, and I'm not letting him get away with it!

"Seriously, Levi? I'm furious with you and *that's* what you're thinking?" Pulling into the parking garage at work, I maneuver my car into one of the cramped spaces and throw it in park. Sighing heavily, I lean forward and bang my head against the steering wheel.

"Okay, okay. Don't be so damn dramatic. Listen, I know I should've told you Tyson was going to be there and I promise that I meant to tell you, but I've been so busy lately that it slipped my mind." He pauses, waiting for me to reply. Hell no! He's going to have to do better than that.

"Ugh," he growls. "I'm sorry, okay? It was a shit thing for me to do, and I should've told you. But I didn't, and I can't take that back. Forgive me?" he pleads.

"Well, that depends," I reply, tapping my finger against my lips.

"Jesus Christ," he mumbles. "On what?"

"You have to come cook for Max and me."

"Done."

"This Wednesday."

"Done."

"And you have to make that spectacular cheesecake thingy that I love."

"Done."

"Good. Then I forgive you," I reply, silently smiling to myself, knowing good and well that I would have forgiven him without the dinner and dessert.

SHRUGGING INTO MY LAB coat, I walk up to Cindy's door, knock twice, and let myself in. "Hey, boss! Where do you want me today?"

Cindy and I started working here at the same time. Last year she was promoted to the position of staff coordinator, and I couldn't be more proud of her.

"I'm not your boss," she replies swiftly, "but that does have a nice ring to it." Cocking her head to the side, she gives me a cheeky grin and continues typing furiously on her keyboard. "Okay. Done with that," she says, closing her laptop and leaning back in her chair. She gestures for me to sit and I do, tossing my bag on the floor and setting my tea on her desk.

"It is way too early to be as busy as your are," I say with a chuckle.

She rolls her eyes. "Tell me about it! I had some call-offs today, so I had to move a few people around. It's going to be one of those days."

Reaching into my bag, I grab the pager that I'm required to carry and slip it into the pocket of my scrub jacket. Looking up, I find Cindy watching me. Her gaze appears both worried and hopeful.

"Why are you looking at me like that?" I ask, instantly suspicious.

"Because you're going to hate me."

"Hmmm...try me."

"I'm putting you in the ER." Scrunching her nose, she cringes, awaiting my reaction.

Throwing my head back against the wall, I growl loudly.

"See, I knew you'd be upset."

I know, I'm a grown adult that's whining like a two-year-old, but I really *hate* the ER. You never know what's going to walk through the door, so I guess it's really the unknown that I hate. It could be something fairly simple like a broken arm or someone needing stitches. Or it could be a mom, dad, or child just pulled from a car accident, barely alive and on the verge of coding. *I. Hate. It.*

Reaching for my tea, I sit up and take a drink. "No, not upset," I reply pointedly. "After all, it is my job. I just really, *really* hate the ER. It's so depressing and it's such a fast-paced environment. I just feel like I don't do well there."

"Nonsense," she says, waving her hand dismissively. "You're a great nurse, the staff down there absolutely loves you, and the head Doc down there adores you. Every time you work there, he raves about how good you are with the patients."

"Ha!" I snort. "I'm not sure it's my nursing skills that he adores as much as it is my ass in these scrubs."

She grins at me and shrugs. "Can't blame him there. It is a great ass."

"Alright, as much I'd love to sit here and discuss the fabulousness that is my ass all day, I really better get to work."

Standing up, she walks around her desk and gives me a quick hug. "Thanks for not hating me...oh! Can you take this with you down to the ER and give it to Nikki for me?" Reaching under her desk, she comes back up holding a large box.

"Sure thing." I grab my bag and throw the strap across my shoulder. I wrap my arms around the large box and then Cindy picks up my cup of tea, waving it around. "Want me to throw this away?"

"Are you crazy?" I scoff. "That's my fix! I need my sweet tea!"

Laughing, she helps me take hold of my beloved tea. Hurrying in front of me, she props the door open with her foot. "Be careful. Oh, and don't drop the box!" she yells at my retreating back.

"Ha! Be careful? Is this some kind of trap? I feel like you are setting me up for failure," I yell at her over my shoulder while continuing for the elevator. Angling my body to the left, I manage to hit the 'down' button with my pinky. "You owe me!" I shout as the elevator door dings and her laughter fills the air.

Peeking around the edge of the box, I make sure that no one is coming before stepping out of the elevator and toward the ER.

"Harley? Is that you?" I can't see Rosie, but I'd know that sweet voice anywhere.

"Yup, it's me, Rosie! Can you get the door for me?" I can hear her feet shuffle across the floor just before the door opens. "Thank you so much!"

"Whatcha got there?"

"I'm not really sure," I reply, continuing down the hall. "I'm just delivering it to Nikki."

"Well, she's back in her office. Just be careful…that box is too big. You're going to fall and break an arm."

"Well," I holler over my shoulder, "at least I'm in the right place if that happens."

Damn, this box is heavy. Cindy is going to owe me for— "OOMPH!" I hear a light grunt as the sudden, unexpected impact causes me to stumble back and drop my tea in the process. I can hear the liquid gush across the floor, and I cringe at my lost sugar high.

"I'm so sorry. Please tell me I didn't bathe you in my tea," I plead as two hands reach out to remove the box from my grasp.

"Nope." I hear a chuckle and my eyes snap up at the sound of his voice. *Tyson*. "Only got my shoes, but lucky for me my shift is ending, so it's no big deal." He shrugs, setting the box down. "Are you okay?" he asks, scanning me for any injuries. His wandering eyes leave a path of tingles and I shift my feet nervously.

Jesus Christ. *What the fuck is wrong with me?* He's back for all of five minutes, and my body is ready to completely forget the past five years and claim him anyway.

"Sorry, I wasn't paying attention to where I was going," he says at my continued silence. "It's been a really long night, and I was kind of in a hurry to get home." I nod at his words but don't respond. I can't seem to form any intelligible words, let alone sentences.

I blink rapidly several times, continuing to stare at the man in front of me. Dear God, he is sexy. Never in my life have hospital scrubs turned me on. *Until now*. The blue material is fitted across his chest. Not to the point that the top looks too small, but enough for me to get a good mental picture of what's underneath. And *GOOD LORD* those biceps are fucking drool-worthy.

Okay, I need to get laid.

Tyson has his stethoscope hanging over one shoulder and his lab coat draped haphazardly across his arm. His scrub pants are hanging low on his hips, and what I wouldn't give to reach under his top and—

He clears his throat, snapping me out of my sex-driven thoughts. It appears that our run-in has rendered me catatonic. I must look like a complete idiot.

"Harley? I asked if you're okay." His eyes are dancing with amusement. Busted!

Wait, *what is he doing here anyway?*

"W-What are you doing here, Tyson?" I stammer, cocking my head to the side.

His eyes light up and the smile on his face makes it look as if he just won the lottery.

"I work here. This is where I'm doing my residency. What are you doing here? You hate the ER; it makes you nervous," he states, furrowing his brow.

His perception causes a dull ache to take root in my stomach. I had forgotten how well he knows me. When I ran into Tyson a few nights ago and agreed to allow him the chance to regain our friendship, I hadn't planned on seeing him again so soon. I thought I'd have a little bit more time to come to terms with everything. And I certainly hadn't planned on having to work with him. So right now I'm feeling a little off-kilter.

I nod, feeling my lips curve into a smile. "I do...and it still does."

"Then why are you working here?" He shifts his feet and leans his shoulder against the wall.

"Well...I don't *work* here, work here...I mean I do work here—in the hospital—but not here in the ER...at least, not all the time, but sometimes—" He smiles as I fumble over my words. Shaking my head, I run a hand through my hair and take a cleansing breath. "I'm a float nurse. They pull me where they need me."

"That's great, Harley. So we might be seeing each other every once in a while." *Great.* This is just what I need—a daily dose of my biggest regret. Lucky me.

Looking down, Tyson chuckles, and I notice the puddle of tea that has now seeped around both of our shoes. "I see you're still a tea addict."

"That's an understatement," I reply, stepping out of the tea puddle.

"How are you ever going to make it through your day in the ER without your tea?" he asks, obviously amused.

"I'm not," I reply, giving him the most hopeless look I can manage. "I'm probably going to die."

He laughs and pushes off the wall. "Well, we can't have that now, can we?"

Silence descends and we both stand there, staring at one another, drinking each other in. We both seem to be taking a visual inventory, noting all of the changes that have taken place over the past five years, while simultaneously reveling in everything that has so perfectly stayed the same.

"Well...I'd better get going," he says, throwing a thumb over his shoulder. "It's been a long night and I'm exhausted. I'll see you around, Harley."

"Yup, see ya around." With an awkward wave, he turns and walks away.

"UGHHH!" I GROAN, THROWING myself into a chair at the nurses' station. "I just got here an hour ago and I'm already ready to go home." Logging into the computer, I click on my patient's name and start charting.

Laura, a nurse about my age, is sitting to my left. Without breaking eye contact from her computer, she grins. "What happened? Did Mr. Wilcox try and *woo* you into submission?" she asks playfully.

I whip my head over to glare at her. She doesn't make eye contact, but I can see the shit-eating grin on her face. When she glances in my direction and sees my narrowed gaze, Laura throws her head back and laughs hysterically.

"You bitch!" I hiss playfully.

"I'm sorry!" she says while continuing to laugh. Reaching up, she puts a hand to her chest. "I really am sorry, I couldn't help myself. Mr. Wilcox is a frequent flier around here. He's felt all of us up at some point and it was your turn, girl."

"Felt up?" I scoff. "The man practically molested me! Look..." Turning around, I show her my butt. "You know what that is?"

"No," she answers, shaking her head vigorously, trying to catch her breath from laughing so hard. "But that's the funniest thing I've ever seen! You have an orange ass!"

"Cheetos. Freaking Cheetos!" I smack my ass and a puff of orange dust fills the air, causing another fit of laughter from Laura. "Jesus, he's in the ER, for God's sake!" I'm not really angry with her. In fact, Mr. Wilcox is a very pleasant man. A drunken man, but a pleasant one, nonetheless. Laura's laughter rubs off, and before long I find myself laughing with her.

"I mean, seriously? It's eight in the morning and he's drunk as a skunk, eating Cheetos. I was trying to get his vitals and start his IV while trying to avoid his grabby little orange fingers. I had to have Nikki come in and occupy him so I could get a vein."

Using the back of her hand, Laura wipes away the tears that linger from her laughing spree. "Good Lord, that just made my day." Reaching across the desk, she picks up a travel cup and a folded piece of paper and turns to hand them to me. "Here, maybe this will help make your day a little bit better."

"What is it?" Picking up the cup, I lift the lid. Hallelujah, it's tea! "This definitely makes up for you throwing me to the wolves...or should I say, Mr. Wilcox."

"Oh, it's not from me," she replies, shaking her head. I furrow my brow in confusion. "That hot-as-hell resident that worked last night dropped it off about ten minutes ago and asked if I would give it to you." Giving me a quick wink, she turns and walks away.

Taking a sip of the tea, I gently unfold the piece of paper. The rush of emotions that hit at the sight of his words is entirely indescribable.

> Can't have you dying on me before I get that second chance you promised!
> Hope your day goes smoothly.
> —Ty

    I floated through the rest of the shift on a high, which carried over into Tuesday and Wednesday. I didn't see Tyson again those next two days, but it's not like I was hoping to see him.
    Was I?

Chapter 5
Harley

"I GOT IT!" MAX hollers at the sound of the doorbell.

"Ma-ax! You know better than to open that—" My words trail off at Max's high-pitched screech as he tears off through the house with Levi hot on his heels. The sound of Levi's teasing and Max's laughing quickly permeate the house.

"Me. Eat. Max. Me. Want. Max." Levi's hands are raised up in front of his face as though he has claws, and his monster-esque voice sends Max into another round of ear-shattering screams. I can't help the smile that overwhelms my face as I watch the two of them make laps around the house, Levi pretending that Max is too fast for him to catch. Reaching out, Levi snags Max around the waist, tossing him effortlessly over his shoulder as he pretends to bite at Max's side.

Happiness. Contentment. That's what this is for me. Don't get me wrong, Max and I live a happy life. But there is a different level of joy that shines through his eyes when Levi is around. He just plays so differently with men than he does with me. I try to roughhouse with him and play 'boy' games and chase him around like a monster, but he doesn't get into it the way he does with my dad or Levi. It must be a guy thing.

Sneaking up behind Max, I quickly throw the back of his shirt up around his neck and pretend to bite at his back while Levi continues at his front. "Max. Taste. Good," I say in my best monster voice. "Me. Want. More." Max stiffens his back and legs, throwing his head in an attempt to escape our attack.

"Done. I'm...stop. Done," he says breathlessly while simultaneously thrashing his body from side to side. We consent to his surrender and Levi lowers Max to the ground. Keeping a hand on his shoulder, he allows Max a second to regain his footing.

Levi raises his hand in the air about two feet above Max's head. "High-five, Maximus, my man!"

"My. Name. Is. Not. Maximus," he replies, each word ringing out between jumps, finally landing with a loud slap of a high-five.

"Alright, bud. I have to get cookin' before your mom here starves to death." Giving me a quick wink, Levi ruffles Max's hair and walks over to the front door, retrieving the bag of food he must have dropped prior to his monster transformation, and heads toward the kitchen.

"Can I watch a movie?" Max begs, bringing his clasped hands under his chin. Max has large, chocolate-colored eyes outlined in thick, black lashes, and he uses those magnificent eyes to get his way.

"Sure, but only until dinner is ready. Deal?" I stick out my arm and Max slips his tiny hand in mine, giving me an exaggerated shake.

"Deal." Scurrying over to the TV stand, he begins rummaging through our collection and picks out his favorite movie, *Cars*.

There's really no point in helping Max start the movie. I'm not sure where kids learn all this stuff, but I swear that Max can work any electronic device in this house better than I can on any given day.

My butt starts vibrating so I reach into my back pocket and pull out my phone. I swipe my thumb across the screen and a text from Quinn greets me.

Quinn: What's up sexy mama? You and Max doing anything cool?

Me: Hey sweet cheeks! Nope just chillin'. Max is watching a movie and I'mwatching Levi.

Quinn: You're watching his ass right? Please tell me you're watching his ass!

Me: Yup! I'm watching his sweet ass cook me dinner.

Quinn: What? WTF! I want to watch Levi cook!

Me: Get your booty over here. Pronto. Dinner in 30.

Quinn: Well I don't want a pity invite.

Me: Shut the hell up and get over here!

Quinn: Be there in 5. I'll bring the wine!

"Quinn's on her way." Walking to the stove, I hip-bump Levi and lift the lid to the saucepan. "This smells amazing! What is it?" He hands me a spoon and I stir the creamy white sauce.

"It's a provel mushroom cheese sauce, and it's to-die-for," he tells me. "That's good, don't stir it too much." Replacing the lid, I hop up on the counter next to the stove and grab the glass of wine next to Levi.

"It's okay, I didn't want that glass of wine anyway," he says with a smirk, not taking his eyes off of the vegetables he's chopping. A comfortable silence surrounds us and Levi loses himself in his cooking as I watch.

A loud growl echoes off the kitchen walls, and both Levi and I turn our heads simultaneously.

"No! You—" Quinn says firmly, pointing to Levi, "—turn back around. I wasn't done admiring your derrière." Levi smirks and turns back around before giving his butt a little shake.

"Max didn't let you in, did he? Because he knows better—" Quinn waves her hand, effectively cutting me off.

"No. No. No. Don't get you're panties in a bunch, Mama Bear, I let myself in. I practically live here anyway."

Setting a bottle of wine down on the table, Quinn makes her way over to me and gives me a quick hug. Turning to the stove, she lifts the lid on the saucepan.

"Mmm...what's this?"

"Stay out of there!" Levi says, slapping her hand away. Quinn pouts her full lips at him, but he's completely immune. "Nice try, but the answer is still 'no.'"

Gripping my waist, Levi lifts me off the counter and guides me to a kitchen chair, pushing me into it. Without a word, he walks over to Quinn and proceeds to do the same thing to her.

Quinn looks at me, raising her eyebrows in question, and I shrug my shoulders. Levi grabs two wine glasses and uncorks Quinn's bottle of wine, pouring each of us a glass. We watch silently as he sets a glass down in front of each of us and then gently removes his wine glass from my hand.

"Uhh..." I start to protest, but Levi quickly raises his finger to my lips and hushes me. My eyes widen and Quinn smiles in amusement.

"This is your space," he says, waving his hands in our direction, "and this is my space." He gestures to the opposite side of the kitchen before continuing. "This is your wine," he says, pointing to the glasses now in front of us, "and this is my wine." Lifting his goblet in the air, he brings the wine glass to his lips before turning and heading back to the stove.

"He's very serious when he's cooking," I whisper to Quinn while keeping a close eye on Levi. "He says cooking is an art and too many distractions will disrupt the beauty of his final product."

Quinn's head slowly turns in my direction and a mischievous grin creeps across her face. "Let's see if we can ruffle his feathers a little bit." Quinn begins taunting him before I even have a chance to respond. "When did you get so damn bossy?" she shouts, her arms crossed over her chest, a smile playing at the side of her mouth. "You're acting like someone pissed in your Cheerios this morning." We both watch as Levi continues to stir the sauce, seemingly oblivious to Quinn's antics.

Quinn looks at me and winks. Our heads whip back toward Levi at the sound of the stirring spoon being dropped on the counter. In three long strides, Levi has Quinn pinned in her chair. With a hand on each of her armrests, he leans in toward her, effectively caging her in.

Quinn's eyes widen and she tilts her head back to look up at him. He stares at her intensely, his deep blue eyes boring into hers, commanding her attention. I can't help but smirk because I've been on the receiving end of this side of Levi, and Quinn has no idea what he's about to do to her.

"First," he says, lifting up one finger. "I don't eat cereal. I am a man, Quinn." He grabs her hand and puts it on his chest, running it across from his left pec to his right. "I am a six-foot-one inch, two-hundred-pound man." Quinn's eyes are riveted to their joined hands and a small gasp leaves her mouth as Levi slowly drags her hand down his chest. "And because I am a man, I eat a man's breakfast, which does not consist of pissed-on cereal. Second," he says, continuing to slide Quinn's hand down his stomach. She whimpers when her hand reaches his rock-hard abs.

I've felt that stomach many times so I know exactly what the fuss is all about. Levi drops her hand and she hesitates before letting it fall limp at her side. Leaning forward, his lips graze the shell of her ear. "I've always been bossy, sweet Quinn. I usually just save my dominating tendencies for the bedroom. And trust me when I tell you...that little scene isn't even a tenth of what I'm capable of." Levi gently nips Quinn's earlobe and then turns back to the stove.

Quinn's head sags back against the chair and she closes her eyes. "I think I need to change my panties," she whispers, squeezing her thighs together. Levi's boisterous laugh rings loudly and I pat Quinn's knee in understanding.

"Yo, Max!" Levi yells. "Dinner's ready!" I drag Quinn out of her chair and we begin setting the table as Levi puts the finishing touches on the food.

"What are we having?" Max sits down and scrunches his nose as Levi puts a helping of chicken and vegetables on his plate.

"It's baked chicken smothered in a provel mushroom cheese sauce," Levi explains proudly.

"Ewww, that's disgusting," Max says, pushing his plate away from him.

Levi straightens his back, crossing his arms over his broad chest, and glares at Max. "Max, have I ever fed you anything that's disgusting?"

"Umm..." Max taps his chin for a moment before he smiles proudly and points at Levi. "That one time at your house. You had that tube of pink stuff, remember?" Furrowing my brows, I cock my head at Levi. *What the heck is Max talking about?*

Levi's eyes widen but before he can say anything, Max keeps talking. "You remember, Uncle Levi? That gooey pink stuff that was supposed to taste like strawberries. It made my lips feel funny. Don't you remember?"

Quinn attempts to muffle her laughter with her hand and my jaw drops open in disbelief. Levi sticks his arm out as though I'm about to attack and he could actually keep me away from him. "Max. Dude. That was our little secret," he admonishes, taking a few steps back. Stupid man, he should turn tail and run!

"Sorry, Uncle Levi." Max shrugs as I push his plate back in front of him.

Grabbing Levi's arm, I yank him over to the doorway. "Really, Levi, nipple butter? You let my son eat nipple butter?" I hiss incredulously.

"It's your fault," he whisper-yells back.

"What?" I scoff, hands on hips. "How was that my fault?"

Levi pushes me further out of the kitchen and into the living room. "Oh God! Yes, Levi! Don't stop!" He moans softly, throwing his head back in exaggeration. "Does that sound familiar to you?"

I stare at Levi. I have no comeback. I did. I said all of that.

His face turns triumphant and he pats me once on the butt before returning to the kitchen.

Damn him!

"I REALLY LOVE THAT little man. He is so precious." Walking up to me, Quinn grabs a towel and starts drying the dishes as I wash them.

"That was nice of you to give him a bath and read him his story. He really loves you, Quinny."

"It really was my pleasure. He fell right asleep too. I think we wore him out tonight," she replies with a smile. "I hope I didn't impose on you though. I know how much you treasure your routine with Max."

"It's okay. You're family, and he needs more than just me in his life anyway." She doesn't respond, but I can feel the weight of her gaze and I know exactly what she's thinking. Quinn thinks I'm lonely. She's convinced herself that I'm pining away for a man to fill a gap in our lives. She couldn't be further from the truth.

Yes, there are times when I am lonely. But five years ago my heart shattered into a million pieces, and that same night I vowed that if ever—by the grace of God—I was able to put it back together, I'd never give it away again. I'd keep it tucked away in a nice, warm, soft place where nothing bad could ever happen to it.

In an attempt at breaking the uneasiness that has settled around us, I dip my fingers in the sudsy water and flick them at her. She squeals, eyes wide, and instantly begins to spin her dishtowel, twisting it as tight as she can. Realizing what she is doing, I fling water at her again and take off around the table. The crack of the towel resonates and a quick sting pinches at my butt.

"Damnit, Quinny. That hurt!" I stop running and rub my butt where she towel-whipped me.

"I'm sorry," she laughs. "Do you want me to kiss it and make it all better?" she asks in a baby voice.

"Yes! Kiss it. Please, kiss it! Harley, take your pants off." Quinn and I turn in sync to glare at Levi and he raises his hands innocently. "Can't blame a guy for tryin'."

I point at Levi accusingly. "I'm still mad at you, Levi Beckford. You have some explaining to do." Rolling his eyes, he refills his wine glass and walks back into the living room.

"Oh snap! He just walked away from you. You're not going to let him get away with that, are you?" Quinn asks, refilling both of our wine glasses.

"No. Way. In. Hell."

"This is going to be good," Quinn murmurs in a sing-song voice, following behind me.

"Don't you walk away from me," I warn, making my way into the living room. Quinn snuggles into the recliner, leaving me standing in the doorway.

"Come here, Harley," Levi says calmly, patting the cushion next to him. "Come sit down. We both know you aren't really mad. You're just pretending to be mad because you're his mom and you feel like it's something you should be upset about."

My shoulders rise and fall on a deep breath and I concede by sitting down on the couch—as far away from Levi as I can get.

"It really is quite funny, Harley," Quinn says, sipping from her glass.

"No, it's not," I reply, shaking my head solemnly. "It's not funny. My son ate nipple butter. The same nipple butter that was used *on me*. What kind of mother does that make me?"

"You're right. You're a horrible mother, and now Max is probably going to grow up to be a porn star that craves strawberry-flavored nipple butter." Levi throws a pillow at Quinn's face in response and she laughs. "It's edible, Harley. No harm, no foul. You really should just laugh about it."

I cast my gaze across the room, staring at Max's baby picture where it hangs on the wall, and I can't help but wonder how many times I've failed him. "Fine. I'll drop it." Levi wraps his arm around my shoulder and pulls me in close.

"You know I'd never let anything happen to Max while he's in my care. Right?" he asks with his lips pressed against my temple. Snuggling in closer, I pat his thigh gently.

"I know, Levi."

"Gag! If you guys are going to start doing your 'friends with benefits' thing, then I'm outta here."

"You have nothing to worry about, Quinn." Tightening his arm, Levi gives my shoulder a quick squeeze. His voice softens, but it's still loud enough for Quinn and I to hear. "I'm fairly certain the 'benefits' phase of our relationship is over," he says with a smirk.

Quinn eyes snap to me and I look at Levi, curious where that came from. How long has he been thinking about this? The idea that we might need to back off has crossed my mind a time or two, but I didn't know he felt the same way. Or maybe...maybe he met a girl. That has to be it! Levi met a girl! I smile at him knowingly, but he immediately begins shaking his head vigorously.

"No! This is not about me. I did not meet someone, so wipe that smile off your face and stop planning my damn wedding."

"Then what's this all about?" Quinn asks.

"Tyson."

"What?" I squeak as Quinn chokes on her wine.

"What about Tyson? Is there something you aren't telling me, Harley? Because if that's the case, then I'm totally pissed at you right now."

"No!" I reply, shaking my head. "I don't know what Levi's talking about. Tyson and I talked the other night outside the bar, but you both know that. I told you what was said, and then we talked again..." My words trail off and I can't help the small smile that begins to form when I remember the tea that Tyson bought and left for me at work the other day.

"When?" Quinn prods when I don't continue. "When did you talk again?"

"At work," I answer softly. "We talked at work." My eyes bounce between her and Levi, waiting to see who is going to react first.

"Whoa! Back up a minute," Quinn says, setting her wineglass down and scooting forward in the chair. "You and Tyson work together?" Nodding my head, I turn to Levi and find him watching me curiously. His eyes are soft and caring and maybe a little...hopeful? I'm so confused right now.

"Yes. He is doing his residency in the ER and I float. We ran into each other the other day."

"Wow. Um. Okay. But you guys already agreed to try the whole friendship thing again, so why does that put a halt to things with you?" Quinn asks, directing her question to Levi.

"Yeah, Levi. What does Tyson being home have to do with us? Are you having blue balls? Is this because I left you unsatisfied the other—"

Quinn grips the side of her head and covers her ears. "Gah! Blah, blah, blah...TMI, Harley. TMI!"

"Nooo..." Levi drags out. "This doesn't have to do with us because there is no 'us,' remember?" Out of the corner of my eye, I notice Quinn lowering her hands.

"Yes, I remember," I answer sarcastically. "But I'm still curious. Why, Levi?"

"Because that boy is head over heels in love with you," he answers, matter-of-fact. Quinn and I both gasp. The only difference is that she has a huge goofy smile on her face and I don't.

"What?" I ask, pushing up from the couch. "He is not! He's only been home for a week, and we've only talked twice. How would you...what makes you..."

"I'm a guy, Harley, and I saw the way he looked at you when you walked into the bar the other night. It wasn't an oh-there's-my-old-friend-Harley kind of look. It was more of a there's-the-other-half-of-my-soul kind of look."

"Oh, it was not!"

"Uh, yeah, it kind of was, Harley. The boy looked at you like you were water and he hadn't had a drink in forty days!"

"Quinny. NO," I reply firmly.

"Not only that, but you should've seen his face when you ran out and I told him to stay put because I was going to go after you," Levi says, shaking his head. "Jesus Christ, I thought he was going to pulverize me!"

I've had enough. "Okay, you guys are fuckin' crazy!" I say, throwing my hands up in the air. "First, I'm over it. Been there, tried that. He wasn't interested. Second, he has a girlfriend, remember?"

Levi cocks his head and looks at me curiously. "You guys really haven't talked much, have you?"

"NO! I told you that! We've barely talked at all. Why? What do you know that I don't? Have you talked to him?" Quinn must sense my increasing level of anxiety because she reaches over and hands me her full wine glass.

God bless you, Quinn. She should really just go grab the whole damn bottle.

"Actually, I have," he answers cautiously, leaning his elbows on his knees. "We've talked a few times since he came home, including when he came into the restaurant last night. We had a late dinner after he got done with his shift." Levi eyes me warily, obviously unsure how I'll react.

This whole conversation has my head spinning. I can't let myself go there. I can't let myself hope for something that I know will never happen. I've done this once before. I've already laid everything out on the line, putting my heart on the chopping block, and the end result was devastating.

"Do you want to know what we talked about?" he asks, looking down at the ground and then up at me.

"Hmm? What? No." Right? I don't want to know. Do I?

"I do," Quinn says excitedly.

Crap. Quinn is looking at me with hopeful eyes, her hands folded under her chin in a perfect imitation of Max, and Levi is staring at me. Damn Levi and his unreadable baby blues.

I sigh and fall back on the couch. "Fine. I give in. Tell me." Actually, I need a drink for this. Picking up my wine glass, I open my throat and down the entire glass. "Okay. Now I'm ready."

"You. We talked about you," he says and I feel my stomach plunge.

Okay, maybe I'm not ready.

Because it doesn't matter what they talked about or what was said. I've got to keep reminding myself that nothing Tyson says will change anything.

Nothing.

Zilch.

Nada.

"Well..." Quinn pleads, urging Levi to continue.

Pushing the magazines to the end of the coffee table, Levi makes a spot for himself and sits down, facing me. "We talked about everything, really. I don't think I ever told you this, but he and I kept in touch off-and-on over the past five years. During that time, he didn't really ask about you at all. In fact, he avoided any and all conversation that could have led to your name being mentioned."

I flinch at his unexpected words; they're a complete slap in the face. It's hard to imagine that I upset Tyson *that* much. Did I seriously hurt him so badly that he couldn't stand the thought of even hearing my name? Swallowing hard, I work to keep my emotions in check, but I can't prevent the small quiver that starts in my chin or the sting in my eyes as tears form.

"Please don't cry." Reaching out, Levi grasps my hands in his and Quinn moves to wrap her arm around my back. "I'm not telling you this to upset you," he soothes. "I'm telling you this because he told me why he acted like that, and I think it's something you need to know."

I wipe away the few tears that manage to escape. "He did?" I ask, unable to control the shakiness of my voice.

Levi takes a deep breath and blows it out harshly. "I'm not sure I should be telling you this, but I can't *not* tell you."

Burying my face in my hands, I try to prepare myself for what's about to come out of Levi's mouth.

Please. Please. Please don't let this break me.

"Harley." Levi's voice is gentle as he removes my hands from my face before lifting my chin so that he can look me in the eye. "He came back for you...five years ago, he came back for you."

"Oh my God!" Quinn gasps, bringing her hand to her mouth. At the same time, I let out a breath I didn't realize I'd been holding.

"*What?* What do you mean he came back for me?" I ask quickly. My mind works to process what exactly he's trying to say. One tear trickles down the side of my cheek and then another and another.

"Sweetheart, I don't know all of the details. Maybe someday Tyson will tell you everything, but he asked to have dinner with me last night because he wanted to tell me what happened when he did come home." I know Levi is trying to take his time and make sure that I'm okay, but right now I just really need him to spit it out. I wipe away my excess tears and raise my eyebrows at him, silently pleading with him to keep going.

He takes a deep breath and rubs his hand across his mouth. "He came back four weeks after Dallas' funeral, Harley. He came by your house, but he never did talk to you because he thought you had moved on."

No. Why would he think that?

I rub my forehead, eyebrows squished together, and stare at

the ground. "I don't unders—" *Oh my God.* My chest tightens as realization dawns.

We fought two weeks before Dallas died, and he came back a month after the funeral. That means he came back...*Oh God.* Six weeks later. He came back six weeks later. My head starts shaking on its own accord and a sob rips from my throat as the memories flood my mind.

My fingers curl inward, tightly gripping my hair. I'm numb. Completely numb. I tug harder, needing to feel something—anything. Rocking my body back and forth, a small groan escapes my mouth.

This isn't happening.

This can't be happening.

Please let this be a dream. Please.

Pulling my head out of my hands, I turn my tear-streaked face up to the sky and contemplate what in the hell I ever did to deserve this. I've always been a kind person; I've always gone out of my way to help people and serve the community. I've gone to church every Sunday and I've never gotten into trouble. I did everything I was supposed to do. I graduated high school and finished all four years of college. I don't understand what I did wrong.

"Please say something." The heat from his breath caresses my cheek. He's been so quiet that I actually forgot he was even sitting next to me. Turning my head, I lock eyes with his and allow the anger that consumes me to pour out.

"What do you want me to say, Levi? What the fuck did I do to deserve this?" I don't mean to snap at him, but I can't help it. I wish he would just fucking leave and let me handle this on my own.

I stand up and start pacing the length of the porch, trying anything that might expel all of this energy coursing through me. Tilting my head back, I stare at the dark, star-speckled sky.

"Where the fuck were you when I needed you?" I shout, allowing my soul to expel six weeks worth of pain. "You fucking *abandoned me! It wasn't bad enough that I was RAPED? I was FUCKING RAPED! WAS THAT NOT ENOUGH FOR YOU?!" My voice cracks on the last word, the tightness building up and clogging my throat.*

Goddamn. Why am I so fucking numb? I clench my fists, allowing my nails to bite into my skin, desperate to feel something... anything. I squeeze my eyes closed, releasing a fresh batch of tears and scream. I scream at everything...and nothing.

Why am I still crying? Don't people run out of tears after a certain amount of time? Was six weeks not enough time for my well to run dry?

"Harley, please. Please calm down," Levi soothes. *He scoots closer, pulling me to him but I jerk away.*

I don't want his goddamn pity.

"I know you're scared but we'll get through this. I promise." *His voice is quiet, and even though I just pulled away, he still reaches out to rub my arm.* "Please don't lose your faith in God. We're going to need him now more than ever." *His eyes roam my face cautiously.*

Is he fucking kidding me? My eyes snap to his, anger and annoyance rolling off of me in waves.

"God," *I scoff.* "There is no fucking God. If there was, he wouldn't have let this happen."

Levi grips my hand tightly in his. He's done that a lot lately, and I welcome the warmth that his touch brings to my cold soul.

"Harley, I know that this might not be the path that you would've chosen for yourself, but you were put on it for a reason. You can do th—"

"Path?" *I yell, yanking my hands from his.* "You think this is my goddamn path? You think this was my fucking fate?"

Leaning forward, he runs a shaky hand over his face. "Yes. I do," *he says hesitantly.* "I know this is the last thing in the world that you want right now and I know that the circumstances aren't exactly ideal, but Harley take a step back and think about this. Think about what's grow—"

My cheeks burn and my body starts trembling as shame washes through me. "Jesus Christ, Levi! You don't think I know what's growing inside of me? Because I do. I know." I snort humorlessly, batting away another batch of tears. I can't be happy about this. He can't expect me to be happy about this. Right? Who in their right fucking mind could ever see the good in this?

"What's growing inside of me is the spawn of an evil bastard," I hiss, inhaling sharply at my first verbal acknowledgement of my pregnancy. The reality of my words sinks in, and the thought of having a baby brings me crashing down to a new low.

Fuck! Where the hell is my fucking rock bottom? I need to see a goddamn light somewhere in here. I can't have a baby. I don't want THIS baby.

Uncontrollable sobs wrack my body and my lungs fight the screams that have been clawing to get out. Levi wraps his arms around me tightly and simply holds me. Bringing my hands up between us, I fist them in the front of his shirt and anchor myself to the one person that has kept me from taking a flying leap out of this god-forsaken life.

I'm not sure how long he holds me. Minutes...maybe hours. Yet I still can't find the solace that I'm searching for.

"I c-can't...I d-don't want to d-d-do th-this," I choke out between sobs. "H-how can I e-e-ever love a b-baby that I d-d-don't even w-want?" Levi continues to rub soft circles up and down my back in a consistent rhythm, attempting to calm the tremors that have overwhelmed my body.

"You will love this baby," he soothes, "because that's who you are, Harley." He pulls back, cupping my tear-stained cheeks in his hands without dislodging my tight grip from his shirt. "You will love this baby because he...or she...is a part of you. And you, Harley, are the most amazing woman I've ever known." I don't reply, simply because I just don't agree with him. I hang my head, not wanting him to see the shame on my face. I'm not amazing, I'm horrible. I'm disgusted at the thought of my unborn child, and that alone makes me a monster.

Gripping his shirt tighter, I move as close to Levi as I can get. I need the close contact right now. I need to crawl inside of him and absorb all of the warmth and love that he has showered me with over the past month. I need to absorb his unwavering faith. Burying my face in his neck, I inhale the warm scent that has become a second home to me.

"Please don't leave me," I beg, my voice cracking.

His lips are soft against the side of my head. "Never. I'll never leave you."

Pulling back, I stare at the man who literally picked me up off the ground after my brutal attack. The man who sat with me at the hospital while I had rocks dug out of the side of my face. The man who has held me and wiped away my tears countless times since that horrible night. The man who has shown me over and over again what it means to love someone, even if that love is one of friendship.

My hand is surprisingly steady as I run it up his neck and grip his jaw in my palm. I graze his bottom lip softly with my thumb and lean in, placing my lips gently against his while maintaining eye contact.

Tilting his head, he pulls back. "Harley, I—" He shakes his head slowly as if trying to comprehend what I'm doing. I can't help him out, because I don't even understand what I'm doing.

A single tear runs down the side of my face. "Please, Levi... just..." My eyes bounce between his mouth and his eyes several times.

Leaning forward, he lays a gentle kiss to one side of my mouth and then the other, halting my words. Pulling back again, he watches me warily for only a brief second before his lips descend on mine in a kiss so sweet and gentle that for the first time in the past six weeks, I have hope that maybe—just maybe—I will survive this.

"I don't know what I'd do without you," I whisper against his mouth.

"You'll never find out, sweet girl. Never."

"Levi, please tell me he didn't—"

"No," he interrupts gently. "He didn't hear anything. From what I could gather, he pulled up outside your parents' house in time to see you wrapped in my arms. He saw us kiss, which is why he ultimately left without talking to you."

I can't believe this. "I don't understand. Why didn't he try harder? Why didn't he talk to me about it? Why did he cut me out of his life for the next five years? Even if he thought I'd moved on, that still doesn't explain why—"

Levi runs his hand through his hair. "I honestly don't know, Harley. Maybe that's something you will have to ask him."

Quinn clears her throat and looks at me, and then over at Levi curiously. "Wait a minute. I don't understand. You guys didn't start your 'thing' until Max was two. Did it start the night you found out you were pregnant?"

"No," Levi and I reply at the same time.

"Crap," I murmur, rubbing my hands over my face. "I don't know what came over me that night...I don't even know how to try and explain it. I was so scared and devastated and...just numb. I was completely numb. And if it weren't for Levi..." Looking up, I reach out and grip Levi's hand in mine. "It was just a reaction. I don't know how or why, but it just felt like the right thing to do."

I look at Quinn and smile. "But to answer your question, no, nothing officially started the night I found out I was pregnant with Max. Levi and I talked a few days later, and we agreed that I had reacted out of emotion and that neither one of us felt anything for each other."

Quinn fails miserably at trying to mask the hurt in her eyes. She thinks I lied to her.

"Quinny, I didn't tell you about the kiss because it wasn't important. You know I'd never lie to you about something like that."

"I know." She sighs, giving me a sad smile as she reaches for her wine glass and takes a small sip. "So that's it?" she asks Levi. "That's all he said at dinner, just that he came back for her?"

"No," Levi replies. There's that damn smirk again. "He wanted to ask me if you and I are together."

This doesn't *change anything.*

This can't *change anything.*

"Well...what'd you tell him?"

"What do you think I told him?" he asks, giving me a classic that-was-a-stupid-question look. "No. I told him no. I told him that he was a fucking idiot for not talking to you five years ago and that he completely misunderstood what he saw. I told him we aren't together and we never have been."

"Did you tell him that you've slept with her...more than once?" Quinn asks with a gleam in her eye.

Levi stands and stretches his arms above his head. "First of all, you two talk too damn much. I don't even want to know what all you know," he says, waving his hand toward Quinn. She looks at me and winks, effectively decreasing the tension in the room. "Second...*hell* no. It's not my place." He turns his gaze to me. "If you choose to tell him about us someday—which I'm certain you will—then that's your choice. I'd never tell him something like that without talking to you about it first."

"You didn't tell him about Max, did you?" I ask nervously, wringing my hands together.

Levi shoves his hands in his pockets and pins me with an annoyed look. "That's a stupid question. Of course I didn't. Again, that's not my story to tell."

"Holy moly, this is like a Jerry Springer show and I'm the live studio audience." Lifting her hands in the air, Quinn acts as though she's a narrator, even altering her voice for optimal performance. "Girl tells best friend she loves him. Best friend leaves girl. Best friend's best friend helps heal girl's broken heart. Best friend returns only to leave again...only to return again." We all chuckle at her impromptu performance. "Wow," she continues, "I did not see all this coming when I came over here tonight. Seriously, Harley, you can't make this shit up."

"You didn't see this coming?" I ask incredulously. "What about me? This changes everything."

WHOA! What? Where did that come from? I've been saying all along that this changes absolutely *nothing*. I've clearly been lying to myself.

"So...now what?" Quinn asks, looking at me curiously and then at Levi. Reaching up, she starts twirling a strand of hair around her forefinger. It's a nervous habit the both of us share.

"Now, Miss Quinn," Levi says, pushing her hand out of her hair. "Now we sit back and watch Harley fumble her way through this. It should be quite entertaining." Levi has a goofy smile on his face and his deep blue eyes are smiling warmly at me. Reaching down, he pulls me up to him, wrapping me in a tight hug.

"I'm gag ewe fine gas runny," I mumble into his shirt.

His deep chuckle vibrates through me. He pulls back and I tilt my head to look at him. "I'm sorry you find my gas runny," he says with a smirk.

"I said I'm glad you find this funny." I frown up at him as Quinn walks up behind me and they sandwich me in a hug. I love these two so much. Tears sting my eyes just thinking about everything they have done to help me get to where I am today. I wouldn't be here if they didn't love me and believe in me as much as they do.

It's after ten o'clock before I end up kicking them out, refusing their multiple attempts to help me clean. "Go!" I say, pushing them out the door. "I need to clean. It'll give me time to think."

Two hours later, I'm still cleaning an already spotless kitchen because I can't seem to keep my mind from going in a million different directions. I've not only cleaned every nook and cranny in the refrigerator, but I also took care of the stove, microwave, and toaster oven.

I force myself to take a shower, fighting off a thousand 'what ifs,' and crawl under my crisp, cool sheets. I toss and turn for over an hour before I finally give up. Reaching across my bed, I run my hand along the underside of the mattress until my fingers hit the edge of what I'm looking for. Pushing myself up against the headboard, I lean back, pulling my knees up to my chest.

I stare at the old, tattered picture. The edges are falling apart and there are numerous smudges and tear stains. I've been able to find comfort in the picture off and on over the past five years, pulling it out when I felt like I couldn't remember what he looked like or what his voice sounded like.

I run my finger across the picture that was taken of Tyson and me when we were twelve. The photo was snapped after a summer co-ed soccer game. It had rained that day, and our jerseys and cleats were covered in mud. My ponytail hung messily across my left shoulder and we both had mud caked to our faces and legs. Our smiles were large and bright as we posed for the camera with our arms wrapped tightly around each other's shoulders.

I would give anything to go back to the day this picture was taken, before high school, boyfriends, girlfriends, and gossip. A time when we were naïve and innocent, and all we cared about was playing ball, winning games, fishing, and catching fireflies. A time before emotions, love, and rejection. I squeeze my eyes closed, hugging the picture to my chest, and allow myself to be absorbed in the memory.

I can feel the tears breach the corner of my eyes, but I don't wipe them away. I let them make their journey down my face because they're there for a reason. Although at this point, I'm not sure if I'm crying because of the happy memories, the sad ones that came years later, or out of fear of what's to come.

Chapter 6

Tyson

"ALRIGHT, MRS. COLLINS, YOU'RE good to go!" I yell, slowly enunciating each word. Sweet Mrs. Collins is completely deaf, even with her hearing aids. "I've sent the prescription to your pharmacy electronically, and don't forget, no more Q-tips in your ear."

"Why would I put Q-tips in my beer?" she yells back, furrowing her brow in confusion.

"No." I shake my head, laughing, and point to my ear. "Not beer. EAR. Don't put Q-tips in your ear."

"Oh. Okay," she says, patting my hand gently and nodding her head. Gripping her walker, she shuffles down the hall with the nurse following closely behind.

I head over to the nurses' station to finish my charting on Mrs. Collins when Avery steps out of an exam room. "Hey, Avery. How's your morning going?"

Avery completed her residency two years ago at a hospital in Indiana. She recently relocated to St. Louis after accepting a job here in the ER.

"It's going okay," she says, wiping her arm across her forehead. "I've done stitches on a head laceration, and I'm fairly certain that the gentleman I just examined broke his hip. How's your day going?" she asks, falling in step with me.

Avery is petite and at least a good foot shorter than me. She reminds me a lot of Brit; they both have straight, blond hair and big, blue eyes. She's really quite beautiful—if that's the type of girl you're looking for. But right now, I've got my sights set on a gorgeous brunette with large green eyes, thick black lashes, and a dimple in each cheek. I can't help but grin when I think about the look on Harley's face after she ran into me earlier this week and spilled her tea. Damn, she looked incredible. The past five years have treated her well. If it's possible, she's even more of a perfect version of the woman she already was.

"Tyson?" Avery shakes my shoulder gently, pulling me from my memory.

"Huh?"

She smiles at me warmly, her perfectly straight teeth on display. "Where'd you go just now?" she asks. "You stopped talking and had a huge smile on your face."

"Sorry," I reply, pulling out a chair at the station for her and then one for myself. We both start thumbing through charts. "What did you ask me?"

"I asked how your day was going."

"Eh..." I shrug. "It's going, I guess. I've had an abdominal pain, a sprained ankle, and I just saw a woman who had the end of a Q-tip come off in her ear canal."

She chuckles lightly. "Mrs. Collins. I heard her yelling something about beer."

"I love my job," I state sarcastically with a grin, turning my head to look at her.

She smiles shyly and pushes a strand of hair behind her ear. "So, you're from around here originally, right?" she asks, turning back to continue her charting.

"Yup," I nod. "Well, I was raised across the river in Illinois, but I grew up in the area. How are you liking it here so far?"

I turn around when someone taps my shoulder. "I took Mr. Cook down for an X-ray of his ankle. I'll let you know when he's done," Callie says as she walks by the nurses' station.

"Thank you, Callie!" I holler at her retreating back and she throws her hand up over her head in response. I turn my attention back to Avery. "So...how are things going?"

She averts her eyes, appearing nervous. *Do I make her nervous?* "It's okay, I guess," she says with a shrug. "I don't really have any friends and I don't know anyone other than the staff here, so I spend most of my time off at home working around the house."

"You'll make friends," I say, nudging her shoulder with mine. "The nurses here are all really great. You just need to get to know a few of them."

"Yeah, I will. I'm sure it'll get better soon." She logs out of her computer and stands up, stretching her arms above her head. When she lowers her arms, she places her hand gently on my knee. I look down at it and frown.

What the hell is that about? Is she hitting on me? The sad thing is that I'm a twenty-eight-year-old man and I'm not even really sure if a woman is hitting on me or not. Jesus Christ, I was with Brit for too long. And she never flirted with me—okay, sure she did in the beginning, but not after we got to New York. After the move, our relationship became strained and we never saw each other. You'd think that would've been a sign that maybe I shouldn't have proposed.

I raise my head when Avery tightens her grip on my thigh. "Wow, you're really bruising my ego here," she says with a hesitant smile.

"What?" I ask.

Her blue eyes dance with amusement. "You keep spacing out on me. You're either preoccupied or I'm really boring."

"No, you're not boring at all." I stand up and her hand slides off of my leg. A slight frown crosses her face before she looks at me, the smile firmly back in place. "I'm just preoccupied, that's all. What were you saying?"

She steps toward me. *Holy fuck, she's bold.* "I asked if I could maybe go out with you and your friends sometime. You know, to get out and meet some new people outside of work." She raises her eyebrows in question and gently bites her lower lip, but what sets off the alarm bells in my head is the hopeful look in her eyes. No way in hell am I going to do anything to mess up the groundwork I've laid with Harley. I hate to be a dick, but Avery needs to know that I'm not interested.

I step back, leaning a hip against the desk. "Sure, we could go out sometime," I say nonchalantly. "I'd be happy to introduce you to some of my friends."

"Great," she says, her smile growing even brighter than it already was. "I can't wait."

I rub my hand against the back of my neck and divert my eyes. *Fuck, I hope this doesn't come out wrong.* "Avery, you and I are friends...and if we go out, it will be *just* as friends."

Her face falls but she quickly recovers, straightening her shoulders and lifting her chin. "Oh. Umm, yeah." She nods slowly. "Absolutely. I wasn't...are you dating someone?" she asks, tilting her head.

I appreciate her audacity. I wish every woman would say what she is really thinking or ask for what she wants. "No, I'm not, but there is someone that I really care about."

Her eyes soften in understanding and her hand grazes my arm lightly. "She's a very lucky woman." Running her hands down the front of her scrubs, she takes a deep breath and sighs before stepping back. "I better get back to work."

I reach in my pocket as she walks down the hall. All this talk has me thinking about Harley. It makes me happy, knowing that she's in the hospital and I could run into her at any time. Pulling up my contact list, I click on Harley's name. I wonder if she ever changed her number? Only one way to find out.

Me: Did you enjoy your tea?

What I really want to say is '*you looked amazing the other night*,' but I don't want to scare her off so I'll stick with the tea.

I make sure my phone is on silent and shove it back in my pocket. "Callie, who's up next?"

I spend the next forty minutes examining an elderly gentleman with chest pain. "Callie, Mr. Pierce is going to be a direct admit to cardio. I've already talked to Dr. Davis and he's writing orders now."

"I'm on it." Callie is a great nurse, but she's not very talkative and prefers keeping to herself. "You're free for a little bit, Dr. Grawe. Dr. Pierce took the next patient."

"Thanks," I murmur, pulling out my phone on my way back to the break room. I unlock the screen and my heart pounds at the sight of her name.

Harley: Who is this??

What does she mean, "*Who is this?*" How many people does she have buying her tea?

Me: Are there other doctors bringing you tea? Give me names so I can kick their asses!

I pour myself a cup of coffee, anticipating her reply. My phone lights up almost instantly.

Harley: How did you get my number?

Me: Shot in the dark. You never changed it. Have lunch with me.

I stir my coffee impatiently, hoping that she'll say yes.

Harley: I can't.

Me: Why not?

Harley: I would but I brought something. I was going to eat on the run.

Me: What did you bring?

My knees bounce nervously under the table. I stare at my phone for a full minute before I realize what I'm doing. *Jesus Christ, when did I grow a fucking vagina?*

Harley: I brought a pack of dog nuts to eat.

Me: Uhh... that's an interesting lunch choice. Do you cook them or eat them raw?

I hit send, chuckling to myself. Her reply is immediate.

Harley: NO! OMG NO! Doughnuts! I brought doughnuts!

I throw my head back and laugh. I can picture her with wide eyes, her fingers typing furiously on her phone.

Me: Thank God! Doughnuts are still a horrible lunch choice though. I'll break about 12:30. Have lunch with me.

She doesn't reply and I tuck my phone in my pocket, disappointed at my failed attempt. She'll come around...I'll just have to give her a little more time.

I see my next two patients, one with pneumonia and one with mono. Afterward, I sit down to finish my discharge paperwork and I can hear Rosie at the front desk, laughing enthusiastically. I can't help but smile to myself. Rosie is such a sweet woman and her laughter reminds me of my mom.

I print off my patient's discharge instructions and walk into his room to give him a rundown of what he can and can't do, things he should watch for, and when to follow-up with his primary doctor. Once I'm certain that he understands the seriousness of the situation if he doesn't comply—college students are notorious for relapses—I give him a note for class and then usher him out. I turn down the hall and walk into the break room, barely crossing the threshold before stopping dead in my tracks. Goosebumps run up my back at the sight of a pair of mossy green eyes that I've dreamt about every night for the past five years. The door slams into my back, propelling me forward.

Harley jumps up and hurries to my side. "Damn, that had to hurt. Are you okay?" she asks, her face laden with concern.

"I'm fine," I snap, straightening my spine and smoothing my shirt. "What are you doing here?" *Damnit, that didn't come out right.* This is what happens when I'm around her. It's like she sucks the air out of the room and my brain loses the ability to function.

She steps back. Her lips are pursed and a quick flash of regret crosses her face.

"I'm sorry," she stammers, taking a step toward the door. "I should have texted you back." Another step. "I got busy and then realized it was almost twelve-thirty." She looks at the door and then back at me before shoving her hands in the front pockets of her scrubs. "I should go."

"No!" I snap, reaching out and stopping her before she makes it out the door. "No—" I shake my head, trying to pull myself together. "I mean, yes. I do want to have lunch with you. Please don't be sorry." I run my hand down the length of her arm and grip her wrist lightly, stepping toward her. My movement causes her to look up and her breath fans my face. She smells of tea and cinnamon, and I would give anything to bend down and have a taste for myself.

I run my thumb over the inside of her wrist several times, grateful when she doesn't pull away. She looks down at my hand, then back up at me.

"I'm really glad you came down here, Harley." She smiles timidly and reaching up, she wraps a chunk of hair around her finger. *Some things never change.* If there is one thing I learned from being friends with Harley for so long, it's her nervous habits. She stammers when she talks and she twirls her hair...incessantly. I'm not sure why, but the fact that I know she's nervous right now makes me smile. It lets me know that she still cares.

I can't stop staring at her. My eyes roam freely from top to bottom and she stands there quietly, letting me take my fill. She's so fucking gorgeous, and the fact that she's completely oblivious to it makes her that much more attractive.

I'm well aware that I have a huge grin on my face and it probably looks ridiculous, but I don't give a shit. *Harley came down here to have lunch me.* This is a huge step. I can't even describe what it means to me that she took that initiative.

Harley leans in, lifting her hand to my bicep and my heart starts pounding on contact. "We should get going. I've only got an hour."

"Right." I open the door and gesture for her to go in front of me. The side of her mouth ticks up and she walks through the door, giving me a slight curtsy once she's out in the hall.

I follow behind her for a few steps and allow myself the chance to watch her. Harley is of average height, maybe five feet six inches. She has curves in all the places that a healthy woman should have curves and they are sexy as hell. My eyes drift downward, catching sight of the way her hips sway with each step. It's like she's floating. *What the fuck is wrong with me? Floating?* A brief shake of my head and two quick strides puts me next to her, and I nudge her gently with my shoulder. "I'm glad you decided to come have lunch with me."

"Me too." She nudges back, a playful smile sliding across her face. Her smile alone makes my heart flop around in my chest. It's infectious, and the two dimples that perfectly frame her amazing mouth only add to the effect. Why the hell didn't I notice all these things five years ago?

Something stirs deep inside of my body—a pull. A pull to be near her and touch her. My arm grazes hers as we walk and she smiles coyly without looking up. Her smile makes me happy...it always has. I dreamt of it several times over the years, and I'm overjoyed to finally see it again. I *need* to see her smile like this every day.

We both walk through the cafeteria line and Harley grabs a turkey sandwich and apple as I reach for the same. She finds us a table while I grab our bottles of water.

"So..." I pull out my chair and sit down as Harley bites into her apple. "This is way better than dog nuts, right?" I ask teasingly. Her eyes widen and she chokes back a laugh as a small piece of her apple flies from her mouth. I can't help but chuckle at the horror that crosses her face as she lifts her hand to her mouth.

"I can't believe I did that," she mumbles while giggling around the apple and through her hand. Her eyes shine with delight and a warm feeling settles in my chest.

"You can't believe you spit your apple at me?" I ask, amused. "Or that you told me you were going to eat dog nuts for lunch?"

"Both! And I didn't spit my apple at you," she says, throwing her napkin at my face. I catch it with a laugh. "And I wish I had actual buttons back, not these damn pictures of buttons." Lifting her hand, she inspects her fingers. "My fingers must be too fat because I think I'm hitting the letter 'd' and I really hit an 'f.'"

"There's not an ounce of fat on your body, Harley." She smiles sweetly but doesn't respond and we both begin eating our lunch in comfortable silence.

I can't believe that I ever thought I could actually walk away from this...from her. I should have fought for Harley. The second she told me she loved me, I should have wrapped her in my arms and accepted what she was offering—her heart.

Instead, I threw it back in her face, making her feel like she did something wrong. The fact of the matter is that I was a scared little shit.

Five years ago, my life was on a different path. I had just decided to make a huge change and follow Brit halfway across the country. I'd already sent the letters and had my residency transferred, and we had already found a place to live. I was too scared to say, *'I change my mind,'* too fearful of what would happen with my residency, too worried about what my parents would think, and too afraid to break Brit's heart. Therefore, I made a split-second decision that I have regretted for years. I would give anything—hell, I'd give *everything*—to be able to go back and do things over.

I've learned a lot over the past five years, the most important of which is that sometimes I have to put me first. I have to fight for what I want and, truth be told, five years ago I wanted Harley.

Her fingers lightly graze my knuckles, catching my attention, and my head snaps up to meet her curious face. "Penny for your thoughts?" she says quietly. Her eyes are wide like she's scared to actually hear my answer. I don't respond right away and she lowers her head to take a bite of her sandwich. I can feel the tension growing between us and I can't let that happen.

I slouch back in my seat and watch her, waiting for her to look at me again. She must notice that I'm staring at her because she lifts her head. I open my mouth to speak, but she beats me to the punch. "I missed you," she blurts and all of the tension instantly drains from my shoulders. Good Lord, I really needed to hear that.

I smile tenderly. Any other woman would have probably been horrified at blurting out such an honest statement, but not Harley. She stares at me openly, patiently waiting for me to reply. "I was thinking about how I would do things differently with you if I could rewind time," I say, itching to divulge so much more. I need her to know that I made the biggest mistake of my life and I have no intention of ever letting go of her again, but I know I need to do this slowly. I want to do this right.

Her eyes soften and appear wistful. Reaching out, she grips

the top of my hand. "We have a lot to talk about. So much has happened since you left, and I really do want to tell you all about it—" Lowering her head, she takes a deep breath. When she looks at me again, her eyes are glistening with tears. "And I will, but not here. I also want to hear all about everything you've done and experienced, but right now...right now I just want this. I want to get reacquainted with the friend that I lost."

I don't miss the fact that she said *'friend,'* which is understandable because that's what we are. That's all I've ever allowed us to be, but come hell or high water, that's going to change.

I scoot forward in my seat, not breaking eye contact. "Harley, I—"

My words are cut off when someone plops down in a chair next to me. Turning my head, I find Laura, one of the nurses in the ER. "Hey, Harley!" she says with a smile. "Dr. Grawe." She nods at me and then turns her gaze back to Harley. "Do you guys mind if I join you?"

Yes, we mind. Find another table.

"Sure," Harley says sweetly. "How are you? Busy day?"

"So-so," Laura shrugs. "How's Max doing?"

Who the fuck is Max? I watch Harley intently. Her face takes on a dreamy appearance and she tilts her head, giving Laura an easy smile. "He's great...really great. Thanks for asking."

Again, who the fuck is Max? And what's so great about him?

Harley looks up and when our eyes meet, she straightens her back. I watch her appearance go from laidback and happy to nervous and uncomfortable. Whoever Max is, she doesn't want to talk about him. Her eyes flit nervously between Laura and me. What's that about?

Laura swallows her food and wipes her mouth. "I need to come by and spend time with you guys. I haven't seen him in forever. I'll bet he is even more handsome than the last time I saw him."

"Yup," Harley replies tersely, as she reaches up and wraps a strand of hair around her finger. "He's handsome."

I can't believe I didn't consider this. Of course she's found someone else. *Crap.* She might even have kids. My eyes snap to her left hand. No ring. Maybe they're just dating. I can feel my happiness from earlier start to dissipate, and I have the sudden urge to get up and leave before I expose my disappointment. I did not prepare myself for this at all. *Goddamn, I'm a stupid fucker.*

My chair screeches as I move to stand and Harley quickly does the same, her face filled with worry and something else I can't quite explain. Fear...that's it, she looks kind of afraid. I don't know what she'd be scared about; I'm the one who walked away from her. I can't fault her for moving on with her life.

The weight of that thought slams into my chest and I grip my shirt tightly, trying to stay calm. I divert my eyes and begin picking up our trash and putting it on my tray. I need to get out of here. I need to finish my shift and hightail it home so I can process this. Not that anything has really changed. I still want to rebuild my friendship with Harley, but now I have to make my heart understand that it will never be anything more than friendship.

"Don't leave," she says, her eyes pleading. Reaching out, she grabs the tray. "We still have..." She looks down at her watch and then back at me. "Twenty minutes."

Laura furrows her brow and glances between Harley and me. Then her face morphs into a look of understanding.

"I should go." Laura shoves the last bite of her lunch into her mouth and takes a drink of water. "I didn't mean to interrupt you guys."

"No. You didn't interrupt anything. Just two old friends having lunch. No big deal," I say awkwardly. "I've gotta get back anyway. Here, I'll take your trays." Reaching down, I grab Harley's tray and then Laura's. I can't help but notice the grin on Laura's face, which catches me slightly off-guard. *What the fuck is she smiling about?* Here I am, trying to keep my emotions in check and she's smiling.

"Thanks for lunch," I mumble, walking away without a second glance. I am a fucking dick. I couldn't even look at her when

I walked away. I know she doesn't understand what my problem is, and I know that I'll have to explain it to her at some point, but right now I have to process this.

This is a really hard pill for me to swallow. I may have walked away from Harley five years ago, but I never really left her. My head and my heart have been with her since that horrible night. There hasn't been a birthday, holiday, or hell, any day that's gone by that I haven't thought about her and wondered what she's doing.

When I came home, I really thought that Levi and Harley still had a thing. But after Levi telling me that wasn't the case, I allowed myself to wander into 'what if' territory. For the first time in five years, I felt my heart come alive at the prospect of making her mine. I was nothing short of excited about the opportunity to reclaim the girl I fell in love with so many years ago.

What I hadn't anticipated was Max. I don't even know him and I already hate him. I hate him because he has what I want. I hope to God he knows what he's got in a woman like Harley and doesn't hurt her the way I did.

No wonder she kept friend-zoning me. Hell, that's probably what she was talking about when she said that there were things she needed to tell me.

Fuck.

Stepping into the lounge, I pull out my phone and dial Levi's number. He answers on the first ring.

"What's up, Ty?"

"You stupid fucker! You could've told me about Max," I snap. The line goes silent. His lack of response is not what I anticipated.

"Levi?"

"Yeah, sorry. She told you about Max?" he asks inquisitively.

"No. But you should have the other night. Instead, I had to sit through a conversation between her and Laura about how handsome the bastard is."

"He's not a bastard!" Levi snaps. *Whoa, what the fuck?* I can hear him take a deep breath through the phone. "If I ever hear you talk about Max that way again, I swear to God that I will fucking strangle you." His voice is low and calm but lethal.

Damn, does everybody love Max? "Sorry," I respond flatly. Running my hand over my face, I lean down and rest my elbows on my knees, hanging my head in defeat. "I just...never mind. I gotta go."

"Wait!" Levi pleads. "You just what?"

"I didn't anticipate any competition. You could have warned me." Levi goes silent again, obviously mulling my words around in his head. He's probably wondering when I lost my balls and grew a fucking pussy.

"What exactly did Harley tell you about Max?" he asks cautiously.

I take a deep, cleansing breath. "Nothing," I answer on an exhale. "Her friend, Laura, sat down and asked how he was, and then they started talking about how handsome he is and I bailed."

Levi's boisterous laugh rings through the phone. "This is fucking hilarious," he gasps. "I can't wait to tell Quinn." I pull the phone away from my ear and stare at it. Hitting 'end,' I sever our conversation and lean back in my chair. A minute later my phone beeps.

Levi: Sorry dude. Wasn't trying to laugh at you. You need to talk to Harley about Max. I promise that when you meet him, you'll love him. Just talk to Harley.

Ha! I doubt that I'll ever love him—he has what I want. I'm not even going to respond to that.

I look up when the door opens and Avery walks in. I watch her move about the room for a few seconds, allowing myself to admire her. She's a little bit thinner than I prefer and I really don't want to be with another blonde, but she's incredibly smart and really sweet. Maybe I should give her a chance after all. And it's a long shot, but maybe if I'm with someone else, I'll be able to forget about Harley.

Chapter 7
Harley

"HEY, DAD!" I SAY, slightly out of breath. I hold up my finger, gesturing for Max to give me a second as I sit down in the grass. "What's up?"

"Hi, sweetheart," I hear my mom say. These two crack me up. They always get on the phone together so that they can each hear what's going on. "Your dad and I were wondering what you and Max have planned for this weekend."

I watch Max climb his rock wall, stand tall, and bring his hand above his eyes, peering out into the yard. "Ahoy, Matey!" he yells at no one in particular.

"Oh, is that Maxy?" my mom croons. "Tell him Nana says hi."

I roll my eyes. I hate when she calls him Maxy. It makes me think of maxi-pads, but I never say anything because...well, because my parents are incredible and they help me out so much. So I just keep my mouth shut.

"Max!" I yell across the yard. "Nana and Papa say hi!"

"Aye!" he growls. "I'm not Max. I'm Captain Hook and you took my treasure." He points at me accusingly and looking as if he expects me to produce the 'stolen' goods.

"Alright...whatever," I murmur, waving my hand dismissively at him.

"Mom, Max is playing but I'm sure he says hello." I smile as I watch him take on a bad guy in a pretend sword fight. Holy hell, I want some of that energy. "Anyway, I don't think that Max and I have any plans for this weekend. Why, what's up?" I ask, lying back to enjoy the evening breeze. The sun is setting and it's at the perfect angle to light up the clouds in deep purples and reds. This is by far the best time of the year.

"Well—"

"Well, what?" I ask.

"We—" Mom and Dad answer at the same time, causing me to chuckle.

"Okay, you tell her," my mom says.

"Honey, I got tickets to the Cards-Cubs series this weekend. There is a Saturday game at eleven in the morning and then a twelve o'clock game on Sunday."

"Oooh, that sounds like fun!" I answer excitedly. "We would love to go."

"That's just it. We only have three tickets and I was hoping to bring Max," my Dad says hesitantly. "But I don't want to hurt your feelings. You know you'll always be my Missy Moo Cow, but Max is young and all of this is new to him and he has so much fun. He loves baseball."

Tears sting my eyes and I squeeze them shut, holding back the emotion that's clawing its way up my throat at the mention of my childhood nickname. Apparently when I was a toddler, I thought that every animal said, 'moo.' I'm not sure how he got the name, but ever since then my dad has always called me Missy Moo Cow.

My dad hasn't called me Missy Moo Cow since the night of my attack.

"He loves everything, dad," I murmur, mostly to myself. "It's okay, you can take him."

"Sweetie," my mom croons. "We aren't trying to take him away from you. We know we had him last Saturday, but...well... we aren't getting any younger and Max is growing up so fast." She sniffs lightly into the phone and continues. "One of these days he won't want to do things like this with us."

"It's really okay, Mom. I understand. It's not a big deal. So what's the plan? What time do you want to pick him up on Saturday and Sunday?" I ask, sitting up so I can keep a better eye on my little pirate.

"Well..." my mom drags out. Oh Lord, this should be good. "The games aren't in St. Louis. They're in Chicago."

I jump up, brushing the grass off my butt. "What? No. Sorry, I'm not ready for that." *What the hell?* I've never been away from Max for longer than a night. There's no way in hell I could go a whole weekend.

"See, I told you, Marie," my dad chastises.

"Oh, sweetie. You're making a big deal out of nothing. We aren't going to let anything happen to Max. We're going to have so much fun! We'll go to the games, and I want to take him to Navy Pier and let him ride that big Ferris wheel," Mom says hopefully.

I grip my phone tighter in my left hand and throw my right hand in the air. "It's not about that, Mom!" I snarl. "You know that I trust you guys more than anyone else. Keeping him for one night is okay when you're just down the road, but keeping him for two nights when you're five hours away doesn't sit well with me. What if something happens?" I ask in disbelief.

"Its okay, honey," Dad says, followed by whispered words that I can't quite make out. *Am I being irrational?* "Your mom and I will go by ourselves; it's not a big deal."

Turning toward the swing set, I watch Max play. He stands about ten feet from his swing and runs at it with full speed. His little arms are pumping furiously and his legs are moving in rapid succession. Reaching his arms out, he leaps onto the swing on his belly and pretends he is flying. I hate missing out on this stuff. I don't want to miss out on anything.

It's not that I don't want Max to go; I just wish I could go with him. Maybe I want to be there when he rides that big Ferris wheel. Did they ever think of that? Ugh! As much as I want to be there for everything, I understand that it's not possible. There are moments in his life that I will inevitably miss, and right now I should just be grateful that I have two wonderful parents who love my son as much as I do. Scrubbing my hand over my face, I growl. "Fine," I concede. "He can go."

"Alright!" my Dad cheers. "Thank you so much, sweetie."

"You're welcome," I reply flatly.

"We love you, darling. Give Max kisses from us, and tell him we're going to come get him Friday afternoon," Mom chirps into the phone. *Damn them. They knew I would give in.*

"Love you too. Night." Ending the call, I toss my phone to the ground and take off running for Max. He catches sight of me out of the corner of his eye and squeals loudly as he takes off in the opposite direction. Halfway around the house, he turns and starts chasing me. We run around for several minutes before I let him tackle me to the ground. His laughter fills the air and joy fills my heart.

"I love you, Captain Hook." I nuzzle my nose into his neck and he laughs at the contact, scrunching up his shoulders.

We finally make our way inside after the sun goes down. I give Max a bath and let him watch a show before tucking him into bed for the night. Now is when I get busy. Call me crazy, but I don't like to do housework when I'm home with Max. I'd rather spend the time with him—everything else can just wait. The drawback is that it leaves me with laundry, dishes, and any other housework to do after he goes to bed, which makes for a long night and an even more exhausting morning.

Flipping on the TV, I start folding a load of laundry. My mind quickly turns to my lunch with Tyson today. When he first texted me, I was terrified. But then I remembered my conversation with Levi and the fact that he and Quinn both thought Tyson was interested in more than friendship. Ultimately, that's what I was thinking about when I walked down to the ER to meet him for lunch.

Initially, I thought they had been right. I noticed him watching me on several different occasions and he even went out of his way to brush up against me, which I thoroughly enjoyed. Tyson is ruggedly handsome with his light brown hair, square jaw, and round, chocolate eyes. His gaze alone makes me feel vulnerable and sexy in a way I've never felt, and I found myself wanting more.

When Laura sat down, everything changed. She started talking about Max and that alarmed me. I don't want Tyson to learn about Max from someone else. I want him to learn about Max from me, and today I realized just how easy it would be for someone to inadvertently spill the beans. I could tell Tyson's demeanor shifted instantaneously and when he walked away hastily without a glance in my direction, my heart dropped.

I can't believe he walked away from me—*again*.

Laura watched me closely after Tyson left, but thankfully she didn't say anything. Meanwhile, I fought back tears while I cleaned up the rest of our mess from lunch. I left right after, knowing she would be able to see the sadness on my face. Knowing Laura, she would try to console me and I'd probably break down and cry. I really didn't want to cry. I can't believe that he said we were just '*two old friends having lunch.*' But he's right, that is what we are—and I hate it. I don't want to be just *two old friends*.

For some reason, I feel the need to make this right. I feel like I need to reach out to him and fix whatever it is I inadvertently broke. Grabbing my phone, I type out a text before I let my nerves get the best of me.

Me: I'm sorry we were interrupted at lunch today. I really enjoyed spending time with you.

Hitting 'send,' I toss my phone off to the side so that I won't sit and watch it. My pulse is racing, and my nerves feel like they're itching to get out. My phone dings almost instantly and I grab it frantically.

Tyson: It's okay. Me too.

That's it? I throw myself out there and tell him I enjoyed spending time with him today, and that's all he says in return? Well fuck, I was hoping for more than that.

Me: Maybe we could try again tomorrow?

Tyson: I usually don't get lunch.

Now *that* pisses me off! Why would he try so hard to spend time with me and then just walk away...and now he's blowing me off? My thumb hovers tentatively over my screen as I contemplate my next move. After my attack and Max's birth, and following my bout with depression, I promised myself that I wouldn't let fear rule my life. I vowed that I would take chances and be bold because tomorrow isn't guaranteed. And I swore that I wouldn't have any more regrets. Those pledges are what spur my next text.

Me: Would you like to go out to dinner with me this weekend?

He doesn't respond right away, and I briefly think that maybe I shouldn't have just done that. *Damnit.* Why can't there be a grace period with text messages so that you have about a minute to hit 'undo' before they're actually sent? That would really be great right about now. Several minutes pass before Tyson replies.

Tyson: Really? You want to have dinner?

Me: Of course I do. I thought that's what we were trying to do, get to know each other again. Did you change your

mind?

What the hell? I'm so confused. He can't change his mind.

Tyson: Okay. Dinner. Will Max be okay with us having dinner?

That's an odd question. Oh God! My hand covers my mouth. Brit. Gah! I groan, throwing my head back on the couch. How could I forget about Brit? That's probably why he was acting so funny at lunch. Maybe I was coming on too strong and I made him uncomfortable. *Wait.* Levi made it sound like Tyson came back for me. Why would he come back for me if he's still with Brit?

Me: Umm... yeah. We're just friends, but I'll still tell him we're going. He already knows about you. He'll probably be upset that he won't get to meet you himself.

Me: What about Brit? Will she be okay with us having dinner?

Tyson: You told him about me?

I frown at my phone momentarily—he didn't answer my question about Brit.
What is going on in that boy's head?

Me: Yes. He's seen pictures of you and knows about our history. He's going to be really excited to meet you.

When we moved into the new house, Max and I were looking through some old albums, and of course they were filled with pictures of Tyson and me. Max asked so many questions...he wanted to know who Tyson was, how I knew him, and basically everything about him. Even though it reminded me just how much I missed Tyson, I enjoyed telling Max about him and reliving those memories.

Tyson: You can bring him to dinner with us if you want. I can meet him there.

Me: He's going to the Cards-Cubs game in Chicago this weekend. But soon. Let's talk more over dinner?

Tyson: Ok. Dinner. Send me your address and I'll pick you up.

Me: I can meet you somewhere. I don't expect you to drive all the way here.

Tyson: On my days off I've been staying in one of Mom and Dad's empty rental houses. It's closer to home.

Me: Ok. 22 Larson. Pick me up at 5?

Tyson: See you then.

Dropping my phone in my lap, I lean back against the couch and close my eyes. *What the hell is happening?* My phone lets out one last chirp, startling me.

Tyson: Brit and I aren't together.

"Yes!" I whisper, pumping my fist in the air.

So I guess I was wrong...Tyson didn't act weird earlier because of Brit. But that still doesn't explain anything. Unless maybe he could tell that I was still attracted to him and he doesn't feel the same way. Oh God, please tell me I didn't creep him out. I close my eyes, trying to remember every detail from lunch today. I don't remember doing or saying anything that would make him uncomfortable.

Me: What happened?

Tyson: We can discuss over dinner. Good night.

Tyson

LOCKING THE SCREEN, I toss my phone aside and flop back on the bed. Did she really think I was still with Brit?

What the fuck just happened? Her text was completely unexpected. I'm the one who acted like a complete douche, and yet she reached out to me? I tried to sound unaffected, not because I wanted to upset her but if we are only ever going to be friends, then I have to maintain some sort of distance in order to keep my heart intact. That strong determination quickly went to shit when she asked me to dinner. I was *definitely* not expecting that.

My first thought was why would she ask me to dinner after the way I walked away from her today. For a brief moment, I found myself wondering if Harley was the type of girl that would go out with me and not tell her boyfriend. I shook that thought off quickly, angry with myself for even thinking it. Of course she wouldn't, and she didn't disappoint. Not only did she say she would tell Max, but said she had already told him all about me.

Fuck. Keeping any form of distance is going to be impossible. I need to burn off some energy before I go insane.

I take off my shirt, slip on basketball shorts and my running shoes, and push my ear buds in my ears. It takes me thirty minutes to run to my gym, where I spend another two hours working off all of the frustrations from today.

Seeing Harley this afternoon was fantastic, but realizing that we could only ever be friends was not. I groan at the memory, hating myself for the way I walked away from her. By the end of my workout, I have myself convinced that I can, in fact, just be friends with Harley. I want that. Very much.

It's going to take time to not look at her as more than a friend though, considering I haven't been able to stop thinking about her sexy, toned legs, killer curves, and picture-perfect rack since I first laid eyes on her again. It probably doesn't help that every time I close my eyes, I picture said legs gripping my hips tightly as I plunge deep into her warm body.

My workout doesn't exactly alleviate my frustrations so I make one last attempt by sprinting home at a fast clip, pushing my body to its limit. I stagger into my condo, my legs loose and unsteady as I strip down, leaving a trail of clothes on my way to the bathroom. Reaching around the curtain, I turn the shower on and let it run briefly to warm the water. Stepping in, I allow the scalding hot water and steam to engulf me, and I relish the way it relaxes my muscles after a hard workout. Closing my eyes, I lean my head back and Harley's beautiful face instantly consumes my thoughts.

Today she was wearing hot-pink scrub pants that sat low on her hips and hugged her tight ass perfectly. Her scrub top had a piece of material that wrapped around her waist and tied in the back, accentuating her kick-ass curves. She had her long chestnut waves wrapped in a loose bun at the base of her neck. A low growl rumbles from my throat and I feel my cock begin to stir.

Reaching down, I fist myself tightly, hating that I'm about to bring myself pleasure by thinking about the one person I can't have. I would have given anything today to pull the band from her hair and watch it cascade down her back. I pump harder at the thought of running my fingers through her thick mane and giving her hair a firm tug, not hard but enough that she knows who's in control.

My hips rock quickly as I allow the fantasy to run wild behind my eyelids. Pushing her against the wall, I dip my hand down the front of her scrub pants. Sliding her panties to the side, I breach her wet folds and plunge my fingers deep inside her soft, warm body. Throwing her head back, she arches into my touch, offering me everything she has. My name leaves her lips in a light whisper and…that's all it takes. My body convulses and my dick continues to twitch in my hand as I ride out the final waves of my orgasm.

I'm fairly certain that I haven't come that hard in years.

Fuck. It's going to be harder than I thought to only be her friend.

Fucking Max. Lucky-ass bastard.

Chapter 8

Harley

I WRAP MY ARMS tightly around his waist and bury my nose in the side of his neck, inhaling his perfect scent. *Crap.* What was I thinking? I can't do this. I squeeze tighter. Honest to God, someone is going to have to pry me off of him.

"Mo-om," Max whines. "You're squeezing all my breath out." Chuckling lightly at his comment, I pull back and start peppering kisses across his face. Scrunching up his shoulders, he collapses to the floor in a fit of giggles.

"Tickles. It t-t-tickles," he squeaks in between laughs. Gripping his hands, I pull him up so that he's standing in front me and I cup his cheeks in my hands. My eyes roam his face nervously, memorizing every little thing about him. Some people would probably think I'm overreacting, but if there's one thing I've learned in my twenty-seven years, it's that bad things can happen in the blink of an eye.

It's that thought that makes my stomach twist in knots and I swallow hard, choking back my emotion. Max doesn't need to see me cry. "I love you, buddy."

"I love you too, mom," he says with a wide, toothy smile.

"Listen to Nana and Papa and don't ever walk away from them. Got it?"

"Got it," he replies with a firm nod.

Bending down, my mom grabs Max's overnight bag and tosses it over her shoulder. "Alright, Maxy, let's get going. We've got a long drive ahead of us."

"Woo-hoo..." Max yells, his voice trailing off as he runs through the house.

Mom wraps her arm around my neck and pulls me into a hug. "He's going to be fine. Stop worrying," she soothes. "Enjoy your Max-free weekend. Get out and do something fun."

Pulling back, I attempt to give her a genuine smile. Her face is full of amusement and her answering grin causes my smile to turn into a sob. My head drops to her shoulder and I hear her laugh quietly as she reaches up to wipe away the wetness from my eyes.

"Stop this...we will be back before you know it." She pats me twice on the back and then walks off, leaving me standing in the middle of Max's bedroom.

Making my way to the living room, I find Max jumping excitedly from foot to foot. "I getta ride a big ferry wheel!"

Dad's mouth lifts into a huge grin and he reaches down, mussing up Max's hair. "Ferris..." he says slowly, "not ferry."

"Who cares," Max yelps, batting away my dad's hand. "It's a big wheel and I get to ride it!"

Squatting down to Max's level, I envelop him in another big hug and give him one last kiss. "Have fun, buddy! I'll see you in a few days."

"'Kay, mom. Bye!" he yells. Grabbing my dad's hand, Max turns and pulls him out the door. Dad turns his head, giving me a quick wink, and mom walks out behind him, stopping briefly to kiss my temple. "Bye, sweetie."

"See ya. Have fun." I shut the door, lock it, and turn around to face my empty house. Pressing my back against the cool wood, I slide to the floor and allow the silence to consume me. I promised myself that I was going to take advantage of my weekend alone. I can do whatever I want; I just have to figure what it is I want to do.

"Now what?" I murmur to myself. My phone beeps in my pocket and I pull it out, smiling when I see Quinn's name. Perfect timing, Quinny.

```
Quinn: Did Max leave yet?

Me: Yup...

Quinn: Are you crying?

Me: Nope...

Quinn: Do you have plans for tonight?

Me: Nope. Wanna get together?

Quinn: Sorry I've got plans.
```

Seriously? I stare at the phone, at a loss for how to respond, when another text comes in.

```
Quinn: Try Levi.

Me: Then why did you ask if I have plans?

Quinn: Cause I was curious.

Me: What are you doing tonight?

Quinn: I've got a hot date.

Me: WHAT?!
```

Screw this. Sometimes I hate texting. I dial Quinn and she answers on the first ring. "Ha! I knew you'd call."

"You have a date? Why am I just now hearing about this?" I

ask accusingly. "Who is it?"

Quinn's laugh rings loudly through the phone. "First, you are just now hearing about it because it just sort of happened. Second...I'm not tell-ing," she sings.

"What?" I scoff. "Damnit, Quinny, I tell you everything. Please tell me," I beg.

"I can't."

"Can't or *won't*?" Pushing up from the floor, I make my way through the house, picking up Max's toys that he left scattered around.

"Umm...both."

What?

"What the fuck, Quinn? Spill the damn beans, 'cause you're starting to piss me off!" I scold.

"Harley," she whines, "please don't push me on this. If you keep pushing, I'm going to tell you, but this is really important to me and I'm not ready to make it public. It's so fresh and new, and right now I just want to enjoy it. If I feel like it's going somewhere, then I promise I'll tell you. Okay?"

Wow. Quinn has always been an open book so this is a huge shock. She is totally the kiss-and-tell type of girl.

"Okay, Quinny. But now I'm worried about you."

"Harley, quit worrying about me. You've got an entire weekend to yourself. You need to go out and do something fun. Tell me what you have planned."

"Well, I'm cleaning right now. I've got some laundry to do, the dishes need to be washed, the floors could use a good scrubbing—"

"Jesus Christ..." she moans, effectively cutting me off. "You're twenty-seven, Harley, not seventy-two. The cleaning can wait. You have no kid and no responsibilities for two-and-a-half days. Do you realize that you could go get shit-faced and sleep in the next day? Seriously, when is the last time you've been able to do that?"

She's got a point. Usually when I go out, I only have a drink or two because I know that I'll have to pick up Max the next day. When was the last time I got drunk? Or even had a buzz? Honest to God, I can't remember.

"You're right!" I announce proudly. "I deserve to have some fun. I'm going to call Levi and make him take me out."

"Atta girl…" she praises. "Now go get all dolled up and have some fun."

"Thanks, Quinn. I'll talk to you tomorrow. Have fun tonight."

"I will, and you have fun too. Bye, babe," she says, hanging up the phone.

I look at my watch—five-thirty. Plenty of time to clean and then jump in the shower. It's easy for Quinn to say 'no housework' because she's never had to pick up after a four-year-old boy. I gather Max's toys and toss them in the toy box and then make quick work of sorting through the dirty laundry before throwing a load into the washer.

I type out a quick text to Levi, telling him that we're going out tonight, and I jump in the shower, relishing the fact that for the first time in a long time I don't have to rush.

I shower until the water runs cold, forcing me of out my slice of heaven. *Crap, that was amazing!* I make a note to do that more often.

Throwing the shower curtain back, I reach for my towel and wrap it around my head before wrapping another one around my body. The red light blinks on my phone, indicating a missed call. I pick it up. *Damnit.* I press 'talk' to call Levi back and make my way into the closet to find something to wear tonight.

"Hey, Harley! I just called you," he says, answering the phone.

"Yeah. Sorry about that. I was in the shower." Reaching up, I grab a few tops and a pair of jeans and toss them onto my bed. "So, where should we go tonight?" I ask, releasing the towel from my grip. "I was thinking we could go get a pizza or maybe Mexican and then hit up some bars. What are your thoughts?"

"Harley," he sighs. "I'm sorry, I can't go out tonight. Marco called in sick and I had to step in and help out in the kitchen." It's obvious when he steps outside the restaurant because the commotion that I'd been hearing in the background disappears, replaced by the faint sound of the wind blowing into the phone.

"Are you serious?" I whine, throwing myself back on the bed.

"I'm sorry, Harley. Call Quinn."

"I already did," I lament. "She has a hot date."

"What? Really? With who?"

"I don't know. She wouldn't tell me. Must be someone special if she's keeping it tight-lipped. Damn, this sucks. I don't have Max for a whole weekend and I'm lying naked on a pile of really awesome clothes that I wanted to try on." Pulling myself up, I shimmy on my underwear.

Levi doesn't respond, but I can hear him murmuring something to himself. "Levi? You there?"

"Yup. I'm here," he responds on a deep exhale. "I'm reminding myself that you're just my friend. *Only* my friend. Nothing more. Right?"

I can't stop the laugh that bubbles up my throat. "Right. If it makes you feel better, I'm putting my sweatpants on now, so I'm not naked anymore."

"What? Why?" he asks. "You have to go and do something. Seriously, Harley, you can't sit at home and clean all weekend."

"Well, what the hell am I supposed to do?" I ask, throwing my hand in the air. "Am I supposed to get all dolled up and go out by myself? You know me better than that. No way in hell."

"Tyson."

"What about Tyson?"

"Call him. See if he wants to hang out tonight. I mean, that's what you guys are doing, right? You're becoming friends again, and friends hang out. Call him."

Sliding the towel off my head, I run my fingers through my tangled hair. "No. I can't call him tonight. We already have dinner plans tomorrow night."

"Who cares? Look, I have to go. I'm really sorry. I'll try and stop by Sunday evening to see Max."

"It's okay. I'll see you Sunday." I move to end the call when I hear him yell my name through the phone.

"What?"

"Call. Him." He hangs up before I can respond to his bossiness and I'm left staring at my phone in confusion.

I can't have drinks with Tyson tonight. *Can I?* Although I can't really deny that I would love to see him again, and it would be really nice to see him outside of work. In fact, since our lunch and brief texting session yesterday, I haven't been able to get him off of my mind.

You know what? Fuck it! I pick up my phone and scroll down to his name. My thumb hovers tentatively over the 'talk' button as I give my self an internal pep talk. *There is no reason to be nervous. We are friends and friends have dinner and drinks.* The only problem is that I can't stop picturing myself shoving Tyson up against a door so that I can rip his pants off, fall to my knees, and worship every inch of his body. And I can't stop imagining him hovering over me and making sweet love to me.

Shit. Where's my damn vibrator when I need it?

I hit 'talk' and tuck my phone between my ear and shoulder as I rummage through the clothes on my bed. The skinny jeans and peasant top I'd contemplated wearing earlier were great when I thought I was going out with Levi. But if I go out with Tyson, I need something a little different...a little sexier. The phone rings four times and goes to voicemail. I end the call with a huff, deciding to shoot him a quick text rather than leaving a voicemail.

Me: Any plans for tonight? Max left earlier than expected and I was wondering if you wanted to go get dinner and have a few drinks with me.

My hair is way too long and takes forever to blow-dry. Standing in front of the mirror, I hold my hair on top of my head and then lower it back down, trying to decide the best way to style it. Down—definitely down.

Tyson always did like it down. He used to tell me that when my hair was down and I walked by, he could smell the soft vanilla scent of my shampoo. Picking up my phone, I double-check that the volume is on high, nervous that I might miss his response.

I gather my hair over my left shoulder and pin it in place so that the silky waves drape over my chest. I pull out a few chunks of hair to frame my face and spray it lightly with hairspray. Perfect.

My attention keeps wandering to my silent phone. What is he doing? Why hasn't he replied yet? My eyes flit nervously to my watch. Get a grip, Harley, it's only been twenty minutes. Maybe he's busy, or at work, or— "Fuck," I grunt, my head hanging low. I can't believe that he already has me tied up in knots like this.

What the fuck is my problem?

I promised myself that I would never get like this over a man again—especially not Tyson—and then look what happens! He walks his fine ass back into my life and within days, he's successfully turned my life upside down. My phone chirps, startling me out of my thoughts, and my fingers itch to grab it and see what it says. A small part of me doesn't want to see the text at all because what if he rejects me? What if he turns down my offer? Or worse, what if he's on another date?

The self-control it takes me to walk across the bathroom without touching my phone is indescribable. "He can just wait," I murmur to myself. Reaching into the drawer, I pull out my make-up bag and begin my ritual. Foundation. Blush. Eye shadow. Mascara. The 'smokey eye' that some girls can pull off is a horrible look for me so I usually stick to my 'less is more' motto. I do, however, apply an extra few extra layers of mascara. If there is one thing about myself that I like, it's my eyes. I was lucky enough to inherit my mom's sage-green eyes and my dad's long lashes.

Looking in the mirror, I do a final once-over, smiling brightly at what I see. Not too shabby, if I do say so myself. Now I just hope that I didn't get all decked out to sit at home and watch reruns of *Friends,* while *my* friends are all otherwise occupied.

My phone chirps again, signaling an unviewed message. Picking it up, I walk through the house to the kitchen, where I pour myself a glass of wine. I mean, why not, right? Giving my glass a slight twirl, I take a sip. My body is humming with anticipation and butterflies have taken flight in my stomach. Fucking hell, what is wrong with me? Grow some balls, Harley!

Swiping my finger across the screen, the beginning of a message appears on my phone.

Tyson: I'm at work but—

My hope plummets. Work. Of course he's at work. He's a resident…he works all the damn time. My fingers quickly unlock the phone to bring up the full message.

Tyson: I'm at work but I get off at 7. I would need to run home and get cleaned up, so maybe 8ish. Is that too late for you?

Hope blooms in my chest once again at his words. Hell no, eight isn't too late.

Me: No, that's perfect. Do you want me to meet you downtown since you'll be at your condo?

The butterflies in my stomach shift from fluttering nervously to quivering in anticipation. Taking a deep breath, I open my throat and down the entire glass of wine. I know, I know…It's very un-ladylike. But I'm nervous, damnit!

Crap. Clothes. I need clothes.

I scurry off the couch, sliding across the hardwood floor as I attempt to run down the hallway to my room. Flipping the light on in my closet, I make my way to the back, completely bypassing the skinny jeans and peasant top. Okay, I need something sweet and sexy. There is nothing I want more than to have Tyson back in my life, but more than that, I really want him to notice me. My hand hovers nervously over a hanger as Levi's words repeat in my head... *"I'm a guy, Harley, and I saw the way he looked at you when you walked into the bar the other night."*

I want to see that look on Tyson's face. Making my decision, I pull a top from its hanger and toss it on the bed next to my skinny jeans. A quick glance at my phone indicates a reply from Tyson.

Tyson: I was going to stay at my parents' rental house since I have the rest of the weekend off. Why don't we meet somewhere near you.

Me: Okay. How about My Dad's Bar?

Tyson: Um. Okay. I didn't know your dad owned a bar. Is that new?

Me: Ha! No. It's a new tavern in town. It's called My Dad's Bar. You'll like it. They have great food too if you're hungry!

Tyson: I ate a late lunch. I'll google the address and meet you there around 8.

Okay. I was really excited when he decided to go with me, but now I'm unsure. I've known Tyson my whole life. He's usually quite happy and talkative so the answers I'm getting seem a little off, which sort of bugs me.

Me: K

My eyes roam over the outfit on the bed and I bite my lower lip, contemplating how I'm going to approach this. It's obvious after the way he left lunch the other day that something spooked him. I'm just not sure what that something was.

Shaking my head, I scoop up the clothes I'd laid out and put them back into the closet. *I really need to make up my freakin' mind*, I mumble to myself. I pull out my favorite pair of faded, boot-cut jeans and shimmy into them. I love these jeans. They're the perfect wash, they have a small tear in the right upper thigh that gives them a rugged look, and they make my ass look three sizes smaller.

I pull my favorite graphic tee out of the drawer and slip it on, and then finish the outfit off with my Converse. Hmmm...something looks off. The hair—it's definitely the hair. The hair is sexy, but I'm now going for casual so I reach up and pull the pins out, run my fingers through it a few times, and let the waves fall down my back. *Perfect.*

If Tyson wants his friend, Harley, back, then by gosh that's what he's going to get. I read the words printed on my shirt through the mirror and smirk. *It's time to get my friend back.*

WALKING INTO MY DAD'S Bar, I notice two things right away. One, Tyson isn't here yet. Two, apparently its 'fight night' and I'm one of only a few females in the entire place. The bar is filled to capacity with groups of men, all watching the TV intently. Every couple of seconds, they all jump out of their seats in anticipation, their fists ready to pump the air.

Men.

I walk to the back of the bar and slide into a booth. It looks a little more private than an open table. A gorgeous waitress approaches and hands me a menu. I order an Amaretto and Coke and she walks off without a second glance. As I silently read the descriptions of the entrées, my stomach lets out a fierce growl and I suddenly realize that I haven't eaten since I made Max biscuits and gravy this morning.

My waitress returns, placing my drink on the table in front of me, and pulls out her notepad. "What can I get you, hon?" I grimace at the nickname; it's almost as bad as being called 'ma'am.' Leaning forward, I read her nametag. Brittany...*oh, how fitting*.

"Yes, can I get a plate of your chicken quesadillas? Oh...and a water, please." She glances at my mixed drink and then back at me with a blank look on her face."Okaaaay," she says slowly. "Anything else?"

My head pops up as Tyson slides into the seat across from me. "Yup. I'll take a Bud Light bottle, please."

Brittany turns her head in Tyson's direction and smiles appreciatively at what she sees. She nods her head slowly. "Sure thing, sugar." Leaning forward, she places her palms on the table, her cleavage on full display. "My name is Brittany. Holler if you need anything."

Bitch. I hate her.

Tyson smiles lightly, his eyes never wavering from hers, and nods his head. My eyes glare a hole in her back as she retreats. Who the hell does she think she is? Can't she see that he isn't here alone? I scoff internally at the nerve of that girl. Shifting in my seat, I reach for my drink and my eyes land on the amused face across from me.

"What?" I ask innocently, taking a sip of my sweet drink.

His smile grows and he shakes his head. "Nothing."

Brittany returns and hands Tyson his beer. Reaching in her pocket, she pulls out a napkin and slides it to him, the movement causing the side of her breast to brush against his arm. My mouth drops open in shock at her blatant flirting.

Smiling sincerely, Tyson grabs the napkin and uses it to wipe the wetness from his bottle before tossing it aside, completely ignoring the phone number she'd scribbled on the back. Brittany stalks off and relief washes through me at his rejection of her.

"So," he says, a smile tugging at his lips. "Should I read the next sentence?" His grin is infectious and I smirk back, reveling in his playful behavior. Growing up, Tyson and I always had a thing for text-based t-shirts. In my attempt to rekindle our friendship, I wore one tonight to see if I'd get a reaction out of him, which thankfully I did. I look down, reading the words written across my chest.

**DO NOT
READ
THE NEXT
SENTENCE**

I look down further at the part that he can't see. In smaller print, closer to the bottom of the shirt, it says:

You little rebel. I like you.

"I don't know. How bad do you want to know what it says?" I've always loved taunting Tyson and vice-versa.

He lifts an eyebrow, briefly studying me. Then, he tilts his beer bottle and takes a drink, his eyes holding mine the entire time. "I'm good. I don't need to know."

I throw my head back and laugh at his poor attempt at indifference. He's dying to read it. "Suit yourself," I shrug.

Brittany returns with my quesadillas and two plates, and then walks off.

"You pissed her off." Grabbing one of the plates, I pile on a few triangles of the Mexican masterpiece and a dollop of sour cream. I push the second plate to Tyson and gesture for him to help himself.

"Who cares," he replies, shoving a bite of food into his mouth. "I can't stand it when women are so blatantly sexual. It's like they think that a sexy smile and large rack will get them everywhere in life. I prefer my women to be more subtle and less flashy."

I'm subtle, I think to myself.

Our conversation is light and comfortable as we finish our food and it leaves me feeling satisfied in a way I haven't felt in years. Tyson leans back in the booth, resting his hand on his stomach.

"I thought you weren't hungry," I tease.

"I shouldn't be. Avery brought in leftover pot roast and cheesecake, and I ate way too much of it," he groans.

"Who's Avery?" Reaching for my glass, I take a drink, trying to appear casual. My stomach twists. *Who the fuck is Avery?*

His eyes flash briefly with an unknown emotion. "She's one of the ER docs. I'm surprised you haven't met her?"

"Who knows? Maybe I have. I've met so many doctors."

"She's really nice, and maybe a few years older than us. She's smart and has been a great mentor. Most of the doctors down there are older, so it's nice to have someone around that's closer to my age. You guys would probably get along great."

Nodding my head, I smile tightly, choosing not to respond. At that moment, loud cheers ring throughout the bar and I stare intently at the action on the big-screen TV, attempting to look interested. Silence engulfs us and guilt rips through my chest. Things just got really uncomfortable and it's totally my fault.

I finish my drink and signal our waitress for another round. Shifting in the booth, I turn toward Tyson. His eyes are trained on his beer bottle as he slowly turns it while picking off the label.

"Wanna play a game?" I ask, intent on alleviating the awkwardness I caused.

His head stays down but he raises his eyes to meet mine. *Why do I find that move so damn sexy?* "What do you have in mind?" he asks as Brittany replaces our empty drinks with fresh ones.

"Can we get eight shots? Four Tequila and four Southern Comfort, please?"

Tyson raises his eyebrows at my request and Brittany merely nods and walks off. "I'm not sure shots are a good idea," he says.

"Why not? Wait...I get it," I croon with mock understanding.

"You've become a lightweight over the past five years, haven't you? You're afraid I'll out-drink you." Tyson has never been one to back down from a challenge, and I'm going to take full advantage of that right now.

"Hell no, I'm not a lightweight," he scoffs. "What are the rules?" I can't help the joy that settles in my chest at the thought that maybe—just maybe—I still know more about him than anyone else, even after five years apart. I wonder how much he remembers about me?

"It's easy." Propping my elbows on the surface in front of me, I entwine my fingers and pin Tyson with a questioning glare. "You want our friendship back, right?"

His face softens and he smiles sweetly. "Right."

"Okay. We each get to ask a question. You either answer or take a shot."

"We can ask anything?" he clarifies.

"Anything." Sliding the sleeves of his shirt up to his elbows, he scoots forward in his seat and rubs his hands together mischievously. My eyes drift down and lock on the roped veins that run from his hands to his elbows, and I watch with rapt attention as his muscles tick with each movement. *Good God, he has sexy forearms.*

I shake my head. *WTF? Sexy forearms?*

"Let's do this. You go first," he says.

Reaching over, I grab the shots that Brittany dropped off and line them up in the middle of the table.

My eyes shift to his. "Okay. I'll start off easy. What's my favorite color?"

"You're kidding, right?" Leaning back in the booth, he crosses his arms over his chest and scowls.

Okaaaay. Apparently I've insulted him.

"What? It's a simple question. I'm asking if you remember my favorite color."

"Of course I do, Harley. I might have been gone for the past five years, but I didn't forget anything." I stare at him, lifting my glass to take a sip, and he sighs. "Purple. And not just any purple... bright purple."

"See? That wasn't so hard, was it? Your turn." Leaning back, I cross my legs and take another drink in anticipation. This game could really turn out to be fun, as long as he doesn't ask ab—

"Are you in a sexually romantic relationship?" Amaretto spews from my mouth and my eyes widen in horror. Tyson laughs and hands me a napkin. Dabbing my mouth and wiping off the table, I avoid eye contact. I mean, HELLO! Who the fuck asks that as a first question?

"Wow. You aren't holding back, are you?" His eyes smile but he doesn't respond. *How the hell do I answer that?* Technically, the answer is no, I'm not currently in a sexually romantic relationship. Then again, I did mess around with Levi a few weeks ago. Does that count? Fuck it.

Reaching across the table, I grab a shot glass. Disappointment flashes briefly across Tyson's face and I hesitate, but I still can't speak past the shock at his unexpected question. Cursing myself, I tip my head back. The cool liquid burns on the way down, and I wipe the back of my hand across my mouth in disgust at the taste it leaves behind.

"Maybe this isn't a good idea," he says. "You're just going to ask easy questions and I'm going pelt you with hard ones that you don't want to answer, and you're going to end up praying to the porcelain gods tonight."

I snap my mouth shut and furrow my brows, feigning insult. "First of all, I'm disappointed at your lack of trust in my ability to hold my alcohol. Second," I say, holding up my hand to stop his interruption, "I'm not just going to ask easy questions, and I'm not going to avoid answering all the hard ones. You caught me off-guard, that's all. This is about getting to know each other again, so no more arguing about question selection. We're starting over. What did you miss most about home while you were gone?"

"You." His answer is quick and the vulnerability on his face leaves me momentarily stunned. My heart flips and constricts in my chest at his raw honesty.

My first instinct is to catapult myself into his arms and never let go, but that might be a bit dramatic. "Good. I missed you too," I respond instead. "See, we're making progress. This is going to be fun. Your turn."

A faint smile tugs at his mouth. "Okay. Hmm." He runs his hand across his chin and I follow his movements. "What's your favorite memory from our childhood?"

Interesting. "Well, let me think. There are so many to choose from," I say, shooting him a wink as he lifts his beer bottle to take a drink. "Got it!" I say, snapping my fingers. "It's nothing too special, but do you remember that summer our parents signed us up for the local kickball league?"

A smile lights up Tyson's face and he pulls his beer bottle back enough to speak.

"Of course I remember. I got chosen to be a captain, and I thought I was hot shit! We were on the same team," he says and I smile and nod at his correct recollection, "and everyone made fun of me because you were the only girl in the league and I picked you to be on my team. Ha! We ended up getting first place."

My eyes burn at the memory and I swallow hard. "That was the best summer for me, and that memory stands out above all the others."

He tilts his head. "Why? I mean it was sort of uneventful. Fun, but uneventful."

"Because you picked me first," I reply wistfully. Tyson watches me carefully, his milk-chocolate eyes searching mine. I can tell he's trying to remember, but it's not clicking. "And, it's the first time you told me I was your best friend."

"You remember that? Why don't I remember that?" he asks disappointedly.

"You didn't care what any of the other kids thought." I smile as the memories flood my mind. "Later that same night, we were sitting on the porch swing and I asked you why you chose me. You looked at me like I had asked the stupidest question and you said, 'Because you're my best friend.' That moment was—is—so special to me. I'll never forget it."

"Wow. I, umm..." he trails off, seemingly at a loss for words.

"My turn!" I chirp, effectively redirecting the conversation away from my sappy memory and giving him the reprieve he needs. "What's your favorite childhood memory?"

My eyes roam the table and land on the seven shot glasses still sitting in the center. "Wait! Let's do a shot."

"Why are you so hell-bent on drinking? Didn't you get all that out of your system...oh, about six years ago?"

"Well, if you must know, I really haven't gotten the chance to indulge myself much over the past five years and now I have the opportunity. I have no responsibilities this weekend and I'm going to take full advantage of it." Tyson's face drops slightly but he recovers quickly, handing me a shot glass. "Cheers." Tapping my glass to his, I take the shot and cringe.

What the fuck is wrong with me? That shit could burn the hair off a bald monkey.

"That," I say, pointing my finger at Tyson, "was another question, so I get to ask the next two." Laughing, he waves his hand across the table, conceding to my demand.

"So, what's your favorite childhood memory?"

I can see the memories flit around in his head based on the nostalgic look that crosses his face, but he doesn't take much time to come up with his response. "I'm not sure I ever told you this, but when I was younger—I can't remember how young exactly—Dallas would hide under my bed. Sometimes he would do it in the middle of the day, other times at night, but he would be really quiet and when I was relaxed or maybe even on the verge of sleep, he would use his hands and feet and bang on the bottom of my mattress." Scooting forward in his seat, Tyson fights back a laugh in order to finish his story. I want so badly to smile back at him but *fuck me*, the mention of his brother is like a punch to the stomach and I pray that he can't see my discomfort. "Damn," he continues, "that used to scare the living shit out of me. I think that one time he scared me so bad, I actually pissed my pants."

"That's a nice memory." A twinge of disappointment flashes through me that his favorite memory doesn't include me, but I quickly shake it off. Tyson worshipped his brother so I shouldn't be surprised.

He shakes his head and takes a drink. "That's not the part that makes it the best. I would always get so mad, but then I would see Dallas rolling around on the floor, laughing uncontrollably with his arms wrapped around his belly. He would laugh so hard that he would cry. That's what makes it my best memory. I don't remember a lot of happy times with Dallas, but that memory stands out. When I think of Dallas being happy and healthy, that's what I think about."

An uncomfortable silence falls between us, the emotions floating off of us are practically palpable in the air. I finish my drink and signal for another round after Tyson finishes his.

"Okay," he says, clapping his hands together. "If that little trip down memory lane doesn't call for another shot, then I don't know what does." I don't respond, instead I smile knowingly and grab a glass, joining him in another shot. "Your turn again."

I look around the bar slowly, contemplating my next question. When did they dim the lights? I look down at my watch and I'm surprised at how much time has passed. The fight on the TV seems to have ended and a band is setting up their equipment on the small stage. I'm glad that we arrived early enough to get our own table, but a small part of me wishes that we were forced to squeeze in next to each other by the bar. That way I could accidentally brush against him or—

Friendship, Harley, I remind myself. *You're supposed to be getting to know him again, not finding ways to molest him.*

"Alright. Next question." Taking a deep breath, I relax back into the booth. I can't believe I'm about to ask him this, but it's killing me. I need to know. "So, what happened with Brit? Why did you guys break up?"

Tyson goes still. His eyes bounce around my face nervously,

and I can't help but wonder what he's nervous about. It's an easy question. There is a reason for the breakup, and I want to know what that reason is. His eyes widen slightly, and I can see the battle ensuing behind his russet gaze. He inhales deeply and runs his hand across his mouth. Reaching for his beer, he takes several long drinks while my mind starts running in a million different directions about what could have happened between him and Brit. I can see it in his eyes—he isn't going to tell me.

Cocking my head to the side, I raise my eyebrows, silently encouraging him to answer the question. My anticipation is quickly slashed when he averts his eyes and takes a shot.

"Now who isn't answering the hard questions?" I murmur sarcastically.

"You have your reasons for not answering my question and I have reasons for not answering yours. No more arguing about question selection, remember?"

I tip my head and glass at him in acceptance of his response, and then what he says next both excites and scares me. "I'm going to tell you what happened with Brit, but now isn't the right time. I need us," he says, waving his hand between the two of us, "to be in a certain spot and we aren't there yet. It may take awhile before I'm comfortable enough to give you that answer, but I promise you, Harley, it will happen."

Reaching up, I twist my finger around a lock of hair and start twirling it in an attempt to calm my nerves. I study Tyson's face, trying to see what's going on behind that dark gaze, but he's closed off. I can't tell what he's thinking. "Your turn."

"Were you and Levi ever together?" *Goddamn, he's making this hard.* I reach across the table and take another shot. "Seriously? You're not going to answer that question either?" he snaps.

"Nope, I'm totally going to answer you...I just needed a shot first. You know, liquid courage and all." I reach down and check my phone for any missed calls. I know I'm stalling, but I need to think this through. He doesn't know I know he came back for me. Maybe Tyson is just trying to figure out if Levi was telling the truth. Picking my words carefully, I straighten my back and prepare for the conversation that I should have known would come.

Tyson casually sips his beer, his eyes trained on mine, watching me curiously. "Levi and I have had an *interesting* friendship," I say slowly, giving myself time to think of the right way to tell him everything. Taking a deep breath, I find my resolve and continue. "We were never in a relationship. But we, umm...we had more of a 'friends with benefits' thing going."

He furrows his brows and his lips clamp together, forming a thin line. Ironically, I find the glare he's giving me erotically sexy. If he gave me this look in bed, I'd expect him to follow it up with a firm smack to the ass. I let my eyes close and internally roll them at myself. I know I shouldn't be having these thoughts, but I can't help it. He's sexy as hell and I've thought about him every day for the past five years. Here he is, sitting in front of me and looking better than I remember...how in the hell am I supposed to keep my thoughts PG?

Okay, I battle with myself. *A little ogling and fantasizing has never hurt anyone. I'll just keep it to myself.*

"Impossible," he says with a shake of his head. "No male and female can have an honest-to-God 'friends with benefits' relationship and keep all the emotion out of it." He's upset. I can tell by the tick of his jaw and the way his arms are crossed over his chest, effectively closing himself off.

"I disagree. You can believe what you want, but I'm telling you the truth. Levi and I have no emotional connection other than that of friendship. We were using each other and that's all. Nothing more."

"Using each other? I don't understand."

"I don't expect you to understand because you don't know what I went through after you left. No," I stop him as he starts to open his mouth, shaking my head, "let me finish." Tyson reaches out and grabs a shot glass, downing the dark content. He lets the glass land roughly back on the table and he watches me...waiting. I reach across the table and grab the final shot glass, keeping my eyes trained on his as I down the clear liquid. A warm sensation rushes to my arms as the alcohol starts to take hold in my body.

"A lot happened after you left, Tyson. I was in a dark place for a long time." My head drops between my shoulders and regret overwhelms me. Tears threaten to slip out but I fight them back.

I can't look up at him. I don't want to see the questions in his eyes. He wants specifics. He wants to know what I'm talking about, but I'm not prepared to tell him tonight. Soon...but not tonight. "There were times I didn't think I was going to make it," I continue finally. "I had a lot of dark thoughts running through my head. There were a few times I thought my parents were going to have me hospitalized—"

"Because of me?" he interrupts frantically, and I flip my head up to find his face awash in panic. "You were like that because I left?"

"Oh, God no," I reply, shaking my head vehemently. I don't think twice about reaching across the table and gripping his hand in mine, and he doesn't move away. Scooting forward on the seat, I need to convey to him that what happened to me was not his fault. "Please don't think that. Several things happened after you left to get me to that point, but you...you were always a light in my life. Don't get me wrong, I was so mad at you for walking away." He opens his mouth, but I shake my head again. "But I was more mad at myself for being the reason you walked away. I hated myself for what I did to us." My voice cracks and I try to pull my hand back, but he grips it tighter, preventing my movement.

He laces his fingers through mine and cups my hand between his. Leaning his head down, he rests his forehead on our joined hands and takes a deep, shaky breath. We sit like this for several minutes, neither of us saying a word. I wish I knew what he was thinking.

His eyes remain hidden from my view and he speaks softly into our hands. "I can't tell you how badly I want to have this conversation, but I really don't want to do it here." Looking up, his dark chocolate eyes swirl with emotion. "And I really want you completely sober when we do talk."

"Okay," I concede. "But can I say one more thing?"

He nods his head solemnly.

"Levi and I are friends. We will never be more than friends. Please believe me. It doesn't matter what we've done in the past, we are just friends—nothing more. I swear I wouldn't lie to you about that." I'm hoping that the conviction in my voice tells him how serious I am.

"Did you love him...when you guys were..." he trails off, obviously at a loss for how to categorize what Levi and I were.

"I wasn't *in love* with him, no. Do I love him? Yes. He's been my rock and he got me through those really dark times, and I will always be grateful for that. But the love I have for him is completely platonic."

His shoulders relax slightly at my words and I can see some of the tension drain from his face.

Standing up, he pulls his wallet out of his pocket and drops a stack of money on the table. "Let's get out of here."

I stare at him awkwardly and reach for my purse. "Neither one of us should be driving."

"We're not going to," he replies, reaching out for my hand. "Your place is only about a mile from here. We'll walk."

I look at him and cock my head to the side, his hand still stretched out for me to take. "How do you know where I live?"

He chuckles softly. "You texted me your address for tomorrow night, remember?"

"Oh yeah. I forgot."

"The rental house is only about a mile from your place, so I'll walk home from there." I place my hand in his, and his strong fingers wrap snugly around mine as he helps lift me from the booth. *Fuck me. Even his hands are sexy.* They're strong, tan, and calloused like he works outdoors, not soft and manicured like I would expect from a doctor.

My head spins slightly with the position change and I lean into Tyson for a second to regain my balance.

"Are you okay? I didn't think we drank that much, but I can call us a ride if you need me to."

I squint my eyes and cock a brow at him. "I'm not drunk. I'm just feeling good. I'll be fine to walk, but first I need to break the seal."

He barks out a laugh. "Are you sure that's a good idea? Right before we have to walk home? Usually once you break the seal you can't stop."

"Oh, I'll be fine." Patting his arm, I walk off in the direction of the bathroom.

When I return, Tyson is leaning against the end of the bar, waiting for me. As I get closer, a bright grin flashes across his face and the sheer joy and beauty of it causes me to stumble. He's so damn gorgeous.

He reaches out but I manage to steady myself. I stop in front of him, noticing that he still has that grin on his face. I look down to make sure I don't have toilet paper stuck under my shoe. "What?" I ask, looking at him questioningly.

"I was just being a rebel." His smirk grows, causing twin dimples to form on his face.

What? Maybe he's the one that's had too much to—*ohhhh.* Understanding dawns and I return his smile. "I knew you'd read it eventually." Swinging my purse over my shoulder, I move past him and sashay toward the door.

"I like you too," he murmurs behind me. I keep walking, but I'm sure I look like a complete idiot with my big, goofy smile.

Chapter 9

Tyson

WE STEP OUT INTO the cool air and a light breeze throws Harley's hair up around her face. She doesn't make a move to fix it but just lets it float around, landing where it may. That's one of the things I love about her—she doesn't care how she looks. Brit would have never walked a mile home from a bar, and if the wind started to blow her hair around, she would've freaked out and instantly began to tame it. But not Harley…nope, she doesn't care.

I needed to get out of the bar before I broke down and did something stupid like gather her in my arms and beg her to leave Max. Not to mention, she had me on the verge of an emotional breakdown when she spoke about how hard of a time she had after I left. When she reached out and grabbed my hand, I was floored. Harley and I have touched a lot throughout our lives, but this time it felt different. I can't explain it, but the light touch of her hand on mine instantly relaxed me, and suddenly I could think straight and everything made sense.

Goddamnit. I've gotta stop this. Reaching down, I adjust myself. I'm really just making sure my balls are intact and I didn't grow a vagina.

In a few quick strides, I catch up to Harley. I nudge her with my shoulder and she stumbles slightly to the right, causing both of us to laugh. "Tell me something random."

She glances at me out of the corner of her eye and smirks. "I read erotica."

My jaw drops. Okay...I wasn't expecting *that*. "You do not!" I respond, shaking my head.

"Oh yes, I do! But I don't care if you believe me or not. I gave you a random fact. Now you."

"I hate bananas because they're slimy in the middle," I share.

She throws her head back and laughs but keeps going. "I'm addicted to chapstick."

"I went streaking with some med school buddies in New York." She stops dead in her tracks and turns to me, eyes wide.

"You did not! I don't believe you."

"I did so, and it doesn't matter if you believe me or not." She smiles knowingly when I throw her words back at her and we keep walking.

"I wear granny panties." Now it's my turn to laugh at her random fact.

"You mean you don't wear thongs?" I ask, feigning exasperation.

"Hell no! I'd be digging that thing out of my ass all night long." *Yup, there's another thing I love about her.*

"I'm scared of owls," I admit.

"Me too!" Her eyes gleam with excitement and in that moment, I see Harley. *My* Harley. The girl I grew up with. The girl I remember before I left. Open, honest, and sweet as hell. The urge to touch her is too strong and I can't fight it. I swing my arm across her shoulders and pull her into me. She hesitates for a brief moment and then snuggles in next to me as we continue our slow walk home.

The one-mile walk, which should have probably taken us about fifteen minutes, ended up taking forty-five. Mostly because we were laughing so hard we had to stop for frequent catch-my-breath breaks. We talked about everything from favorite flavors of ice cream to future dreams. But something felt off. Even though she opened up, telling me both things I already knew and a few that I didn't, I still felt like she was holding something back. I felt like I was missing...*something*.

"This is me." Her words pull me from my thoughts and I look up to find us standing in front of a small, brick, ranch-style house. The porch light is on, bathing us in a dull yellow glow, and I pause for a second to take in my surroundings.

Her yard is manicured and several bushes line the front of the house. A small yard swing sits off to the right under a large oak tree, and a pinwheel spinning in circles is nestled in the landscaping. An overwhelming sense of pride runs through me, knowing that *she* did this—she got herself here.

Turning my gaze to her, I find her watching me tentatively. She wants my approval and that makes my heart clench and then soar. Hell yes, she's got my approval!

"This is beautiful, Harley." Tension visibly releases from her face. "I'm so proud of you. I wish I would've been here to see you get to this place in your life."

Her green eyes soften and her timid reply causes my heart to constrict again. "You're here now." She looks so innocent and sweet right now that I'm tempted to fall to my knees and confess my undying love for her.

I nod, afraid that if I speak I may say the wrong thing and undo all of the progress that we've made tonight. I don't want to push my luck. We made more headway tonight than I expected, and I really want to end the evening on a good note. We have tomorrow, or any day after that to get into the hard stuff.

"I'm really glad that you called me tonight," I finally tell her.

"Me too." A hesitant grin pulls at the corner of her mouth.

"I had a really great time, Harley."

"Me too." The grin tugs up a little bit more, revealing a shallow dimple in her right cheek. I have the urge to lean forward and kiss that dimple, but I restrain myself—barely. Her cheeks turn a soft pink and she casts her eyes downward.

I can't take it anymore. Reaching out, I pull her into my arms, startling us both. She reacts instantly, wrapping her arms around my shoulders, nuzzling her face in my neck. The faint scent of her vanilla shampoo draws me in, and I bury my face in her hair and hold on for dear life.

It doesn't take long for my body to recognize and appreciate our close proximity. *Fuck.* That's the last thing I need, her thinking I'm taking advantage of the situation. I shift slightly so she can't feel the bulge growing behind my zipper.

Damn, she's perfect. This is perfect. I'm not an idiot, and I realize instantly that right here, in my arms, is exactly where she needs to be—where I need her to be.

The thought of letting go of her terrifies me, but the idea that another man gets to hold her like this regularly terrifies me even more.

Screw it! I need to feel more of her...I need to hold her closer. In a slow, calculated move, I slide my hand up her spine and grasp the base of her neck, holding her against me, molding our bodies together. The move causes a shiver to run through her and I revel in the fact that I'm the one who caused it.

"I missed you so much," I murmur into her soft hair, my voice thick with emotion. She tightens her grip at my words and doesn't seem to think twice about her reply.

"I missed you too. *So much.*" Her sweet breath feathers across my neck and her soft curves relax into me, eliciting an internal groan. We stand this way for several minutes, neither of us wanting to let go.

So many things are being said during our period of silence... so many emotions are being conveyed in our tight embrace. Pain. Regret. Acceptance. Relief. Comfort. Happiness.

Closing my eyes tightly, I fight to take it all in. I've held Harley several times throughout our lives, but this is different. We aren't just holding onto each other, we're letting go of the past, accepting the present, and opening ourselves up for the future. I just wish I knew what the future holds for us. Did I already miss my opportunity?

Her grip loosens. Her soft hands slide up my shoulders and she cradles my neck between her palms. Our bodies are still flush against each other, and the placement of her hands causes a level of intimacy that I hadn't expected. She lifts her face from my neck and I feel empty at the loss of her warm breath against my skin. Pulling my head from her hair, I rest my forehead against hers, trying to drag this out for a few more minutes. I've waited five years to hold her in my arms, and although I was hoping to be holding her as my girlfriend and not my friend, I'm still not ready to let her go.

Her head dips, our noses brush together lightly, and she takes a deep, shuddering breath. I can't explain it, but in that moment, something shifts. The air surrounding us feels warm and thick, causing me to lose my breath. Her once soft touch seems to be producing some sort of electricity that makes me want to push her away and pull her in closer, all at the same time. When she lets out a breath, the faint smell of Amaretto drifts across my face and I can't help but wish that we hadn't had those drinks tonight. I need to know that every move on her part is completely intentional and not driven by alcohol-induced courage.

Fuck me. This woman is going to be the death of me.

It's hard enough to hold myself back after feeling her soft, warm body against mine, but when her mouth is this close to mine, it's nearly impossible. I need to pull back and break the connection. Our friendly, emotional hug is quickly turning into a not-so-innocent embrace that I need to stop before my heart digs in deeper than it already is...and before she does something that she'll regret.

Her sweet breath feels warmer against my face when she dips her head a bit more, causing her top lip to rest lightly against mine. I lift my eyes to her face, but her eyes are closed and her breathing is now shallow and ragged.

What is she doing?

What am I doing? I can't let this happen.
One name pops into my head. *Max.*

It takes every ounce of willpower I have to reach up and grip her wrists in my hands. I don't pull my head back quite yet—one thing at a time.

"We can't do this," I whisper softly against her mouth, screaming at myself to pull the fuck back.

She sucks in a breath and holds it as her body stiffens against mine. She releases her grip from my neck and steps back quickly like my words just slapped her. The look of surprise and embarrassment that flashes across her beautiful face is like a punch to the gut.

Why is she surprised?

She was about to kiss me...how did she expect me to react? She has a boyfriend, for Christ's sake.

A battle ensues—my heart begging to pull her back to me, and my head telling me I did the right thing. Even though I'd like to tell my head to fuck off, I know what would happen if I allow her to kiss me. One of us is going to end up hurt and it's going to be me.

She lifts a shaky hand to her mouth and rubs it lightly with her fingertips.

Maybe I made the wrong decision? I would never come in between a relationship, but fuck me, I would totally do it for a shot with Harley.

She stumbles back, her gaze bouncing around, landing on everything but my face. She sucks her bottom lip into her mouth, attempting to stop the quiver that I'd already noticed in her chin. My heart rate increases and a nervous feeling settles in the pit of my stomach as my mind searches for something to say.

What did I do? Why won't she look at me? I was doing the right thing. Right? We

can't go backward...we just can't. I *need* her.

"I...I'm so sorry," she whispers. I don't miss the cracking of her voice and my body reacts. I reach my hands out to her cautiously.

"Harley, please—" Before I can finish what I was going to say, she manages to unlock her front door and slip inside with one last *'I'm so sorry'* before the door shuts in my face.

What the hell was that?

I stare at her front door for several minutes, trying to wrap my head around what just happened. It doesn't take long to come to the conclusion that I'm a fucking idiot. The woman I've thought about and dreamt about for the past five years was going to kiss me and I stopped her—*I fucking stopped her.*

I fight with myself momentarily. I consider pounding on her door until she opens it and then making her sit down and talk about what the hell just happened, but I know that's not what she needs right now. It's evident that she did not expect me to pull away, and that alone leaves me even more confused. *Did she want me to kiss her?*

I walk slowly to the end of her sidewalk and turn around in time to see her front porch light switch off. Something inside of me breaks, shattering into a million little pieces. Taking a deep breath, I turn around and head home. Right now, I need hot shower and a beer, and then I need to sit down and figure out how to fix whatever the hell I just messed up.

Chapter 10

Harley

"HELL. NO. HAVE YOU lost your freakin' mind?" I shove my fork into my eggs and take a bite, staring at Quinn like she's crazy. Because she is.

She shakes her head and laughs, which pisses me off even more. "Don't laugh about this, Quinn. This isn't funny. It was embarrassing and humiliating and there is no way I can go out to din—"

"Maybe you're overreacting," she interrupts smoothly, shoving a bite of sausage in her mouth. "Maybe he was nervous. Maybe you came on too strong."

Me? Come on too strong? She's officially lost her damn mind.

"I did *not* come on too strong. He led me on!" I scoff. "He gave me every signal that he wanted it just as much as I did, and when I finally grew a pair of balls and made a move, he totally shut me down." I know I probably sound like a crazed lunatic and my words are flying out of my mouth faster than I can think them, but I'm genuinely upset about what happened last night.

"Okay. First of all," she says, waving her fork in the air, "don't ever say that again! Balls are not strong. Growing a set of balls will not make you stronger. Now, a vagina, that's strong. Take your vagina, for example. You pushed out a ten-pound baby without a lick of medicine. That," she shoves a bite in her mouth, "is a strong vagina. You've got like the superhero of all vaginas!"

I'm at a loss for words. Quinn is known for her random rants, but this is way off-the-wall. I keep staring. What the hell do I say to that? She's right. My vagina freakin' rocks!

A deep cough sounds behind me and I turn around to see a woman about my age, slapping her husband on the back. Said husband is looking at Quinn and I with a horrified expression and an extremely red face. I can't help but smile when his obviously pregnant wife slides out of the booth, tosses some money on the table, and high-fives me on her way out of the diner.

I turn to Quinn and her eyes are wide with amusement. We both let out a snort of laughter before she continues. "Anyway," Quinn says, trying to catch her breath, "I still think you shouldn't cancel on him tonight."

It takes me a minute to remember what we were talking about and I shake my head, erasing all thoughts of strong vaginas. "Quinny, if you would have been there—if you would've seen what happened—you'd agree with me. There is no way I can have dinner with him tonight."

She pushes her empty plate to the edge of the table and picks up her cup of coffee. Leaning back in the booth, she pins me with her okay-convince-me eyes. "Tell me exactly what happened."

I tell her all about our conversation at the bar and the game we *tried* to play. I also disclose the small, emotional breakthrough we had, which ultimately led to our decision to leave the bar and walk home. Then, I give her a quick rundown of the random facts we shared on the way home.

"But it wasn't just what we said, Quinn. He found small ways to touch me or bump into me, and at one point he shocked the hell out of me by wrapping his arm around me and pulling me to his side."

"So? What's the big deal about wrapping his arm around

you? How is that leading you on?"

"Well, if you'd stop interrupting me and let me finish, I might get to that part!" I snap. She snorts out a laugh and keeps smiling. *Damn her.*

"He didn't just pull me to his side. He pulled me to his side and then nuzzled my hair!" My voice is rising with each word, trying to get her to understand that I didn't misread the situation.

"You're right," she nods, "that was a more intimate move. How did you react?"

The waitress brings back my sweet tea and I chug half the glass, needing my sugar fix this morning since I didn't sleep a wink last night. I take a deep breath and then let everything else fall out.

"I hesitated, for just a second. Then, I thought to myself, *'Why the hell not?'* It's no secret I've lost all of my resolve with him. So I figured that if he wanted to take the initiative and get close to me, then I wasn't going to stop him...or myself." I wait for Quinn to respond but she doesn't. Instead, she raises her eyebrows, urging me to continue.

"When we got to my house, he told me he was proud of me and we sort of had an awkward moment. Then, he pulled me into a hug...but it wasn't just any hug, Quinn!"

"Of course it wasn't," she murmurs with a smirk.

"What the hell? What's that supposed to mean?" *Now she's just pissing me off.* My best friend, who is *supposed* to have my back, is finding this whole situation funny. It's not funny. I'm hurt and embarrassed, and I need her to tell me I'm not overreacting. I'm half tempted to get up and leave her ass here with the bill, but her face softens and she grabs my hand that is currently balled into a fist.

"I didn't mean anything by it. It's just...this is you and Ty. Harley and Tyson. We've always known this was going to happen. You two are destined to be together and it's *finally* happening. I'm just so happy for you, Harley." I glare at her, not wanting to respond in fear of giving myself false hope. "I'm going to call you guys 'Har-son,'" she says, laughing at the name she created before she keeps going. "Ty-ley. Oh...Har-ty!" She thinks she's being funny. She slaps the table and laughs while I keep glaring.

"Sorry," she says, catching her breath and holding her hands up in surrender. "Sorry. I'm a little slap-happy. It was a long night and you got me out of bed way too early. Please continue. What happened next?"

"Well, now I don't even want to tell you." I'm dying to tell her, but I need her to take this seriously. This isn't a game, it's my heart!

"Oh good Lord, Harley, stop being childish and get on with it."

"Fine," I concede. "It wasn't just any hug, Quinn. God, I feel like an idiot saying this, but sparks flew. Like *literally* flew! As soon as my body touched his, it felt like we were meant to be together and we just...fit. I squeezed him tightly and buried my face in his neck, because the thought of being anywhere else scared the hell out of me. I didn't want to let him go." I swallow hard, pushing back the emotion that starts clawing its way up my throat at the memory of how that moment made me feel.

"I know he felt it. I know he did. Then—and here's the kicker—he buried his nose in my hair, and in a move so sensual and sweet, he moved his hand up my back and held the base of my neck. My neck, Quinn! You don't just run a hand along someone's spine and grip their neck if it's not meant in a romantic way. Right?"

"Right. I can see how you'd think that." She aimlessly stirs her coffee, seemingly unaffected by anything I've said.

"Am I totally off the mark here?"

"Nope," she says with a quick shake of her head, "keep going. Tell me the rest."

I run my hands over my face roughly, not wanting to relive the embarrassment I felt with Tyson's rejection. "I was elated that he did that. It was intimate and it made my entire body break out in goose bumps. Quinn, it felt amazing." I roll my eyes in exaggerated pleasure, causing her to chuckle. "I haven't felt like that in...I don't know how long. I didn't want it to end so I decided to take it a step further. I cupped his neck in my hands and pulled back a little bit. I wanted him to know that I was open to whatever was happening.

"I totally thought we were on the same page because he pulled back and rested his forehead against mine. It was so sweet and we just stood there, breathing the same air, soaking in the moment, and then..." *Good Lord.* And then I made a horrible mistake. A low groan rips from my throat and I bury my head in my hands. *What the fuck did I do?* It's not possible that I misread that whole situation. Right? I mean, realistically, I know that I've been out of the dating loop for quite some time, but come on!

"Then what happened?" Quinn asks.

"Then, apparently I made a huge mistake. I lowered my head—I was trying to go slow because I didn't want to rush the moment—but before I could go any further, he grabbed my wrists. At first I didn't realize what he was doing, but then he said..." I swipe away a tear that falls down my face. "He said 'we can't do this' and I froze, Quinn. He completely shut me down and it was like...it was like I was reliving that horrible night all over again." The tears become too heavy and start spilling over my lashes. I bat them away, looking up to find Quinn watching me. I can see it...she remembers what I went through after he rejected me the first time.

"Harley." Her voice is low and raspy, and she slides out of her side of the booth and into mine. Quinn wraps her arms around my shoulders and holds me as silent sobs rip through my body.

Thank God we are sitting in the back where no one can see us. "Harley," she whispers into my hair. "I can't even imagine how that made you feel, but I want you to look at me." I sniff lightly, but my head remains down. I don't want to look at her. I don't want to feel this way. How could I put myself back in that situation? What was I thinking? "Look at me." At the sharp sound of her voice, I raise my eyes to her.

"Harley, I know it may have seemed bad at the time, and I hate that it took you back to that horrible night, but there has to be a different reason why he pulled away. Did you guys talk afterward? Did you ask him what was wrong?"

"No...no, I didn't." There is no way that I could have talked to him afterward. I was so embarrassed and mad, mainly at myself. Plus, would it have made a difference? Would he have given me an acceptable reason? "I freaked. I dashed through the front door and shut it in his face before he had the chance to say anything."

Now that I say it out loud, I feel sort of bad. Maybe I did overreact. "What do I do, Quinn? Now I feel like an idiot."

"Well, that's because you are," she quips, causing my sob to turn into a laugh. I pull back and Quinn dries my face with the pads of her thumbs. I vow to never take Quinn for granted; I couldn't ask for a better friend.

"I'm just kidding. You know that, right?" I nod once, taking a deep breath. It's time to put on my big-girl panties, pull my head out of my ass, and fix this mess. "But seriously, Harley, you need to talk to him. You need to find out why he stopped you, because I really don't think it's because he doesn't want you."

She's right. I know she is, but that doesn't change the fact that I feel like an idiot and having dinner with him tonight is going to be awkward as hell. "I hope you're right."

"I am right, you just wait and see. So, does this mean you aren't going to cancel on him?"

"No. I won't cancel on him tonight." *That is, unless I change my mind after you drop me off at home.*

"Good." We signal for the waitress and pay our bill. The ride to my house only takes about five minutes and as we are pulling into the driveway, my phone chirps. I grab it out of my purse and my stomach, along with my heart, falls.

Tyson: I got called into work, heading there now. Can I get a rain check on dinner?

Me: I understand.

I don't comment on the rain check because, at this point, I'm not really sure how I want to respond.

"What's wrong? You look like someone kicked your puppy." Quinn's voice pulls me out of my thoughts and I turn my tear-streaked face to hers.

"He canceled."

"What?" She rips my phone out of my hand and reads the text. "Harley, he got called in to work."

"I know," I nod.

"Then why are you crying? He has a good reason to cancel."

I shove the heels of my hands into my eyes and groan. "I know! I think I'm getting ready to start my period or something."

"Period," she says, putting her car in reverse and backing out of my driveway. "Girl, with all the tears you've shed, it's more like an exclamation point!"

I shove her shoulder, thankful that she can always make me laugh. "Where are we going?"

She glances in my direction, her eyes full of mischief. "I'm not going to let you sit at home tonight and dwell on what happened. What kind of friend would it make me if I let you do that? I'm taking you to get a mani-pedi, and then we're going to go shopping, buy smokin' hot outfits, and hit up the town!"

My phone vibrates in my hand again and I look down.

Tyson: I'm sorry, Harley.

What's he sorry for, canceling on me or rejecting me?

Me: Me too.

Miley Cyrus' *Wrecking Ball* filters through the speakers—*how fitting,* I think to myself—and my eyes close as her sultry voice fills the air.

"I love you, Quinn." I don't open my eyes to look at her, but I know that she's looking at me. I can feel the weight of her stare.

"Of course you do. What's not to love?" Yup, that's Quinn. A laugh rips from my throat and I can practically hear her smile.

"NOPE," I SHAKE MY head vehemently, "I can't."

Her eyes narrow and she slides the shot glass in front of me. "You can and you will."

I take the shot because there really is no point in arguing with Quinn. When she has her mind made up, there is no way she's going to change it.

We enjoyed our day at the nail salon and had a blast shopping. It's been a long time since I've felt my age and today I felt young and carefree. Quinn looks smokin' hot in a denim shirtdress that she paired with leopard-print heels. Me, I'm not so confident with my wardrobe, but I did manage to find an awesome pair of white lace shorts that I paired with a gauzy, pale pink top and nude heels. All in all, I was pretty damn pleased with how we looked when we walked out the door two hours ago.

Our intention was to hit up a few local bars, have fun, and enjoy the rare chance of getting to hang out. We walked into the first bar and never even made it to a table before Quinn and I made the joint decision that it just wasn't going to cut it. I put a call in to Levi and he hooked us up with a table in the VIP section at Blue.

Don't get me wrong. Quinn and I have no problem hanging out at our old stomping grounds. But tonight we preferred to be ogled by thirty-something businessmen and not twenty-something boys, who couldn't deliver an orgasm if it was handed to them on a silver platter.

"Alright. Check out the guy at three o'clock." I chuckle at her attempt to be stealthy. Leaning back in my seat, I cock my head to the left. Well, hello there! Mr. Three O'clock is tall, dark, and handsome, and has a set of broad shoulders that would put any linebacker to shame.

"Nope." Picking up my empty glass, I wave it at the bartender, Ryan, signaling for another drink. He tilts his chin in acknowledgment and I turn to Quinn, who is staring at me like I've grown a third head.

"What?" I ask.

"What do you mean, *nope*? He—" she says, waving her hand dramatically at Mr. Three O'clock, "—is not a 'nope' kind of guy."

"Quinn, I told you, I'm not going to go hit on some guy because Tyson rejected me last night."

"Why not?" she whines. "He could be the one."

"Trust me, he is not the one," I scoff as Ryan puts my drink on the table.

"How do you know? You won't even go talk to him. Is this because you haven't been on a date in four years? Because if that's the reason, then I promise you, it's like riding a bike!"

"I've been on dates," I pout.

"Um...Harley, that was called fucking, not dating." She lifts her glass of dark liquor and takes a sip.

"Jesus, Quinn, why do you have to be so crude? Did you see the guy next to Mr. Three O'clock?" I ask, diverting the conversation away from my lack of dating skills.

"Mmmm." A low rumble rolls from Quinn's throat and she uncrosses her legs and stands, adjusting the hem of her dress.

"What are you doing?" I whisper hiss.

"I'm going to talk to the Adonis." She winks and then spins on her five-inch heels and walks away. I don't know how in the hell she walks in those things. My heels are three inches at best, and usually I just wear kitten heels. If I put those spikes on that she wears, I'd bite the dust.

Quinn is smooth and graceful as she glides across the floor, drawing the attention of every man in the room. Her blond hair is cut in a long stack, starting at the base of her hairline and tapering down past her chin. The inside layer of her hair is black and pops under the platinum blonde top layer. It's sassy and sexy, just like Quinn. Her body is slammin' and her legs go on for miles. I'm completely jealous. No really, I am! My once perky breasts now hang, thanks to Max's constant appetite as a baby, and the stretch marks on my stomach are distorted in an unattractive way. Sure, I can hide all of that with a good push-up bra and a pair of Spanx, but eventually those have to come off!

My eyes widen in horror when I notice Quinn, Adonis, and Mr. Three O'clock making their way over to our table. Adonis glances at Quinn's ass as she walks, and based on the smirk on her face, she knows exactly what kind of effect she's having on him. I take notice that Three O'clock isn't watching Quinn's ass. No, he's watching me. I grab my drink, using it as a distraction. *What the hell is she doing?*

SOME TIME LATER, I find myself immersed in testosterone and loving every freaking minute. It turns out that Mr. Three O'clock, who actually *was* a linebacker in college, has a name, Brady, and Adonis is really Ben. Shortly after they joined the table, Levi and his brother, Mason, showed up. Turns out that it wasn't a coincidence Brady and Ben were here tonight. Apparently, Levi and Mason are thinking about expanding their business and Brady and Ben are here to discuss the possibility of opening up a restaurant\ bar in both Chicago and Nashville.

Of course, Levi gave Brady a hard time, threatening to break both of his hands if he so much as looked at me the wrong way, and Brady answered by throwing his head back and laughing. At some point, Cooper and one of his co-workers showed up and joined the group—looks like Quinn and I hit the hot-guy jackpot tonight!

I now find myself squished between Brady and Levi, listening as all the men share stories of their craziest one-night stands.

I'm wiping the tears of laughter from my eyes at Cooper's most recent experience when Quinn stands, excusing herself to go to the bathroom.

Brady cocks his head and leans in to me. "Aren't you going to go with her?"

I can't help the easy smile that slides across my face. He looks genuinely concerned that I'm not going with her. "No, believe it or not, there's no rule that says girls have to go to the bathroom in pairs," I say with a laugh.

He smiles at me, relaxing back in his chair. Conversation dies down and a comfortable silence descends on the table when Cooper leaves to get another round of drinks. I really should stop, but the drinks are going down really smooth...and well, I don't want to stop. The shrill sound of a phone interrupts the light conversation and we all look around to see who the important person is. Levi smiles and digs his phone out of his pocket.

"Hey! What's up?" he answers, taking a drink of his beer. I don't mean to eavesdrop on his conversation, but I have nothing better to do.

"I'm actually here now, you should come on up." He looks at me and smiles, draping an arm over the back of my seat. He laughs, nodding his head a few times, and then he sits up and twists away from me, the unexpected movement catching me off-guard.

I can't hear what's being said so I lean a little closer to Levi. "Ummm...are you sure that's a good idea?" He notices that I'm listening in and gives me the stink eye, which of course I return. "Yeah, you're right. It's fine. Alright man, see you soon." Levi ends the call and shoves his phone in his pocket. He looks everywhere but at me as he raises his hand, motioning for Ryan to bring a round of shots to the table.

I slap his arm playfully to get his attention, even though I'm feeling anything but playful. "Who was that?"

"No one." His smile is too bright and his answer is too quick. "How drunk are you?" he asks.

I narrow my gaze at him. "What's your deal? What are you up to?"

"Nothing. How drunk are you?" he asks again.

"Eh..." I shrug my shoulders, "...maybe halfway there."

"Good," he says, sliding a shot in front of me. "I'm in the mood to dance.

Chapter 11

Tyson

I CAN'T BELIEVE THIS is happening. *Of course* I get called in to work on the one fucking night that I need to be off. After the way things ended last night, I fully expected Harley to try and pull some bullshit and cancel on me. I was determined that I was going to fight her on it, until *I* was the one who had to cancel.

Her short replies and lack of attention to my request for a rain check bothered me. But when I told her I was sorry and she replied 'me too,' I had a horrible feeling she wasn't referring to me canceling on her and that gutted me. I'm still mad at myself for doing whatever I did to put that wounded look on her face last night.

So, needless to say, here I am in the ER and we're fucking slammed. I typically don't mind being busy because it makes the time go by faster, but today has been disastrous. At least Avery is here today; she always makes things a little more fun.

As soon as my shift started, we had a motor vehicle accident roll in. It was a husband and wife, and the husband coded on me twice before they were both rushed into surgery. My next patient had a gunshot wound to the abdomen. The kid was only twenty years old and he was shot in the fucking abdomen for a drug deal that went horribly wrong. *What the hell is wrong with the world today?* And to top my morning off, I just finished taking care of a woman who tried to overdose. Apparently, she thought swallowing a bunch of her psychiatric medicine and chasing it with a bottle of Jack was the best way to convince her son that he wasn't, in fact, attracted to men.

I rip off my gloves, wash my hands, and push my way out the door. Avery is standing at the end of the hall, staring at the ceiling with her hands on her hips. I haven't had much time to talk to her today because we've been so busy, but I heard that she was working on a tough case.

"Avery?" I grip her shoulder gently and her head drops as a small sob rips from her throat. Her shoulders begin to shake and I step up behind her so she knows I'm here, but I don't say anything else. It's obvious to me that she doesn't need to talk right now... she needs to grieve. I've been in her shoes. I know what it's like to become emotionally attached to something or someone, and it doesn't turn out the way you wanted. It's devastating and often leaves you feeling like you've failed.

A couple of minutes pass and her shoulders stop shaking. She is still facing away from me, but I don't need to see to know that she is hurting. She takes a deep breath and raises her head. Her hands wipe furiously against her face and she slowly turns to look at me. When our eyes meet, all of her emotions resurface. Tears re-form and breach the confines of her lashes without notice. Her chin quivers and I know she's doing everything in her power to hold it in. "Come on, you need to take a minute." Placing my hand at the small of her back, I lead her into our break room and lock the door.

I reach for her arm and she doesn't resist. Pulling her to me, she buries her face in my chest and allows herself to lose control. "I lost her," she cries, her tears soaking through my shirt. Raising her head, she peers up, my scrubs bunched up in her fists. Her sad, bloodshot eyes stare back at me and my heart breaks. "She was a mother." Her last word cracks on another gentle sob and her head falls against my chest. "She had two kids, Ty. Two. They're five and seven, and now their mom is gone." I don't say anything because I'm really not sure what to say. I've lost kids, parents, grandparents...you name it and I've seen it. I know it's hard but it's just something that you have to grieve and move past, or the 'what ifs' will eat at you and break you down.

"She'll never see them graduate high school or go on their first dates. She'll never see them kick the final goal to win a soccer game or go off to college." A strangled cry flies from her mouth and I pull her in tighter. "They're going to go through their whole lives without the one person who is supposed to be there to support them and protect them. Now who is going to do those things?" she asks, raising her grief-stricken face to mine.

"Their dad is going to do it." I normally would never presume that the kids have a dad or that he's actually capable of taking over, but I saw the family she is talking about in the waiting room and the guy looked like a stand-up guy. I understand that looks can be deceiving, but he looked devastated and I saw him holding his two boys tightly as they all prayed for the woman that they love with all their hearts.

"He is going to step in and fill those shoes as best he can. He is going to remind them of their mother every day, and he is going to love those boys with everything he has because they need him and that's what a dad does." At least that's what my dad would have done.

"Do you have kids?" she whispers into my shoulders.

"Nope. You?" I respond quietly, continuing with the slow circles my hand is making on her back.

"No. But someday..." She trails off, sniffing a few times, and after several more minutes, her shoulders stop shaking.

"Are you okay?" I pull back from her, gripping her shoulders in my hands. Her eyes are still sad, but her tears have dried. She tries for a genuine smile but fails miserably, and I chuckle lightly at her attempt.

"I will be. Thanks for that," she says, waving at my tear-soaked scrub top. Laughing, I wrap my arm around her shoulder and pull her into me.

"Yes. You will be. Look, I know that this is hard—losing anyone is hard—but you've got to allow yourself to move on. Not only for your own sanity, but because there are still patients sitting in those rooms," I say, pointing out to the hall, "that need you completely focused when you go in to take care of them."

Fuck. I probably sound like a cold bastard, but when you're around this type of thing every day, you learn to deal with it. It doesn't mean you forget about it, but you learn to live with it.

A genuine smile lights up her face. "Aren't you just the resident and I'm the Doc? I'm the one that supposed to be helping you deal with these things." Her voice is light and seems unaffected, but I can tell it bothers her that I saw her lose her shit like that.

"It doesn't matter, you needed to grieve and I was here. Maybe I'll let you buy me lunch for acting as your human tissue!" She slaps my chest playfully and moves to walk out. "Is that a yes?" I yell down the hall after her. She lifts her hand above her head, waving me off and I laugh quietly.

"NO, NO! I GOT it!" she says, pushing me aside to hand the cashier her employee card.

I attempt to block her, but she's a tough little thing. "Avery, I was joking. I don't expect you to pay for my lunch."

"Oh no! I'm not going to fall for that one. You'll hold that shit against me someday!" she says, pointing a celery stick at my face.

We opt to take our lunch back to the break room because Avery is still feeling a little raw over what happened this morning.

"So...do you want to talk about it?" I ask, popping a fry into my mouth.

She shakes her head firmly. "Nope. In fact, I'd very much

like to talk about anything that doesn't have to do with healthcare. Hey," she says, smiling brightly and wiggling her eyebrows suggestively, "how are things going with that girl you care about?"

Well, shit! She doesn't want to talk about healthcare, and I don't want to talk about Harley. But I will because, fuck me, I've got to tell someone, and I sure as shit can't tell Levi...he's just too close to her. It kills me to think about just how close they really were.

"We had drinks last night," I say, shoving my cheeseburger in my mouth.

"That's great." She smiles around her soda and I know she's being sincere. I can tell by the open admiration on her face that she genuinely wants me to be happy.

"She tried to kiss me." Her eyes widen and she grins.

"She seems bold, I like that!" she says excitedly.

"Yeah, well, I screwed it up," I reply.

Avery's eyebrows rise and she looks at me amusingly. "How on earth can you screw that up? It's really easy, Ty. The girl you care about tries to kiss you...you kiss her back. What did you do?" she asks with a laugh.

My eyes lock onto hers and I stare at her condescendingly. *I don't need this.* I don't need some chick telling me what I did wrong. I'm not an idiot, I know what I did was wrong. Sitting quietly, I take a few more bites, determined not to have this conversation. Fuck this...this is chick shit, and there's no way in hell I'm going to sit around and gossip about my feelings.

Avery continues to stare at me. I'm able to stay strong for a few seconds, but her questioning gaze is unwavering and it pisses me the hell off.

"Fine," I blurt. "If you must know, I pulled away from her!"

Avery sets her sandwich down and tilts her head to the side. I hate it when women do that shit; it drives me crazy.

"Why?"

"Because she has a boyfriend," I reply sharply, instantly regretting my harsh tone. Sitting back in her chair, she crosses her arms over her chest. I keep shoving food in my mouth, hoping like hell it will keep me from talking.

"Did she tell you she has a boyfriend? Have you actually met him?" she asks, scrunching her brows.

Shit.

"Well, no—" I answer slowly, contemplating the possibility that I've completely misread every fucking thing that has happened. *No way.*

"Then how do you know she has a boyfriend?"

I've had enough. Tossing my burger onto my tray, I glare at Avery. "This conversation is over. I don't want to talk about Harley, and I don't need you telling me how to—"

"Whoa!" she says, cutting me off. I snap my mouth shut, pissed that she interrupted. "Listen, I'm sorry I upset you. That wasn't my intention." Her voice softens, and she rests her joined hands on the table. "But I'm a woman, and I think you've got this all wrong."

I don't have this all wrong, but right now I'm so damn tired of thinking about Max that I just need her to finish what she wants to say so I can get the hell out of here. "Fine. I'm listening. Then we're done talking about this."

She nods her head, a small grin playing at her lips. "If this Harley is as wonderful as you say she is—and you're an incredible person, so I'm sure she is—then there is no way she would ever cheat on her boyfriend. Therefore, if she tried to kiss you last night, then I'm about ninety-nine-point-nine percent certain that she doesn't have a boyfriend. So you need to pull your head out of your ass and get your girl before someone else realizes how amazing she is and snags her up!"

With that, Avery stands and tosses her plate in the trash. She walks to the door and then turns back to me. "And do me a favor, when you do get the girl...grovel like hell for pulling away from her last night, because I can't even imagine all the insecurities that must have caused."

Fuck. The look of embarrassment that washed over Harley's

face last night pops into my head and I rub my hands over my face roughly, trying to get that image out of my mind.

What if Avery is right? What if Harley doesn't have a boyfriend and I was wrong? That would I've been wasting my time and worrying for no reason. All I know is that this has to end. I either need to know she's single and beg her to give me another chance, or I need to meet Max and see for myself that I really did fuck things up five years ago.

Tomorrow. I'm going to get through this shift and then this ends tomorrow.

"THANK GOD THIS DAY is over." Grabbing my stethoscope, I drop it in the bag with my scrubs. I always bring a change of clothes to change into before I go home. Tossing my bag on the table, I walk over to the coffee pot. It's way too late in the evening for me to be drinking coffee, but I need *something*.

"I know, right?!" Avery says, shedding her lab coat. She looks completely exhausted and her eyes are still mildly puffy as though she's been crying off and on throughout the day.

"You okay?" I ask, handing her a cup of coffee.

She grabs the mug and takes a few sips, her eyes trained downward. "I will be. It's just been a shit day and I really don't want to go home, and...hey—" She looks at me hopefully. "You wanna go grab a drink somewhere?"

Fuck. No. All I really want to do is go home and crash. Looking down at my watch, I see that it's ten o'clock. It's been a long day and I'm exhausted, but I can tell that Avery doesn't want to go home, probably because she'll spend the rest of the night thinking about that family.

"Sure," I answer. "Let's go have a drink."

"Great. Thank you," she sighs, patting my arm as she walks past me to drop her cup in the sink.

"But just one," I say, pulling my phone out of my pocket. "My friend, Levi, owns a bar a few blocks away. Let me call him and see if they're out."

I hit 'send' and Levi answers almost immediately.

"Hey! I was seeing if you were going to be at Blue tonight. I was thinking about coming out for a drink or two," I reply.

"I'm actually here now, you should come on up," he answers.

"Great. I'm just getting off my shift, and it's been one hell of a day. Avery had an even worse day than I did, so I told her I would have a drink with her. Plus, she's been wanting to meet some people from around this area anyway." Avery smiles at me, mouthing that she is going to the bathroom to change before we leave, and I nod.

The line goes silent and for a second I wonder if the call was dropped, but then Levi starts talking again. "Ummm...are you sure that's a good idea?" he asks quietly, as though he's trying to avoid anyone overhearing him.

What the hell? "Why wouldn't it be a good idea? We're just friends. We work together, and she had a shitty day and asked if I'd go have a drink with her. Is that not okay?" I ask sharply.

"Yeah, you're right. It's fine," he sighs.

"Okay. Good. You're really going to like her. We'll see you soon."

"Alright, man, see you soon," he says, ending the call. Slipping my phone in my pocket, I can't help but feel like something is off. I'm not sure what it is, but I have this weird feeling in the pit of my stomach that something unpleasant is about to happen.

"Are we all set? Is your friend at his bar?" Avery asks, pulling her bag up over her shoulder.

"All set." Reaching out, I open the door for her, shoving the uneasy feeling away, intent on getting Avery's mind off of what happened today. One drink, that's it. Then, I'm getting a good night's sleep and tomorrow I'm going to talk to Harley.

We decide to leave our cars and walk since it's only a couple of blocks. It's beautiful out this time of year. There's a light, cool breeze and I take a deep breath, enjoying the fresh air and being away from the hospital and this shitty-ass day.

"Wow!" she gasps when we walk in the door, her hand gripped to her chest and her eyes taking in her surroundings. "This place is fantastic." Levi's bar really is spectacular, even more so when the dance floor is littered with gorgeous people grinding their sexy-as-hell bodies together in rhythm with the music, like it is tonight.

I glance up to the third level, but I can't see Levi—it's too packed in here. Placing my hand at the small of Avery's back, I lead her to the bar, where a seat just opened up and I motion for her to take it. We order our drinks and when they're handed to us, I turn to face her, propping my elbow up on the bar. She tips her beer back, practically chugging half the bottle.

"God, that's good," she sighs, slamming her bottle down on the bar, eliciting the attention of a few nearby patrons. "I need about ten more and I think I'll be set."

I turn toward the bar, intent on ordering Avery another drink, and find myself face-to-face with a familiar set of blue eyes.

"We meet again."

"Blaire," I state with a smile. She grins at me, probably happy that I remembered her name. "I thought you were a hostess?" I ask, leaning forward on the bar.

A mischievous look spreads across her beautiful face and she leans her elbows on the bar, completely ignoring the other patrons who are trying to order drinks. "I do hostess. I also bartend, and sometimes when I need extra money, I let Levi put me in one of those things." She nods her head in the direction of the hanging cages, but I don't have to follow her gaze—I already know what she's talking about. "In fact, I'll bet there are a lot of things that you don't kn—"

"I said, excuse me!" Blaire's eyes harden and she turns her gaze to Avery. Her brows furrow slightly, a look of confusion flashing across her face at the sight of the woman sitting next to me. Avery blatantly rests her hand on my forearm, giving it a light squeeze as she looks at me adoringly, attempting to flutter her eyelashes.

It takes everything I have not to bust up laughing at the look on her face, but I manage to succeed.

What the hell is she doing?

Blaire's eyes follow Avery's hand, and then they bounce from me to Avery a couple of times before she blinks. She nods her head once, looking like she understands something...I'm just not sure what.

"What can I get you, Mr. Grawe?" *Yup, I've still got it.* I smile smugly to myself, completely oblivious to whatever the hell just happened. Blaire remembered my name. And I'm not going to lie, the fact that she called me Mr. Grawe instead of Tyson was really fucking hot. Only now, Blaire's eyes aren't soft like they were before. They're not hard either; it's more a look of...indifference?

Avery slides her free hand along my back and wraps her arm around my waist, her other hand still resting on my arm. I stare at her in amusement as she pins Blaire with a hard look and answers before I have a chance.

"Sweetie," she says, dragging her eyes back to me. "Do you want another beer?" I can't help the laugh that slips from my mouth as I nod my head in agreement.

Blaire turns around without a second glance, grabs us each another beer, and then slides them across the bar. As soon as Blaire turns to the line of customers waiting to order their drinks, Avery removes her arm from around my waist and leans back in her chair with an arrogant look on her face.

"What the hell was that?" I laugh, taking a swig of my beer.

She cocks her head to the side, winks, and tips her beer in my direction. "You're welcome."

"For what?"

She looks confused. *What the hell is she confused about?* "For what?" she asks, sitting forward in her chair. "For saving your ass!"

"Okay. I'm totally lost." Setting my beer on the bar, I face

Avery, my arms crossed in front of me. Her eyes wander from my face, across my chest, and down to where the fabric is stretched tight around my arms, and I can't help but smile. *Women.* "Either the first bartender spiked your beer with something, or you've just totally gone insane." Her eyes snap to mine and she has the nerve to look at me like I'm the one that's crazy. "Okay, let me spell this out for you." She crosses her legs and sets her beer on the bar. Turning toward me, she raises her hands as she starts to tick off what I did wrong. "All I've heard you talk about for the past week is Harley—Harley this and Harley that—and then you're telling me that she tried to kiss you but you didn't let her...which I still think was a huge mistake on your part. Anyway," she waves her hands in the air as though she got off track, "so now you come here and start flirting with the first hot little number you see. I'm not going to lie, Ty, I'm really disappointed. I expected more out of you."

Okay, now I'm mad. "First of all...I know Blaire. We met last time I was here. Second, it's none of your damn business who I flirt with, and it certainly isn't your place to step in and pretend that we're 'together' so that she would stop flirting."

"You're right," she snaps. "It's not my place, but I probably just saved your ass from fucking *that*," she points to the end of the bar, "up."

I turn around to see what she's pointing at and my eyes instantly find Harley, who is looking straight at me. I can't help but smile at the sight of her—that's just how she makes me feel—and goddamn it's good to see her beautiful face. Wait...she's not smiling back, and are those—

"Wait! Where are you going?" Avery asks, grabbing my arm when I start to walk away.

I look down at her hand on my arm and then back at her. No one is going to keep me from going to Harley. "That's Harley, and she looks like she's about to cry so if you'll please let go of my arm..." I'm trying to keep my cool with Avery, but I'm still sort of confused about everything that just happened and now she's trying to stop me from—

"Because of you!" Her voice and eyes harden, but she lets go of my arm. "She's probably crying because of you." She rolls her eyes and takes a drink of her beer. "Good God, men are stupid," she mumbles around the bottle.

"Me? How in the hell did I make her cry? I didn't even know she was here until you pointed her out. Wait a minute, how did you know that was Harley?" I ask. "You told me you guys have never met."

"We haven't. But I recognize her from the hospital. She was sitting there watching us, and then when you started flirting with Blaire, her eyes got really sad. I just put two and two together. Plus, I'm a woman...I know these things."

She was...she saw...I whip back around, intent on finding Harley, but she isn't there. My eyes scan the room, but there are too many people.

"I *wasn't* flirting with Blaire. I was just being nice and—" Avery cocks her eyebrow, giving me a classic you're-full-of-shit look. "What? I wasn't flirting. She might've been, but I wasn't," I defend, poking myself in the chest.

Avery nods in understanding. "You're right, but a couple more seconds and you would have. And..." She drags the word out, preventing me from butting in. "Harley doesn't know that! All Harley knows is that last night she tried to kiss you and you rejected—"

"I didn't reject her!"

"Yes, you did," she says, matter-of-fact. "She tried to kiss you, you rejected her, and now she finds you here at the bar, which is totally my fault," she mumbles the last part absently before continuing. "She was probably excited to see you until she saw Blaire practically shoving her very large, very fake rack in your face."

Fuck. I screwed up—again. I've got to find her.

"That's why I played the doting girlfriend," she says, making another attempt to flutter her eyelashes at me. "I was trying to stop the trainwreck before it happened. So I'm sorry if I upset you, but

I saw Harley watching you and I felt like I needed to stop Blaire... and you, before it went any further."

"It wasn't going to go any further. I told you, I don't like Blaire like that." Jesus Christ! What is the big fucking deal? So a girl was flirting with me and I didn't stop her, who cares?

"And I'm really glad to hear that. But if you don't like her like that, then what was up with the whole leaning-on-the-bar, flirty voice act?"

"What do you expect me to do, Avery? Harley. Has. A. Boyfriend," I yell, instantly feeling bad for raising my voice at her. I know this isn't her fault, but I'm pissed that she's making me feel like I did something wrong. I didn't sleep with Blaire, for fuck's sake...I didn't even touch her.

"You're wrong," she says calmly. Tipping her head back, she finishes her beer, sets it on the bar, and slides off the stool.

"Where the hell are you going?"

Avery glares at me and I snap my mouth shut. No need to piss off another woman. She starts to walk away and then turns around briefly. "I'm going to try and fix your mess."

Great. This is just great.

Chapter 12

Harley

"ENOUGH! ENOUGH, ENOUGH, ENOUGH!" Quinn weasels her way between Levi and me, grabbing onto my hand. "I love you both and you're both hot as hell, and it's sexy watching you dance, but I need my girl back." Quinn starts yanking me off the dance floor and I turn to look at Levi, but he already has another girl wrapped in his arms. I smile warmly...he needs that. He winks once and then spins the lucky girl in the opposite direction.

I've had several more drinks and a few shots so my mind is a bit foggy, but it feels good to let loose. "Quinn. Slow down. I can't keep up with your ostrich legs!" A small laugh leaves my lips and I stumble, ramming into Quinn's back when she stops in her tracks.

She turns to look at me with a huge smile on her face. "Did you just call me an ostrich?" she asks.

I furrow my brow. "Uhhhh...no?"

She shakes her head and laughs. Turning around, she pulls my hand and starts dragging me behind her again. "You're drunk and I LOVE IT!" she sings over the music as we step up to the bar.

"No." I shake my head swiftly. "No more drinks. I need to

function tomorrow."

"Pfffff." She waves her hand, dismissing my protest. "But you're right, no more drinks." Oh God. She doesn't give up that easy. What the hell is sh—

"Yo, Mike!" The sexy, tatted-up bartender looks our way and tips his chin. What the hell is up with that? Why do guys tip their chin? It's official...I don't like the 'chin tip.' "I need two Tijuana Hookers. PRONTO!" My eyes widen and my head, along with every other head at the bar, spins in Quinn's direction.

"What the hell is a Tijuana Hooker? I don't want a Tijuana Hooker. What's in a Tijuana Hooker?" I rapid-fire questions at her.

"You'll love it! Trust me," she says dismissively.

"Seriously, Quinn, when I said 'no more drinks,' I didn't mean let's do shots."

"Lighten up, tight-ass," she quips, smacking me hard on the butt and then rubbing the sting. I swat her hand away and she laughs. Mr. Tatted and Sexy—yup, I named him too—slides four shot glasses in front of us. Wait a minute. Didn't she order two shots? Leaning forward, I peek in the glasses and sniff.

"What. The. Fuck. Is that pickle juice? You're out of your ever-lovin' mind if you think I'm going to—" Quinn covers my mouth with her hand and I resist the urge to lick it. Who cares if I'm twenty-seven, it would still be funny as shit!

Leaning in close, she whispers in my ear. "Listen. You know I have no problem making a scene. In fact, I've already got the attention of almost every man at this bar. So you have two choices. One, you take the shot of tequila and chase it with your pickle juice." I try to make a disgusted face, but her hand prevents my nose from crinkling. "Or two, I'm going to kiss you in front of all of these men." *She wouldn't, would she?* Oh shit, she totally would!

"Nod once if you understand." I nod once. Lord knows I don't want to piss off a woman who wants to drink a Tijuana Hooker. Seriously, where the hell does she come up with this shit? "Blink once for the first choice or twice for the second." She sits back, her hand clamped tightly around my mouth and winks at the guy sitting next to me. I turn my head slightly and see him smiling suggestively at the two of us. *Creeper.*

Well, shit. I don't want tequila with pickle juice, but Quinn knows I would shit a brick if she actually kissed me in front of all these people. I blink once.

"Damn. I was kinda hoping you'd pick number two." She grins, removing her hand from my mouth.

"You were?" She must be wasted. Quinn loves men more than anyone I know.

"Nah…I only offered the second choice because I knew you wouldn't take it. But you should've seen your face—priceless," she says, letting out a deep throaty laugh. She slides me two shot glasses before lifting her own shot of tequila. I follow suit and we tap glasses and drink. HOLY SHIT, that burns! Reaching for my shot of pickle juice, I throw my head back. HOLY SHIT…hey, that's good. Like really good!

I push the shot glasses away from us. "Wow. I actually liked that."

"Oh. My. God." Quinn throws her head back with a deep moan, eliciting the attention of every male within a ten-foot radius. "This is the best Tijuana Hooker I've ever had. Ever. I needed this." She smacks her lips and looks around, noticing for the first time the attention that she has garnered. Quinn loves it—of course she does—so she smiles, turning her attention to me.

"See, I knew you'd love a Tijuana Hooker. Now, let's do another one." Partly jealous that she has a dozen pairs of eyes watching her every move and partly because my lips are too tingly to protest, I nod my head in agreement. I'm already half cocked so if I'm going to do this, I might as well do it right.

"But after this, we really need to stop," I say as I regain feeling in my lips. "Do you know how long it's been since I've drunk like this. I'm going to have a three-week hangover." I know I'm being a worrywart, but I can't help it. I'm a full-fledged, panties-in-a-bunch, Type A personality, 'nervous Nelly.' I think first and act second. Sometimes I wish I could be more like Quinn, who acts first and then worries about the consequences later.

Her head rolls back on her shoulders and she sighs dramatically. "Fiiiiine. One more and then we're done." She turns to look at me. "I'll let you pick, since it's your last shot."

"Ummm...how about something with Irish Cream? I love Irish Cream." She purses her lips in contemplation, then leans over the bar and snaps, "Yo, Mike!"

A beautiful blonde—I'll call her Barbie—walks up and rests her hands on the bar. I cock my head to the side, examining her face. I'm fairly certain I've met her before, but right now my brain is in an alcohol-induced fuzz and I can't really put my finger who she is. "Mike's busy. What can I get ya?" Damn, she's pretty. Her eyes are two deep blue pools of water.

"You can get me Mike," Quinn replies tightly, but Barbie doesn't miss a beat. I take it she's used to women asking for Mike all the time.

"I said—"

"I got this," Mike says, resting a hand on Barbie's shoulder. "There's a guy down there you can take care of. Blue shirt." She rolls her eyes and walks away.

"What can I get you beautiful ladies?" he says, shoving the sleeves of his shirt up to his elbow, effectively putting on display the sleeve of tattoos adorning his left arm. Yup, not only does Mike have sexy-as-hell ink, but he's also got a shitload of charm. His bright blue eyes dance with trouble as he stares at Quinn. My eyes snap to her and I find her staring back. He grins. She grins. He leans forward, resting his elbows on the bar. She bats her eyes, which I totally didn't realize women could actually do, but she does.

My head continues to snap back and forth between the two of them. Okay...now I know I'm a little tanked, but if I didn't know better, I'd think that the two of them are having a conversation, promising each other all sorts of pleasure and other dirty things.

Good God, that's hot. Shit, now I'm kind of jealous.

I clap my hands between the two of them and Mike laughs, turning his handsome face to me. Quinn pipes up before I even have a chance to order.

"We'll take two Clit Lickin' Cowgirls." She raises two fingers and smiles suggestively. Mike flashes us a huge, white smile and turns to the bar.

Did she just say Clit Lickin' Cowgirls? Who the hell comes up with these shots?

"Okay. Who are you? What's a Clit Lickin' Cowgirl? And how do you even know what a Clit Lickin' Cowgirl is?" It's like a damn tongue twister...pun intended. I laugh softly at the little inside joke I just made, and Quinn stares at me like I've lost my mind before answering.

"I'm Quinn James, your BFF, and a Clit Lickin' Cowgirl is Butterscotch Schnapps, Irish Cream, Grenadine syrup, and...you don't want to know what else."

Mmmm...that actually sounds good. So far.

"I do want to know."

Quinn's eyes lock onto something over my shoulder and her face goes stone-cold sober. Her eyes flick nervously to me and she opens her mouth, but nothing comes out. *What the hell?* Turning in my seat, I look toward the opposite end of the bar and scan the crowd to see what caught her eye.

"Quinn, what are you loo—" The words clog in my throat when my eyes land on the beautiful Barbie bartender from earlier. She's leaning over the bar talking to...Tyson? I cock my head to the side, hoping to get a better look. I have had a few drinks tonight and maybe my eyes are playing tricks on me. Maybe I've been thinking about him so much that *poof,* here he is.

"Harley, come on. Let's go." Quinn grabs my arm but I pull it back, refusing to turn away. *What is he doing here?* He canceled on me because he had to work. If he got off and wanted to go out, why didn't he call me? Maybe he talked to Levi. Maybe he knows I'm here. I move to stand, intent on talking to him, when my whole world falls apart. Okay, maybe that's a bit dramatic, but well…I'm drunk and feeling a bit dramatic.

The scene in front of me unfolds in slow motion and my stomach plummets in defeat and embarrassment. A beautiful woman leans forward, peeking around the side of Tyson, and her eyes meet mine. She watches me intently for several seconds and her brows dip down in confusion, as if she's trying to figure out how she knows me.

My eyes jump to Barbie, who is leaning over the bar trying desperately to shove her tits in Tyson's face. I feel Quinn tug on my arm a few more times, but I'm frozen. Barbie's head snaps up and watches the girl next to Tyson, whose hand is now resting on his arm. She's looking up at him…lovingly? I'd give anything to hear what she is saying.

The movement of her hand catches my attention and I watch as she slides her arm across his back and grips his waist intimately. I'm hyperaware of every move the two of them make and the more I watch, the more I feel like I've been sucker-punched in the stomach.

"Alright beauties, here's your shots." Reluctantly, I turn my head and stare at the shot in front me.

I'm an idiot. Scratch that, I'm a *fucking* idiot.

Reaching forward, I grab the shot, taking it without waiting for Quinn. Emotion burns deep in my throat as I turn back around to watch Tyson and the woman who now has her arms around him. Maybe this is why he pulled away from me…he's with someone else. I don't know why I'm surprised. After all, he is the whole package. He's perfect and wonderful and…I can't do this to myself anymore.

I *need* to see this. I need to watch him with someone else so that maybe, once and for all, I can allow myself to accept that we simply aren't meant to be. Tyson isn't mine and he never will be. The realization causes something inside of me to clench and then break, causing hot tears to burn the back of my eyes.

The woman next to Tyson points in my direction and he twirls around. Our eyes lock and a small smile tugs at the corner of his mouth. I can't smile back. I swallow hard, determined to make it out of the bar before I completely break down. Tyson's smile fades and he takes a step away from the bar and for a split second I have hope that maybe he's coming to me.

But that miniscule piece of hope is ripped away when a delicate hand grabs onto his arm. I watch as he looks at her hand and then turns his back on me. I don't have to say anything. Quinn watches me lose the fight as a lone tear rolls down my cheek. Wiping it away gently, she reaches down, grips my hand securely in hers, and leads me away from the bar, just as Barbie turns her back on Tyson. I strain my neck to keep watching—to keep tormenting myself, really—as Quinn pulls me deeper into the crowd.

Unfortunately, I don't make it out of the bar, but I manage to make it to the bathroom so I'll consider that a success. Quinn pushes open the door, confirms that no one else is in the bathroom, and flicks the deadbolt, locking us in. When Levi built Blue, Quinn and I told him to double the number of female bathrooms he originally intended to have and right now I thank God that he listened to us.

Gripping my shoulders, Quinn gently pushes me down onto the couch in the powder room. Letting my head fall back, I give myself the green light to cry. Streams of tears fall out of the corner of my eyes and disappear, wetting my hair. Quinn wraps her arm around my shoulders, pulling me into her side. She rests her cheek against my head and takes a deep breath.

Wait for it...it's coming...wait for it...

"Quinn, you're scaring me," I say in a hoarse whisper, not moving from the cocoon she has me wrapped in.

"Mmm...why's that?" she mumbles softly.

"You're supposed to say something smartass and funny," I say, my voice cracking. "Something to make me laugh or cry harder. Why aren't you saying anything?" I rub a finger across my eye, removing the excess moisture, and push myself up so I can look at her.

This isn't like Quinn. Don't get me wrong, she'll comfort

me and I'm sure that tomorrow you'll be able to find us curled up on my couch watching *The Notebook* and eating an array of junk food, but right now I expect her to be telling me to 'buck up' or 'put on my big-girl-panties.' I assume she'd say that he's just a guy and there are tons of fish in the sea. Why isn't she telling me that?

"Harley, I—" Someone bangs on the door, jiggling the handle to the bathroom. Quinn slides her arm out from behind me and stands, leaning into the door. "This bathroom is occupied. Go away!" she yells, turning back toward me. "Now where was I?"

"There's more than one stall in there! Open the damn door!" The angry voice outside stops Quinn in her tracks and she spins on her heel, marching back to the door, hands on her hips.

"I'm takin' a shit. Now take a hint and LEAVE!" Quinn seethes.

"Seriously?" The woman laughs, and Quinn's eyebrows rise in shock. People don't usually talk to Quinn like that, so I'm sure it caught her off-guard. "That's all you've got? You're taking a shit? That's about the wor—"

"What the *hell* do you want?" Quinn asks, flinging open the door. I can't see who it is because the couch is positioned so that the open door is blocking my view, but I can tell by the way Quinn straightens her spine and then cocks her hip that she isn't happy.

Just as Quinn moves to slam the door, a woman flings her arm out, stopping it from shutting. "Wait!" she says frantically. "I need to talk to Harley!"

What? Who the hell is that? I sit up instantly and my whole world tilts violently to the left. My hands grip my head tightly, trying to stop the spinning. Fuck me, I didn't need that last shot. Standing slowly, I give myself a few seconds to get my bearings and I walk to the door. My heart stops—literally fucking stops. *What is she doing here?*

Quinn notices the look of panic on my face and positions herself in front of me.

"You have thirty seconds to say what you have to say, or I'm going to have to throat punch you." Quinn's face is stern, her eyes narrowed and lips tight.

The woman's eyes widen. "Throat pu—" She shuffles back and looks at me. "Did she just say throat punch?" I nod once, examining the woman in front of me who has won Tyson's heart. She's classically beautiful...perfect, in fact. "What's a throat punch?"

"Avery," I whisper as I step around Quinn, who is eyeing me warily. I reach my hand out hesitantly. "You must be Avery?" Some of the horror leaves her face as she slides her delicate hand in mine.

"You know who I am?" she asks, dropping her hand down to her side.

"Uh, yeah." My eyes flit nervously around the room and I take a deep breath. *Damnit.* I do not want to have this conversation. "Tyson has told me about you."

Her eyes widen in confusion and she crosses her arms across her chest. "He has?" I nod my head because that seems to be the only thing I can do tonight. "We haven't even met, so how did you know who I was?"

I shrug my shoulders. "I just put two and two together. I've seen you around the hospital, and I remember him saying he's really glad the two of you work together." I offer her a timid smile, which she returns. "I just never really knew who you were, and then I saw you guys at the, uh, at the bar—" I wipe my hands nervously on my thighs before continuing, "—and I just sort of knew it had to be you."

"Okay," Quinn interrupts, shoving me to the side. Her hand snaps out and she yanks Avery into the bathroom and locks the door. She walks to the sink, steadies herself, and leans forward to slip off her stilettos. Standing up, she rolls her head and stretches her arms like she's about do some hot yoga or something.

I can't help the laugh that bursts out of my throat. "Quinn... what the hell are you doing?"

She pushes past me and says, "You're obviously too nice and

too drunk to handle this situation, so I'm going to handle it for you." Avery sucks in a sharp breath and takes another step back. I purse my lips and shake my head at Avery, trying to reassure her that Quinn won't do anything, but she doesn't look convinced.

"Alright." Quinn cracks her knuckles. "No hitting above the neck—I just had a facial. And no hair pulling, because that shit's just not cool," she says, pointing her manicured finger at Avery.

Reaching out, I grip Quinn's arm, spinning her around. "Quinn, you don't have to fight Avery. It's okay." The amused smile falls from my face as the words leave my mouth. A warm feeling crawls up my spine and tears clog my throat when I realize that it's true. This is okay…I will be okay. All I've ever wanted is for Tyson to be happy, and if Avery makes him happy, then that's what I want.

Fingers snap in front of my face, pulling me from my thoughts. "Remember our freshman year when I found Ben kissing Allison in the parking lot?"

"Yeah," I reply. *Where is she going with this?*

"You hit him for me. You stood up for me, and now I'm repaying the favor," she says, looking at me like I should know why she's acting like a madwoman.

I shake my head slowly. "I didn't hit Ben."

"Yes, you did!" she snaps. "I got mad and pushed Allison, called Ben a few choice names, and then stomped off. When I turned back around, Ben was holding his cheek and you were standing in front of him." I continue to shake my head slowly, discrediting what she's saying. Her face falls and I almost feel bad for telling her the truth. "Yes, I specifically remember I cocked my eyebrow at Mason and he pointed his finger at you, indicating that you did it."

"I'm not the one that hit Ben. I'm sorry, Quinn. I hate that you thought I stood up for you like that and I didn't. I mean, I totally would. You know I'd smack the shit out of any man that hurt you, but I didn't smack the shit out of *that* man."

"Who did?"

"Mason."

"Mason?" Her jaw drops and she stares at me, but I can tell she isn't looking at me. She's looking *through* me, trying to remember the events of that day.

"I'm sorry." Avery approaches the two of us cautiously. "I really don't mean to interrupt your trip down memory lane, but does this mean that you aren't going to throat punch me now?"

Quinn is still staring at me, dumbfounded. "No," I answer for her. "There will be no women's bathroom MMA fight tonight."

Quinn seems to snap out her funk and she whips her head around. "Damnit, Harley. She stole your man! You have to *fight* for him!" Avery opens her mouth to talk, but Quinn and I both raise our hands at her and she snaps her mouth shut.

"No, Quinn. She didn't steal my man. Tyson is not mine. He never was." The last part is whispered because it physically hurts to say.

"Ummm…" Avery raises a hand and tries to interject, but Quinn and I keep bickering.

"You're wrong. He *is* your man. He was yours five years ago when he walked away and he is yours now." I appreciate that she's fighting for us, but there's really no point. I'm done fighting. Done dreaming. I'm just done. I've spent the last five years being regretful, mad, sad, angry, and hopeful…I want to be happy. I want to be normal. I want to fall in love. I want to find a nice man, one who will love Max and me the way we deserve to be loved. And that man might not be Tyson—like I'd hoped—but that man is out there...somewhere. I just have to find him.

"Quinn," I whisper, touching her arm gently. "You are the *best* best friend a girl could ever ask for." The emotions, mixed with the amount of alcohol in my system, prove to be too much and tears start dripping from my eyes. I bat them way. "I wouldn't be here if it weren't for you. You've been with me through everything. You've held me, cried with me, and laughed with me. And the fact that you are willing to fight for me tonight…" I gesture toward Avery, who appears to be fighting to hold back her own set of tears. "Well, it just reiterates what I already know. You are amazing and wonderfully loyal and I will love you forever. But this thing with Tyson...I need you to let it go. Please," I beg when she opens her mouth. "Please, for me. I can't do this anymore." My voice thickens and then cracks, and my hand fists my blouse over my heart. "I. Cant. Do. This." Quinn steps forward and engulfs me in her arms, holding me like she's done so many times before.

"Can I just say someth—" Avery starts to speak when the door handle turns and Levi walks in, key in hand, followed by Tyson. "Goddamnit. Why do I keep getting interrupted? I need to fix this," Avery says as Levi and Tyson walk further into the room, trying to gauge what the hell they just walked in on.

Tyson is watching me. I can tell he wants to say something, but I'm on a roll. May as well get this over with.

I pull back from Quinn. My face is throbbing, but I'm not sure if it's from the alcohol or the crying. I tend to be one of those ugly criers. You know the kind...red face, snotty nose, puffy eyes. Yup, that's me. I'm sure I look extremely unattractive right now. Regardless, I wipe my face and turn toward Tyson, who is now standing where he should be—next to Avery.

"There is nothing to fix," I say to Avery and then turn toward Tyson. Quinn stands next to Levi, and for some reason I feel like I'm on a stage and they are all my audience.

"Harley?" Tyson whispers, taking a hesitant step forward. "Are you okay? What's going on in here?" he asks, looking at both Quinn and Avery before turning back to me.

"No." I let my lids droop over my eyes and cast my gaze down. "Everything is *not* okay." I don't want to him to see how he affects me. I showed him my hand five years ago and he walked away. I showed him again last night what I was willing to give him and he rejected me. I'm done handing him my heart, just to have him throw it right back in my face. I take a deep breath and search for the resolve that I lost the night I saw him again for the first time...here at this very club.

"We can't be friends, Tyson." There. I said it. It's out there.

And now I feel even worse.

"What? Why not?" he asks. I look at him, surprised to see that he appears angry. I'm not going to lie, I was hoping he'd look a little sad.

"Why? *Why?* Are you a damn idiot? Why can't I be your friend?" I yell incredulously, throwing my hands in the air, then letting them fall back to my side. "Because…" I swallow back the lump in my throat and push forward. "Because you *hurt* me, Tyson. You know what?" I shake my head swiftly. "Hurt isn't even a good word for it. You fucking *wounded* me." Jesus Christ, these fucking tear ducts are getting on my nerves. My eyes have met their threshold, but I wipe them before any tears are able to fall.

"I know I did, Harley!" Tyson yells back, pounding his fist into his chest. "I know I fucking hurt you. And it fucking killed me, I told you that! I thought we were past this. I thought you forgave me and we were moving forward." His hands are fisted at his side and his shoulders are tense, but some of the anger has drained from his face. Now he just looks lost, and maybe confused.

I hate that we've come to this point. We shouldn't be fighting—this just isn't us. I soften my voice, trying to diffuse the situation. "We were, and I thought I could move past it. But you've given me so many mixed signals this past week that I don't know whether I'm coming or going."

"I gave *you* mixed signals? What about y—"

"I'm not done talking," I snap. He rubs his hands over his face in frustration but lets me continue. "Maybe I was the stupid one. Maybe I misread everything. But you did—you gave me mixed signals. You flirted with me. You found small ways to be close to me and touch me. You were persistent in wanting us to spend time together. And then you pulled away from me and started acting funny. I thought it was me. I thought maybe I was giving you mixed signals, so I wanted to make it clear."

Goddamnit. Remind me not to have these conversations again when I've been drinking. I stop trying to prevent the tears from falling. What's the use? My therapist told me once that I need to let things go, that it's not healthy to hold it all in. So this is me…letting things go. Tyson's body instantly reacts at the sight of my tears and he reaches forward, gripping my arms gently.

"Harley…"

I twist my arms out of his grasp and his eyes flash with pain. I'm hurting him. *Ironic, huh?*

I'm surprised how steady I'm able to keep my voice when I state, "I tried to kiss you last night, Tyson." This obviously hits a note with the silent trio standing off to the side, because the three of them speak at the same time.

"What?" Levi gasps, eyebrows raised.

"Yup," Quinn responds without taking her eyes off of us.

And I swear I hear Avery murmur, "Jackass."

Tyson's face twists in anguish and his chocolate eyes flash with regret. He reaches his hand out but drops it immediately when I shift away from him. "Harley, I made a mistake. I'm sorry. I wasn't rejecting you. God, I would never rejec—"

"And then," I interrupt, not wanting to rehash the embarrassment I felt last night, "I show up tonight and see you with her." I wave my hand at Avery. "She had her arm around you and the way she was looking at you…my God, I'd be an idiot not to notice—"

"Actually, that's why I came in here to talk to you," Avery interjects softly. Frankly, I don't care. I don't want to hear what she has to say…this is between Tyson and me. I continue talking, not even acknowledging her and not caring that I'm being rude either.

"At first, I was bothered because you got called into work and had to cancel our dinner. But then when I saw that you came here with her instead, and the way you looked at her…" I take a deep breath, willing myself to talk through the tears. "You looked happy, Tyson. You were smiling and I realized that it's been a really long time since I've seen you smile like that." My throat is burning and scratchy and I want nothing more than to run out of here and save face, but this is good for me—I need to get this out.

Tyson is watching me. His face is guarded, but his eyes are hard. I hate that I can't tell what he's thinking or feeling, but I have to finish this. "So I'm done. I can't be your friend. It's too hard," I sob, "I can't be your friend when I'm still completely in lo—"

"Enough!" he yells, stepping into my space. I stumble back, bumping into the sink. "Enough. Don't make this my fault, Harley. Don't play the fuckin' martyr, because it isn't attractive on you."

"What?" I ask, feeling like he just slapped me in the face. "What the fuck are you talking about?"

"Oh, come on, Harley. You want to know why I pulled away from you? You want to hear me say it?" His voice starts to shake and he twists away from me, running his hand across the back of his neck. "Because I was fucking jealous, okay? I was mad at myself that I had the chance to be with you and I blew it, and someone else stepped up and I was fucking jealous."

What? He's jealous? Okay, I know I've had a few drinks, but I have no idea what he's talking about. Who the hell is he jealous of? Despite my complete confusion, I don't miss the fact that he never told me I was wrong about Avery.

He turns back to me. "I want it to be me, Harley. I want to be with you." His voice is strong and firm, and his determined eyes bore into mine. "I want to be the one that gets to kiss you good night. I want to be the one to make you breakfast in the morning. Not him. Not Max," he says, shaking his head angrily.

Thoughts...meet brick wall.
What the what?
What the hell is he talking about?

He lowers his head in defeat at my silence and wipes a hand across his face while my heart clenches in my chest.

"Max?" I ask slowly, trying to make sure I heard him correctly.

"Yes, Max. You know...oh-he's-so-handsome, he's-doing-great, Max." His voice is laced with hurt and sarcasm, and it pisses me off because he is oh-so-fucking wrong. I glance at Quinn and she cocks an I-told-you-to-tell-him eyebrow at me. Then it hits me...this is my fault. I never told him I have a son. I never told him about Max.

I'm mad and hurt and pissed and every other negative emotion known to man. But mostly, I'm angry with myself. Maybe if I had been up front with him, none of this would have happened. But his sarcastic words ring in my ears, and as much as I know I should be gentle and truthful, I just can't.

"Oh my God, you're joking, right?" I ask mockingly. "You're jealous of *Max*? You don't even know who Max is," I spit.

Tyson's eyes swirl with emotion. He's watching me, waiting to see what I'll do or say next. Well, I hope he's watching closely, because I'm about to rock his fucking world and then he's going watch me walk right out that door.

"Uh-oh," I hear Levi whisper. "She's going to do it."

"She is soooo doing it," Quinn replies.

"What? What's she doing?" Avery whispers.

"She's going to tell him who Max is."

"I was right," Avery says, a smile playing at the corner of her mouth. "Max isn't her boyfriend." Levi and Quinn both shake their head. Tyson appears completely oblivious to the conversation that just took place behind him.

Well, let's go down in flames, shall we? With tears racing down my face, I open myself up, allowing him to see every emotion that I'm feeling. In fact, if he looks close enough, I'm fairly certain he could see my soul.

Stepping up to Tyson, I take a deep cleansing breath, which doesn't really help. "Max isn't my boyfriend." My voice is laced with venom when I go in for the kill, "He's my son."

Tyson's face pales. His chocolate eyes darken and nervously roam my face, looking for some sign that I'm lying. He's not going to find one. His body sags as the truth sinks in, and I can see tears glisten in his eyes under the dim lighting. He doesn't move. He doesn't respond or try to touch me. He just stands there—frozen.

Just before I push past him to walk out the door, I see a million emotions flash across his grief-stricken face: disbelief, pain, grief, regret, acceptance, hope, and then confusion. But I don't wait. Shameful tears prick my eyes as I push my way out of the bathroom and through the throngs of bodies, trying to exit the bar.

I should have stayed. I should have let him come to grips with what I just threw at him. I'm sure he has a million and one questions and he's going to want answers. But I've had enough for tonight. I want to go home, curl up in bed, and go to sleep. I'm going to spend tomorrow wallowing in my pain, and then I'm going to pull myself together, pick myself up off the ground, and dust myself off. Because let's face it, this is my fault. I should have been up front with him from the beginning.

I unlock the car, drop into the front passenger seat, and lean my head against the window. So much for a fun night out. I know Quinn won't be long, and since we've been drinking, I'm certain Levi will be hot on her heels.

Just before Levi slides behind the wheel and Quinn gets in the back, I remind myself to never let Max leave for the weekend again. Leaning forward, Quinn gently strokes my hair. Levi reaches across the center console and squeezes my thigh reassuringly before he starts the car and pulls away. Neither one of them says a word— they don't have to. They've been down this road with me before, and they're prepared to go down it with me now. I just pray to God that I never have to go down it again.

Chapter 13

Tyson

IT'S BEEN TWO DAYS since Harley told me that Max is her son. *She has a son.* I'm still trying to wrap my head around that. I can't believe I never found out about him. I mean, my parents are friends with her parents, for Christ's sake. Granted, they moved out of town after Dallas' death, but I'm sure they still keep in contact. And Levi—fucking Levi. I shouldn't be surprised that he never told me. It's obvious that his loyalty lies with Harley, and if I had to guess, she probably told him to keep his mouth shut.

I've spent the last eighteen hours thinking about him…thinking about Max. What does he look like? Does he have Harley's green eyes? Does he look like his dad? Who *is* his dad? Is the guy still in the picture?

I want to meet him. I *need* to meet him. It's the weirdest thing, but once she told me she has a son, I got this incredibly strong urge to spend time with him. It's almost as though we have this strange connection and I'm being pulled to him. At first, I thought the urge was simply because Harley has always been a huge part of my life and it's natural to want to know her children. But I…I just don't know how to explain it. I just need to meet him.

And I need to talk to her.

Christ, I was so wrong. I should have just asked. I should have put her on the spot and asked who the hell Max was. Instead, I pulled away. The look on her face when she said I rejected her is burned into my memory. I don't ever want to see that look on her face again, and it kills me that I'm the one who put it there. She needs to know how I feel; she needs to know I would never reject her again. *Ever.*

I've called her at least a dozen times, left several voicemails, and I've even texted her. No response…nothing. Well, I'm done giving her the option to ignore me because it's going to be kind of difficult when I show up at her door. Thank God I didn't have to work today, because I'm not sure I could've waited much longer. I should have fucking showed up the next morning. But I'm an idiot—pretty sure we've already established that.

Putting the car in park, I take a deep breath and wipe my hands down the front of my pants. Why am I so nervous? This is Harley and her son. Nothing to be nervous about. I know I'm going to catch her completely off-guard and she probably isn't prepared for me to meet Max, but I just hope she doesn't slam the door in my face.

Walking up the sidewalk, I notice a kid's bike propped against the side of the house and a ball in the middle of the yard. Were those here last time? I knock softly three times and steel myself for Harley's wrath. *Crap, this is going to piss her off.* Who am I kidding? Right now, I don't give a shit. This is going to happen sometime, so it might as well happen now.

"Welcome to my dungeon!" I hear a little voice roar. "You must answer three questions right or you must go!" I can't help but smile…I already love this kid!

"What are the questions, good sir?" I ask, using the deepest voice I can muster. I can hear him giggle through the door and it's such a great sound. I want to hear it again.

"What president is on the United States penny?" he asks with authority.

"That would be the sixteenth president of the United States. President Abraham Lincoln," I answer proudly. There's that giggle again.

"What great Cardinals player wore the number six?" Yup, he's definitely Mr. Thompson's grandson. Thank God I spent enough time at Harley's house growing up to acquire plenty of Cardinals baseball trivia.

"Stan Musial," I reply, adding a "DUH!" at the end, which elicits an even bigger laugh from the opposite side of the door.

"What is the name of a butterfly's tongue?"

"It's called a tongue?" I half-ask, half-state, hoping that I didn't get outsmarted by a child.

"Ehhhh!" he yells, doing his best impression of a buzzer. *Well shit.* I'm not sure how old Max is, but he has to be younger than five, so how in the hell would a five-year-old know the name of a butterfly's tongue?

"It's called a proboscis," he yells through the door. "Now, I unleash the dr—"

"Wait!" I holler. "You have to give me a bonus question, it's part of the rules!"

"Hey!" he scoffs, flinging open the door. My whole body is frozen in place as I take in the little ball of fire in front of me. His eyes…his eyes are what completely catch me off-guard. I know it's impossible, but his large, coffee-colored eyes and thick black lashes are exact replicas of my brother, Dallas. *Holy shit.* I rub my fists over my eyes quickly, thinking that maybe I'm just missing Dallas so much that now I'm seeing him everywhere I go.

"You can't make up rules!" he says firmly, pointing his Styrofoam sword at my chest.

"Max!" My head snaps up when I hear Harley's voice, and Max drops his chin in defeat. She's coming around the corner while wiping her hands off on a towel, so she hasn't seen me yet. "Max, what did I tell you about opening the do—" Her words cut off when she finds me standing in her doorway. She inhales sharply and her mouth forms the most perfect 'O.' Max uses the silence to his advantage.

"Hi!" he says cheerfully, sticking out his hand. "My name is Max, and don't you dare call me Maximus." He's attempting to give me the 'stink eye,' but it's just so damn cute that I laugh.

"Hello, Max." I grip his hand firmly and pump it dramatically a few times, causing him to giggle. "My name is Tyson, but you can call me Ty." I quickly glance at Harley, who is watching Max and I with a look of horror, and for a moment I feel like maybe I've overstepped my boundaries.

I look back down when Max taps my arm. "I know you!" he says excitedly.

"You do? But we haven't met until now. How do you know me?" I ask, squatting down to his level.

"You're in the picture book," he chirps, grabbing my hand and tugging. "Follow me, I'll show you." I turn to Harley, who is still watching us. Some of the terror has drained from her face, but she still looks incredibly uncomfortable. I stop dead in my tracks at the thought that I'm causing her more pain, because that isn't my intention. Her eyes flit from Max to me and then to our joined hands.

"Is this okay?" I ask her. "I can leave if—"

"No, no," she says, waving the towel that's gripped tightly in her hand. "Go ahead. It's okay." Her voice is timid and soft and I'm not sure if it's really okay with her, but I'm not going to argue. She's letting me stay so I'm staying. I smile softly and nod my head.

"Okay, buddy, let's go." I pull on his hand and Max jumps in step beside me, a big, toothy grin on his face.

He instructs me to sit on the floor and then he takes off running down the hall. I sit down and let my eyes wander around the room. A beautiful brick fireplace sits against the far wall and it's adorned with photos of Max, Levi, Quinn, and Harley's parents. I notice that there aren't any photos of another man—a man who could be Max's father. Against the adjacent wall is a large entertainment center with a big-screen TV nestled in it, and I spot a

Nintendo Wii tucked in there too.

There's a large chest tucked in the corner that is overflowing with toys, and a plush gray couch and rocking chair sit on the opposite side of the room. From what I can see, the entryway, living room, and hallway are all covered in a deep brown hardwood floor, and her walls—with the exception of the deep red wall that holds the fireplace—are a warm mocha color. Her home is warm and inviting and...cozy. Not for the first time, pride swells in my chest when I think of what Harley has accomplished. I find myself playing the 'what if' game as Max comes sliding back into the room.

"Got it!" he cheers, holding an album above his head. Sitting down on the floor, Max scoots as close to me as he can get and opens the photo album, so half of it is on my lap and the other half is on his. He doesn't waste a second as he starts showing me pictures of himself when he was a baby.

I can see his mouth moving, but as my eyes take him in, his voice fades deeper into the background. His hair is dark like Harley's and a bit wavy, almost curly. It's slightly unruly, and I watch as he bats a chunk of it out of his eyes. His cheeks are a little chubby with two perfect dimples. He has Harley's thin nose and his eyes...those eyes. They must belong to his father, because they sure as hell don't belong to Harley. Don't get me wrong, her eyes are gorgeous and I could stare at them all day. But for some reason, Max's eyes are stunning and surprisingly...familiar.

"Do you?" Max says, nudging me in the side.

"What? Sorry, bud. What'd you say?" I ask, pulling myself out of my head. He rolls his eyes at me and points to a photograph.

"Do you remember this picture? It's my favorite." I look down, shocked to find myself staring at picture after picture of Harley and me when we were kids. How did she get all of these?

She kept them. *She kept them.*

"Of course I remember that! Your mom and I both got new bikes for Christmas." I rub the picture absently, remembering how excited I was to get that bicycle. "We were so excited to ride them, we couldn't wait." Max looks at me, his eyes full of wonder. "It might have been winter, but it hadn't snowed and the sidewalks were still clean, so we begged and begged until our parents finally let us ride our bikes." I smile to myself when I remember how we only lasted about ten minutes in the freezing cold weather, but it was best ten minutes I'd ever had. "We bundled up and rode up and down the sidewalk, over and over. We only stopped because your mom's nose started running and the snot was freezing to her face!" Max throws his head back and snorts with laughter.

"That's not how I remember it." My head whips around, where I find Harley standing in the doorway, her hip propped against the frame with a small smile playing on her perfect lips. "If I remember correctly, you started crying that your toes were going to fall off and your mom made us go in. So see, it's all your fault."

"I have a bike," Max interjects, sitting up. "Wanna see it? It's a *Cars* bike. It even came with a tool kit for when I have to make a pit stop. It's really cool. I'll let you play with it if you want. My mom said she would get me a bell to put on it. Maybe I'll get one for Christmas and then I can ride my bike outside like you did." Harley's eyes dance with amusement as she watches Max talk my ear off. I can't really get a word in edgewise so I follow behind him, nodding my head and oohing and aahing when I feel it's appropriate.

Harley watches us in the backyard from the kitchen window. Every time I look up and catch her staring, she quickly ducks her chin, averting her gaze. I'm not sure why, but that makes me happy. If I didn't know better, I'd think that she likes seeing me with Max almost as much as I like being with him.

I'm not sure how much time passes, but it must be getting late because Harley comes into the backyard, ordering Max to get cleaned up for bed. This of course, elicits an eye roll and loud groan from the feisty four-and-a-half year old. Yup, I figured out how old he was. Well, actually he corrected me when I called him a five-year-old.

"Don't roll your eyes at me, Max. It isn't nice," Harley scolds, rolling her eyes at me when Max isn't looking. I shoot her a quick wink and she smiles in return.

I can't help but feel like things are going way too smoothly. Harley is probably waiting for Max to go to bed so that she can try to kick me out of her life again, which I've already decided isn't even an option. I'm here to stay, and there isn't a damn thing she can do about it. I just pray that she doesn't fight it too hard, because I'm not sure how much longer I can wait to make her mine.

"But mo-om, I don't want to go to bed. I want to play with Tyson." She picks him up, tossing him over her shoulder, and he keeps talking into her back. "We played with my tool set, and he put a baseball card in the wheel of my bike so that it sounds like a motorcycle when it goes around. And then we played soccer. I was the goalie and Tyson didn't score one goal. I'm that good, mom!"

"You *are* that good," she croons and then turns back toward me. "You can wait in here while I give him a bath, if you want." She looks nervous and I know it took a lot for her to tell me that. "I mean…unless you have to go. That's okay too."

"I have nowhere else I'd rather be," I reply, ruffling Max's thick hair as I walk by. She smiles and tells me to make myself at home. I pick up the photo album we left sitting on the floor and start thumbing through it, laughing to myself about how excited Max was to show me each and every picture.

I learned one very important thing about Max tonight—he loves to talk. The kid does not stop talking. I don't even have to say a word, he just talks for me. But it's awesome. He is awesome. I'm not sure if it's normal to instantly connect with a kid that isn't even yours like that, but it felt…normal. It felt right.

After a few minutes, Max emerges from the bathroom in Teenage Mutant Ninja Turtle pajamas, which I didn't even know were still around. Growing up, they were one of my favorites. His wet hair is parted and combed perfectly to the side. It definitely looks like a woman fixed it.

"Come here, Max." I pat the seat next to me on the couch

and he jumps up and looks at me. "Have you ever heard of a faux hawk?" I ask.

His cute little nose crinkles in confusion and he cocks his head to the side, as if actually trying to remember if he's ever heard of it. "I know what a hawk is!" he answers proudly, his eyes widening with excitement.

I laugh at his innocence and pull him to stand in front of me. Running my hands through his hair, I start pushing it around and styling it. When I'm done, his hair is pulled together in the center and he has a full-on mohawk going from his forehead to the back of his neck. Christ, this kid has a ton of hair, almost like—

"Wow. Cool," he says, gently running his hand along the top of his spikey hair.

"It won't stay. It'll fall when it dries, but next time I'll bring some gel and we'll style it for real. Now go have a look at it in the mirror."

"Alright! Mom, look!" he yells, running out of the living room. They round the corner at the same time and Max plows right into Harley. He scowls at her and reaches up to make sure his hair is still intact. "Careful, Mom!" he scolds. "Don't mess up my hawk!"

"Oh gosh, I would never want to mess up your very manly mohawk," she says, squatting down to his level, just as he barrels past her to find a mirror. Harley shakes her head and laughs, walking toward the couch. She sits down on the opposite end, and I want nothing more than to pull her down here by me.

She's watching me, her face expressionless. Is this that look they say that mothers give? I keep watching her and she keeps watching me. *Yup, this must be that look.*

"You gave my son a mohawk." Her face is stone cold, but as I watch her for a few moments, I can see her fighting a grin that is pulling at the side of her mouth.

"Hell yes, I did! Did you see his hair?" I ask, leaning back against the couch and pointing down the hall at Max. "He looked like a choir boy."

She throws her head back and laughs, exposing the length of her neck. *Fuck me, everything about her is perfect.* All I can think about right now is what I wouldn't give to feel that silky skin against my lips.

"There is nothing wrong with a choir boy," she gasps, trying to stop from laughing. Her eyes smile at me and it's an incredible feeling. I don't ever want to go back to the place we were two nights ago.

"No, there isn't. But your son has an amazing personality and he needs an amazing hair style to go with it!"

"Okay. Okay. He can keep the mohawk," she says as Max comes barreling back into the room. Holy crap, does that kid ever slow down? He's go, go, go all the time.

"I love it! Did you see my hair, mom?" he asks, and she nods. "Do you like it? It's *so* cool. Andy is going to be so mad that he doesn't have a hawk! Tyson said he was going to bring gel over next time and do it for real. Can I read you a book before I go to bed?" he asks, looking directly at me. I love how he so easily goes from talking about hair to asking to read a book in the same breath.

I point a finger at myself in question and he nods. "Do you mean, can I read *you* a book before bed?"

"No," Max replies, staring at me like I'm crazy. Both he and Harley are watching me, and I swear my whole body warms under their gazes. I've had such a great time tonight; I really don't want it to end. "I'm going to read you a book. How about *Goodnight, Goodnight, Construction Site*?" Max whips around on his heel and takes off for his room, obviously expecting me to follow behind.

"Really?" I ask, raising my eyebrows in question. "He can read already?" *Is that normal?*

"No." She laughs, shaking her head. "I've read him that book so many times that he has the words memorized. He knows exactly which words are on which pages and it *looks* like he's reading."

"Your kid is too smart for his own good," I say, pointing a finger at her. "He's going to give you a run for your money. You know that, right?"

"I know," she says dramatically, tossing her head back on the couch as I make my way back to Max's room—which is totally awesome, by the way.

The far wall from where I walk in is painted with red seams to make it look like a baseball and there is a mural on the south wall, painted to look like a stadium full of people. There is a large St. Louis Cardinal baseball rug in the middle of the room. *Surprise, surprise.* A small bookshelf sits in the corner and it's overflowing with sleeved baseball cards, bobble heads, a few signed baseballs, and a replica of a World Series ring…at least I think it's a replica. I'm going to be shocked if this kid doesn't end up becoming a baseball player himself someday.

Like Harley said he would, Max 'reads' me the entire book from start to finish without missing a word. Whenever he's done, he shuts the book, tosses it on the floor, and crosses his legs. "Did you like it? It's my favorite book. My mom bought it for me. She's my favorite mom, but she's not very good at playing freeze tag. She told me that you're her best friend. Are you still her best friend?" This kid can rapid-fire questions quicker than anyone I know. Forget the baseball player, maybe he'll be a lawyer.

His face is full of innocence as his oversized chocolate eyes bore into mine, waiting for me to respond. "Yes, your mom and I are still friends," I answer, wondering to myself how much you should tell a four-and-a-half-year-old. He seems to be incredibly perceptive, so I want to be very careful about how I answer him.

"Why did I never meet you before?" he asks openly.

"Well…" I stop, trying to come up with the most appropriate answer. I decide to go with the truth. "Did your mom tell you that I'm a doctor?"

He smiles, nodding enthusiastically. "I want to be a doctor someday, but don't tell my papa," he whispers, leaning in to me. "I think he wants me to play baseball."

I scoot off his bed and onto the floor, propping my elbow on his bed so that I'm closer to being at his level. "Well, when I was going to school to be a doctor, I decided to go to school in New York. Do you know where New York is?" He nods his head and I continue. "My classes were really tough and New York is so far away that I didn't come back home as much as I should have."

"Why not?"

Because I was an idiot. I was scared. I was mad. I could literally give a million reasons.

"I don't know. A lot of reasons, I guess. But I'm back now and I'm not leaving." I don't know why I felt the need to tell him that. It's not like he cares, it just sort of slipped out. "But yes, your mom and I are still friends and I really, *really* wish I would have come back home sooner so that I could have met you. Because you, my man," I say, reaching out and ruffling his hair as he snuggles down under his blanket, "are a really awesome kid, and I had a blast playing with you tonight."

He doesn't say anything to that, but when I stand up and move toward the door he says, "Good night, Tyson. I'll see you soon, okay?"

"Goodnight, Max." I flip off the light and watch in amazement at how fast his eyes start to drift shut.

It's mind-blowing. I came here tonight in hopes of talking to Harley and hopefully getting to meet Max. Never in a million years did I think I would end up playing with the kid for two hours and then tucking him into bed.

I take a deep breath, steeling myself for the conversation that is yet to come. Walking down the hall, I head toward the kitchen where I find Harley standing at the sink, washing dishes. She's staring mindlessly out an open window and a light breeze flows through, tossing strands of her hair up around her face. She's an angel, pure and simple.

A pair of pink cotton shorts showcases her mile-long legs and her bare feet are tapping out a light rhythm on the floor. I know from seeing them earlier that she has her toenails painted hot pink and I find it sexy as hell.

And there goes my vagina again...it must be getting bigger!

Who the hell notices the color of a woman's toes?

She's wearing an oversized t-shirt, and I can't help but wonder who it belongs to because it's obviously too big to be a woman's shirt. The neck of the shirt has fallen down on one side, exposing the length of her neck and the top of her right shoulder.

She's perfect. How in the hell did I walk away from this woman? I loved everything about her five years ago, but now... now I appreciate all of those things that I loved. She's funny and tenacious, but at the same time she can be incredibly quiet and shy. She's graceful and charming in a classic sort of way, and it's utterly impossible for anyone who meets her to not fall in love with her.

And good God, let's not forget her body. Harley has the kind of curves that are meant to be worshipped for hours on end, which is exactly what I plan to do when she finally gives me a second chance at more than friendship

I watch quietly as her shoulders rise and fall on a deep breath. She's such an incredible woman, and the fact that she has raised such a wonderful little boy makes me admire her that much more. My head knows that Harley and I need to talk, but my heart...my heart is screaming at me to go get my girl. Well, five years ago I listened to my head; tonight I'm going to listen to my heart.

I wait until she's rinsing the soap off of the dishes before I make my way across the kitchen. She doesn't hear me approach, but when I step up behind her, placing my hands on the counter on either side of her, her back stiffens. I stand there for several seconds and then decide that there's no better time than the present.

I lower my head alongside hers, my front pressed lightly to her back. My cheek is resting next to hers, and even though they aren't touching, I can feel the warmth radiating off of her body. I hate that she's so rigid, but I'm hoping that if I can manage to get out a few things I have to say, she might relax just a little bit.

"Max is asleep." My words are soft and spoken over her shoulder. "What are the chances that he'll get up?"

She shakes her head slowly. "He won't." *Good.* That's what

I was hoping for.

"Well, it appears I was wrong." When my breath fans across her face, I notice her neck break out in goose bumps and I smile to myself, loving the way her body is reacting to me. "It turns out Max isn't your boyfriend."

A soft laugh slips from her lips and she shakes her head, lowering it. I'm not sure if she's looking down to see the dishes in front of her, or if she's dropping her head at the memory of us fighting the other night at Blue. Either way, at least I made her laugh and I really want to do that some more.

"I was wrong and I'm sorry." She lifts her head and angles her face slightly to the right. Her eyes flit to mine and she nods, a sad look on her face.

"I'm sorry too. I should have told you about Max sooner. I was going to, it ju—"

"Don't. It's okay. You have nothing to apologize for. This was all me. And now it's my turn to talk, okay?" She nods, turning her gaze back to the window.

"Do you have a boyfriend?"

She hesitates, making me fear the worst and then answers, putting me out of misery. "No."

"Do you have any sort of relationship with Max's father?"

"No," she answers, quieter than before. *Thank God!*

"Is Max's father in the picture?" She squeezes her eyes shut and quickly shakes her head. *Damnit. I hate to hear that.* That stupid prick has no idea what he's missing out on. I make a note to spend some extra time with Max doing 'guy' stuff. And I'm going to circle back around to discuss Max's father, but right now there are more important things we need to talk about.

"I'm really sorry to hear that. You've done an amazing job raising him. He's an incredible little boy," I say with as much conviction as I can.

Harley releases a quick breath and some of the tension drains from her shoulders. I can feel her back soften against my front and I'm thankful that I'm making some progress. *This is good.*

"Avery and I are not together." Harley doesn't say a word. I can feel her back rise and fall against my front, her breathing steady and even, but other than that, she doesn't move an inch. I can tell she wants to believe me, but she's not convinced.

"I can't look at anyone else, because all I see is you." Her eyes close and I can feel her relax into me. "I've thought about you every day, Harley, and I should have never walked away from you five years ago. I don't want Avery; I don't want any other woman. I just want you. I. Want. You," I whisper, my words spoken directly into her ear. When I see a single tear slide out of the corner of her eye, I lower my head a little more, lightly brushing my nose against the side of her cheek.

"I made the biggest mistake of my life when I walked away from you that night. I may be an idiot, but I learn from my mistakes and if you give me another chance, I swear to you...*I swear*, I will never walk away from you again." Tears are now streaming down her face—I just pray that they're happy tears.

"You need to know that I was not rejecting you the other night. I thought you had a boyfriend and I was trying to do the right thing, but I need you to know that pulling away from you was so fucking hard, Harley." She's breathing faster and her hands are gripping the counter so tightly that her knuckles are turning white. "Do you believe me?" I whisper, gently prying her hands off the counter. I hate asking her that, but I need to know if my words are getting through to her.

"Yes," she whispers, her voice cracking. She wipes the tears from her eyes and turns in front of me. I don't move. I like having her close, caged in my arms.

She stares at my chest, and I can tell by the expression on her face that she's trying to figure out what she wants to say. I keep quiet because I really want us to be on the same page...but I need her to get there on her own.

She lifts her face and the softness in her eyes cracks my heart wide open."You're sorry?" she asks timidly, her eyes wide with hope.

"More than I could ever tell you."

"And you aren't with Avery?"

"Never. Avery who?" I answer, pulling a small smile from her lips.

She looks at my chest again, trying to find her words. Releasing my grip on the counter, I wrap my hands around her neck, my thumbs caressing the sides of her jaw. At first she looks startled, but then her body relaxes and she catches me off-guard when she grips the bottom of my shirt, fisting it in her hands.

"Ask me, Harley."

Her eyes blur with tears and I can see the slightest quiver in her bottom lip, but my brave girl doesn't back away. "You want me?" she says, so softly that I barely hear it.

"I want you more than I've ever wanted anything in my entire life." I'm laying it all on the line. There's nothing else I can do. I have to open myself up to her and hope to God she believes me. I'm trying with everything I have to display every emotion I'm feeling on my face right now.

"Ask me something else, Harley." My voice is firm when I repeat myself, but I can hear it cracking when I say her name. Her eyes close, causing a few more tears to leak out. I lean forward and gently kiss them away. Her body shudders at the contact and I rejoice.

Do it, pretty girl. Ask me.

Chapter 14

Harley

"ASK ME SOMETHING ELSE, Harley."

I can literally feel the emotion rolling off of him. He's nervous. What is he afraid of? Does he think I'm going to reject him? Because I'm fairly certain I've already proved that I have absolutely no willpower when it comes to him.

Okay, to be honest, that's sort of what I was prepared to do when he showed up at my door tonight. And even when he held me hostage against the sink—which was totally fucking hot, by the way—I was prepared to give him a very polite send-off. Then, he opened his mouth and started saying some of the sweetest things—things I've wanted to hear for as long as I can remember. I should have known I wouldn't be able to hold my ground, not when the only man I've ever really wanted was bearing his soul to me. And who am I kidding? I don't want to hold my ground because I want him too.

I. Want. Him.

I take a deep breath and let that sink in for a second. *This is happening.* This is *really* happening. Wait a minute...what does he want me to ask him? Because I can think of about a million things to ask…kiss me? Make love to me? Get naked with me? Marry me? Okay, it may be too soon for the last one, but you can bet your ass that if I thought there was a chance in hell he'd say yes, I'd ask. No joke.

I'm watching him watch me and he seriously looks like he could throw up. I've probably been quiet for too long; I guess I need to put him out of his misery. If he wants a second chance, then that's what he's going to get. *But first…*

"I'm sorry," I say, fighting back a smile. Gah, this is so mean of me but I can't resist. "I can't."

His eyes close and he drops his forehead to mine. His shoulders rise and fall on a shaky breath. He looks completely defeated.

"I can't ask you to marry me." His head snaps up and his eyes are shining. A huge smile lights up his entire face. "It's too soon. We should probably just date for a while. Don't you agree?" His hands are still wrapped intimately around my neck and he tilts my face to his.

"You're amazing, you know that?" Just when I thought my tear ducts were starting to dry up, another tear trickles down the side of my face. Tyson extends his thumb and wipes it away.

"And for the record, I would've said yes." His eyes shimmer with emotion I can't quite place and we both start laughing. This is such a great feeling. Never in a million years did I think I would be standing here—like this—with Tyson. *My* Tyson.

The way I feel right now, I wish I could bottle it up and save it for a lesser day, but I know I can't so I need to make the most of this moment. Letting go of his shirt, I slide my hands around his back, pulling him to me, and the smile on his face fades. In its place is a look of pure need.

My eyes flit between his and then they drop to his mouth… his perfect mouth. The mouth that I've dreamt of kissing for years. His tongue flicks out, wetting his bottom lip, and I drag my eyes back to his. "Please kiss me," I whisper, hoping that this time I'm going to get what I want.

He gently tugs me forward until the front of our bodies are

melded together, and my heart starts racing on contact. I close my eyes, wanting to memorize everything about this moment. I don't ever want to forget the rhythmic way his soft thumbs brush across my jaw, the steady beat of his heart against my chest, the way his breath feathers across my face as he dips his head lower, or the way I feel his hardened length press gently into my belly. This moment can't possibly be any more perfect. At least that's what I thought, until I feel his lips brush against mine for the first time.

Now it's perfect.

His soft lips brush against mine once…twice…and a third time before he pulls his head back a fraction, waiting for me to open my eyes. I lift my heavy lids to find him watching me with open wonderment, and the words that flow from his mouth make my heart soar.

"I've been waiting for this kiss for the past five years, and I want you to know that it hasn't completely happened and it's already the most amazing kiss I've ever had." With those final whispered words, he proceeds to rock my fucking world.

In an unbelievably smooth motion, he pulls my face back to his, tilting it slightly to the left. My lips part and the moment his open mouth descends on mine, an entire swarm of butterflies take flight in my stomach. Our tongues intertwine, sliding against one another in the most natural way, and I swear…I swear I just died and went to heaven. I don't think anyone has ever kissed me in such an intimate way, but something inside of me snaps and I instantly want—no, I *need*—more.

My hands glide up his back and I tangle my fingers in his hair, tugging gently. He smiles against my mouth, pulls back a little, and my mouth follows his for a beat, trying to reconnect. A groan rips from my throat in disapproval, and he chuckles. Okay, now I'm a little pissed. I was really enjoying th—

"I'm not going to lie…I wasn't expecting you to be a hair puller."

"I'm a hair puller. Is that going to be a problem?" I'm talking as fast as I can because the quicker I talk, the quicker I can get his delectable mouth back on mine.

"Good God, no," he says, sliding his hands to the back of my head.

"Great. Now a little less talking and little more of whatever it was that you were do—" My words are cut off as he slams his mouth against mine, our lips and tongues moving together in a fiery passion.

I need to be closer to him. I need to feel more of him. A deep groan rumbles from his chest when I slide my hands down his stomach and under the bottom of his shirt. Fuck me…he has a six-pack. Wait…oh God, it's an eight-pack. He pulls back again and I growl at him.

"Stop doing that," he mumbles against my mouth.

"Doing what?" I ask, slightly perplexed. "Stop kissing you?"

"No! Fuck no! Don't ever stop doing that! But you have to stop counting my abs…it tickles."

"Okay, no ab-counting," I answer with a grin, my breath coming out in small pants, mostly because I'm a little—okay, *a lot*—turned on. "But listen to me…I've waited too damn long for this moment, so if you don't stop pulling away from me, I'm going to spank you. Now kiss me."

A mischievous grin spreads across his face. "We are going to be so perfect together," he says, kissing the spot below my ear, right before he takes my mouth in another heated kiss.

His hands glide down my back and he grips my hips firmly, lifting me up on the counter. My legs wrap around his trim waist and he pushes into me, grinding our bodies together. Our tongues start delving deeper, exploring every inch of each other's mouths. Our movements become more intense and my body feels like it's going to explode. I've felt pleasure before, but never anything like this. It's like he's trying to climb inside of me and I'm more than willing to let him.

"Fuck. You feel so amazing wrapped around me," he says, trailing kisses down my neck, stopping at the base to bite it gently before he makes his way back up. "I don't want to stop, but I'm afraid that if I don't—"

"Ty," I whisper, dislodging my hands from his warm chest. Cradling his face in my hands, I place a delicate kiss against his mouth. I open my eyes when his lips don't respond to find him watching me. "What? What's wrong?"

The look on his face is filled with pure affection, and my heart starts to slam inside my chest. "Please tell me what's wrong," I whisper again.

His face softens when he realizes that he's making me nervous and he pulls my forehead to his. "You called me Ty. You haven't called me Ty since I've been back."

I grip his face a little tighter and close my eyes, thankful that's all he said. "I'm sorry," I say, letting out a breath I didn't know I'd been holding. "I don't know why, I jus—"

"It's okay," he says with a laugh. "It's okay. I'm just so damn happy right now that I don't even know what to say or do. I just know that this feels so…"

"Perfect?" I say, finishing his sentence.

"Perfect."

"You know what would make it more perfect?" I ask suggestively.

"Mmmm, what's that?" he says, nuzzling his face against my neck. I pull his head back and he groans. Placing my lips gently against his, I whisper, "If you touch me."

Thank you, Jesus! The man needs no more direction.

His large warm hands slide under the back of my shirt, causing my entire body to shiver. Our mouths dance together and our movements become more intense with each passing second. His hands skim across my skin before he cups my heavy breasts, and his thumbs brush against my nipples in slow, circular movements. I moan with the intensity of the sensations that he's eliciting.

"That is the sexiest sound I've ever heard," he mumbles, trailing open-mouthed kisses down my jaw to the hollow spot below my ear. "Touch me." His voice is raw with passion and I squeeze my thighs together at the warmth that's starting to settle there. *Well shit, he doesn't have to ask me twice.*

I guide my hands under his shirt and lightly caress his chest, stopping briefly to tug on his nipples. He grunts at the sensation and I smile to myself, allowing my fingers to trail down the planes of his stomach. My hands flirt with the front of his jeans, aching to touch him. My movements are quick when I hook my left arm around his neck, pulling his mouth down to mine, while simultaneously trailing my right hand down the front of his pants and gripping him snugly through his jeans.

Tyson moans against my mouth and slides his hands up the front of my bare thighs and under the hem of my cotton shorts. When he reaches the apex where my thigh and hip bone meet, he squeezes and pulls me forward on the counter. My mind is telling me to pull back and watch—I want to watch him…I want to see his hands tucked under my shorts—but I can't stop thinking of how this man can kiss, and I just can't pry my mouth away from his.

A few seconds pass with fevered movements and deep kisses, and when I feel like my entire body is going to shatter, he slips his fingers under the edge of my panties and gently caresses my heated flesh. "Ty," I moan, throwing my head back as Tyson's mouth attacks my neck. His extremely talented hand starts torturing me with slow, rhythmic circles. He shifts his body, allowing his hand to delve deeper, and I feel two thick fing—

"MOM! MO-OM!" Max's ear-piercing scream halts our actions. Ty watches me for a moment, eyes wide, before he rips his hand out of my pants, pushes my hand off the front of his erection and steps away from me. I can't help it—it's clear that he's never been cock-blocked by a child before—and I can't stop the deep laugh that rips from my throat.

"What?" he asks, bewildered. "What are you laughing at? This isn't funny," he says, shaking his head. "Max could've walked in. How in the hell would we have explained my hand down your pants?" he whisper-yells. His movements are jerky and fast, and his hands are shaking. I'm hoping that this doesn't scare him away, so I approach him gently. He runs his hand through his hair and takes a deep breath. I push him down into a chair and kiss him gently on the lips.

"Let me go check on Max. Don't move," I say, pointing at him as I begin to walk away. He doesn't respond but watches me with a terrified look on his face. In three strides, I'm back in his face. Gripping it tightly, I tilt my mouth over his and give him the quickest, most heated kiss I can manage. When I pull back, he has a goofy grin on his face, and I'm fairly confident my kiss served its purpose. "Now, don't move!" I demand, walking back to Max's room.

It turns out that Max had a bad dream, something about dragons and leopards. I listened to him tell me about it, and then I held him, soothed him, and reassured him that he was safe. It was only a matter of minutes before he was sound asleep again, nestled under his comforter.

When I walk back into the kitchen, Ty's seat is empty—*completely empty*—and tucked in neatly under the table. I take a deep breath and blow it out slowly, resting my hands on top of my head. A lump forms in my throat and I can feel the tears start to burn my eyes when I feel two warm arms wrap around me from behind. A light sob rips from my throat and a few tears manage to escape. "Hey... " Ty says, turning me around. He cradles my face in his hands and brushes the tears away. "Why are you crying?"

"I don't know, I just—" I shake my head, trying to find my words. "I just saw the empty chair, and after Max interrupting us, I guess I thought...I don't know. I guess I thought that maybe you changed your mind."

"I had to use the bathroom," he says, watching me carefully. "And never again...I am never going to leave you or walk away from you again. Got it?" he says, leaning down so we're eye to eye.

"Got it," I answer feebly. He slides his arms down to my butt and lifts me up. I wrap my legs around his waist and bury my head in his neck as he walks us to the couch and sits down with me still attached.

He pulls back, and I sit up and face him. "Harley…I know we still have a lot to talk about—and we're going to—but I'm not sure I made myself clear earlier. When I asked you for a second chance, I meant it. But probably what I should have said is that I want you and absolutely everything that comes with you, including Max. I'm not going to run because he interrupts an intimate moment or because he throws a fit out in public or whatever crazy thing he will inevitably do, but I need you to remember that this is new to me. I've never really been around kids before. I've never been interrupted unexpectedly like that and it scared me, which obviously scared you. But I'm not going anywhere, okay?" I smile and nod as he leans forward and kisses me tenderly.

Chapter 15

Tyson

HARLEY'S ARMS ARE WRAPPED so tightly around my neck that I'm afraid she might seriously cut off my airflow. But there is no way in hell I'm making her move because this—right here, right now—is absolutely perfect and wonderful and any other sappy word you could come up with.

I hate that she thought I'd left, but I won't lie—Max scared the shit out of me. I'm going to have to be more conscious of him being around. It's going to kill me if I can't touch Harley or kiss her anytime I want, but I know she'll want to take things slow when it comes to Max and I'm more than okay with that. If we're going to do this, I want to do it right.

"I thought you said he wouldn't wake up," I murmur, running my fingers through her silky hair.

She sits up and rests her hands on my chest. "Well, technically he didn't get up."

"Okay," I chuckle. "But close enough." She's watching her hand as her fingers draw little circles and shapes across my chest. The light graze of her nails makes my arms break out in goose bumps, and she laughs when she notices. I can tell she's getting lost in the moment, taking it all in and trying to absorb everything that's being said and everything that's happening. I know because I'm right there with her.

"He had a bad dream. It's totally my fault though," she says, waving her hand in front of us. "The kid's a little vagina-blocker." Wait…did she just say *vagina-blocker*? "I totally should've known that the second you decided to even get near it, he would find some way to interrupt."

My face feels like it's going to break from smiling so much. "Did you call your son a vagina-blocker?" I ask through a laugh.

"Absolutely!" she replies, her face stone-cold sober and her head nodding like a bobblehead. "It's the truth! He's done it before!" *Okay, I don't really want to know that.* It fucking guts me to think of Harley with someone else.

"No, that's not what I meant," she says, shaking her head gently and stroking her knuckles down the side of my face. *How did she know what I was thinking?*

"I'm a single mom, and sometimes I have to find ways to, um…to, uh…enjoy myself. And there has been a time—maybe two—where Max has walked in." Her eyes fall to her lap as though she's embarrassed, which she absolutely should *not* be. God, the thought of Harley touching herself makes me instantly hard. "He's never seen anything," she adds quickly, "I'm always in my bed under the covers…or in the bathtub."

I tilt her chin up. I don't ever want her looking down like that again…I don't like it at all. "Don't be embarrassed, Harley. I think it's fucking hot, and one of these days I'm going to watch." Her eyes snap to mine and brighten with mischief. She likes the thought of that…I'm going to have to remember that for future reference. *How did I not know about this little fiery side to her?*

"We're just going to have to be a little more careful," I state, trying to keep my wits about me around this girl. "I don't ever want Max to walk in on anything."

"I agree," she nods. "I got carried away. I mean, I've waited for that for…well, forever, and—"

"Don't," I say, putting my finger up to her lips. "Don't ever be sorry for getting carried away with me. In fact, feel free to get carried away with me anytime. Well, almost anytime." She smiles softly and nuzzles her face in my neck. I can feel her warm breath against my neck when she yawns, and I realize that it must be getting late.

"What floor are you on tomorrow?" I ask, running my hands up the back of her shirt, needing to feel her soft skin one more time.

"7 West," she mumbles.

"Pediatrics. That seems perfect for you."

"I love it," she says, yawning again.

"Have lunch with me tomorrow?"

"Okay." She sits upright, rubbing at her tired eyes, and cocks her head to the side. "Are you leaving? Please don't leave," she begs, pushing out her bottom lip.

I pull her face toward mine and laugh against her mouth. I suck that sexy-as-hell bottom lip into my mouth and bite it playfully. She groans, closing her eyes. Damn, I shouldn't have done that, because now I want to do it again. Only this time I want to add a little hand action and—

Now I have to leave before I act on these thoughts. "It's late. You're exhausted, I'm exhausted, and we both have to work tomorrow. Plus," I kiss her nose, "I'm coming over to make you and Max dinner tomorrow night, so I need you nice and rested."

Her face brightens with the most gorgeous smile I've ever seen, and I make a mental note that making dinner for her and Max makes her a very happy woman. And making her a very happy woman is at the top of my to-do list.

"But I just got you," she grumbles, her smile slowly fading. "I'm not ready to let go quite yet." *Isn't that the truth?*

Maybe it's the way her eyes misted over when she said that or perhaps it was the way her voice softened, but something snapped inside of my chest. Something powerful and way beyond anything I've ever felt. As though she felt it too, Harley leans forward, lowering her forehead to mine.

"I don't want to go either," I say, grabbing her hand, linking our fingers together. "But we've literally been together for—" I lean back, looking at the clock on her wall "—three hours. I think it's a little too soon to have sleepovers." She bends forward, pressing her entire body against mine, and claims my mouth. I open up for her, grip her neck in my hand, and we kiss wildly, breaking contact only when we're both panting and out of breath.

"Tomorrow." I say, kissing her nose, each eyelid, and her chin. "And every day after that. Okay?"

She huffs out a breath. "Okay."

WE SPEND THE NEXT two days at work texting back and forth, eating lunch together, and both days I pulled her into an empty exam room, locked the door, and we made out like two horny teenagers. Both nights after work, I arrived at her house to find Max ready and waiting for me.

Max and I played soccer, freeze tag, built a fort, played Candy Land—he totally cheated, by the way—and then both nights he stood on a chair at the counter and asked a million and one questions while he helped me make dinner for his mom.

After tucking Max into bed, Harley and I stayed up late into the night—both nights—getting reacquainted. We alternated between deep sensual kisses and heartfelt conversations that left both of us either on the verge of hysterical laughter or tears. It's been fun getting to know her again, and I enjoyed telling her about my time in New York. She said she's never been so I vowed to myself that someday soon I would take her and Max.

We both learned that not a whole lot about either of us has changed. When asked, Harley danced around what happened with her during the first couple of years after I left, and I let her get away with it—for now.

One thing I've learned is that Harley is a very physical person, which is something I never would have guessed. She likes to be touched, and if I'm not touching her, then she is touching me in some way or another. But don't get me wrong, I'm not complaining—that woman can touch me any damn time.

I've also learned that she loves when I talk dirty to her. No joke, it sends her from zero to sixty in two seconds flat. The first time I did it she ended up straddling me, shoving that delicate little hand of hers down the front of my pants. The second time, she let out a noise so fucking erotic, I had her flat on her back with her shirt and bra bunched up around her neck before she could even register what had happened. Both times I had to diffuse the situation before it went too far.

Honestly, I'm not sure how much more I can take though. I don't want to stop her, and I know that one of these days I won't be able to. There is a passion between the two of us that is unexplainable. It's something I never felt with Brit—hell, with anyone—and I know that if we aren't able to act on it soon, one of us is going to combust.

I've always enjoyed work and have never been bothered by back-to-back shifts...until Harley and Max. Now I hate working the long hours and spend the entire time thinking about them and wondering what they are doing. We text and talk, and she and Max send me a few goofy selfies, but it's not the same. I want to be with them.

Today is my day off and waiting for Harley to finish her shift has been hell. I watched a baseball game I had recorded, thought about Harley, did laundry, thought about Harley, went for a run, thought about Max...and Harley.

I finally got fed up and drove to the sporting goods store. If I couldn't stop thinking about them, then I was going to do something for them. I remembered Max telling me that he was going to ask for a soccer goal—one of those little portable ones—for Christmas. Well, he won't need to ask for it. Not only did I buy two goals, but I also got him shin guards and a new ball. I would have gotten him a new pair of cleats, but I didn't know what size he wore.

The two goals are lined up in their front yard and I'm sitting on the porch, tossing the ball around, when they pull into the driveway. Max jumps out of the car, running over to one of the goals at full speed. "Wow," he says, rubbing his little hand along the orange pole. His sparkling eyes find me and a wide grin splits his face.

He looks at the goal and then at his mom, at the goal again, and then finally at me. His voice is innocent and full of wonder as he walks toward me, asking, "Is this for me?"

"It is," I confirm, squatting down to his level. "So is this," I hand him the new ball, "and these." When I hand him the shin guards, he looks at his overflowing arms and then back at me. His smile is beaming and spontaneous laughter bursts from his mouth. The look of pure joy and amazement about drops me to my knees. I've known Max for less than a week and already there isn't a thing I wouldn't do for him.

Dropping the equipment out of his hands, Max propels his little body at mine with so much force that he knocks me off-balance, causing both of us to tumble backward. His arms latch around my neck as little fits of squeals and giggles fly out of his mouth.

"Thank you, thank you, thank you. This is so cool. You're the best. I love it! I'm gonna play with it all the time, like all the time." He takes a deep breath, pulling back to look at me. "Can I play with it now? Will you play with me?" he asks, bouncing from one foot to the other.

I pick up his equipment and hand it to him. "Absolutely. Go get your shin guards and cleats on."

"Yes!" he shouts, bouncing into the house. Straightening, I turn to Harley, and all of my excitement dissipates at the look on her face. Her eyes are misty and a trembling hand covers her mouth.

Two strides and I'm in front of her. "What's wr—oomph."

This family must have a thing with throwing themselves at people. Before I can find out what's wrong, she slams her mouth against mine.

MAX, HARLEY, AND I spent the next two hours playing three-man soccer, and ended the night eating pizza and watching *How To Train Your Dragon*.

"Mmmm...I missed you." Harley nuzzles my neck, peppering kisses along the outside of my jaw, and my cock stirs.

Max's head is leaning awkwardly against my arm, and if the small, wet spot forming on the sleeve of my shirt is any indication, I'm fairly certain he fell asleep. I can't really move, but I have no desire to anyway. I like it here, wedged between a snoring four-year-old and a beautiful woman that can't seem to keep her hands off of me.

"I missed you too," I say, shifting my arm carefully, trying to lower Max's head to the couch without waking him up.

"Here," Harley says, standing up and reaching down to pick Max up off the couch. "Poor little guy wore himself out. I'm going to put him in bed." She walks off down the hall, a limp Max hanging from her arms, and I can't help but smile. It's a beautiful sight and it kills me that someone was actually stupid enough to walk away from the two of them.

"You look really tense," she says softly, making herself comfortable on my lap. I grip her hips tightly and lean forward to sweep my lips against hers, which are always so damn soft. "I think I can help relieve some of that tension." Her voice is low and seductive, and I want nothing more than to let her relieve my tension...but I can't. For some reason, I can't get that stupid fucker out of my head.

The words spill from my mouth before I even have a chance to second-guess myself. "Who is Max's father?"

Her body stiffens against mine and she leans back, releasing her grip from my hair. I know I'm making her uncomfortable, but I have to know. I *need* to know what happened…why he left. Harley stares at me, blinking absently several times. Her vibrant green eyes have grown cold and distant, and I hate that I put that look on her face. Reaching up, I thread my fingers through her hair, hoping to salvage the moment.

"Please don't pull away from me," I sigh. "I can see that this is hard for you, but I *need* to know." I rest my forehead against hers, willing her to come back to me, but I can tell it's already too late. She pulls backs, dislodging herself from my embrace, and stalks off toward the kitchen. I follow behind her quietly and watch as she grabs two water bottles out of the refrigerator. She doesn't say a word, just continues past the stove and out the sliding glass doors into the backyard.

She hands me a bottle, but I shake my head. I don't want something to drink. I want her to talk, that's what I want. She shrugs her shoulders, twists off the cap, and takes two long swigs. Her eyes are trained on something in the distance, but I can tell by the far-off look on her face that she isn't really looking at anything…she's thinking. *What the hell is there to think about?*

She bites the inside of her cheek and blinks several times, obviously trying to keep from crying. When she finally speaks, her voice is laced with contempt. "I don't know who Max's father is," she says, avoiding eye contact.

Wait. What? "I don't understand."

"It's not difficult, Tyson," she snaps, throwing her hands up at her sides. When she sees the questioning look on my face, she closes her eyes and drops her chin. "Just think about it for a second," she murmurs.

It's a simple question. *How in the hell could you not know who the father of your child is?*

"Did you have a one-night stand?" I ask, confused.

She scrunches her eyebrows and glares at me. "No, I didn't have a one-night stand."

My eyes stay locked on hers, but for the life of me I can't come up with any other reason. Again, how do you not know? "You're gonna have to spell it out for me, Harley. I don't—"

"I was raped, Tyson," she yells. Her words slam into me like a freight train and my heart starts pounding against my ribcage. No...*NO!*

This isn't happening.

Please God, please tell me that didn't happen.

I rush over to her, fighting back the lump forming in my throat. I grip her arms firmly, jerking her to me. "Who, Harley?" I demand. "Who was it?" The roaring in my ears is pounding in sync with my heart. I clench my jaw as my mind focuses on nothing other than destroying the motherfucker that hurt *MY* girl! I know I need to calm down, but she needs to tell me who did this. *I'll fucking kill him.*

What kind of sick fuck—?

"I said I don't know." Her shrill voice rings loud, and through my rage I finally register her ashen face and trembling body.

Closing my eyes, I take a deep breath, trying to calm the anger that's boiling inside. I slide my hands up her arms, cradle her face, and gently pull her to me. My thumbs tip her face toward mine, and when our eyes collide, all I see is...fear.

No. No, no, no. "Harley," I soften my voice, pushing my anger aside. Her eyes drop. "Look at me, please," I say, nudging her chin softly. She raises her face, meeting my gaze. She blinks rapidly several times and lifts her hands to grip my wrists.

FUCK!

I fucking scared her.

My hands slide to her shoulders, down her arms, and then I turn her hands over, linking them with mine. I lower my forehead so we're nose to nose.

"I would never—*never*—hurt you." My words are pointed yet soothing, and a gush of air rushes out of her lungs.

Her chest heaves several times and she squeezes my hands. "I know," she whimpers. "I know you wouldn't. I'm sorry, I didn't mean to—"

The guilt and pain in her voice is my undoing. "No. You have nothing to be sorry about. Just please don't ever fear me," I beg, bending down so that we're eye level. "I will *never* hurt you." She nods once and I lean in, stroking my lips over hers.

"I know this is hard for you…" I pause, my eyes glancing around the yard, trying to find my words. Guilt burrows deep in my gut and my stomach rolls. I know it isn't fair to ask her about that night, but I have to know. "I still have questions," I say softly. "Is that okay?" I raise my eyebrows questioningly and she nods once.

Her strength amazes me.

"You don't know who did this?" I ask again, this time keeping my rage in check. She shakes her head slowly and tries to look away, but I don't let her. *Why won't she look me in the eye? She's told me no three times and each time she looked away.*

Chapter 16

Harley

I'M NOT SURE WHAT the fuck just happened, but when he jerked me toward him, I could *see*—no, I could *feel*—the anger rolling off of him. In that moment, when those same chocolate brown eyes met mine, all I saw was Dallas. Fortunately, his gentle touch quickly brought me back to reality.

I hate doing this. I hate lying to Tyson. This is no way to start a relationship—I *know* that—but I can't tell him. I won't do that to him, I just won't. The look in his eyes is already heartbreaking enough. He's hurting for me and I can't stand to see him like this. I know he would blame himself if I told him, and that's the last thing I want.

"Harley," he whispers, leaning in close. I can see the tears pushing at the confines of his eyes, begging to be let free, but he's doing it…he's holding them back. "Baby, you didn't see who attacked you?" He's pleading with me, his eyes desperately searching mine, wanting me to change my mind. I shake my head. "Are you sure?"

I squeeze his hands, holding on for dear life and hoping that he doesn't see right through me. "I didn't see his face," I lie. "It was dark out and he came at me from behind."

I'm going straight to hell.
Please. Please forgive me for lying.
I have to protect him and this is the only way.

"Please say something," I beg, tugging him forward. He disentangles our fingers and runs a hand through his hair and over his face in exasperation. He walks a few steps away from me to take a deep breath. His chin quivers and he swallows hard. When his eyes reconnect with mine, he loses the battle and a few tears roll down his grief-stricken face.

"I don't know what to say." His voice cracks as he holds his arms out to his side in confusion. "*When? Where? Fuck!*" He grips his hair and turns away from me, facing the horizon. "*Fuck!*" he grunts, low and hard. I want to reach for him and hold him, but I don't.

This is new, it's fresh, and he's going to have to go through all of the emotions like I did. I've had five years to be mad, yell, and get angry. I've battled it, I've lived with it, and I've come to accept it. The past cannot be changed, and no one knows that better than I do. It doesn't mean that the pain, fear, and anger don't consume me, because some days they do. It just means that I've learned to take one day at a time and deal with those days as they arrive.

"Harley," he says desperately, slowly shaking his head, "*when*? When did this happen? Why didn't you call me?"

I inhale deeply and then blow it out slowly. I know that when he finds out I did call him, he's going to flip his lid. But I also know that there's no way to avoid this. Tyson is no dummy…once he finds out Max's birthday, he'd figure it out anyway.

"I did, Tyson. I did call you." The memory of that night—the memory of calling Tyson over and over, just for the calls to go to voicemail—prove to be too much, and I feel the emotion roll in my gut. I close my eyes, remembering my desperate words, begging Tyson to call me. I push back the anger that starts to creep forward and remind myself that it's in the past.

It's. Over.

I've accepted it, I'm stronger because of it, and I'm not going to let it take him away from me.

"What?" he gasps, shaking his head vehemently. "No. No. No!" he barks, shoving his finger into his chest. "If you would have called…if you needed me…I would have been there. I would never abandon you during something like that, Harley!"

Oh, God, this is going to be hard. *Please, God…please don't let this drag me back down. I've worked too hard to get where I am, and right now I need you to give me the strength to get through this.*

I walk over to Ty and link my fingers through his. He doesn't resist, but he doesn't look at me either. "Look at me," I demand, throwing his words from earlier back in his face. I can see the battling emotions swirling deep in his still-averted eyes. He doesn't know whether to be angry or devastated, but he's trying to stay strong—for me.

"If we're going to do this, I need you to look at me." His eyes lock with mine. *Good.* "I need to know that this isn't going to destroy us. I've worked too hard to get where I am, and I'll be damned if I let this come between us. I *will not* lose you over this."

His eyes widen with shock at my pointed words and he pulls me to him. "You're not going to lose me," he confirms resolutely, "but I need answers, Harley. I hate to push you, but—"

"It happened the night you walked away from me." *Crap. Shit. Crap.* I didn't mean for it to come out like that, and I instantly regret my words when utter devastation consumes his beautiful face. "I'm sorry," I say, reaching out for his other hand. "I didn't mean to say it that way." I pray that he believes me…the last thing I want to do is hurt him.

His nostrils flare and his chin quivers, but he's fighting—he's fighting like hell to hold himself together. I can see the questions flashing across his face, but it's obvious he can't bring himself to ask any of them. That's okay…it's my turn to be strong.

"I should have followed you inside, but I didn't. That's my

fault, Ty, not yours." His eyes stay locked on mine, his thumbs rubbing soothing circles across my knuckles. I'm unsure if he's soothing himself or me, but at this point I don't care.

"I stayed out back at the picnic table...and—" I shake my head jerkily as the memories flood my mind. "It just happened so fast that, in the beginning, I don't even think I registered what was happening. I kept praying that someone would come back out—"

Ty yanks away from me, bending at the waist, a deep sob ripping from his throat. His shoulders heave roughly several times before he puts a hand over his eyes and begins to pace, moving further away from me. I cover my mouth with both hands. *I can't handle this.* I've never seen Tyson cry, and watching him fall apart is like a knife to the fucking chest. I don't ever want to see him hurt like this again, but I *need* to finish and he needs to hear it.

"When it was over," my chest heaves in and out several times, "when it was over, I just laid in the alley, sobbing, and in total shock. I don't think I could have moved if I wanted to. I'm not sure long I laid there, but Levi found me. He took me to the hospital to get cleaned up." I squeeze my eyes shut, remembering how scared I was when I refused a rape kit, but he doesn't need to know that. "When I got home, the first thing I did was call you, and when you didn't answer Levi tried calling you."

"FUCK!" Tyson growls, folding into himself. "*FUCK!*"

The anger and self-loathing rolls off of him in waves, but I sit back on the shore, watching—waiting—to see what he'll do. My body aches to move toward him and my hands ache to soothe his pain, but I'm frozen. I'm stuck in my own hell, where the memories of my past are battling my future—and there isn't a damn thing I can do to stop it.

Suddenly, Tyson stands, smoothing his hands down the front of his pants. He takes a few deep breaths and clears his throat. When he walks over to me, he doesn't reach for me. No, he stands in front of me, his eyes bouncing around my face for several seconds before his words come out, rough and raw.

"What do you need from me?" he asks. "Tell me what you

need and that's what I'll do. You need me to find out who it was and kill him? Done." I grimace. "You need me to get on my knees and beg you to forgive me? Because I'm already certain that's going to happen. But I need to know," he sucks in air, "because I don't want to make this harder for you."

My future just kicked the ass of my past!

I take a sure, steady step toward Tyson, his words still fresh in my head. *Tell me what you need and that's what I'll do.* Everything from our chests down to our thighs is touching, but it's not enough. I need more—I'll always need more.

I waste no time throwing my arms over his shoulders, pulling him closer to me. Tyson doesn't miss a beat. His strong arms wrap around my back as he gathers me against his body. His beautiful face is buried in my neck, and when I feel his tears gather there, I squeeze him tighter.

"This is what I need, Ty. *I need you.* I've always needed you." My words are nothing but a jumbled mess mumbled against his shoulder, but I know he hears them. A deep sob roars from his mouth. He lifts me and when my feet leave the ground, I wrap my legs around his waist.

We stand there for several minutes, both of us crying. "I'm so sorry. I'm so fucking sorry. Please, please forgive me. If I could rewind time, I—"

Doesn't he know that I would never undo what happened? Because despite the crippling fear and unimaginable anger, the attack resulted in the one person who I truly could not live without—Max.

I pull back, gripping his cheeks in my hands. I wipe away his tears and give him a watery smile. "No," I whisper, shaking my head. "I wouldn't want you to rewind time because that night, as horrible as it was…that was the best night of my life." His head rears back, his face scrunched in confusion. He's giving me that are-you-smoking-crack look and I chuckle, losing a few more tears in the process.

"What happened to me that night," I say, pausing to wipe my

face, "was hands-down the worst thing I've ever been through. But that night gave me Max." He drops his forehead to mine and I hope that's a sign he understands. "So you see, I don't want to rewind time. Max is my silver lining…he is what got me through this. That little guy is the best thing to ever happen to me, and I'd go through what I went through a million more times if it meant that in the end I was going to get Max."

Tyson captures my mouth with his, but this kiss is nothing like any kiss we've shared before. This kiss is wrapped in acceptance, forgiveness, and *hope.*

"You are the strongest, most amazing woman I've ever met," he mumbles against my lips.

"You forgot kind, beautiful, spectacular…" His mouth tilts over mine in another kiss, this one so powerful that my entire body trembles. When he finally pulls away, I'm left heaving and breathless. He rubs his nose against mine before kissing it softly.

His sweet breath fans my face when he talks. "I'm fairly certain the world hasn't yet discovered the word that best fits everything that you are, Harley." I smile against his mouth, kissing him again and again. I love that I can do that whenever the hell I want.

"You're perfect." His words are soft, firm, and they're the sweetest words I've ever heard. "I love you, Harley, *so much.*" All of my thoughts come to a complete halt… *What? He…what?*

Is it impolite to beg—demand—he say it again?

Chapter 17

Harley

"OH. MY. GOD," QUINN moans, licking the ice cream off her spoon like it's a damn lollipop. Two teenage boys are sitting in the booth next to us and when I see one of them reach under the table, I decide I've had enough.

"Ouch! Damnit, Harley, that hurt," she scolds, bending down to rub her leg.

"Quinn, you just moaned 'Oh my God' with your head thrown back as you sucked on a spoon...in public." She stares at me, her face saying, *'And your point is?'*

I shake my head, returning to my lunch. "Never mind."

She shrugs her shoulders and pops her spoon back in her mouth, completely oblivious. "So...spill it."

"Uh, spill what?" I ask, feigning ignorance.

"Oh, come on." She rolls her eyes. "It's been three weeks. I know you've done the deed and I want details," she says, singing the last word. "That hunk of a man of yours is fucking hot," she says, fanning herself with her napkin. "Like H-O-T, hot! His body is rockin' and please, *please* tell me he knows how to use it."

Well, shit. This is awkward. But I don't have any details to give. I want details...I really, really want lots and lots of details. But damnit, Max's vagina-blocking abilities seem to be getting stronger.

Quinn watches me, understanding flashing across her face. "Wait!" she says, putting her chocolate sundae down. How the hell she gets by with eating ice cream for lunch and still manages to look like she does, I'll never know.

"You haven't slept with him." I don't answer because it's not a question. She chuckles humorlessly and leans forward. "Why the hell haven't you slept with him?" Her face is serious. Quinn is actually concerned about my sex life.

I shrug my shoulder and pop a bite in my mouth. "I don't know. It just hasn't happened," I mumble.

She leans back, crossing her arms over her chest. Quinn can read people better than anyone I know and she can smell a lie from a mile away, which is how I know that I haven't gotten away with my little fib.

"Fine," I say, throwing a chunk of my bread at her face. She bats it away playfully before it can smack her in the head. "It's hard to get to that point when Max is around. When he's awake, we're always waiting for him to walk away so we can steal a kiss, and when he's asleep, we only make it so far before something happens to stop us."

"Interesting." She keeps lapping at her sundae before waving her spoon in a gesture that clearly indicates I should continue.

I sigh, pushing my half-eaten lunch to the side. "Okay. For example, the other night, Ty was watching TV so I decided to jump in the shower after I put Max to bed. Well, Tyson slipped into the bathroom, climbed into the shower with me and we started making out. His hands were everywhere and it felt so good," I say, rolling my head back. "At least it did until Max started banging on the door, which thankfully Ty had locked on his way in. So there I was standing in the shower with Tyson's hand between my legs, two seconds away from—" I lean down and whisper, "—the best orgasm ever." I sit up and Quinn laughs. "The poor guy hadn't even been touched and there was Max, bangin' on the door."

Thank God, this time Ty didn't freak. Nope, we've been interrupted so many times that he was cool as a cucumber. I, on the other hand, was not. Tyson merely laughed, dried himself off, and pulled his pants on, while I squeezed past the bathroom door in my robe and stuttered my way through a quick conversation with Max.

"So what happened?"

"Max had to pee, and then he wanted a drink of water. By the time I got him back in bed and took a shower, our flame had officially been doused."

Quinn clicked her tongue several times. "You guys need some alone time."

"Um…HELLO! You don't think I know that?" Tyson's birthday is in five days and I would love to get some alone time with him. Unfortunately, mom and dad already have plans that night, so I was kind of hoping I could rope either Quinn or Levi into watching Max for me.

"Harley," Quinn purses her lips. "Why didn't you just ask? You know I'm always more than happy to help out with Max." *Christ, I love this girl.*

"Thank you, Quinn." Reaching across the table, I give her hand a firm squeeze. "It's hard sometimes for me to ask for help, especially from you and Levi. You're both still single and have your own lives."

When my head drops, she snaps her fingers in front of my face, and I look at up her. She's smiling, her eyes dancing with amusement. *Well, I'm glad she finds this amusing.*

"Harley, you and Max are part of my life—end of story. It doesn't matter if I'm single or attached. Someday, if I find someone—"

"Wait. What happened to that mystery guy you were telling me about?" I can't believe I forgot to probe her about that.

She waves her hand dismissively. "Nothing. It didn't go anywhere."

Seriously? That's it? She's going to have to give me more than that. "Who was it?" I ask, leaning into the table.

Her eyes study me for a beat, and then she looks down and shoves a bite of ice cream into her mouth. "It was Mason," she mumbles, swallowing hard.

My eyes widen and I scoot forward in my seat. "*What?* You and Mason?" Honest to God, I had no idea they even had a thing for each other. "How long were you guys..." I trail off and her eyes snap to mine.

"Not long. Really, it was nothing," she says, her voice flat. Her eyes bounce around the room and when they land back on me, I notice the spark that's normally there is gone.

My heart squeezes inside my chest. Quinn may come off rough and tough but deep down she's a sensitive—soul, she just doesn't express it that well. "Quinn, if it was Mason, then it wasn't nothing. Mason doesn't do *nothing*."

She nods slowly, but doesn't say a word. I can tell by her rapid blinking and the shoveling of ice cream into her mouth, that she's trying to keep from showing any emotion. "Quinny." Reaching across the table, I try to grip her hand, but she pulls away before I have the chance.

"I really don't want to talk about this, okay?" Her chin quivers and I relent, not wanting to push her too far.

"Okay," I nod. She takes a deep breath, blows it out slowly, and just as quickly as she disappeared, happy Quinn resurfaces.

"Okay. So like I was saying before you so rudely interrupted me," she shoots me a wink, "someday, if I find someone—"

"*When*," I interject, and she rolls her eyes in response.

"*If* I find someone, they'll have to be okay with the fact that you and Max are a package deal." A lump forms in my throat. Hands down, I couldn't ask for a better girlfriend than Quinn.

"So, when do you want me to watch him?"

Clearing my throat, I ask, "Can you keep him this Friday? It's Ty's birthday and I was hoping—"

"Done!" she declares, beaming at me. "Want me to keep him

for a few hours, or do I get to keep the handsome little devil for the night?"

"Um...for the night?"

Quinn straightens her back. "Harley," she snaps. "No. Just no. You need to give me more conviction and a little less of whatever *that* was."

Oh, Quinn...always trying to make me stronger. Little does she know that she is this rare breed of woman who all other women strive to be. But I'll humor her, just this time. Straightening my back, I pin her with a firm gaze. "You'll keep him for the night. Pick him up at three so I have time to plan something, and don't bring him back the next day until I call and tell you to."

She bursts out laughing, laying her hand across her chest. "I am so proud. My little girl is all grown up," she says with an exaggerated sniff.

"You're so weird, Quinn." I pick up my tray, wrap my purse over my shoulder, and slide out of the booth.

"Weird...but awesome," Quinn replies, following behind me. "So, what are you going to get that sexy man of yours for his birthday?"

Well, shit. I hadn't thought about that. Don't get me wrong, I knew I was going to give him...well...me, but I probably need to give him something else too.

"Not sure yet. I'll come up with something though." Quinn nods in agreement.

Three hours later, my phone beeps just as we are sliding into Quinn's car. I unlock the screen and smile at what greets me. I shove my phone in Quinn's face and she rips it out of my hand.

"Holy shit, he's hot!" I yank the phone back and smile. Yes, he is quite hot.

"Quinn, did you even see the picture?" I ask, looking at the picture Ty sent of him and Max. Tyson is smiling his million-dollar smile and Max has his cheek squished against Ty's, making a silly face. My heart melts—literally melts.

"I saw it," she replies. "Max is cute and Ty is freaking gorgeous. Was it weird leaving Max with him this morning?" she asks, glancing at me and then back at the road.

Quinn and I haven't spent any time together since Tyson and I reconnected. So when she called and wanted to spend the afternoon shopping, I wasn't about to tell her no. Ty was more than happy to spend a few hours alone with Max, and by the look of it, they're having a great time.

"Honey! We're home!" Quinn yells, stepping into my house.

Max comes barreling around the corner and throws himself at Quinn. "We made you guys dinner!" he chirps excitedly.

"Max!" Ty laughs. "It was *supposed* to be a surprise!"

"SORRY!" he yells back.

Tyson walks into the living room, a dishrag hanging over his left shoulder. He looks at Max and then at me, and smiles. My heart flutters at the adoration displayed on his face. It takes every ounce of willpower I have—plus some—to keep from throwing myself at him.

We decided right off the bat that we weren't going to be affectionate in front of Max. We also didn't want to try and explain anything to him until we were certain that this was going in the right direction. But if the daily sight of my son wrapped up and giggling in Ty's big, strong arms isn't a sign of good things to come, then I don't know what is.

"Come on, Ty!" Max hollers. "Let's finish dinner." Tyson scoops up Max, tossing him over his shoulder, and Max lifts his head, waving at Quinn and me. A snort slips from his nose when Tyson tickles his side.

Quinn and I watch the two of them walk into the kitchen and she nudges me with her elbow. "Please tell me that turns you on," she says, still staring in the direction they just walked. I know exactly what she's talking about. Watching Tyson and Max interact and get to know one another has been the most awesome experience. He is so good with Max, and it's clear that Max already owns a little piece of his heart. Watching Tyson with Max is, in fact, a huge turn on—for me, anyway.

"It does," I exhale. "It so does."

"What does Max think?" she asks, turning toward me.

We should tell him. He's too perceptive not to pick up on it, but it's such a big step, and up until about five seconds ago, I wasn't sure I was ready.

"We haven't told him."

Quinn's eyes widen. "Why the hell not?"

"I want to…" I say, not answering her question. My eyes dart into the kitchen. Max is standing on a step stool in front of the sink, washing vegetables, and Tyson is next to him, encouraging and praising him for doing a good job. My heart squeezes at the sight of them together and something snaps.

"I'm going to," I confirm, stepping away from Quinn. I make my way to the kitchen and Quinn follows behind. *I'm such an idiot.* Tyson has become such a huge part of my life—not to mention, Max's—and I've been keeping him at arm's length, denying to everyone except the two of us what he means to me. Well, not anymore. If he wants in, he's in.

"What's going on in here…" I ask suspiciously. Tyson throws a wink over his shoulder and ruffles Max's hair.

"Max here is—" His words cut off when I press against his back, my hands resting at his sides. Panic flashes across his face as I slide my arms around his middle, flattening my palms against his stomach. I smile at him reassuringly and his face lights up with understanding. With his right hand still firmly planted against Max's back, all other sensations fly out the window when I feel his rough hand slide along my forearm. When his hand reaches mine, he stops, gripping it gently.

Thank you, he mouths, his neck cocked back and to the side so that he can see my face. My eyes burn with happiness and I drop my chin to his shoulder. *You're welcome,* I mouth back.

This *is* right.

It's *so* right.

I can feel it in my bones. Deeper than that, I can feel it in my *soul.*

"What?" Max demands, looking at Tyson. "You said 'Max here is' and then you stopped. You can't do that." His brows are dipped low in frustration as he watches Ty.

Reaching up, Tyson ruffles his hair again. "Max here is washing the vegetables so he can make a..." he trails off, encouraging Max to finish his sentence.

"A salad!" Max answers proudly, beaming his white smile up at me. "I'm making you and Quinn a salad. DO YOU LIKE SALAD, QUINN?" he bellows over his shoulder, obviously assuming that Quinn is in the other room.

"I LOVE SALAD," she yells, right behind Max. He startles, his body jerking, and a fit of laughter spews from his mouth.

"You scared me!" he says in between giggles. She sidles up next to him and starts to help him wash the vegetables, giving Tyson and me a moment to relish the huge step we just took.

Turning in my arms, Ty laces his fingers through mine and wraps our joined hands around my back, pulling me flush against his chest.

"Hi." His smile is infectious and I'm so grateful I was finally able to pull my head out of my ass.

"Hi yourself," I whisper back. Tyson leans forward, placing a gentle kiss on the end of my nose.

"EWWWW!" Max snickers, looking from us to Quinn. "He kissed her nose!" Then he turns back to Ty, pointing his little finger. "You kissed her nose!"

"Oh my gosh!" Tyson reaches up, dramatically wiping his arm across his mouth. "Does your mom have cooties?"

Max throws his head back and snorts with laughter. "*You* have cooties." We all start laughing at Max's antics and Tyson turns a serious face to me.

"Did you give me cooties?" he asks accusingly.

"Who me?" I hold my hands up, feigning innocence. "Never. Besides...you have to kiss someone's lips to give them cooties. Like this!" Grabbing Max's face, I slap a kiss against his mouth.

"Ewwww!" Max squeals, jumping off the stool. He wipes furiously at his mouth as Tyson, Quinn, and I watch with amusement at the simplicity of the moment.

What I wouldn't give to go back in time and have nothing to worry about except whether or not someone gave me cooties.

"Alright! Enough cootie passing. Max and I have a dinner to make."

I don't put up a fight when Ty puts a glass of wine in my hand and pushes me into the living room, along with Quinn. When I'm settled on the couch and Quinn is flipping through channels, Tyson comes barreling back in. Leaning over me, he pins me against the couch, his hands on either side of my head. Tenderness and passion are warring for a spot on his face as his eyes bore into mine. He drops his mouth, capturing mine, and gives me a sweet kiss.

"Thank you," he murmurs against my mouth. "Thank you for doing that."

"You're welcome," I respond with not an ounce of regret. His lips trail over to my ear and his tongue darts out, sucking my lobe into his mouth. When he bites down, every nerve ending in my body tingles, shooting warmth and pleasure straight to my core.

"I love you," he whispers, kissing my cheek before he walks back into the kitchen.

This man owns me.

Chapter 18

Tyson

I NEED TO SEE one last patient and then get out of here...this has been the day from hell.

"Hey!" Avery walks up, shrugging on her lab coat.

It's horrible, I know it is, but I don't even want to talk to her—or anyone, for that matter. I'm exhausted and crabby, and I'd give just about anything to go home and pass out for a day... or two.

"Hey," I respond, rubbing my hands over my face, a last-ditch effort to keep myself awake.

"Wow. Rough day, huh?" she asks, handing me a cup of coffee. I shake my head, refusing to drink anything that will keep me awake.

'Rough day' doesn't even begin to describe it. "You have no idea."

"Go home," she says, patting my back. "I've got this one." She reaches out, grabbing the notes I'd jotted down on a piece of paper.

Yes! "Are you sure?" I look down at my watch. "Your shift doesn't even start for another twenty minutes."

"It's fine," she says, waving me off. "Consider it your birthday present. How old are you again?" she snickers. "I swear I heard you're pushing thirty."

Ever since they shared tears in the bathroom at Blue, Avery and Harley have become fast friends. "You guys talk way too much."

"You going over there tonight?" she asks nonchalantly, logging into her computer.

Just thinking about seeing Harley and Max makes me smile. "Do you even have to ask?"

She shakes her head and laughs. "I'm so happy for you two." Her fingers rest on the keyboard and she smiles, a wistful look passing over her face. "The two of you give me hope that true love is possible." Her eyes find mine when she states, "You make me believe that happily ever after really does exist."

Okay, this is not my forté. I don't talk about 'true love' or 'happily ever after'…with anyone. Well, with anyone other than Harley. What the hell am I supposed to say? Do I console her and tell her that she'll find that special someone?

Hell. No. I'm not going there. That's what girlfriends are for.

"Jesus Christ. Just leave," she says, pushing me out the door. "Forget I said anything."

"Oh, thank God," I mumble, eliciting an eye roll and shove from Avery.

I walk briskly through the hospital, hoping to avoid anyone who may try and stop me. The elevator dings and I step into the parking garage.

If it's nice out, I usually walk to work since it's so close. I'm thankful I was called in early and decided to drive, because I would hate to walk home after the day I've had.

My phone rings as I'm starting up the car, and when I slide it out of my pocket and see Harley's beautiful face light up my screen, my entire body comes to life.

"Hey, beautiful."

"Happy birthday!" she says excitedly. "I've been waiting all day to tell you that, but you never called. I'm guessing you had a rough day?"

I drop my head back on the seat and moan. "You have *no* idea. Sorry I didn't get a chance to call you. I barely got a lunch."

"No worries," she replies casually. "If anyone can understand what a horrible day in the ER is like, it's me." Harley amazes me around every turn. Just another one of those little things I love about her.

"What's Max doing?" I ask, yawning on the last word.

"He, uh…he, um…he's outside. He's outside playing." She sounds off—distracted almost.

I can hear pots clanging in the background and then a huge thud. *"Shit!"* she hisses, the phone going static.

"Harley? You okay?"

"Yup! Yup, all good." Her reply is rushed and she sounds out of breath. "What time are you coming over? I was hoping maybe sixish," she grunts. *What the hell is she doing?*

Fuck. I was hoping to get a nap in before I head over there. I look down at my watch—four-thirty. "Can we make it seven?" I ask hopefully.

"Seven?" She sighs, her disappointment evident. "Umm… sure. Okay. Yeah. No problem." I hate that she sounds upset. I know it's my birthday and she wants to celebrate—which, believe me, I'm all for—but I'm fucking exhausted.

"Are you sure?" I question. "Because I can come sooner if—"

"Nope. Don't even worry about it. I'll see you at seven."

I hate the thought of disappointing her. I'll just wait until Max goes to bed and make it up to her then. Just thinking about what I want to do to her turns me on. *Fuck.* I should just stay awake and go over there now. But then I'll probably fall asleep at the same time Max does, and that's just not going to work. "Alright, baby. I'll see you at seven. I love you."

"See you then." She ends the call and my heart constricts. Harley still hasn't said those three little words, and I've wondered several times if I said them too soon. *Who wouldn't?* Her reaction to my declaration of love is always positive—she nuzzles in close and makes the sexiest little purring sounds—but I just wish she would say it back.

I don't want her to tell me she loves me if she doesn't mean it, but I know she feels the same way. I can *see* it in her eyes when they soften at my voice. I can *feel* it in the way her hands cradle my face, and in the way her lips move gently over mine when she needs to be close. I *hear* it every time her heart pounds in her chest when I tell her I love her. I just need *her* to see it, and feel it...and say it.

Patience. I need to have patience. This is part of the process. I asked for the opportunity to make things up to her, and this is part of that. I need to build and gain her trust, proving to her that *this* time, when she hands me her heart, I'm going to cherish it like the special gift that it is.

I punch in the code and the gate to the underground parking garage at my condo rises. Walking through the door, I toss my keys on the counter and throw my lab coat on the couch. Walking down the hall, I tear off my scrub top and then undo the drawstring on my pants, letting them fall in a heap on the floor. I'm not usually one to leave a trail of clothes, but I'll get them later—after I nap.

Sleep, I sigh, falling face-first onto my mattress, wishing that I would've taken the time to strip off my boxers. Reaching over, I slap my hand against the nightstand until it connects with the fan remote. I flick it on low and everything goes black.

HOT. IT'S FUCKING HOT in here. I turn over roughly, kicking the sheet off of me, and sit up, rubbing my heavy eyes. I probably could have slept straight through the night, but I need to get to Harley's. Reaching across the bed, I search for my phone, sitting up abruptly when it's not in its usual place. *Crap. It's in my lab coat*. I slide out of bed and jog into the living room, where I hear my phone alarm going off.

"DAMNIT!" I growl, noticing the time. Eight o'clock. *Fuck*.

I shoot Harley a quick text, letting her know that I overslept and that I'll be there shortly. Peeling off my boxers, I turn on the faucet and step in once the water is warm. I rush through my routine, easily taking the quickest shower I've ever taken, all the while chastising myself for oversleeping.

"Idiot. I'm an idiot," I mumble to myself, reaching for the pair of jeans that I know is Harley's favorite. I yank on a light blue polo, step into my Chucks, and I'm out the door in ten minutes flat.

Merging onto the interstate, I pull out my phone, hoping to see a response from Harley. *Nothing*. I should have gone straight to her house after work. My hands tighten on the steering wheel in frustration while my foot pushes lightly on the gas pedal, needing to get to her faster.

I hit 'talk,' praying that she isn't pissed and hoping like hell that maybe she just didn't see my text because she was busy putting Max to bed. Her phone rings several times and then goes to voicemail. I hang up, immediately hitting 'talk' again. *Nothing*.

"Hey, babe," I say when her voicemail picks up the second time. "I'm so sorry I overslept, but I'm on my way now. I'll be there in about…" I glance at the clock, "…thirty minutes. Do me a favor, will you? If Max is still awake, will you keep him up so I can see him before bed? Okay. Love you. See you soon."

Ending the call, I toss my phone on to the passenger seat and growl in disappointment. The thirty-minute drive feels more like an hour, and when I pull up to her house, I nearly sprint to the front door. A week or so ago she told me that I didn't have to knock before entering, but this situation feels a little different and I'm praying that she doesn't want to take my head off as soon as she sees me. Her house looks dark, but I can see a lamp on through the front window. I knock twice softly, just in case Max is already in bed. Then, I wait…and wait…and nothing. *What the hell?*

Digging my phone out of my pocket, I call hers again. I can hear my ringtone through the front door, but she doesn't answer so I hang up.

"Harley? Baby? I know you're in there," I say, knocking a few more times. "Please open up," I plead, hoping I didn't totally fuck things up. "I'm so sorry I overslept. Please don't be mad." Threading my fingers through my hair, I pace the length of her porch a few more times, trying to decide what the hell I should do. I peek in her window—nothing. The damn curtains are in the way.

My forehead falls to the front of her door in pure self-loathing and exasperation. *What the fuck am I going to—*

The front light porch flickers on and I hear the lock on the door click. The heavy wood creaks open just a bit, and Harley peeks around the corner. She's rubbing her eyes as though I woke her up and her hair is piled on top of her head. As always, she looks sexy as hell. Her hand stills and her eyes widen with something that isn't shock—relief maybe?—before she opens the door wide.

"Tyson," she exhales, looking down at her pink cotton pants. "I, uh, I didn't think you were coming." Forget the pants, Harley's wearing a white tank top that doesn't leave anything to the imagination. When she registers what she's wearing, she tugs self-consciously on her shirt, covering up the sliver of skin that was peeking out above her waistband. My hand itches to reach out and put it back where it was.

She clears her throat and I drag my eyes to hers. She opens the door further in invitation, and I slide past her. "Did you get my text?" I ask, taking her hand in mine. I walk over to the couch and pull her down with me.

She shakes her head, causing a piece of her hair to fall around her face. I tuck it behind her ear, letting my knuckles graze the side of her cheek before I pull away. "No," she says, her body trembling with the contact. "I didn't get it. I think I fell asleep waiting for you."

"I'm so sorry I'm late. My phone alarm was set to wake me

up at six, but I left it in the living room and didn't hear it go off." She rests a hand on my chest, instantly calming my nerves. "I texted you as soon as I woke up and headed straight here."

Pulling her hand to my mouth, I kiss each of her knuckles, thankful that this amazingly kind and wonderful woman is mine.

Mine.

"When you didn't reply, I thought for sure you were pissed at me." Her eyes drop to our hands and she takes a shuddery breath.

"No…" she says, climbing out of my lap, "not mad." My body shivers at the loss of her heat, and I stand to follow her when she walks toward the kitchen. "Would you like a drink?" she asks, not turning to look at me.

"No, I—" Everything comes to a complete halt when I step into the kitchen and take in the scene in front of me. I'm speechless. I don't deserve her. If there is one thing I know, it's that she can do so much fucking better than me. My eyes find hers and she looks away sheepishly. Her hands are twisting around the bottle of water she's holding and she makes a move to step away, but my arm shoots out, stopping her.

"This is for me?" I ask, my voice full of emotion and disbelief. She nods once but still won't look at me.

A lacy white cloth runs the length of the table. There are two plates, right next to each other, both overflowing with heaps of steak, potatoes, and vegetables. There are two wine glasses, one full and one empty, and the sight alone causes a small piece of my heart to crack. Sitting atop two glass stands in the middle of the table are two no-longer-lit pillar candles with wax dripping off the sides. Another fissure in my heart. *I'm not sure how much more the damn thing can take.*

One long stride and I'm cupping Harley's face gently in my hands, tilting it up to mine. "You did all of this…for me?" My voice is full of wonder because no one has ever done anything like this for me before. She nods again and I slam my mouth down on hers, claiming her with a fiery passion I didn't even know I had in me. Blood starts rushing through my ears as my body temperature rises, and only when I'm breathless do I pull away gently, continuing to pepper her swollen lips with kisses.

"I'm so sorry." Kiss. "I don't deserve you." Kiss. "Please forg—"

She pushes her fingers against my mouth and shakes her head. "Don't. I don't want to hear it." My heart plummets straight to my feet and a sharp pain slices through my stomach as though I've been shot. She's done. She gave me another chance and I screwed up.

"Stop," she says, laughing. "Whatever is going through your head right now, just stop." I sigh with relief and she pulls me to her, until there's no room left between us.

She rises on her toes and wraps her arms around my neck, a playful smile pulling at her lips. "I'm not mad, I'm relieved. And maybe a little disappointed," she says, holding her fingers an inch apart, scrunching up her nose.

I kiss her nose and then rub my thumb along the soft spot between her eyebrows, smoothing out her frustration. "Keep going," I whisper, kissing her again.

She sighs, her mouth following mine when I pull away. "I wasn't sure what happened, but I should've known you wouldn't stand me up." I kiss her again because, well, I can't stop, and because I have to. My body aches for her.

"Never. I'll never stand you up." She nods once and then walks to the table, picking up both plates.

"Let me reheat these and we can eat." Her words gut me and guilt rises, thick in my chest. She and Max went out of their way to plan something nice for me, and I repaid them by completely screwing it up.

Following her to the microwave, I grab the plates from her before she can put them down and I set them on the counter. Her curious eyes follow my every move. "I'm not hungry," I inform her. "At least not for food."

Turning around, I stalk back to her, grinning at the shocked look on her face. She takes a step back but ends up against the counter. Using that to my advantage, I cage her in, placing my hands on either side of her. Her eyes widen in surprise, and I guide my lips to the crook of her neck and whisper, "Where's Max?"

Her surprise quickly transforms into desire and her hands reach up, gripping my shirt. "He's gone."

"What do you mean, *gone*?" I ask, snapping my head up. I'm watching her face carefully, but there is no concern there, only lust…for me. As much as that realization causes my heart to race, I need to know that Max is okay. "Is he alright?"

Harley sucks her bottom lip between her teeth and averts her gaze, but that isn't going to work for me. I grip her chin, pulling her face back to mine. "Where is Max?" I repeat, this time more firmly. She's really starting to fucking scare me. If something happened to Max, I need to fucking know…*now*.

"He's with Quinn." I glance at my watch, noticing the time.

"Did they go to a movie or something? Do we need to go pick him up?"

Harley's eyes stay trained on mine and she shakes her head. "Is she going to drop him off?" I ask, wondering how much alone time we might have left. Her eyes flicker with mischief and she grins, shaking her head again. My stomach flutters with anticipation, desire pumping through my veins.

"So we're alone…" I pause and she nods, "…all night?" When she nods again, I take a deep breath, trying to bring myself back down from the nervous high I seem to have ended up on. Harley and I have waited for what seems like forever to be truly alone. Now that the time has come, I'm a complete ball of nerves. I need this to be perfect…for her. I've told her a thousand times how much I love her, and now I'm going to get the chance to show her.

"You're being awfully quiet," I whisper, turning her so that our positions are switched. Leaning against the counter, I widen my stance, pulling her between my legs.

She smiles shyly, a deep flush staining her cheeks, and my cock twitches. Her bright eyes glance down at her trembling hands and she opens her fists, splaying her fingers across my chest. This time when she lifts her face, her gaze is full of anticipation.

Chapter 19

Harley

I'VE DREAMT OF THIS moment for so long that I never considered how I would feel if it ever actually came true. What if he doesn't find me attractive? What if his expectations are too high and I somehow disappoint him? My heart rate speeds up. *This is going to change everything.* How we proceed right now is going to directly affect every single moment between us from here on out. *Oh God.*

"Are you okay?" Tyson asks, his gentle voice breaking through my thoughts.

I take a deep breath. "I...I'm not sure I can do this," I confess. My chest quivers as a sob threatens to rip from my throat. Tears dampen my eyes as fears resurface. "I...

I mean, I can do this. I want to." I glance away as I struggle to form the words.

This should be easier. I want this. I want us—but I'm scared.

"Talk to me," he whispers, linking his hands behind my back. "I need to know what's going on up here," he says, kissing my forehead. "I don't want to push you into doing something you're not ready to do."

"I am ready," I insist, not sure if I'm trying to convince him or myself. "I just don't want to disappoint you."

He flinches and then ducks his head so that we're eye to eye. "Why would you think you would disappoint me, Harley? I'm in love with you." His hands trail up my body, framing my face. "You cannot disappoint me."

"But what if I do? What if I'm not what you expect?" I ask, raising my eyebrows. "What if you don't feel the same way about me when this is over?" I swallow hard, my eyes shifting between his.

"Harley," he says softly, gliding a hand down my cheek. "There is no way you could ever disappoint me." I sigh, closing my eyes. "I need you to trust me," he says. "I need you to trust that I will *never* hurt you."

I lean into him, bringing my forehead to his lips again. "I know you won't. I didn't mean it like that, I just…"

I can't believe I'm doing this. I'm letting my fears and insecurities taint the one thing that I've waited for my entire life. Truth slams into me like a freight train. Butterflies take flight in my stomach as hope blooms. Ty has proven himself to me repeatedly. Not only has he been here for me, but he's also been here for Max, proving to us that he is here to stay.

Beyond that, I love him. I've always loved him. My lungs suck in the air between us, letting all of my worries go when I exhale.

Lifting my face so I can look deep into his eyes, I lock my hands behind his neck. Kissing his chin softly, I bring my nose to his. "I do trust you," I confirm. "I believe in you, and I believe in us." His body sags with relief, but I'm not done. "I love you, Ty."

"You…" Eyes wide and voice full of shock, he stands to his full height. "You love me?" he asks slowly, as if he's afraid that he didn't hear me right.

I chuckle, loving the weight that has been lifted off my shoulders. The look of pure joy on Tyson's face is the only thing I need to know that I made the right choice. "I *love* you, love you." His face sobers upon hearing the same words I said to him five years ago.

His hands, which have been resting on my lower back, trail down to my ass. Lifting me, he twirls around and sets me on the countertop. His body claims the space between my legs and then strong hands slide up my spine, stopping to tangle in my hair. Nose to nose, he whispers, "I *love* you, love you, too." I whimper hearing his words.

My tongue slides across my lips, parting them as Ty's mouth descends on mine. His lips feather across mine and my heavy eyelids drift closed, reveling in the feel of his tongue as it gains entrance into my mouth. Our tongues tangle, sensual and searching, like we're exploring each other again for the very first time. My hands twist through his hair, tugging gently. We kiss until our lips are swollen and numb and we're both fighting for air. Ty pulls his mouth away from mine and our eyes lock.

"Don't stop. Please don't stop," I beg, needing his hot mouth back on mine.

His eyes search mine. I'm not sure what he's looking for, but I hope to God he finds it soon. "You have to tell me what you want, Harley," he says, his voice firm. "I need to hear you say it."

My grip tightens on his hair. "I want *you*." My body is trembling with anticipation, adrenalin pumping through my veins. He leans forward, pressing his body closer to mine so he can trail kisses down my neck. A low growl rips from my throat when he bites down gently, immediately soothing the same spot with his tongue.

"That's a good start," he mumbles, sliding my tank strap down my shoulder so his mouth can continue its torturous path. "But you're going to have to be a little more specific."

His lips are scorching hot and feel fucking fantastic against my skin. I close my eyes, letting my head drop against the cabinet behind me, allowing myself to be absorbed in—

I whimper when a cold draft blows over my bare shoulder... right where his lips should be. He laughs. "Concentrate," he says, bending forward to nip at my bottom lip. "Tell me what you want."

"I want your mouth on me," I pant, and he slams his mouth to mine. Our tongues battle for control while his hands roam my body, sliding up my thighs, over my stomach, and teasing the material at the swell of my breast. He pulls away much too soon and my mouth follows his, begging for more.

"There? Is that where you want my mouth?"

I shake my head. "You're warm."

He cocks an eyebrow, a mischievous grin pulling at his mouth. "Well, warm isn't going to work, now is it?" His tongue darts out, tracing a path of open-mouth kisses across my chest and over my collarbone.

"Warmer...you're getting warmer," I say, my voice low and husky. I should be embarrassed that he's worked me up this fast, but I'm not. His erection is cradled firmly between my legs and he thrusts against me. I want more. I *need* more.

Looking down, I watch him cup my breasts, my nipples puckering until they ache. He yanks the top of my shirt down, freeing my heavy breasts. His mouth descends, attacking and sucking. By the time his mouth moves to the opposite side, I'm writhing against him, a deep warmth settling in my belly.

"More...I need more."

"Patience," he mumbles. I jerk his mouth back to my aching chest and I can feel him smile against me. *He knows I don't have patience.* I grip his erection through his pants and his hips buck against my hand. He is hard and ready for me. I rub him several times, feeling the thick steel grow and stretch behind the tight confines of his jeans. I squeeze my eyes shut, imagining how good he will feel deep inside of me. Popping the top button of his jeans, I slide my hand in between his boxers and soft, warm skin. A low groan vibrates from his chest and I gasp at the feel of him hot and heavy in my hand. I stroke up his length, gripping his girth. The fire burning between my legs inflames with desire.

In the blink of an eye, Ty yanks my hand away, and I find myself being hauled off the counter. I wrap my legs around his waist, my mouth devouring his as he storms down the hall. He kicks open the bedroom door and wastes no time settling me on the bed. Reaching back, he pulls his shirt over his head in that sexy way that men do. My eyes ogle his bare chest, appreciating every line and groove of his toned stomach. Leaning down, he reaches for the hem of my shirt.

"Wait!" I blurt, tugging desperately to cover my marred stomach. "I have stretch marks." My heart rate kicks up. I frantically search his face for any sign that I just completely destroyed the moment. Reaching up, he tenderly strokes a hand down my cheek. His eyes are full of compassion, and there is no trace of disappointment anywhere on his beautiful face.

"So you have stretch marks." Tyson drops to his knees, slowly peeling the flimsy material out of my hand. He lowers his mouth to my belly, and his tongue traces the first mark. My hands fist his hair as my heart flutters from his intimate touch. "Let me love them." He trails kisses along my belly. "They're a remnant of the life you carried inside of you." His fingers graze over each line he'd kissed and he looks up into my glassy eyes. "And I love that little life just as much as I love you."

If I wasn't already head over heels in love with him, I would be now. His words cause my heart to soar higher than I ever thought possible. My body catapults forward, slamming into his. Our mouths fuse together, my lips parting against his, and unlike before, *I'm* the hungry one. I stroke my tongue against his, letting him have all of me, letting him know that I'm his to have. Our kiss is passionate, demanding, and destroys all other kisses before it.

Breathless, he pulls away from me, his eyes burning with desire. With steady hands he lifts my shirt up, pausing briefly to give me the chance to back out. I raise my arms and he yanks the material over my head, dropping it behind me. Chocolate eyes greedily roam my naked chest. My breathing turns to a light pant when he runs a finger down my breast, pinching my nipple. I clench my thighs together, desperately trying to calm the incessant throbbing. Seeing him between my legs, drinking me in, leaves me desperate for him.

"Lie back," he demands, his tone soft. I comply without question. Ironically, I find this demanding side of Tyson to be a huge fucking turn-on. "On your elbows." I prop myself up at his authoritative tone. Watching him undress me throws my body into a frenzy, my excitement and anticipation growing so thick that my clit starts pounding. Sitting back on his haunches, he examines me, his eyes blazing as he seemingly memorizes every line and curve of my body. I'm now lying before him naked, vulnerable and unashamed.

"I'm going to take my time with you," he whispers, his breath warm on my skin as he lowers himself between my legs. I squeeze my eyes shut, a harsh moan falling from my lips when I feel his tongue slide across my apex, mere inches from my core. His hands spread my lips apart and I wait for him to devour me.

"Watch. Me," he growls and my eyes snap open. With a devilish grin on his face, he lowers his lips to my clit. The pad of his tongue slides down my core. My toes curl and my heels dig into the bed. With each lick and every suck, my moans grow louder.

Ty's shoulders press against my thighs, spreading my legs further apart. Goosebumps run up my body when he slides a thick finger deep inside of me, thrusting slowly several times before adding a second. My eyes roll to the back of my head as he continues to bring me closer and closer to the proverbial edge. He alternates between his tongue and hands, tasting and teasing, sucking and stroking. My legs begin to tremble, my skin igniting with intense heat. I'm trying desperately to keep my eyes trained on him, but I can't—the pleasure is just too intense. His name falls from my mouth in a strangled cry as waves of pleasure crash through me. My body jerks, convulsing forcefully against his face and hand. I beg and plead for him stop, but he doesn't.

Instead, his tongue works faster against my tender clit. My gyrating hips, gripping hands, and hoarse pleas…he's immune to it all, determined to bring me back to the crest once again. He moans erotically several times, the vibrations bringing to the table a new sensation, and the feeling alone is enough to push me over the edge once more. I writhe against his mouth, my hips bucking and my hands fisted in the sheets, as my second orgasm plows through my body.

"Oh, God!" Squeezing my eyes shut, I throw my head back against the mattress as Tyson works my body to its breaking point. He continues to suck and nip my sex as the pulsating slows and my body floats leisurely back down to earth.

A cool draft flows through the open window, caressing my damp and still sensitive skin, and I peel my eyes open. Pushing up on my elbows once again, I watch Tyson work the zipper of his jeans. His eyes find mine as he pushes his jeans and boxers down his long legs in one smooth motion, and I suck in a breath as his thick cock springs free.

My heart pounds in my chest. His erection bobs when he leans down to grab a condom out of his pocket and my mouth waters. I've never found the act of giving a blowjob appealing, but for some reason—with Tyson—I want to do it. I want to bring him to the brink with my mouth like he did for me. I want to taste him on my tongue, and I want to feel him lose control as his body submits to me.

I kick off the bed and drop to the floor in front of him as he stands to his full height. My hands slide up his legs, feeling his warm skin against mine. I stroke him once, twice, and a pool of pre-cum forms at his tip. I twirl my tongue around the thick head before I take him deep into my mouth, surrounding him as far as my throat will allow.

"Fuck!" he gasps, gripping the side of my face. I slide my tongue along the underside of his shaft and suck hard, causing him to buck against my mouth. My sex is still throbbing from having his mouth on me, and when he lets out a deep growl, I slide my hand down my stomach and over my clit, trying to calm the impending storm.

"Harley." His voice is rigid. Under hooded eyes, I glance up at him, shifting my body back enough so that he can see what I'm doing.

"Fuck. Stop…Harley…stop." Tyson yanks back and I release him with a wet pop.

"What? What's wrong?" I pant, hoping like hell I didn't somehow screw that up. I know I haven't given many blowjobs, but seriously, how hard can it be?

"Sweetheart, I have a massive amount of self-control, but the sight of you rubbing yourself while sucking me off is too much for any man to handle." He reaches down for my arms, lifting me onto the bed, and then pushes me back as he crawls up my body. "Don't get me wrong," he says, trailing kisses along the length of my neck. "One day soon I'm going to fuck that sweet little mouth of yours, but I've waited too damn long to make you mine. Tonight, I want to be buried deep inside your hot little pussy when I come."

His words cause a tremble to course through my body and I wrap my hand around his neck, slamming his mouth on mine. His tongue plunges deep and I run my free hand down his back, digging my nails into the globe of his ass. He thrusts against me once, his long cock sliding against my crevice.

"Ty," I breathe against his mouth. "I…I…" *Why the fuck can't I talk?*

"Harley?"

My eyes find his, and my heart swells with anticipation and pure desire. "I'm clean."

"Me too," he says, swallowing hard, looking down at the condom. "The hospital tested me when I started."

"I'm on the pill," I offer hopefully. "And I haven't been with anyone since I was last tested." He looks shocked and then his surprised gaze morphs into a stunning smile as he drops the condom on the bed. "I don't want anything between us," I whisper, reveling in the feel of his heavy body pressing down on mine.

"Never. There will never be anything between us." His words are like an arrow straight through my heart and my blood heats, settling in my core. *I need him. Now.*

With a surprisingly steady hand, I grip him gently, guiding

him to my entrance. Ty's hand slides over mine, taking control of our movements. My body arches, seeking his touch, but instead of sliding into me, he rubs himself slowly against my swollen clit.

"Ty...please...I need you in me," I beg.

He drags himself to my opening and I shiver, my breath hitching in my throat. With slow movements, he enters me—inch by delicious inch—and my entire world comes to a complete stop.

This is heaven.

Right here in this moment, my life is perfect. There are no regrets and no guilt, only happiness. And based on the bright-eyed look Ty is giving me, I'm certain he is feeling the same way. My heart freezes and then pounds furiously as blood rushes to my ears.

I groan, writhing underneath of him. He moves, slowly at first, letting me adjust to his size and girth. Our mouths meet in a frenzy, tasting and teasing. With one hand cradling my neck, he slides the other down my body, stopping to grip my hip. His sensual touch sparks fireworks low in my belly. He squeezes my hip and I wrap my legs around his waist.

"Perfect, baby," he breathes harshly into my neck. "You are perfect." I lift my hips, meeting him thrust for thrust, pushing against him, needing all of him. Strong fingers grip my thighs, lifting me to achieve a better angle. With each thrust, he pushes deeper and deeper, and I cry out when he hits a spot that I'm certain has never been hit before.

My fingers rake down his back, over his ass, and then back up over his shoulders, trying to decide where I want to touch him... needing to touch all of him.

"Please," I moan, digging my nails into his shoulders. My body is stretched to its limits, so overwhelmed with sensations that I'm certain it's going to explode. Sensing my needs, Tyson reaches down, swirling his thumb several times over my swollen clit before pressing down—hard. With a deep groan, I ignite like fireworks on the Fourth of July, blasting off into the abyss and then exploding beautifully into a million colorful pieces. My back arches, curving into his strong chest, and he wraps his strong arm around my waist, holding me to him as my body convulses violently around his.

"That was incredible," he growls, pounding into me harder. "Christ," he grunts. "You're body is heaven. Your pussy hugs me like...*fuck*!" His words spur me on and I reach up, squeezing my heavy breasts. I pinch and pull at my nipples, trying to ride out the wave of my orgasm. Tyson's hungry eyes devour every twist and turn of my fingers, and he sucks his bottom lip into his mouth and bites down. His body stiffens against mine as a string of incoherent words fly from his mouth. He buries his head in my neck, rocking several more times as my body milks him for every last drop.

Holy shit. I've never actually watched a man get off, but after watching that, I'm fairly certain I'll never look away again. That was the hottest damn thing I've ever seen! And to know that I'm the one that brought him to that place is intensely satisfying.

Tyson's warm breath fans against my cheek and he pushes up, resting on his elbows. My face is cradled in his hands, and the tender look he's giving me melts me straight down to my soul.

Leaning forward, Tyson peppers kisses across my face while his thumbs rub soft circles against my temples. With each gentle kiss and every caress, he heals my damaged soul. I lock eyes with his. *I love you*, he mouths, cracking my heart wide open. Tears clog my throat, but this time I don't fight to hold them back.

"Why the tears?" His eyes are soft and curiously inviting as he swipes away my tears. "You should be smiling, baby."

"These are happy tears," I hiccup, lifting to graze my mouth against his. "I'm just...I just..." There are so many things I want to tell him, like how complete I feel and how it's never been like that with anyone ever before. I want to tell him that somehow every negative feeling I had has completely dissipated, and in its place is this overwhelming amount of love that I can't seem to put into words.

"I love you...*so much*," I say slowly, enunciating every word.

Tyson smiles lazily and leaning down, he kisses my nose. "I love you more," he whispers.

"Show me." My words were meant to sound seductive. I'm not sure if I succeeded, because when Tyson's lips slide across mine and our tongues collide, I lose all train of thought.

Chapter 20

Tyson

A LOUD THUD WAKES me and I jolt upright, breathing heavily. Rubbing my sleep-ridden eyes, I look around the room trying to remember where I am when my gaze lands on a white, lacy bra hanging carelessly off the end of the bed. *Harley.* Throwing myself back on the pillow, I look at the ceiling, a slow smile creeping across my face.

Show me, she'd said. And I did. I spent the remainder of the night and well into the early morning hours showing her over and over how much I love her.

The smell of bacon filters through the house at the same time I hear what sounds like a wounded cat screeching to the tune of... *no way.* Jumping out of bed, I yank on my jeans, forgoing my boxers because I can't miss this. My eyes quickly sweep the floor for my shirt, but when I don't immediately see it, I take off quietly down the hall, cringing when that horrific sound starts back up.

Slowly I peek around the wall, and the sight that greets me about knocks me flat on my ass. Harley is standing at the counter, her messy hair piled on top of her head and my shirt from last night hangs loosely off her shoulder. She sashays her sexy little hips to *I Want You To Want Me* by Cheap Trick, and when the chorus comes on, Harley throws a hand up in the air and belts out the words. I wouldn't call whatever she is doing singing though, and I'm reminded that Harley has never been able to carry a tune. I flinch when she attempts to hit a high note, and then my jaw goes slack when the hem of my shirt rises with her movements and the round globes of her bare ass peek out from underneath.

Christ, she's beautiful. Her arms lower so that she can tend to the bacon frying on the stove, but she continues to sway and bump her hips to the beat of the music. My feet unconsciously move toward her, because the pull she has on me is so great that I have to be near her. My hands land on her hips, sliding down her bare thighs, and my cock swells at the same time she startles before twirling around to face me.

"You scared the shit out of me!" she scolds, trying to hold back her smile as my fingers skate up the silky skin of her thigh and under the hem of my shirt. She loses her resolve and dissolves into a fit of giggles, and my fingers trace up her sides and over her abdomen. Her tight little body curves into mine and I relish the sound of her tinkling laughter as it bounces around the room. She jerks back, trying to get away from my wandering hands, but there is no way in hell I'm ever letting her go.

"Stop!" she yells, choking out a laugh. "I ca—I can't breathe," she gasps, tears of laughter rolling down her face. My fingers trail a little bit higher and when they meet the warm flesh of her breasts, I squeeze gently, rubbing my thumb across her taut nipples. She whimpers, the amusement draining from her face, and then wipes the wetness out of her eyes right before they flash bright with desire.

I nuzzle my nose against her neck, breathing in her sweet vanilla scent. "I didn't mean to startle you, I just couldn't resist." She purrs, tilting her head to the side, offering me her neck. I nibble and suck the soft skin, smiling when I feel goose bumps prickle underneath my mouth and hands. It floors me to know that my touch can create such an immediate response from her body.

"I'm making bacon," she says on a breathy moan.

I shake my head and murmur, "I don't want bacon. I want you."

She chuckles, stepping forward so we're chest to chest. I wrap one arm around her back, grip her ass in the other hand, and pull her against me. I grind my erection against her apex and watch as she sucks in a deep breath and holds it. Reaching around me, she tucks her hands in my back pockets, holding me against her so that she can rub her core against my zipper. My hand slides down the back of her ass and when my fingers meet the soft, wet skin of her sex, she drops her head to my shoulder, a soft groan falling from her mouth.

"You're soaked." I slide my middle finger over her swollen clit and then back to her entrance where I stop, teasing her with the tips of my fingers. She pulls back, her hooded eyes full of desire. Her tongue licks a slow path along her bottom lip. "You're very perceptive this morning, Dr. Grawe," she says, her voice low and husky. *Sonofabitch. She called me Dr. Grawe.* My cock swells against her belly and a triumphant little grin spreads across her face.

"Are you wanting to role play, Nurse Thompson?" I ask, sliding two fingers deep inside of her. Her hips buck against my hand and I twist my fingers, rubbing the swollen tissue that I know will make her squirm.

"Oh God!" she grunts, her eyes rolling back into her head right before her lids drift shut. I increase my pace, pumping faster and harder in sync with her gyrating hips. She reaches behind me, grips my hair, and tugs. "I need you." Her words tear right through me and my cock swells even more, throbbing against my jeans, threatening to bust through. Reaching up with my free hand, I cup the nape of her neck, drawing her mouth to mine. "I need you too, baby."

"Now," she pants, her fingers digging into my shoulders. Her body squirms against mine as though she's trying to climb me like a tree. "I need you now."

Well, shit. She doesn't need to tell me twice, and she sure as hell doesn't need to beg. I pop the button on my jeans and yank the zipper down, pushing the faded material over my hips, letting it pool at my feet. Harley's eyes roam my body and she licks her lips, gripping the hem of my shirt as she tugs it over her head.

Holy shit! This woman is a fucking goddess.

Reaching behind her, I flick off the burner to the stove. The bacon can wait…right now the only thing making my mouth water is the thought of sinking deep into Harley's tight pussy.

With one hand buried inside of Harley, I use my free hand to grip my aching cock. Her eyes widen with surprise and flick to mine before she looks back down, where she stops to watch as I stroke myself in a slow, fluid motion. Her eyes cloud over and she squeezes her thighs around my hand, trying to rub them together.

"Turn around." Her mossy eyes snap to mine and she sucks her bottom lip into her mouth. She stands there for several seconds without making a move, just staring at me. "Harley, turn around," I demand softly. This time she obeys and then leans forward, splaying her hands out on the counter. I walk up behind her, pressing my front against her back, and she inhales quickly, her body jerking as though I startled her. Something inside of me cracks.

"Are you okay?" I ask, needing to know that I didn't frighten her. She looks at me over her shoulder and nods once, her eyes trailing hungrily down my body as if trying desperately to see what I'm doing behind her. "Good. If you want—"

"Tyson?" she interrupts, pushing her hips back against mine.

"Hmm?" *I can't talk.* I can't form one goddamn word when she grinds that creamy white ass against my pelvis.

"What I want," she pauses, "is for you to put *that*," she says, glancing down at my rigid cock, "in me." Her words stun me into silence and I watch in awe as she wiggles her ass against my crotch. "Now would be good."

I bring my hand down against her butt and she squeals at the quick slap. Her skin instantly flushes a deep red where my hand made contact and I rub it in slow, smooth circles. Leaning forward, my mouth grazes her ear. "You're a demanding little thing today, aren't you?" She shifts on her feet and drops her head when I suck her earlobe into my mouth and bite down.

If I had any sense about me—which I don't, because every last drop of blood in my body is pooled between my thighs—I'd take a moment and appreciate Harley in all her naked glory. I mean, for Christ's sake, the woman is fucking delectable. She's buck-ass naked in the middle of the day, propped against the counter, offering herself to me on a fucking silver platter. My control snaps when I see her slide her hand down her stomach, stopping when she reaches her throbbing clit.

Lining myself up at her entrance, I thrust at the same time she slams her hips back, and I'm completely engulfed in her tight heat.

"*Fuck,*" I groan, at the same time she dislodges her hand from between her legs and slaps her palms against the counter. My hands keep her seated against me and I close my eyes, trying to calm my body. She's got me wound so tightly that it's taking every ounce of control I have to keep from blowing my load.

"Yes. Fuck. That's good. Let's go with that." My hands are gripped tightly around her hips, and once again, the words coming out of her smart little mouth are my complete undoing. Suddenly, I can't claim her fast enough.

I grip one of her thighs, lifting it to get a better angle as I start pounding against her. With each thrust, I burrow myself deeper and deeper, and her soft moans are doing nothing but fueling my fire.

Dropping her leg, I reach my hand around to rub her swollen clit. Her breath hitches as I stroke the tender bud, which continues to swell as my hips slam against hers. The loud slap of skin against skin fills the air, drowning out her hoarse pleas. Without dislodging our connection, she pushes upright, letting her arms fall behind her head until they drape around my neck.

Her porcelain skin is on display, and she hums low in her throat when I trail hot, wet kisses across her bare neck. "Nothing has ever felt as good as being wrapped up inside of you." Her head drops back on my shoulder, her soft pants fanning the side of my face. Her body clenches, squeezing me tight, and I curse. "Does that turn you on?" I pause after thrusting hard. "Do you like it when I talk to you?"

She nods jerkily against my shoulder. I watch as her lips part and a crimson flush creeps up her heaving chest. "You're an angel, Harley." I feel a quiver start deep inside of her pussy and it triggers a deep ache in my spine. "Your body is heaven on earth. It's a fucking shrine, Harley, and I'm going to worship it every day for the rest of my life."

"Please," she groans, looking at me through lust-filled eyes. My mouth captures hers, drinking in every pant and cry as my hips flex, thrusting against hers several more times. I increase the pressure of my fingers against her clit and rub vigorously. I feel her body tense against mine, and when I slide my hand back to feel my cock sliding in and out of her pussy, she falls apart. Her body convulses, trembling against mine, and I thrust against her once more before groaning out my own release. Her body goes slack against mine and I wrap my arms around her, whispering sweet words into her neck in between kisses.

I love you.
That was perfect.
You're so beautiful.

Chapter 21

Tyson

"I AM SO MAD."

Rolling over onto my side, I slide my hand around until it reaches Harley's warm body. Wrapping my arm around her waist, I tug her against me, nuzzling my nose into her soft hair. The faint sound of giggling rings in my ears, but I'm so damn tired I can't talk myself into caring enough to look and see where the sound is coming from.

Harley wore me out today. This girl is a fucking tiger in the sack. My dick is probably going to hurt for days, but I don't give a shit because it was worth it...*she* was worth it. After our afternoon romp in the kitchen, we ate dinner and then I ate dessert...off of Harley. It was the best fucking dessert of my entire life. Then, we curled up together on her living room floor and fell asleep watching our favorite childhood movie *The Goonies*.

"Shhh..." I hear someone whisper way off in the distance.

"I am. I'm so mad. I can't believe this, Quinn!" This time the voice seems closer, but I don't have time to think about it because Harley stretches her lithe body and rolls over beneath my arm. She buries her head under my chin and I shiver when her soft hand slides up my stomach and settles on my chest.

"Get up. Get up. Get up. Get up. Get up." Stretching my arm out, I let it flop across my face. "Get up. Get up. Get up. Get up." Harley rolls out of my arms and I groan at the loss of her warm body against mine.

"I'm so mad at you, mom!" My eyes snap open when a sharp jab hits my ribs. Pushing up on my elbow, I rub my face.

"I'm mad at you too!" Looking up, I find myself face-to-face with a fuming Max. My gaze wanders to Harley, my mind still trying to wake up enough to understand what's going on. Her wide eyes glance nervously down to my naked chest and...that's all it takes. Sitting up, I tighten the blanket around my stomach, praying to God that Max—or Quinn—didn't see more than they should have.

Please let me have pants on.
Please let me have pants on.

Shifting my legs I feel the harsh scratch of my jeans against my skin and I sigh with relief.

"This is great," Quinn says, pulling her phone out of her pocket. Harley growls at her and Quinn throws her hands up in defeat as Max continues to stare daggers at us.

"I can't believe you guys!"

Harley kneels in front of him, gripping his hands in hers, and he jerks away. *Fuck.* I probably just scarred the little dude for life. Granted, we weren't doing anything but sleeping, but judging by the frown on his face, he isn't happy about what he walked in on.

"Max, honey—"

"You camped out without me!" he yells, looking between Harley and me. "You had a campout, and I wasn't invited!" Max's little hands are balled into fists and they're planted firmly on his hips. Throwing my head back, I laugh, relief washing through me. He wasn't upset about finding me asleep with his mom, he's upset because he thinks we were camping out and he was missing out on the fun.

"Max, this was *not* a campout." Some of the anger drains

from his face and he drops his arms to his sides. Harley looks at me, her eyes begging me not to screw this up.

"It's not?" he asks.

"Heck no!" I shake my head. "I don't camp out with girls."

"Because they have cooties?" he asks hopefully.

I nod once, chuckling when Harley scoffs at Max's 'cootie' comment. "That, and because I only camp out with really big, strong men, like you."

Max's eyebrows shoot to his hairline and he licks his lips, his big brown eyes bouncing from my face to Harley's several times. He offers me a slow smile. "Y-you would camp out with me?"

My stomach hardens and my heart stomps wildly in my chest when I consider the fact that Max has never had another guy ask him to go camping. Shit, I use to love to go camping when I was his age. Some of the best memories I have with my dad and brother are of us pitching a tent in the backyard and roasting marshmallows over the fire pit while my dad told us scary stories. I know I'm not his dad, but I love this little boy, and I can tell deep in my heart that this is a pivotal moment between the two of us.

"You bet your as—er, butt I would!" Harley slaps my arm at my word fumble. "There isn't anyone else I would want to go camping with."

"Not even my mom?" he asks quickly, bouncing up and down on his toes.

"Nope," I say, glancing at Harley and winking, "not even her." I scrunch my nose as though the thought of camping with Harley disgusts me, and Max erupts in a fit of giggles right before he throws himself against my chest. Two little arms wrap around my neck, and for a split second I'm stunned still. Then I do the only thing I really want to do…I hold him.

"Thanks, Ty," he says sincerely against my neck, right before he wrenches free from my arms. Jumping to his feet, he takes off down the hall.

"Wait! Where are you going?" I yell after him.

"To get my sleeping bag!" he hollers back.

Harley laughs, reaching her arms out to pull me against her. "That was so sweet of you," she says, kissing the side of my neck.

"Sweet isn't the right word," Quinn quips. "More like sexy as fucking hell. I don't think I've ever wanted to rip your clothes off as badly as I do right now."

I grin, waggling my eyebrows suggestively as I look at Quinn. "So you've thought about ripping them off before?" I ask, cocking my head to the side. Harley's head whips back and she glares at Quinn, pointing a finger at her.

"Quinn..." Harley warns with a smile.

"What?" she asks innocently. "He's fucking hot. Of course I've thought about ripping his clothes off. In fact," she pauses, a mischievous grin spreading across her face as she kneels down to whisper so only Harley and I can hear her, "how do you guys feel about a ménage?"

"I—" Harley throws a hand across my mouth before I can finish.

"I don't even want to hear what you have to say," she scolds. I know she isn't really upset because her bright eyes are smiling and I can see a grin tugging at the corner of her mouth. Removing her hand, she kisses me softly before turning to Quinn. "And that would be a 'no,' in case you were wondering." She high-fives her friend before grabbing the blanket off the floor to fold it. "But nice try."

Quinn curtsies, shooting me a wink as she walks toward the kitchen. Reaching out, I grab the folded quilt from Harley and leaning down, I kiss her cheek and whisper, "I was only going to say that there was no way in hell I was willing to share you."

When her eyes find mine, they are full of adoration. Cupping my free hand around her neck, I pull her to me. Her lips part on a sigh and she pushes her tongue into my mouth. This kiss isn't rushed or desperate like the ones from earlier today. No, this kiss is soft and gentle, and I almost lose my own footing at the promises it holds.

"Ty, you really have cooties now." Harley pulls away, holding her hand to her mouth, embarrassed that she was caught kissing me in front of her son. Her face flushes crimson right before she turns to go find Quinn.

"Watcha got there, buddy?" I ask, sitting down on the floor next to Max.

"It's my backpack. I'm going to pack it for camping," he says excitedly, and I hate that I have to tell him we can't go tonight.

"Max?" He looks at me, stopping the movement of his little hands. "We can't go camping tonight." His face falls and I hurry to explain, "You have daycare tomorrow, and your mom and I have to get up early for work. But I promise you, we will go camping this weekend. How about Friday?"

He opens his backpack and pulls out a thick envelope. "Okay," he sighs, pinning his chocolate eyes to mine. "But you promise?"

Sticking my hand out, I offer him my pinky. "I pinky swear." His tiny lips purse and he furrows his brow.

"What do I do with that?" he asks, looking at me, then down at my pinky, and then back up to me.

"It's a pinky swear," I say, amazed that he has no idea what I'm talking about. He continues to stare at me like I'm an alien, so I reach out and wrap my pinky around his.

"See," I say, shaking our joined pinkies in the air. "It means neither one of us can back out because we made a pinky swear."

"Cool!" he says, beaming up at me, right as Quinn and Harley walk back into the room. Max scoots toward me and holds out the envelope in his hands.

"This is for you," he says quietly, his hands fidgeting in his lap after I take the envelope.

"For me?" I ask, smiling when he nods vigorously.

"I made it for you for your birthday."

"Wait!" Harley jumps up off the couch. "Don't open it!" She takes off in a sprint down the hallway and when she runs back into the living room, her socks slide across the floor and she lands back on the couch with an amused smile.

"Camera!" she says, waving the case in the air. I notice her tuck another white envelope under her leg right before she fumbles with the case, trying to get the camera out. "Okay, ready!"

I laugh nervously, wondering what in the hell she seems so excited about, and Max nudges my leg.

"Open it," he says, scooting closer to me.

Sliding my finger underneath the flap, I rip it open and a handful of colorful papers fall out. Each one is about the size of a 4x6 picture and they're individually decorated with stamps, stickers, and drawings that appear to be done by Max.

I smile, looking over at his expectant face, still trying to figure out exactly what they are. "Turn them over," he says excitedly. "They're coupons!" Reaching out, he turns them over for me. "See?"

Harley's camera starts flashing beside us, but I don't pay attention—the scribbled writing on the cards makes me momentarily forget everything else.

I swallow hard and my heart clenches tight in my chest as I read through the first few coupons. Each one says *'GOOD FOR'* at the top and underneath that, each card says something different.

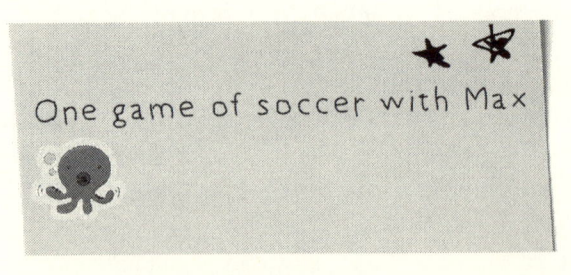

One game of soccer with Max

One movie night out with Max

> One pizza party with Max

    My red-rimmed eyes find his and Max offers me a nervous smile. My hands tremble, but I manage to not drop the colorful pieces of paper that have rendered me speechless. I look back down and keep reading.

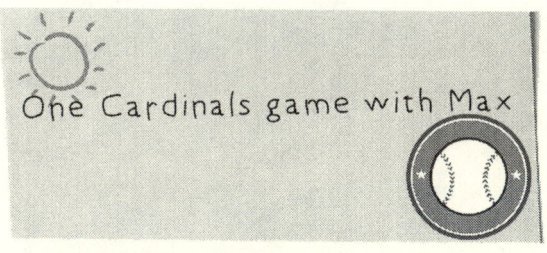

> One campout with Max

> One Cardinals game with Max

> One swimming party with Max

Warmth radiates throughout my body. My heart is racing so fast that I'm certain it could shoot straight out of my chest. I glance over at Harley to find her and Quinn both observing me closely. Harley's hand is covering her mouth, tears brimming her eyes, and if I'm not wrong, I swear I just saw her chin quiver. She's watching me nervously, obviously unsure of how I'm going to perceive the coupons. I offer her a slow smile and she drops her hand and smiles back.

Gently tapping my leg, Max clears his throat. "There's one more." Looking down, I see a bright green piece of paper gripped tightly in his hands. He offers it to me and I gently take it from him. I notice that he's not smiling. He's looking at me, but it's more like he's looking *through* me. Glancing down, I see that the coupon is blank. The stickers, stamps, and drawings are all there, but no words. I flip it over, and when I find that the other side is blank too, I look back at him.

"It's good for anything," he says quietly, glancing nervously at Harley before turning his chocolate eyes on me.

Leaving one card out, I stack the others and neatly tuck them back into the envelope. "I love it, Max," I say, swallowing past the lump he unintentionally put in my throat. "It's the best birthday present anyone has ever given me." His eyes widen, a grin tugging at the side of his mouth.

"Really?" he asks hopefully. I hear a light sob and I know it's probably Harley, but I can't look. Right now all of my attention is riveted solely on this one little man, who has me completely wrapped around each and every one of his fingers.

I reach out, yanking him into my arms, pulling him against me. He wraps his arms around my neck and laughs when I tighten my hold. Burying my head in his messy brown hair, I whisper, enunciating every word, "The. Best. Ever." He nods against my shoulder and I pull back, framing his face with my hands. Leaning forward, I place my lips against the top of his head for a brief second before I pull back and hand him a bright blue coupon.

He scrunches his eyebrows and looks at me questioningly.

Standing up, I reach out my hand to pull Max to his feet. He's smiling up at me, his eyes bright with joy. "I want to play soccer. How about you?"

"Yeah!" he says, jumping up. He fist-pumps the air and then turns toward the door. Stopping abruptly in his tracks, he runs back to me and shoves the blue coupon back into my hands.

"Keep it. This one is free," he says before running off into the kitchen. "I'm gonna get my shoes on and I'll meet you outside," he yells.

Quinn walks up and wraps her arm around me, pulling me in for a hug. "You were great," she whispers before pulling away from me. "I'll give you two a second." I watch her retreating back and then turn to Harley. She's sitting on the couch, her feet tucked neatly underneath her butt. I can tell she's been crying because her eyes are red and puffy and she has tear tracks running down her face.

"I love him," I say softly. Unfolding herself, she walks over to me and strokes a hand down the side of my face.

"I know you do," she says, grazing her lips across my mouth. "He loves you too." Wrapping my arm around her neck, I pull her to me, kissing the side of her head. "It really is the best present I've ever gotten."

Harley chuckles and turns her face to mine. "You haven't seen my present yet," she says seductively.

"Mmmm," I mumble into her hair. "You already gave me my birthday present...like five times."

She laughs, swatting my chest playfully. "Not *that*. I made you something too."

"Can I have it?" I ask. Walking to the couch, I tug her down next to me and pull her legs onto my lap. Reaching across to the end table, she picks up an envelope and lays it in my lap.

"I hope you like it," she says, biting her lower lip.

Once again, I find myself opening a sealed envelope. Small cards are stacked neatly in the envelope and I slide them out. They are very similar to the ones Max gave me, only these are littered with little hearts and flowers around the edges. Sifting through the cards, I notice that there are five—and they are all blank.

My curious eyes find Harley's. "They're blank."

"They are." Her eyes are smiling at me, her straight, white teeth framed by her dimples.

I look at the papers and then back up to her. "For whatever I want?" I ask with a hint of suggestion. One eyebrow raised, she slowly nods at me.

Suddenly, I feel the need to confirm. "Like *anything*, anything?"

"Apart from giving you Max," she laughs, "they're good for absolutely anything." Her hand slides up my chest and wraps around my neck, tangling in my hair. She strokes my scalp several times, her tiny nails causing the hair on the back of my neck to stand up. "I trust you," she whispers against my mouth. "So yes, they're good for anything."

Her soft lips close over mine and her tongue enters, instantly tangling with mine. I groan into her mouth and gently fist my hand in her hair at the nape of her neck.

"TY! COME ON!" Max yells through the back door. Harley giggles as she pulls back, and I close my eyes, dropping my forehead to hers.

"Cockblocker," I murmur. Tossing her head back, Harley lets out a throaty laugh that makes my cock twitch.

Her phone pings and she slides off the couch, grabbing it from the coffee table. A smile spreads across her face as she types furiously on the screen. "Who is it?" I ask, curious who put that look on her face.

She glances at me briefly before turning her attention back to her phone. "It's my friend, Celeste. She was just checking in to say 'hi.'"

"Do I know her?" I ask. "I don't think I've ever heard you talk about her."

Harley's face softens before she says, "We met in an online support group."

A heavy weight settles in the pit of my stomach and I cock my head her. "I didn't know you were in a support group."

She takes a deep breath and blows it out slowly. "There's still a lot you don't know, Tyson." *And there are some things you'll never know.* "It was a long time ago. Celeste and I connected almost instantly, bonded by the fact that we've both been through some terrible things."

My stomach rolls with regret. I wasn't there for Harley when she needed me most, and I'm not sure I'll ever be able to forgive myself for that. "I'm glad you have one another," I say sincerely.

She smiles, but there's no humor in it. "Me too. Quinn and Levi have been unbelievable, but my friendship with Celeste has definitely been another silver lining."

I nod, at a loss for words. Seemingly done with the conversation, Harley reaches a hand out to help me up. Her words spark something deep inside of me, but I can't give it much thought... right now, I have a birthday present to cash in on.

"IT'S OKAY, MOM, DON'T worry about it...yes, really...no, I'll find someone...Quinn, maybe...okay...love you too, bye." Rolling her eyes, Harley tosses her phone on the table.

"What was that about?" I ask, bending down to pull Max's shoes off. The second I'm done, he jumps up and runs to the refrigerator, grabbing a bottle of water.

"Can I take this in my room?" He's looking at me, but I'm not sure why. I glance at Harley and she cocks an eyebrow and shrugs. Max is still watching me, waiting for an answer. "Can I?" he asks again.

"Uh...sure, buddy." I look at Harley and she nods. "Just be careful, don't spill it."

"I won't!" I watch, frozen in place, as Max bounds off down the hall. He asked me for permission to do something. Me—not

Harley. I rub a hand across my chest where I feel my heart flipping over.

Harley pats my arm. "You did great."

"Yeah?" I confirm.

"Yeah." Pushing up on her tiptoes, she kisses my cheek before moving to the sink.

"Who were you talking to when I walked in?" Pulling a towel out of the drawer, I grab a plate and start drying it.

"My mom," she sighs, handing me another plate. "She was supposed to watch Max for me this Saturday since I have to work, but she had something come up and she can't do it."

"So what are you going to do?"

She shrugs. "I don't know." Glancing at me, she frowns. "Maybe I'll ask Quinn."

Hello? Am I invisible? "I'll keep him." Harley's eyes snap to mine and she hands me another plate, her eyes roaming my face as though she's trying to gauge my sincerity.

"Really?" she asks slowly, propping a hip against the counter.

"Yes, *really*. Why not?" I question, mocking her position.

"I don't know," she says, glancing around the room. "Do you think you can handle keeping Max all day?" I know she doesn't mean that in a bad way, she just knows that I've never watched a child for any extended period of time.

"Sure," I nod. "Max and I have fun together. I can handle it."

"You don't have to work?" she asks.

"Nope."

"Are you on-call?"

"Nope," I chuckle. "But it's okay, I understand if you're not comfortable with me watching Max for a full day."

"No. No, that's not it." Dropping her dishrag into the soapy water, she steps closer to me. "That's not it at all. I just wanted to make sure you wouldn't get called into work. If you want to keep him, he's yours."

"Yo, Max! Get in here, bud!" I yell, giving Harley a quick peck on the lips.

"What?" he asks breathlessly, skidding into the kitchen.

"You're going to stay with me this Saturday while your mom works. What do you think about that?" His eyes go wide as he sidles in next to his mom.

"Really?" he asks. She nods, and Max busts out in a little dance.

"Cool!" he booms. "Can we do something fun?"

"Uh, yeah," I say, looking at him like he's crazy for even asking that question. "Now go get ready for bed, it's getting late." Once again he bounces off down the hall, and I briefly think that I would give anything for just a fraction of his energy.

Harley waits until Max leaves the room and then picks up her rag and starts absently washing a dirty pan. "So, are you still going to camp out with Max on Friday?" she asks timidly.

"Of course. I pinky swore." Her eyes shift to mine, an amused grin gracing her face. "And I don't break pinky swears," I add, right before I snap her butt with the dishrag.

Chapter 22

Tyson

"HAVE YOU HAD FUN tonight?" Harley asks, zipping up Max's sleeping bag.

"Yup," he says, turning his head to face me. His eyes are sleepy, and I can tell that it's only going to be a matter of minutes before he's fast asleep.

"Are you gonna sleep here with us, mama?" he asks with a yawn.

Harley kisses his cheek and runs a hand through his hair. "No baby, I'm going to sleep in the house. This is a boys' night, remember?" She winks at me and Max nods. "But I'll stay here until you fall asleep." Kissing him one more time, she scoots over to me and I pull her between my legs, resting her back against my front. We watch patiently as Max's eyelids blink heavily several times.

"Ty?" he whispers, prying his eyes back open.

"Yeah, buddy?"

"I had fun camping out with you."

"I had fun camping out with you too," I whisper, leaning around Harley to run my hand through his hair. "It was the best campout ever."

A lazy smile tugs at the corner of his mouth, but he's too exhausted to keep it there. His eyes drift shut and when I think he's finally dozed off, he mumbles four little words that rock my world to its core.

"I love you, Ty."

I thought that when Harley told me she loved me, I had won the fucking lottery. But that doesn't even compare to how it feels to hear Max say the exact same thing. There's just something so innocent about it, and the way the words easily fell from his lips has left me stunned and fighting for air. I can't explain it...it's nothing I've ever felt before and something I want to feel again every single day.

I pick a shocked Harley up out of my lap and set her down next to me. Leaning forward, I swipe my hand across Max's face, pushing his hair out of his eyes. Kissing him gently on the forehead, I whisper, "Max?" His drooping lids peel open, bobbing several times.

"Hmmm?" Waking him back up probably isn't the best thing to do, but I need him to hear me.

"I love you too, Max." I swallow hard past the lump in my throat as tears prick my eyes. My chest is heaving with the overwhelming sense of love I have for this perfect little boy lying in front of me.

"I know you do." And just like that, everything in my life clicks into place. Every bad choice I've made falls by the wayside because they've all led me here. And there isn't anywhere I'd rather be than in this tent on a cool fall night, where I just bared my heart to a perfect four-year-old boy. I know that Max is not biologically my son, but this love I have for him is all-consuming. It's...it's indescribable. I can only hope that someday I will love my own kids as much as I love Max.

When I turn around, I see Harley brushing away the tears that are streaming down her beautiful face. I pull her into my arms, burying my face in the crook of her neck.

"Thank you." My words are strained with emotion and I

tighten my grip on her, using her as an anchor. "Thank you for giving me another chance. Thank you for raising such an amazing little boy. And thank you for letting me be a part of your lives."

She sobs, her arms squeezing my neck. It's obvious that this is as emotional for her as it is for me. Without a doubt, this is a turning point for us. Harley and I have come so far, and this feeling of finally having come full circle is one that I never want to go away.

Right now, I need to hold her...I need to absorb what all of this means. So I tuck her in next to me underneath the thick down material of my sleeping bag. Snuggling in close, she nuzzles her head under my chin and wraps an arm around my stomach. We don't talk because we don't need to. Instead, we fall asleep wrapped in each other's arms with a snoring Max beside us.

MY PHONE BEEPS AND I pull it out, smiling when I see Harley's name. This morning was chaotic, to say the least. We forgot to set an alarm for Harley, and by the time Max woke us up, Harley had all of one hour to get herself ready and get to work.

Harley: Made it. Have fun today.

Me: Good. See you tonight. Love u.

"How much longer?" Max asks, bouncing around in the backseat.

"Almost there, kiddo. Sit tight," I say, glancing at him in the rearview mirror. When I packed him up in the car this morning, I double and triple-checked the booster seat and seat belt, my nerves getting the best of me.

What if something happens? Is he safe? Is the strap too tight...is it too loose? Max finally pushed me away and told me he was fine and to get a move on. So here we are on our way to the City Museum. I wanted to do something fun with him today—something that he would remember—and one of my favorite places to go when I was a kid was the City Museum. It's a child's dream playground, full of tunnels, caves, and slides. There's an aquarium, rooftop Ferris wheel, a railroad, and a skateless park, which happens to be my favorite part. I can't wait to see Max's face as he explores it all.

We pull into the parking lot and Max instantly starts rapid-firing questions at me.

"Is that a school bus hanging off the roof? Is it gonna fall? Are there kids in there? Should we call 911?" I laugh, putting the car in park. Reaching back, I unbuckle Max and he squirms in his seat, trying to get a better view of the school bus.

"Nope, no need to call 911, it's part of the museum. You get to play in that school bus." His eyes widen with horror.

"But it's gonna fall off the roof!" he screeches.

"No, it's not," I assure him, gripping his hand tightly as we make our way to the entrance. "Trust me, it's perfectly safe. You're going to have a blast."

"TY!" he yells, tugging on my arm as soon as we walk through the front door. "Look at that slide, IT'S HUGE!"

His excitement is infectious and I find myself smiling like a kid when I step forward to pay for our wristbands. "Okay, Max, here are the rules." His wide eyes are bouncing around the museum as he hops from foot to foot. I snap my fingers and he looks at me, though I can tell there about a million other things he'd rather be looking at. "I have to know where you are at all times, okay?" He nods enthusiastically. "You don't run off without telling me, and if a stranger tries to grab you, I want you to kick and scream as loud as you can."

His movements still and he looks at me, shocked. "Is a stranger going to grab me?"

"No, but—"

"Because I don't want to get stolen!" The look on his face is priceless, and for a split second I feel bad for scaring the little fart.

"If you stay by me and I know where you are, nothing will happen. Got it?"

"Got it. Now can we go ride that slide?" he says, yanking my arm as he runs for the stairs. "Look at that!" he hollers, pointing to the ceiling, where a bunch of kids are climbing in a hanging tunnel. "Do I get to do that too?" he asks hopefully as his little legs plow up the steps.

"Whatever you want, little dude, we have all day." He looks at me and grins, his face flushed with exhilaration. We finally make it to the top of the slide and he lets out a loud *'WHOOP'* as he sends himself flying down the three-story slide.

Three hours later I'm exhausted, hungry, and fairly certain that I may have pulled a muscle in my groin. *Note to self: I'm no longer a kid.* Max, on the other hand, seems to just be getting started. This kid has run, jumped, climbed, ridden, and slid up and down this entire museum a hundred times, and he's still jumping on his toes, begging for more.

"Let's get a bite to eat, and then we'll play some more," I say, desperate to sit down for a couple of minutes. He reluctantly agrees and we head over to the mezzanine to grab some grub.

"What's your favorite thing at the museum?" I ask, shoving a bite of pizza into my mouth.

"Ummm…" He taps a finger against his chin and then his excited eyes go soft. "The skatepark. I like the skate park."

I nod, elated that we share the same favorite part. "Me too," I say. "What do you like about it? Do you like running up the ramps, or sliding down them?"

He takes a long sip of soda and then shrugs nonchalantly. "Neither. I like it 'cause Mom told me my dad use to skate." My hand stills on its way to my mouth. His words are completely unexpected and I'm not really sure how to respond. Maybe Harley told him a little white lie about the piece-of-shit dad he will never know. I wouldn't blame her…of course she would want her son to have some good memories of his father.

"Did he rollerblade?" I ask hesitantly, unsure how far I should push this.

He pops a piece of pepperoni into his mouth. "Nope. Skateboard." I smile softly at him, thankful that he doesn't seem upset about the shift in our conversation.

"My brother and I use to skateboard. That's why I love the skate park here. It reminds me of him."

"Were you any good?"

"No," I snicker, remembering how many times I fell before I could even stand up on one. "But my brother was. Dallas could do all sorts of cool stuff on his skateboard."

Max's jaw drops and he lets his slice of pizza fall to the table. "That's my dad's name!" He eagerly scoots forward in his seat. "How cool is that?"

I stare at him in shock for a few seconds, his words repeating in my head. *That's my dad's name.* What does he mean, that's his *dad's name*? My skin heats with frustration, blood rushing through my ears, and suddenly I'm finding it hard to breathe. Harley assured me that she didn't know who Max's father was…was she lying to me? Was she really attacked? Did her and Dallas have an affair, or is she just using Dallas—since he's deceased—to give Max a father? A growl threatens to rip up my throat, but I fight it back, desperate to keep Max from seeing my reaction. I rub a hand roughly over my face, digging my thumb into my eyes. Pushing back from the table, I stand abruptly and snake my hand out to stop our sodas from tipping over when the table shakes.

"Are you okay, Ty?" Max asks, his head cocked to the side.

"Yeah," I wave him off, my mouth going dry. My arms feel heavy when I pick up our plates and toss them in the trash. "Let's go play some more." He smiles at me and starts skipping off toward the skateless park without a clue that he just set off a spark that will more than likely explode into a full-on firestorm.

Chapter 23

Harley

"SO HOW DO YOU think Tyson did with Max today?" Avery asks, shrugging out of her lab coat. "Do you think he survived?" We both laugh and I pull my phone out of my pocket, surprised that there isn't a missed call or text from Ty. I was certain he would let me know how his day went, or at least give me a call when they were on their way home. I smile to myself at the thought that maybe they're having so much fun that they lost track of time.

"I'm fairly certain that Ty will pass out as soon as he hits a bed tonight," I say, tossing my stethoscope into my satchel. I heave the strap over my shoulder and then Avery and I make our way out of the hospital. "He had absolutely no idea what he got himself into."

She snorts with laughter and we talk idly until we reach the parking lot, where she gives me a quick hug before we go our separate ways, promising to catch up for dinner some time soon.

The drive home drags by. I've tried calling Ty several times, but his phone keeps going to voicemail. I decide to call my mom and she answers on the first ring.

"Hi, sweetheart," she croons. "How was your day at work?"

It's so nice to hear her voice. Sometimes you just need your mom, and I feel like lately I haven't needed her as much as I did before. "Hi, Ma! Work was good...busy, but good. Have you heard from Ty? I was curious how his day went, but I haven't been able to get ahold of him."

"Yes, in fact he dropped Max off here a couple of minutes ago." Her words startle me and I find myself sitting up straighter in my seat, my grip tightening on the steering wheel.

"Is everything okay?" I ask hurriedly, needing confirmation that nothing bad has happened.

"Oh yes, dear. Everything is fine. I think that Max wore Tyson out." My shoulders relax as relief washes through me. Deep down, I knew that Tyson could handle it.

"So, why do you have Max?"

She rustles around and a loud clang indicates that she's getting ready to cook dinner. "Uh...I'm not really sure. He called me and asked if he could drop Max off, said he needed to talk to you about something right when you get home. I'm going to bring Max home shortly, so if you two are planning on...you know—"

"Mom," I scoff, rolling my eyes.

Her boisterous laugh rings through the phone. "Well, honey, I'm just—"

"Okay," I interrupt. "Let's talk about something else, other than what I may or may not do with Ty when I get home."

"What are you and Tyson doing?" my dad asks, causing me to choke on the tea I just took a drink of.

"Uh, nothing dad. Where's mom?" I hate it when they do this. She'll just pass the phone off and next thing I know I'm talking to my dad about...nope, not going there.

"She's making dinner. Do you and Tyson want to come over and eat?"

"No, but thanks. I'm exhausted. Just tell mom to bring Max home after he eats, or I can come get him...whatever works for you guys."

I hear him whisper something and then I hear Max laugh.

I smile even though I have no idea what they're talking about. "Okay. See you soon, honey," his rich voice booms, right before the line goes dead.

When I pull in front of the house, the first thing I notice is Tyson sitting on the front step. He stands as I pull into the driveway and park my car next to his. He has a key to the house, so why is he sitting outside? Walking to the car, he opens the door and reaches out to help me with my bag and lunchbox.

"Thanks," I offer, pecking his cheek. He doesn't respond and a shiver runs through my body at the cold vibe he's putting off. "Why didn't you wait inside?" I ask, trying to ease the tension that I feel creeping in around me.

He shrugs once and offers me nothing more than 'I didn't feel like it.' Pushing through the front door, he sets the bag down and then immediately turns to me.

"We need to talk," he says, shoving his hands deep into his pockets. *Oh God, here it is.* He's finally decided this is too much. He spent the day with Max and decided a ready-made family just isn't for him. My hands tremble and I feel tears burn my throat, but somehow I manage to make it to the couch.

"Okay. What do you want to talk about?" I hate that my voice is timid and shaky, but I'm scared to death of what's going to come out of his mouth. I mean, I sort of always expected that this was too good to be true, but now the thought of being without Tyson makes me want to throw up.

"You told Max his dad's name is Dallas," he blurts, his eyes boring into mine. *Okay.* That is not *at all* what I was expecting, and I'm sure as hell not prepared to have this conversation with him. My defenses rise and like usual, when I'm nervous I turn stupid, my words coming out a jumbled mess.

"I...uh...I, um..." I close my eyes and swallow hard, trying to regain my composure. When I open them once again, I find that Tyson's lips are in a flat line and his face is devoid of any emotion.

"You what, Harley?" he says suspiciously, raising his voice. The strong arms that I spent last night wrapped up in and are now splayed out at his side, and I ache to be tucked between them again.

"Just give me a second," I yell, standing up to nervously pace the living room. Annoyance runs thick through my veins, but it's more at myself than at him. I knew that I'd have to answer this question at some point, and I should have just been up front with Ty from the beginning. But how in the hell do you tell the man you're in love with—the man you want to spend the rest of your life with—that his brother is the one who raped you? How do you tell him that your son, the little boy he's madly in love with, is really his nephew?

My silence must be mistaken for deceit because Tyson growls deep in his throat and steps toward me. It's not an aggressive move but it startles me, and when I take a step back I stumble over the coffee table. Surprisingly, his eyes aren't full of anger, which is what I expect to see. Instead, they are wide with pain.

"How could you do this, Harley?" His jaw is clenched, brows dipped low. His eyes gloss over and my stomach twists at the pain I'm about to cause him.

I reach for him but he steps back, preventing me from touching him. "I didn't mean for you to—"

"You didn't mean to *what*?" he roars, fisting his hands in his hair. "You didn't mean to fuck my brother?" My mouth drops open in shock. "You didn't mean to forget to tell me, or you didn't mean to lie to me about what happened to you?" *And that's all it takes.* His discredit of what I told him happened that night makes my blood boil with rage and my body instantly tenses.

"Are you fucking kidding me right now?" I hurl at him. My heart is pounding wildly against my ribs and adrenaline is coursing through my veins so profusely that my body is shaking. "You think I fucked your brother, had a kid, and then lied to you about who the father is? You think I fucking lied to you about what happened that night? What kind of person do you think I am?" I sneer.

"I don't know what to fucking think because you haven't told me a goddamn thing! You told me you didn't know who Max's father was, and now I found out it may or may not be Dallas. What the fuck, Harley?" he yells, the vein on the side of his neck popping out. I hate that I'm causing him so much turmoil. I hate that the strong, gentle man I'm madly in love with is full of so much anger right now—and it's completely my fault.

"What do you want to know, Ty?" I shout, instantly regretting the words that are already falling from my mouth. "Do you want to know that your brother raped me?" His eyes widen in shock, but for some reason I can't seem to shut my damn mouth. "Do you want to know that he yanked me by my hair and shoved my face into the ground so hard when he *fucking raped me* that I had rocks embedded in my *GODDAMN CHEEK*?" Hot tears are coursing down my face and my throat burns from screaming.

Ty's cold eyes are watching me with equal parts anger and disbelief. His nostrils are flared, hands fisted tightly at his side, and his eyes are shooting daggers in my direction. For some reason, that makes me want to piss him off even more.

"Do you want to know that while he was ripping my panties off, I was begging him to stop?" I seethe. My words are meant to hurt him and when he jerks back, I know I hit my mark. He swallows hard, slowly shaking his head in apparent denial. "Do you want to know that I was praying for you to come back—"

"STOP!" he bellows, the deep timber of his voice causing the mirror on the wall to shake. My mouth snaps closed, my chest heaving uncontrollably and my head throbbing from crying. We stare at each other for several seconds as our relationship and all of the trust we've built teeters precariously on the brink of disaster.

His shoulders rise and fall with a deep breath. I can't believe I said all of that to him. My eyes drop in shame and I notice his hands trembling at his sides. When he speaks, his tone is controlled, and it sends a tingle of dread shooting through me. "I..." He shakes his head. "I can't believe this."

Pain flashes across his face and tears pool in his eyes, but he holds them back. "Dallas was a good person. He wouldn't do this, I know he wouldn't." I'm not sure he's talking to me, because his eyes are staring a hole through the floor. I grip my chest tightly at his words because my heart just fucking splintered in two, and I double over in pure agony. *He doesn't believe me.*

His shoulders hunch and I watch the rage drain from his body. Ironically, as his anger fades, mine is building with each passing second. For a brief moment, I consider the fact that maybe he needs a minute to come to grips with what I threw at him. Then I remember the words that just fell from his mouth, and that moment quickly passes. *He wouldn't do this, I know he wouldn't.*

His confused gaze finds mine and he takes a hesitant step forward. "Are you sure, Harley?" he asks, his eyes desperately searching my face for any sign of hope. "Maybe... maybe it was a misunderstanding. You had been drinking, so maybe things didn't happen the way you—"

"*Get out.*" My words are eerily calm as I walk to the front door and yank it open. He dismisses me, instantly shaking his head as he steps further into the room.

"No, I'm not leaving. We need to talk about this," he says urgently, and I laugh humorlessly at how easily he was able to shift from anger to desperation. His eyes plead with mine as he reaches out, touching my arm. I jerk away from the warm hand that I'm certain could bring me loads of comfort if I wasn't so fucking pissed off.

"There's nothing to talk about. Get out." I gesture wildly at the open door, and his mouth flies open at my refusal to discuss this further. I avoid all eye contact because I know that if I do, I'll lose every ounce of resolve I have left.

"No...no!" he says, frantically shaking his head. "Give me a second to process this, it's all just too m—"

"What is there to process?" I snap. "You either believe me or you don't."

"It's not that I don't believe you, it's just that I know Dallas, and there's no way—" I refuse to let him finish that sentence. I should have known that he wouldn't believe me. Dallas was his best friend and confidante, and even though he fucked up in unimaginable ways, Tyson will always see him as the proverbial older brother. Cutting my losses now seems the best way to go about this because there is no way *in hell* I'm going to sit through anyone telling me that Dallas is a saint, and I've come too far to let Ty drag me back down that road. I'm a fucking idiot for even thinking this whole situation could end differently.

"GET. OUT." My words are slow and concise, and right when he opens his mouth to respond, my mom pulls up in front of the house and Max jumps out of the car. Taking a shuddering breath, I turn away so I can wipe my eyes and I see Tyson do the same.

"Tyson!" he hollers, bouncing up the sidewalk. "Did you tell mom how much fun we had today?" Ty rushes to Max and bends down in front of him. I watch silently as his eyes flit anxiously across Max's face, and I know exactly what he's doing…he's looking for the similarities that have been there all the time. He is cataloguing everything about Max that is unmistakably identical to Dallas.

"I didn't," he says gently, patting Max's arm. "I thought you would want to tell her."

"I do!" Max responds, jumping over to me. "Mom, do you want to hear what we did today?" My head nods on its own accord and my distant eyes find my mom.

Are you okay? she mouths, looking back and forth between Ty and me. I nod feebly and she pushes past us to take Max into the house. "Let your mom and Tyson finish up, and then you can tell her all about it."

"I'll see you soon," Ty declares and Max turns around, offering up his pinky.

"Pinky swear?"

The quiver in Tyson's chin is small, but I see it. "Pinky swear." His voice cracks as he locks pinkies with the tiny person he now knows is his nephew. Max smiles, and after he walks away, Tyson turns toward me and marches right into my personal space. His eyes lock with mine, full of determination, and when he speaks, his voice is low and unwavering.

"I'm going to leave because we both need to calm down, but this is *not* over." My watery eyes meet his, and I watch a tear streak down the side of his face. He cups his hand behind my neck and lowers his mouth to mine, and I wonder briefly if he can feel my resolve slipping…if he can feel my heart thundering in my chest at his close proximity.

His mouth descends but pulling away isn't an option, because I know that this is the last time I'll ever kiss Ty. He is so very wrong if thinks that this isn't over. Little does he know that this is something I cannot—and will not—budge on. My eyelids drift shut, pushing out a few more tears, when his soft lips find mine. He kisses me once, twice, and a third time before he whispers, *'I love you'* and walks out the door.

Chapter 24
Harley

SEVEN DAYS.

It's been seven long days since I've talked to Tyson, but it hasn't been for a lack of trying on his part. I plop down on the coach, pull an afghan over my legs, and flip on the TV as I shove a bite of ice cream in my mouth. This is what I've done every single night since he walked out my front door.

That same night, he sent me a text that read, **I'll call you tomorrow.** I ignored it, along with his call the next day. He left two voicemails, both of them pleading for me to '*please call me back*,' which of course, I didn't.

Tossing my head back on the couch, I growl, wondering if I'm making a terrible mistake—quite possibly the biggest mistake of my life. *No*, I tell myself, shoving another heap of ice cream in my mouth. *I mean what the fuck did he think I was going to say when he practically called me a liar and whore all in one breath?*

"He was confused," Quinn answers, causing me to sputter at the realization that I said all of that out loud.

"He was a dick," I retort, a little taken aback that she defended him. She shrugs once and tosses a piece of popcorn in her mouth.

"Can you blame him?" My head rears back and my hand freezes in the air, halfway to my mouth.

"Yes!" I scoff, letting the spoon clatter when I drop it in the bowl. "Yes, I can blame him. Jesus Christ, Quinn, whose side are you on?" Suddenly, I'm feeling overheated underneath the fuzzy blanket. Tossing it to the side, I take off for the kitchen, not sparing a glance in Quinn's direction. The soft shuffle of her feet tells me she's following me, but I don't turn around. Opening up the cabinet, I grab a wine glass and slam the door a little too hard, causing the glasses on the shelf to clatter. I pour myself a glass of wine and chug half of it in the first sip, because Lord knows if I have to battle Quinn on this, I'm going to need some alcohol in my system. In fact, this wine may not be strong enough.

"Can I have a glass?" she asks softly, and I hand her one without making eye contact. She reaches for the bottle, filling the goblet half-full, then pulls out a chair and sits down at the table.

I can feel her eyes burning through me like a hot poker, but I refuse to turn around. I keep my eyes trained on the window as I peer into a dark canvas of emptiness. My eyes gravitate to the tent that is still pitched in the backyard from the campout, and my gut twists in a tight knot.

I miss him.

And worse than that…Max misses him. I'm definitely not winning any mother-of-the-year awards right now. Over the last five days I've come up with every reason in the book as to why Tyson hasn't come over and why Max can't call him. Last night he cried when I tucked him into bed, wanting to know if Tyson still loved him. His words shot straight through my heart, and that was the first time I truly *believed* that I was making a mistake. Before it had just been a fleeting thought that I was able to justify in my head as being false. But as Max sobbed over missing Ty, my heart cracked and something inside me changed.

"Are you done being an idiot yet? Because that's how you're acting…you do know that, right?" My head swivels in Quinn's direction and she meets my gaze head-on.

"Fine. You want to take his side? Go on, convince me that I'm wrong." Her eyes soften at my false bravado and she kicks a chair out, motioning for me to sit down. I fall into it with a huff and she laughs, scooting closer to me.

"Why did you get so mad at Ty?" she asks without missing a beat.

I tip my glass, draining it, and she pushes hers across the table to me.

"We've gone over this, Quinn."

"Humor me."

"Ugh. Fine," I huff, crossing my arms over my chest, simply because it makes me feel less vulnerable. Knowing I'm about to rip open some wounds that haven't seen the light of day in quite some time, I need all the help I can get. "Once Dallas," I cringe at the mention of his name, "was brought into the picture, Tyson lost all faith in me. In the blink of an eye, everything I told him became a lie. He couldn't believe that Dallas was capable of doing something so heinous, and he said so himself."

Quinn nods. "And when he second-guessed you like that, how did that make you feel?"

"What are you, a goddamn psychiatrist?" I ask, receiving only a pointed look in response. "Fine," I sigh. "It made me feel terrible. That was the worst night of my life and to this day, every time I close my eyes I can still—" My voice cracks and tears start dripping from my eyes before I even have the chance to stop them. "I can *still* smell him. I can *still* feel his weight against my back. His breath *still* fans across my face like it did when he—"

"Stop," Quinn whispers, snatching up my hand to cradle it in hers. My watery eyes blink several times and I furrow my brows in confusion. *Isn't this what she wanted?*

"I don't want you to relive that night, Harley. You've lived it once and somehow, by the grace of God, you were able to come out on the other side, and I don't *ever* want you relive that moment again." I take a deep breath and squeeze her hand tightly like the lifeline that it is.

"Let me rephrase my question, so I can get you to see what I see." I nod, knowing I don't really have a say in the matter. This is Quinn we're talking about, and if she wants to have this conversation, then—like it or not—we're having this conversation.

"Why do you think Ty instantly thought Dallas was innocent?"

I laugh mirthlessly, but her cool demeanor doesn't budge. "Because he has Dallas on a pedestal. He's idolized him for as long as I can remember."

"Okay, what if Levi walked up to you right now and told you that I killed someone?"

"This is ridiculous, Quinn." Pushing up from the table, I grab my bowl of ice cream, which is now a heap of melted cream.

"Why is it ridiculous?"

"Because you wouldn't do that," I answer, hating that I'm finally seeing where she is going with this.

"But how do you know I wouldn't do it?"

"Because I know *you*, Quinn. I know the kind of person you are. I know that even though you're crazy and reckless, you don't have *that* in you."

"Don't you think that that's how Tyson feels about his brother? That the brother that he thought he knew wouldn't have *that* in him?" My hands fly to my mouth and my swollen eyes widen as realization slams into me. A heavy sob slithers up my throat and busts free. "You didn't give him a chance to accept what you were telling him," she finishes.

"I get it, Quinn." I hate that she's right, and more than that, I hate that I was wrong…but I was. My body, weak with exhaustion, flops down into the chair that I had just vacated, and I drop my head onto the table as my body rids itself of seven days worth of anguish.

"He needed time to process this, Harley. Trust me, that boy believes in you and he trusts you, and he knows that you wouldn't lie about something like that. But you should have given him the opportunity to talk through it and accept the fact that the brother he thought he knew was not who he thought he was."

"I said I get it!" I yell.

"Do you?" she questions skeptically. "Because I don't think you do." I bury my face in my hands, resigned to take the beating that she's about to give. "He is destroyed right now, Harley." I flinch at her words, but she pushes on. "That man has bent over backward, trying to get you to talk to him. He's left you message after message and text after text. Hell, he even wrote you something." My head twists to face her and I wipe my eyes as hope slowly starts to bloom in my stomach.

"That's right," she nods at my questioning look. "And I'm going to give it to you, but not for your sake…for his. I know he has screwed up before, and I know that he didn't handle it well when he found out about Dallas, but right now *you're* in the wrong. Right now, you need to swallow your pride and fight for the love that that man is trying so desperately to give you." Quinn pushes away from the table and walks into the living room. When she comes back into the kitchen, I see a bright red piece of paper clutched in her hand. She stops in front of me and smiles.

"I love you, Harley, and as much as I want to see you and Tyson end up together, I don't want that if it isn't going to make you happy." She drops the piece of paper on the table in front of me. I inhale sharply when my gaze lands on one of the coupons I gave Tyson for his birthday. My chest physically hurts as though a bullet was shot straight through it.

Never in my life did I think I would cry at the sight of a piece of construction paper, but as my shaky hand reaches for it, my eyes flood with tears. A hard lump has taken up permanent residence in my throat, and I struggle to swallow past it as a million emotions rush through my body. Closing my eyes, I flip the paper over in my hand. I take a deep cleansing breath and peel my lids open, instantly honing in on the scribbled writing on the coupon.

> *You promised*

Two words.

It takes two little words from our past for me to see what's been staring me right in the face for the past seven days. Tyson and I are meant to be together. We have come so far. We have fought, and we have won…at least we had *almost* won until I decided to screw things up. My head drops in shame at how I've handled things this past week. I am a horrible excuse for a girlfriend, and the fact that I completely shut him down without giving him any chance whatsoever to come to grips with what actually happened just proves what type of person I am.

My shoulders lurch with a deep sob and I bury my face in my hands. Quinn's arms wrap around me and she holds me as I expel all of the hurt and anger that I've been carrying around for the past seven days. When I finally start to calm down, she slides a piece of neon-pink construction paper in front of me and I instantly let go of another round of tears. I watch the piece of paper absorb the wetness that falls from my face as I read his final note.

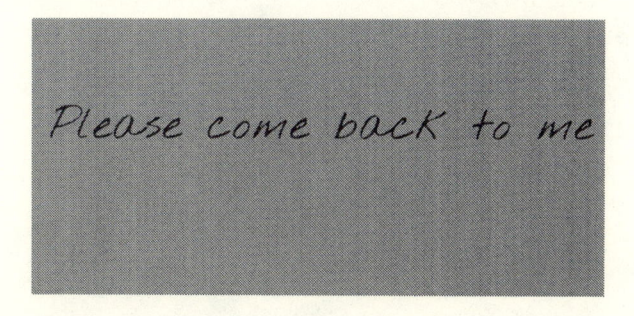

> *Please come back to me*

I'm an idiot. Running my arm across my puffy eyes, I wipe away the moisture. "Can you watch Max?" I ask hurriedly, because suddenly I need to talk to Ty. I need to see him, and it can't wait one more minute.

An I-told-you-so-grin is plastered on Quinn's face. "Go get your man." She raises her hand and I slap it before grabbing my jacket and bolting out the door, all the while hoping and praying that the damage I've caused isn't irreversible.

I'm sure I break every law imaginable on my drive to Tyson's, but I don't care. My car skids to a stop in front of his house, and I send a silent prayer to the man upstairs that I picked the right one. I know he has the day off tomorrow, and usually when he's off, he stays at the rental house here in town.

Looking at the clock, I notice that it's eight fifty-five and I fist pump the air, thankful that I made it on time. Every night for the past week at exactly nine o'clock, Ty has sent me a text...and tonight I'm going to reply back. I turn on the radio and Christina Perri's *A Thousand Years* starts playing. My eyes drift shut as I drink in the lyrics that so perfectly resemble my love for Tyson. When my phone beeps, I sit up frantically, and waves of relief crash against my body when I see his name on my screen. *This is it...time to fight for my man.*

Tyson: I miss you

I smile at the simplicity of his text.

Me: I miss you too

My phone beeps almost instantly and I laugh, picturing him startled at the sight of my name on his phone.

Tyson: Harley?

Me: Yes...

Tyson: I miss you, Harley. I love you.

Hope blooms in my chest and my heart swells with love. My hands are shaking with anticipation, but I manage to reply before stepping out of the car.

Chapter 25

Tyson

HOLY SHIT! SHE'S TALKING to me! Jumping off the couch, I sprint into the kitchen and throw on my shoes, fumbling when I try to tie them. I can't help it...I'm fucking excited and I need to be ready. I need to see her like I need my next breath. Reaching for my phone, I see her reply '*Yes...*' and my fingers scurry across my phone.

Me: I miss you, Harley. I love you.

When it comes to Harley, I've done nothing but fuck up. I made a mistake when I walked away from her five years ago and I made another mistake last week when I ruthlessly confronted her about Dallas. But you can bet your ass that I'm done screwing up from here on out. This girl means the world to me and she needs to know that there is nothing—absolutely nothing—that I wouldn't do for her.

Not that it's even remotely an excuse, but I can't begin to describe how overwhelmed I felt after I heard Max talk about Dallas. It's like my brain had gone foggy and all I could focus on was finding out the truth. Unfortunately, I went about it the wrong fucking way.

At first, I didn't think it was possible for Dallas to do something like that, but the more and more I thought about it, I started to change my mind. When I looked back, I realized that toward the end of his life, I didn't really even know who Dallas was. The drugs and alcohol had changed him so much that I'm sure that he was capable of anything at that point, no matter how horrific it was.

As much as I *hate* my brother for what he did to Harley, I'm still thankful that she has Max. It's going to be hard to look at that little boy and know that Dallas is his biological father, but it's comforting to know that Max truly is a part of me—that my blood runs through his veins. That alone makes this just a little bit better, because I love him like he is my own, and if given the chance, I will spend every day for the rest of my life showing him what it's like to have a real dad.

I'm not naive; I know that things aren't going to be easy. The guilt alone will probably eat at my soul…guilt for walking away from her in the first place and guilt for not going back to check on her that fateful night. Guilt for what my brother—my own flesh and blood—did to my best friend, the woman that I love.

My eyes snap to my phone when it beeps and my heart starts thrashing around in my chest. Hope that I had temporarily lost comes back to life in full force, and I punch my fist in the air when I read her words.

Harley: Can we talk?

Responding isn't an option, because right now I just need to see her. Running for the door, I fling it open, and come face-to-face with Harley. *My beautiful Harley.* She's standing before me, her once vibrant green eyes now dull and puffy, her cheeks shimmering with tears. My hands itch to reach for her, but I can't—not yet.

My phone pings again, but I hesitate to check it, afraid that if I look away she might disappear. Is it possible that I've thought about her and wished for her so many times that somehow my mind was able to conjure her up?

"You've got a text," she says with a small grin, pointing to my phone.

"Is it from you?" I ask cautiously, afraid to get my hopes up. Her small grin turns into a shy smile and she nods.

"What does it say?"

"It says, '*I love you too*,'" she whispers.

Relief floods my body, and this time I don't think twice about yanking her into my arms and smashing her to my chest. She half laughs, half cries when she buries her face in my shoulder. "I'm so sorry," she hiccups, sniffing her nose.

I pull back a fraction and look down into the face of my forever. "Did you just snot me?" She snorts with laughter, tightening her grip around my waist. Sliding my hands up the length of her delicate back, I cup her face between my hands.

"Do you forgive me?" she asks.

Tilting my head forward, I brush my lips across hers and she whimpers. "There's nothing to forgive." She tries to protest, but I seal my mouth over her lips, drinking in her words. Her tongue tangles with mine, and with each glide she manages to soothe my aching soul. I pull my mouth from hers just enough to see her eyes, which are now shining with love. "I think the more important question is, do you forgive *me*?" She opens her mouth to respond, but I lay my finger against her lips. "I'm so sorry, Harley. I know I fucked up—again—the other night. I should have never accused you of the things I accused you of." Tears start running down her flushed cheeks and I wipe them away with my thumbs. "I believe you. Of course I believe you. I just wasn't ready to accept it. I was upset and angry and I took it out on you, and I'm so very sorry for that."

"It's okay," she cries, tightening her hands around my back. We stand there, in the doorway to my house, holding onto each other for dear life. Her tears slowly stop falling and she kisses me gently. "I forgive you, too," she whispers against my mouth. "So we're good now?"

"We're better than good. You came back to me and nothing else matters. We've got this." Her answering smile is all I need to know that she feels the same way, but her next words are what seal the deal.

She unwinds her arm from around my back and sticks her hand in the air. "Pinky swear?"

Epilogue

Several months later

Tyson

"I'M NERVOUS."

"You got this!" I look down into a set of chocolate eyes. Every time I look at Max, I now see Dallas—and that isn't necessarily a bad thing. Don't get me wrong, if my brother wasn't already dead, I'd fucking kill him for what he did. But after *a lot* of talks and *a lot* of tears with Harley, I've learned to accept it.

Suffice it to say that not everything has been peachy keen after the night we reconciled on my doorstep. We've both battled through the guilt and regret of everything that we've been through, but we made it. Sure, we've had disagreements and arguments along the way, but what couple hasn't?

Our biggest one was over why she didn't call the cops after her attack. It warmed my heart to hear that she did it to protect my family and me, but I still wish she had turned the bastard in. Of course, I won't tell *her* that because she's convinced that she's right and it's just easier to agree—and more importantly, it doesn't make a difference at this point anyway.

"What if she says no?" *What the hell is wrong with me? I'm talking to a kid in kindergarten.*

Max reaches up to smooth his hands down the front of my shirt, and I can't help but laugh. *He's such a little grown-up.* "Then you should throw a fit," he says, matter-of-fact. I raise an eyebrow, cocking my head. I'm not going to lie: I'm slightly terrified to hear what's going to come out of his mouth next.

"A fit?"

"Yeah," he shrugs. "That's what I do." Bending over, I grab Max around the waist and toss him over my shoulder.

"You're a genius, little dude!"

"I know," he mumbles into my back as we walk to the car. "Are we going to Grandma and Grandpa's now?"

"Yup," I reply, opening the car door so that Max can climb in. I love that he likes going to my parents' house. That was another source of contention between Harley and me. It took me a long time to wrap my head around why she chose to keep Max away from my parents, and to be honest, I'm still not sure I understand her reasoning. But I can't change it—the past is the past—and we pinky swore to put the past behind us.

Together, Harley and I had a very delicate conversation with my parents. We told them about the attack—and about Max. It was an emotional gathering, with a few cuss words, lots of hugs, and even more tears. But my parents harbor no ill feelings about it; they're just happy to have Max—and Harley—in their lives.

Max doesn't officially know that my parents are his biological grandparents; that's just too much for his little mind to comprehend. He calls them grandma and grandpa because they're my parents, and well, he's been calling me dad, so to him it just makes sense. My parents are on cloud nine every time they get to see him, and between them and Harley's parents, we pretty much have free childcare any time we want it.

My parents are waiting outside when I pull up, and Max flies out of the car and up the front walk, slamming directly into my dad's chest.

"See ya tomorrow, bud!" I yell at his retreating back. He stops and turns, a magnificent smile lighting up his face.

"Good luck!" he hollers. Shooting my parents a quick wave, I hop in my car to head back home. *Home.* I love that word. There's nothing in the world better than coming home every night to Harley and Max, and everyday I thank the Lord that Harley gave me a second—and third—chance.

Harley's car isn't in the driveway when I pull up to the house, so I rush inside to put a few last-minute touches on my big surprise. I'm just finishing up when I hear the front door slam shut.

Harley

"HONEY! I'M HOME!" I chuckle, walking in the front door. The house is quiet—too quiet. Shrugging off my coat, I toss it on the back of the couch. I walk into the kitchen, stopping in my tracks when I see a dozen roses presented beautifully in a crystal vase on the table. But it's not the roses that catch my attention...it's the green coupon tucked in the center.

On wobbly legs, I walk to the table. My hand shakes as I pull the coupon out of the bouquet. I run my finger along smooth paper, slowly turning it over in my hand.

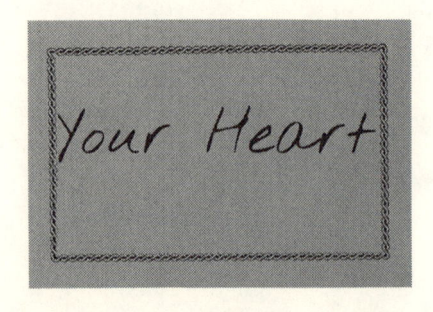

> Your Heart

"I want your heart." His raspy voice startles me and I jump, clutching the coupon to my chest.

"You scared me," I whisper, taking a deep breath. He smiles, taking a couple steps forward, stopping in front of me.

His soft eyes are boring into mine when he repeats himself. I grip his hand, pulling it up to rest over the left side of my chest.

"It's already yours." He swallows hard as tears spring to his eyes. "Are you okay?" I ask, suddenly nervous about why he's acting so strange.

"I will be." With his free hand, he reaches into his back pocket and pulls out a blue coupon. He holds it out in front of me, and my eyes flit nervously between him and the coupon before I drop his hand and take it.

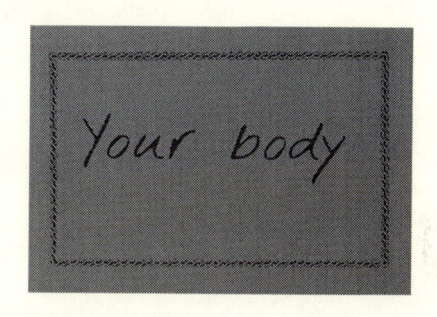

> Your body

My watery eyes find his. "It's already yours," I whisper, choking on my words when I see him pull another coupon out of his back pocket. This time it's purple—my favorite color.

"You've got my heart, and my body is yours. What more could you want?" I quip, causing him to laugh.

"Just one more thing," he replies, handing me the purple card. I turn it over, and after reading the most beautiful word ever, I squeeze my eyes shut.

Forever

Tears drip down my face and I take a shuddering breath. When I open my eyes, Tyson is kneeling before me on one knee and my hand flies to my mouth. A sob rips from my throat as I look into his dark brown eyes, which are swirling with love.

He peels my hand off my shocked face. His hands are trembling and his palms are sweating, but when he speaks, his voice doesn't come out shaky…it comes out strong and unwavering.

"You've given me your body, Harley. You've even given me your heart. But that isn't enough." I shake my head, confirming that '*no, that isn't enough.*' My shoulders bob as I cry silently in front of the love of my life. "I want your future, Harley. I want your forever."

His eyes are full of love, anticipation, and maybe a little fear. I think it's time to put him out of his misery. I drop to my knees, and he lets out a harsh breath. "Yes," I whisper, peppering kisses across his face. "Yes! Yes! Yes!"

"Yes?" he asks, his bright eyes roaming my face. I nod once and he glides his fingers up my arms, stopping when he has my neck cradled between his warm hands. I watch in slow motion as his mouth descends on mine. Our tongues collide, but this time it isn't a lust-fueled battle. It's sweet, sensual, and full of more love than I could ever convey with words.

Tyson pulls away all too soon. I whimper at the loss of his mouth against mine and he chuckles. "This is perfect," he says, waving his hand between us. "This…it's…"

He's obviously at a loss for words, so I interrupt him. "It's perfect, because we're together—in each other's arms—right where we belong."

The End

Please keep reading for a preview of Nevaeh Lee's debut solo novel *Defying All Odds*.

Acknowledgements

I'M GOING TO BE wordy because I have a ton of people to thank, so please forgive me. This book has been a dream come true for me, a literal bucket list check-off, and hands down I could not have finished it without the support of my amazing husband. Honey, thank you for ignoring the messy floors, loads of unfolded laundry, and sink constantly full of dirty dishes. Thank you for getting up with the kids every morning and letting me sleep because I stayed up way too late writing or editing. Your endless stream of encouragement means more to me than I could ever tell you and I love you so very much!

Alexis—oh Alexis. 'Thank you' seems so insignificant. One of the best things I got out of writing this book was your friendship. You took me under your wing, guided me, plotted with me, encouraged me, and laughed with me. Thank you for always being there for me, no matter the question or concern. I promise not to be so crazy the next go around!

My soul sister, Nevaeh Lee. I am thrilled that we somehow managed to find each other in the chaotic Facebook world. We learned quickly that we totally suck at buddy reading, but oh boy, did we have fun! Our connection was instant on so many levels—you know the ones—and I've told you a thousand times that fate brought us together!

S.G. Thomas, my amazing editor. When we met, you didn't

know I was writing a book, and I had no idea you were an editor. After you read my prologue, you sent me a message on Facebook—a message I will never forget. 'Holy-cow girl, you can write.' And that was all it took. Your opinion means the world to me, and I am so grateful that you edited this book.

To Jackie and Michelle. You two have been my rock. I've never laughed harder than I do when I'm talking to the two of you. We literally spend every single night together, and it's because of those nights that I was able to finish this book. You pushed me, cheered me on, and picked me up, and your friendship means the world to me.

Barbara, I feel like we were insta-friends! I've absolutely loved getting to know you, and your kind words, encouragement, and friendship has been the highlight of many of my days. It's never a dull moment when we get together online—or on the phone! And I can't forget the way you swooped in and saved my tushy. In fact, I'm certain I'll never be able to repay you for that!

Livia and Ana, both of you only knew me for five minutes, and yet you jumped right in to help me with a scene—or scenes. Your generosity and kindness are inspiring, and I am so thankful to each of you. Elisabeth, Keshia, and Mia, thank you for answering question after question after question. The three of you opened yourselves up to me when no one else would and for that, you guys rock!

To the girls at *Three Girls and a Book Obsession*. Thank you so much for rocking my cover reveal! I've loved working with you and getting to know each of you. You girls are wonderful at what you do!

Lastly, thank you to the bloggers that participated in my cover reveal and blog tour. Thank you for sharing my teasers and sending me messages of encouragement. It's because of you that indie authors like myself get their books noticed.

About the Author

K.L. Grayson resides in a small town outside of St. Louis, MO. She is entertained daily by her extraordinary husband, who will forever inspire every good quality she writes in a man. Her entire life rests in the palms of six dirty little hands, and when the day is over and those pint-sized cherubs have been washed and tucked into bed, you can find her typing away furiously on her computer. She has a love for alpha-males, brownies, reading, tattoos, sunglasses, and happy endings…and not particularly in that order.

Defying All Odds
by Nevaeh Lee

Chapter 1

Celeste

He shot my damn dog.

This could not be happening.

Granted, that dog was annoying as hell and did bark his head off when the guy forced his way inside the house. *But still....*

If he had waited half a second, he would have realized that the only threat that stupid dog posed was maybe licking someone to death.

I guess it wouldn't help to point that out now.

Especially since there were more pressing matters at hand, namely the gun barrel pressed in between my breasts. And the beyond creepy-looking delivery guy who I'd bet my favorite pair of skinny jeans wasn't really a delivery guy, but who was looking at me like he just struck gold.

Shit.

Time for a quick assessment of this situation.

The creepy delivery guy-who-probably-wasn't-a-delivery-guy was holding a gun, and he's obviously not afraid to use it. He didn't even hesitate before killing my dog, and my best guess was that he didn't think much more highly of me. He wasn't wearing a mask, which meant that whatever he had in mind—and I'm afraid I knew *exactly* what he had in mind—he would kill me when he's done. There would be no reason to leave me alive and his self-preservation dictated my death.

Unfortunately for him, my self-preservation instincts were kicking in too. But even though everything in my body was telling me to fight like hell, I wouldn't.

My assessment complete, I began to focus once again on the guy in front of me. Not that I had much of a choice in the matter with the gun now pressing harder into my sternum, forcing me backward.

"What do you want?" I asked with the steadiest voice possible.

"What do you *think* I want?" he returned, a creepy voice to match a creepy guy.

I hated being right sometimes.

"Alright, buddy—"

"Name's Joe, not buddy."

Yup, definitely not planning on leaving here with me alive, I thought. Randomly, I also wondered if his name really was Joe. Probably.

"Okay, Joe...let's talk about this."

"No need. Nothin' to talk about. In fact, talkin' is not on the agenda. Finding the bedroom is, so let's start walkin'."

Right.

"Well, since I know your name, it's only fair that you know mine," I said in introduction, as if we were having a casual conversation. One where there wasn't a gun pointed at me.

"Again, no need."

So appealing to his humanity was obviously not going to work. I didn't think so, but figured it wouldn't hurt to try. Time to negotiate then. Probably the less he knew about me the better, anyway.

"Um, I'd like to make a deal with you," I began, rushing on before he got the chance to interrupt. "What if I said I won't fight you?"

"I'd say you won't fight me anyway. I've got the gun," he replied, pushing it into my chest. *As if I needed the reminder.*

"Yes, but since I know that you have no problem using it," I stated, indicating Hero lying on the floor nearby, "then I don't have anything to lose, do I? Might as well go down fighting."

"So what are you offerin'? Besides, of course, what I'm already gonna take."

I'd have given just about anything to wipe that nasty smirk off his ugly mug, but instead I respond with the absolute last thing I want to say. "What I'm offering is my full cooperation, which I assure you, will be much more enjoyable for you," I said, raising my eyebrow.

His eyes widened, then immediately narrowed. "Why would you do that?"

"Because I want to live," I said simply. "So when you're done, you leave, and I live. It won't do me any good to report it, since I'm a willing participant. Therefore, there's no need to kill me when you're through."

Creepy-guy Joe appeared to think about this for a few seconds and apparently his pea-sized brain couldn't find any reason to argue, so he agreed. "Okay, deal. Now move it."

"Shake on it."

"Lady, you're pushin' your luck."

"Sir," I said, trying to keep the sarcasm out of my voice. "I don't have any luck…obviously." This was seriously the understatement of the century. "Just please," I pleaded, with as little desperation as possible, "shake on it. I want your word."

"Fine," he said, shaking my hand with his calloused one. I fought back a shiver, knowing that within minutes, that same hand would be on my body. "Now let's go."

Looking into his cold, nearly black eyes, he seemed sincere, albeit in a hurry. And really, what choice did I have at this point but to believe him?

I hated turning my back, but knew I was safe as long as he

still wanted something from me. And the sight of him licking his foul lips told me it was time for that *something* to happen.

With a heavy sigh, I took one more look at Hero and turned to march up the stairs, as if to my execution. *I prayed to God that it wasn't.*

When I entered my bedroom, I went straight toward the bedside table, opened the drawer, and pulled out a condom.

"Oh, hell no—" he started.

"Look," I interrupted, "unless you want me to hunt you down to pay child support for the next eighteen years, then you will wear this. Got it?"

He didn't even appear to think about it this time. Guess he knew how much child support costs.

"Damn woman, you're even more of a pain in the ass than my ex."

Yup, he definitely knew.

"Fine, I'll wear it," he conceded. "No more negotiations. I'm in charge here. I've got the gun *and* the swingin' dick. So get undressed—now."

***

I lay on the bed, shaking, allowing myself a few minutes to pull my shit together. I knew he had left because, after hearing the door slam shut, I dragged myself off the bed long enough to look outside the window and watch him drive away in a non-descript white van. I couldn't see the license plate and my Jell-O legs wouldn't have carried me down the stairs, even if I did care enough to go and try and make out the plate number. But I didn't…there was only one thing on this earth that I cared about. Well, two really.

After a deep breath, I glanced at the clock. *Time's up.* The less thinking I did, the better off I was anyway. I reached across the bed and picked the phone up from the nightstand. After two rings, my friend, Ana, picked up. "Hello?"

"Hey," I said, trying to control the unsteadiness in my voice.

"Celeste, what's wrong?" she asked immediately. *Damn.*

"Ana, I need a favor. You know I hate to ask—"

"Done," she interrupted.

"You don't even know what it is yet."

"Doesn't matter. Whatever it is, consider it done. Now tell me what's going on," she demanded.

I loved Ana dearly and needed her more right now than I ever had and hopefully ever would, but I couldn't get into it. Especially not over the phone.

"I promise I'll explain everything later. In the meantime, I need you to pick up the twins. You are listed as my emergency contact, but I'll call the school just in case, since they've never been picked up by anyone else before. After that, could you take them to your house and watch a movie or whatever until I can come and get them? Oh, and they might have homework, but then again, they're in kindergarten so if they miss one night, it probably won't destroy their academic records," I rambled on. When she didn't say anything, I added, "I don't know how late I'll be."

"*Dios mio,* now I know something is really wrong," she said quietly.

"What makes you say that?"

"Besides the fact that you never ask for help from anyone? You're not giving me the rundown about what they can and can't watch, what snacks they're allowed to have, and to watch my language around them... Just please tell me you're alright, Celeste."

"I-I- will be." It was all I could say. I knew I would be. *I just had to be.*

"Okay," she said after a pause, "I'll get the twins. Call me when you can." She hung up and I sent up a quick 'thank you' that I had a friend I could count on, one who didn't badger me with questions when she could tell that the time wasn't right. Someone who I trusted implicitly with Paisley and Parker, even if I did question her judgment about the men in her life. Still, I hated relying on her. I hated relying on anyone. But if there were ever a time I needed to, it was now.

After hanging up with Ana, I called the school. Once I knew that the kids would be taken care of, I made the one call that couldn't be put off any longer.

***

"So let me get this straight," the detective said, doubt and incredulity clear in his voice. "You made a deal?"

The shock of what had happened was wearing off, my adrenaline plunging to ground zero. Irritation had begun to settle in and unfortunately, this guy was in the line of fire.

"Detective—?"

"Westlake."

"Okay, Detective Westlake. Do you have children?" Based on appearances, I didn't think so. But then again, most people assumed I didn't have kids either.

"No, I don't. And I also don't see how that's relevant."

"Well, it is," I informed him. He arched his brow in response. "Because if you did have kids, then you would know why I made the deal that I did. Had I not made a deal, I wouldn't be sitting here talking to you right now. My five-year-old twins would have waited at the school for me to pick them up until someone—probably from Social Services—arrived to tell them that I would *never* be coming home…oh, and that their beloved dog was also dead. If you did have kids, Detective, then you would also understand that a parent would do anything, and I mean *anything*, to keep their children from having to experience something like that."

He seemed to think about this for a few seconds. "So, can you tell me about your…um, negotiation?" he asked.

"Sure," I said after a deep exhale. "After Joe forced his—"

"Wait, Joe?" he questioned, arching his eyebrow once again.

"That's what he said his name was. Sorry, I didn't check the guy's ID so I couldn't tell you if he was telling the truth or not."

Detective Westlake gave me another incredulous look. I continued, undaunted. "But I figured if it was his name, then he wasn't planning on letting me live long enough to pass that information along." He nodded his head as if this were an accurate statement.

"Anyway, first thing he did was shoot Hero...I know, I know, you don't have to tell me. Terrible name for a dog, and not much of a 'hero' when it came down to it. But at that point, I knew two things: his gun was loaded and he wasn't afraid to use it. He wasn't wearing a mask, so the fact that I could identify him and he readily told me his name, I knew my chances of surviving this... um, encounter...were next to none."

"You were probably right," he said, nodding again. Good, a detective who was honest and not full of bullshit.

"I know." Another arched eyebrow. Damn, he was good at that. And worse, he looked good doing it. *Moving on, Celeste.*

"Because I knew this, I made a decision. I wasn't going to let my kids grow up without a mother because of Joe-the-mother-fucking-delivery-guy-who-probably-wasn't-even-a-delivery-guy. They need me and I..."

I couldn't go on, not with the Texas-sized lump in my throat. Looking away from the detective, I tried to gain control over the tears I could feel burning the back of my eyes, begging to be released. I didn't want to cry because it made me feel weak and powerless, which was exactly how I felt at that moment.

I focused on the one wall that wasn't covered in pictures of Parker and Paisley; seeing their perfect little faces would undoubtedly unleash the threatening torrent. My blurry eyes concentrated instead on a framed Ernest Hemingway quote, and I felt the corners of my mouth turn up slightly, though it was difficult to say whether it was because of the irony of those words or the strength I derived from them.

The world breaks everyone, and afterward, some are strong at the broken places.

When I knew I had stuffed any semblance of fear or pain as deep inside as it could go, I glanced back at the detective, who was now looking over at the quote himself with a curious expression on his face. Before he could ask any questions, I cleared my throat to draw his attention. He looked back at me quickly, his face a blank mask that I'm sure mirrored my own.

"After he made it clear what was going to happen," I continued, "I told him that if he would let me live, I wouldn't fight him."

"And he agreed?" he asked.

"Yes, and he shook on it."

"He shook on it?" he repeated dubiously.

"Yes, and before you say anything, I know he could have been lying or could have changed his mind. But it's not like I had a lot of options at that point, right?"

After staring at me for what seemed like hours but was probably only a few seconds, he answered slowly. "Right. So you went with him to your bedroom?" he prompted.

"Yes," I responded, without elaborating further.

"Ms. Logan," he prodded gently. "I promise that I don't want to ask this any more than you want to answer it, but I need to know what happened next."

Feeling more put out with him than I should, considering I knew he was only doing his job, I answered, "Well, if you must have a play-by-play, let's go upstairs—"

His eyes widened immediately. "Are you okay to go back in there?"

"Sure, why not? And probably the sooner, the better. 'Getting back on the horse' and all that…" I trailed off, then turned and started up the stairs. I could hear the detective following behind, happy that he was following me instead of creepy Joe, and that this time, there wasn't a gun barrel pointed at my back. Oh, and that I wasn't about to be raped. *Ah, the little things in life.*

As soon as we entered, an involuntary shiver shot through my body. I began speaking quickly in hopes that he didn't notice. "The first thing I did was go directly to this side table," I said, indicating the one beside the king-sized bed where I sleep. *Slept was more like it.* No way was I ever getting in that bed again, despite what I just told the detective.

"I pulled out a condom and—" I noticed that his jaw had

dropped and wondered if his shock was due to the fact that I kept protection in my house. If only it had been another form of protection…now *that* would have been helpful.

"You got a condom?" he asked disbelievingly.

"Yes."

"And he agreed to use it?" he questioned, not attempting to hide the doubt in his voice. *What, did he think that I forced the guy to wear one?* I tried to subdue my frustration.

"Not at first. But I threatened him with eighteen years of child support if I ended up pregnant, and after telling me that I was more trouble than his ex, he agreed."

"You're shitting me," he deadpanned.

"No, I assure you I'm not."

"Unbelievable. Not that I don't believe you," he quickly corrected himself. "But the fact that you were able to get him to use a condom or listen to you at all, for that matter, is unheard of. I can't think of a single case where this has happened."

"Well, I did what I had to do, and with my luck, I definitely would have ended up pregnant. And since this guy was ugly as sin, it wouldn't bode well for my future child, now would it?" I added, trying to lighten the tone of the conversation.

He stared at me and then shook his head slightly, as if to clear it. "So after he agreed to wear a condom…"

"He told me that he was through talking and to get undressed. I had promised to cooperate, so I did what he said. He wanted me to undress him, so I did." I said this in an almost clinical fashion, hoping he could just use his imagination for the rest. Evidently, he couldn't.

"I'm sorry, but I have to ask…" And he truly did look sorry. In any other situation, I probably would have felt bad for the guy.

"I know," I said with a heavy sigh. *Deep breath, Celeste.* Then I began….

***

After reliving what had happened for hopefully (but not likely) the last time, I finally looked up into his eyes and saw pure, unadulterated compassion. Since it wasn't pity, I could deal with it. Pity just pissed me off. He didn't seem to be able to speak, and I was ready to get going, so I asked, "Where do we go from here?"

Snapping out of it, he answered, "Well, I need you to meet with our local forensic artist, who will sketch a facial composite based on your description of the attacker. This will be crucial to our investigation, so please provide every detail you can remember. As glad as I am that he wore a condom, for your sake, it makes our job a hell of a lot harder without a semen sample. Not saying that it's impossible though, and maybe the hospital can—"

"DNA won't be a problem," I interrupted him. He looked at me questioningly, so I continued. "Even though he didn't seem like the brightest crayon in the box, I knew that if he had half a brain, he'd flush the condom down the toilet...which he did. So, I raked my fingernails down his back. Of course, the dumbass probably thought it was an act of passion. Regardless, I haven't washed my hands since it happened, which has been extremely difficult for me not to do, I might add."

"You're shitting me."

"Nope, still not."

"What would make you think to do that?"

"You mean, do I watch *CSI*? No, actually, I don't even have cable, even though I am well aware of what a great babysitter the TV could be. But I would much rather read or play games with the twins or spend time outside or—"

"You didn't answer my question, but those are nice things to know," he interrupted gently. I couldn't help but notice when one of side of his mouth barely turned upward.

I sighed. He was probably going to find out anyway before this whole nightmare was over. "Let's just say that this isn't my first rodeo," I answered quietly and looked away, but not before catching the look of horror that swept over his face as recognition hit him as to what my statement meant.

"This has happened to you before?" he breathed, barely above a whisper.

"Yes. State of Texas v. Jared Kyle Young. You're welcome to look up the case if you want, not that it's relevant. The two incidents are nothing alike."

"I'll decide if it's relevant," he said, sounding almost angry. Which, of course, was making me angry. What the hell was he getting upset about? That was the past, and the past was exactly where it should stay.

"Fine, if you must know—and because you'll find out soon enough anyway—I was the victim of date rape when I was younger...much younger. I fought like hell, and it didn't turn out well. There wasn't a gun involved but I was beaten pretty badly." I continued quickly, hoping he wouldn't ask any more questions, "That's how I knew that this time I didn't stand a chance. And obviously I didn't have kids then. Speaking of which, I would really like to get out of here so I can go get them. Can we head to the hospital now?"

If it were possible, he looked even angrier than he did before. I'm not sure if this anger was directed at asshole number one, dickhead number two, or me, for jacking up his whole day.

"Thompson! Price!" he yelled, startling my still-raw nerves. When the two guys entered the room a minute later, the detective spoke to them in what was definitely not his talking-to-a-victim voice. "Take Ms. Logan to the Med. They'll know what to do. Make sure they get the skin cells from under her fingernails before she washes her hands. After that's done, bring her to the station and I'll have the artist ready to sketch. The faster we get a look at this fucker, the better."

"Yessir," Thompson or Price answered.

"Ma'am," the detective said, now looking at me. "I'm sure I'll see you again today. I've got to get back to the station." His clipped tone made it seem like he couldn't get away from me fast enough. Then he turned and walked away, leaving me to wonder what was so damn important that he couldn't be bothered going to the hospital with me himself. If I didn't know it already—which I obviously did—there was one truth I knew, without a doubt: *men suck.*

Made in the USA
Charleston, SC
28 September 2014